T0200809

A NOVEL WITH AWESOME IMPLICATIONS FOR THE WORLD OF TOMORROW

I WILL FEAR NO EVIL
ROBERT A. HEINLEIN

Books by Robert A. Heinlein

I WILL FEAR NO EVIL

Robert A. HEINLEIN

ACE BOOKS, NEW YORK

ACE

An imprint of Penguin Random House LLC
penguinrandomhouse.com

I WILL FEAR NO EVIL

An Ace Book / published by arrangement with G. P. Putnam's Sons

ACE® is a registered trademark of Penguin Random House LLC.
The "A" design is a trademark of Penguin Random House LLC.
For more information, visit penguin.com.

ISBN: 978-0-441-35917-2

PUBLISHING HISTORY
G. P. Putnam's Sons edition / 1970
Berkley edition / November 1971
Thirty-eighth printing / March 1986
Ace mass-market edition / April 1987

PRINTED IN THE UNITED STATES OF AMERICA

Cover art by James Warhola.

Penguin
Random
House

*To
Rex and Kathleen*

I WILL FEAR NO EVIL

1

The room was old-fashioned, 1980 baroque, but it was wide, long, high, and luxurious. Near simulated view windows stood an automated hospital bed. It looked out of place but was largely concealed by a magnificent Chinese screen. Forty feet from it a boardroom table also failed to match the décor. At the head of this table was a life-support wheelchair; wires and tubings ran from it to the bed.

Near the wheelchair, at a mobile stenodesk crowded with directional mikes, voice typewriter, clock-calendar, controls, and the usual ancillaries, a young woman sat. She was beautiful.

Her manner was that of the perfect unobtrusive secretary but she was dressed in a current exotic mode, "Half & Half"—right shoulder and breast and arm concealed in jet-black knit, left leg sheathed in a scarlet tight, panty-ruffle in both colors joining them, black sandal on the scarlet side, red sandal on her bare right foot. Her skin paint was patterned in the same scarlet and black.

On the other side of the wheelchair was an older woman garbed in a nurse's conventional white pantyhose and smock. She ignored everything but her dials and a patient in the chair. Seated around the table were a dozen-odd men, most of them in spectator-sports style affected by older executives.

Cradled in the life-support chair was a very old man. Except for restless eyes, he looked like a poor job of

9

embalming. No cosmetic help had been used to soften the brutal fact of his decrepitude.

"Ghoul," he was saying softly to a man halfway down the table. "You're a slavering ghoul, Parky me boy. Didn't your father teach you that it is polite to wait for a man to stop kicking before you bury him? Or did you have a father? Erase that last, Eunice. Gentlemen, Mr. Parkinson has moved that I be invited to resign as chairman of the board. Do I hear a second?"

He waited, looking from face to face, then said, "Oh, come now! Who is letting you down, Parky? You, George?"

"I had nothing to do with it."

"But you would love to vote 'Aye.' Motion fails for want of a second."

"I withdraw my motion."

"Too late, Parkinson. Erasures are made only by unanimous consent, implied or overt. One objection is enough—and I, Johann Sebastian Bach Smith, do so object . . . and that rule controls because *I* wrote it before you learned to read.

"But"—Smith looked around at the others—"I do have news. As you heard from Mr. Teal, all our divisions are in satisfactory shape; Sea Ranches and General Textbooks are more than satisfactory—so this is a good time for me to retire."

Smith waited, then said, "You can close your mouths. Don't look smug, Parky; I have more news for you. I stay on as chairman of the board but will no longer be chief executive. Our chief counsel, Mr. Jake Salomon, becomes deputy chairman and—"

"Hold it, Johann. I am *not* going to manage this five-ring circus."

"Nobody said you would, Jake. But you can preside at board meetings when I'm not available. Is that too much to ask?"

"Mmm, I suppose not."

"Thank you. I'm resigning as president of Smith Enterprises, and Mr. Byram Teal becomes our president and chief executive officer—he's doing the work; it's time

10

he got the title—and pay and stock options and all the perks and privileges and tax loopholes. No more than fair."

Parkinson said, "Now see here, Smith!"

"Hold it, youngster. Don't start a remark to me with 'Now see here—' Address me as 'Mr. Smith' or 'Mr. Chairman.' What is your point?"

Parkinson controlled himself, then said, "Very well, *Mister* Smith. I can't accept this. Quite aside from promoting your assistant to the office of president in one jump—utterly unheard of!—if there is a change in management, *I* must be considered. I represent the second largest block of voting stock."

"I did consider you for president, Parky."

"You did?"

"Yep. I thought about it . . . and snickered."

"Why, you—"

"Don't say it, I might sue. What you forget is that *my* block has voting control. Now about your block— By company policy anyone representing five percent or more of voting stock is automatically on the board even if nobody loves him and he suffers from spiritual bad breath. Which describes both you and me.

"Or did describe you. Byram, what's the late word on proxies and stock purchases?"

"A full report, Mr. Smith?"

"No, just tell Mr. Parkinson where he stands."

"Yes, sir. Mr. Parkinson, you now control less than five percent of the voting stock."

Smith added sweetly, "So you're fired, you young ghoul. Jake, call a special stockholders' meeting, legal notice, all formalities, for the purpose of giving Parky a gold watch and kicking him out—and electing his successor. Further business? None. Meeting's adjourned. Stick around, Jake. You, too, Eunice. And Byram, if you have anything on your mind."

Parkinson jumped to his feet. "Smith, you haven't heard the last of this!"

"Oh, no doubt," the old man said sweetly. "Meantime my respects to your mother-in-law and tell her that Byram will go on making her rich even though I've fired you."

11

Parkinson left abruptly. Others started to leave. Smith said mildly, "Jake, how does a man get to be fifty years old without acquiring horse sense? Only smart thing that lad ever did was pick a rich mother-in-law. Yes, Hans?"

"Johann," Hans von Ritter said, leaning on the table and speaking directly to the chairman, "I did not like your treatment of Parkinson."

"Thanks. You're honest with me to my face. Scarce these days."

"Removing him from the board is okay; he's an obstructionist. But there was no need to humiliate him."

"I suppose not. One of my little pleasures, Hans. I don't have many these days."

A Simplex footman rolled in, hung the vacated chairs on its rack, rolled out; von Ritter continued: "I have no intention of being treated that way. If you want nothing but Yes men on your board, let us note that I control much less than five percent of the voting stock. Do you want my resignation?"

"Good God, no! I need you, Hans—and Byram will need you still more. I can't use trained seals; a man has to have the guts to disagree with me, or he's a waste of space. But when a man bucks me, I want him to do it *intelligently*. You do. You've forced me to change my mind several times—not easy, stubborn as I am. Now about this other—sit down. Eunice, whistle up that easy chair for Dr. von Ritter."

The chair approached; von Ritter waved it back, it retreated. "No, I haven't time to be cajoled. What do you want?" He straightened up; the boardroom table folded its legs, turned on edge, and glided away through a slot in the wall.

"Hans, I've surrounded myself with men who don't like me, not a Yes man or trained seal among them. Even Byram—especially Byram—got his job by contradicting me and being right. Except when he's been wrong and that's why he needs men like you on the board. But Parkinson— I was entitled to clip him—publicly—because he called for my resignation—publicly. Nevertheless you are right, Hans; 'tit for tat' is childish. Twenty years ago—even ten—I would *never* have humiliated a man. If a man operates by reflex, as most do instead of using their noggins, humiliating him forces him to try to get even. I know better. But I'm getting senile, as we all know."

Von Ritter said nothing. Smith went on, "Will you stick?—and help keep Byram steady?"

"Uh . . . I'll stick. As long as you behave yourself." He turned to leave.

"Fair enough. Hans? Will you dance at my wake?"

Von Ritter looked back and grinned. "I'd be delighted!"

"Thought so. Thanks, Hans. G'bye."

Smith said to Byram Teal, "Anything, son?"

"Assistant Attorney General coming from Washington tomorrow to talk to you about our Machine Tools Division buying control of Homecrafts, Ltd. I think—"

"To talk to *you*. If you can't handle him, I picked the wrong man. What else?"

"At Sea Ranch number five we lost a man at the fifty-fathom line. Shark."

"Married?"

"No, sir. Nor dependent parents."

"Well, do the pretty thing, whatever it is. You have those videospools of me, the ones that actor fellow dubbed the sincere voice onto. When we lose one of our own, we can't have the public thinking we don't give a hoot."

Jake Salomon added, "Especially when we don't."

Smith clucked at him. "Jake, do you have a way to look into my heart? It's our policy to be lavish with death benefits, plus the little things that mean so much."

"—and look so good. Johann, you don't have a heart—just dials and machinery. Furthermore you never did have."

Smith smiled. "Jake, for you we'll make an exception. When you die, we'll try not to notice. No flowers, not even the customary black-bordered page in our house organs."

"You won't have anything to say about it, Johann. I'll outlive you twenty years."

"Going to dance at my wake?"

"I don't dance," the lawyer answered, "but you tempt me to learn."

13

"Don't bother, I'll outlive *you*. Want to bet? Say a million to your favorite tax deduction? No, I can't bet; I need your help to stay alive. Byram, check with me tomorrow. Nurse, leave us; I want to talk with my lawyer."

"No, sir. Dr. Garcia wants a close watch on you at all times."

Smith looked thoughtful. "Miss Bedpan, I acquired my speech habits before the Supreme Court took up writing dirty words on sidewalks. But I will try to use words plain enough for you to understand. I am your employer. I pay your wages. This is my home. I told you to get out. That's an order."

The nurse looked stubborn, said nothing.

Smith sighed. "Jake, I'm getting old—I forget that they follow their own rules. Will you locate Dr. Garcia—somewhere in the house—and find out how you and I can have a private conference in spite of this too faithful watchdog?"

Shortly Dr. Garcia arrived, looked over dials and patient, conceded that telemetering would do for the time being. "Miss MacIntosh, shift to the remote displays."

"Yes, Doctor. Will you send for a nurse to relieve me? I want to quit this assignment."

"Now, Nurse—"

"Just a moment, Doctor," Smith put in. "Miss MacIntosh, I apologize for calling you, 'Miss Bedpan.' Childish of me, another sign of increasing senility. But, Doctor, if she *must* leave—I hope she won't—bill me for a thousand-dollar bonus for her. Her attention to duty has been perfect . . . despite many instances of unreasonable behavior on my part."

"Uh . . . see me outside, Nurse."

When doctor and nurse had left Salomon said dryly, "Johann, you are senile only when it suits you."

Smith chuckled. "I do take advantage of age and illness. What other weapons have I left?"

"Money."

"Ah, yes. Without money I wouldn't be alive. But I *am* childishly bad-tempered these days. You could chalk it up to the fact that a man who has always been active feels

14

frustrated by being imprisoned. But it's simpler to call it senility . . . since God and my doctor know that my body is senile."

"I call it stinking bad temper, Johann, not senility—since you can control it when you want to. Don't use it on me; I won't stand for it."

Smith chuckled. "Never, Jake; I need you. Even more than I need Eunice—though she's ever so much prettier than you. How about it, Eunice? Has my behavior been bad lately?"

His secretary shrugged—producing complex secondary motions pleasant to see. "You're pretty stinky at times, Boss. But I've learned to ignore it."

"You see, Jake? If Eunice refused to put up with it—as you do—I'd be the sweetest boss in the land. As it is, I use her as a safety valve."

Salomon said, "Eunice, any time you get fed up with this vile-tempered old wreck you can work for me, at the same salary or higher."

"Eunice, your salary just doubled!"

"Thank you, Boss," she said promptly. "I've recorded it. And the time. I'll notify Accounting."

Smith cackled. "See why I keep her? Don't try to outbid me, you old goat, you don't have enough chips."

"Senile," Salomon growled. "Speaking of money, whom do you want to put into Parkinson's slot?"

"No rush, he was a blank file. Do you have a candidate, Jake?"

"No. Although after this last little charade it occurs to me that Eunice might be a good bet."

Eunice looked startled, then dropped all expression. Smith looked thoughtful. "It had *not* occurred to me. But it might be a perfect solution. Eunice, would you be willing to be a director of the senior corporation?"

Eunice flipped her machine to "NOT RECORDING." "You're both making fun of me! Stop it."

"My dear," Smith said gently, "you know I don't joke about money. As for Jake, it is the only subject sacred to him—he sold his daughter and his grandmother down to Rio."

15

"Not my daughter," Salomon objected. "Just Grandmother . . . and the old girl didn't fetch much. But it gave us a spare bedroom."

"But, Boss, I don't know anything about running a business!"

"You wouldn't have to. Directors don't manage, they set policy. But you *do* know more about running it than most of our directors; you've been on the inside for years. Plus almost inside during the time you were my secretary's secretary before Mrs. Bierman retired. But here are advantages I see in what may have been a playful suggestion on Jake's part. You are already an officer of the corporation as Special Assistant Secretary assigned to record for the board—and I made you that, you'll both remember, to shut up Parkinson when he bellyached about my secretary being present during an executive session. You'll go on being that—and my personal secretary, too; can't spare you—while becoming a director. No conflict, you'll simply vote as well as recording. Now we come to the key question: Are you willing to vote the way Jake votes?"

She looked solemn. "You wish me to, sir?"

"Or the way I do if I'm present, which comes to the same thing. Think back and you'll see that Jake and I have *always* voted the same way on basic policy—settling it ahead of time—while wrangling and voting against each other on things that don't matter. Read the old minutes, you'll spot it."

"I noticed it long ago," she said simply, "but didn't think it was my place to comment."

"Jake, she's our new director. One more point, my dear: If it turns out that we need your spot, will you resign? You won't lose by it."

"Of course, sir. I don't have to be paid to agree to that."

"You still won't lose by it. I feel better. Eunice, I've had to turn management over to Teal; I'll be turning policy over to Jake—you know the shape I'm in. I want Jake to have as many sure votes backing him as possible. Oh, we can always fire directors . . . but it is best not to have to do so, a fact von Ritter rubbed my nose in. Okay, you're a

16

director. We'll formalize it at that stockholders' meeting. Welcome to the ranks of the Establishment. Instead of a wage slave, you have sold out and are now a counterrevolutionary, warmongering, rat-fink, fascist dog. How does it feel?"

"Not 'dog,' " Eunice objected. "The rest is lovely but 'dog' is the wrong sex; I'm female. A bitch."

"Eunice, I not only do not use such words with ladies around, you know that I do not care to hear them from ladies."

"Can a 'rat-fink fascist' be a lady? Boss, I learned that word in kindergarten. Nobody minds it today."

"I learned it out behind the barn and let's keep it there."

Salomon growled. "I don't have time to listen to amateur lexicologists. Is the conference over?"

"What? Not at all! Now comes the top-secret part, the reason I sent the nurse out. So gather ye round."

"Johann, before you talk secrets, let me ask one question. Does that bed have a mike on it? Your chair may be bugged, too."

"Eh?" the old man looked thoughtful. "I used a call button . . . until they started standing a heel-and-toe watch on me."

"Seven to two you're bugged. Eunice my dear, can you trace the circuits and make sure?"

"Uh . . . I doubt it. The circuitry isn't much like my stenodesk. But I'll look." Eunice left her desk, studied the console on the back of the wheelchair. "These two dials almost certainly have mikes hooked to them; they're respiration and heart beat. But they don't show voices as my voice does not make the needles jiggle. Filtered out, I suppose. "But"—she looked thoughtful—"voice could be pulled off either circuit ahead of a filter. I do something like that, in reverse, whenever I record with a high background db. I don't know what these dials do. Darn it, I might spot a voice circuit . . . but I could never be sure that there was *not* one. Or two. Or three. I'm sorry."

"Don't be sorry, dear," the lawyer said soothingly. "There hasn't been real privacy in this country since the middle of the twentieth century—why, I could phone a

17

man I know of and have you photographed in your bath and you would never know it."

"Really? What a dreadful idea. How much does this person charge for such a job?"

"Plenty. Depends on difficulty and how much chance he runs of being prosecuted. Never less than a couple of thousand and then up like a kite. But he can do it."

"Well!" Eunice looked thoughtful, then smiled. "Mr. Salomon, if you ever decide that you must have such a picture of me, phone me for a competitive bid. My husband has an excellent Chinese camera and I would rather have *him* photograph me in my bath than some stranger."

"Order, please," Smith said mildly. "Eunice, if you want to sell skin pictures to that old lecher, do it on your own time. I don't know anything about these gadgets but I know how to solve this. Eunice, go out to where they telemeter me—I think it's next door in what used to be my upstairs lounge. You'll find Miss MacIntosh there. Hang around three minutes. I'll wait two minutes; then I'll call out: *'Miss MacIntosh!* Is Mrs. Branca there?' If you hear me, we'll know she's snooping. If you don't, come back at the end of three minutes."

"Yes, sir. Do I give Miss MacIntosh any reason for this?"

"Give the old battle-ax any stall you like. I simply want to know if she is eavesdropping."

"Yes, sir." Eunice started to leave the room. She pressed the door switch just as its buzzer sounded. The door snapped aside, revealing Miss MacIntosh, who jumped in surprise.

The nurse recovered and said bleakly, to Mr. Smith, "May I come in for a moment?"

"Certainly."

"Thank you, sir." The nurse went to the bed, pulled its screen aside, touched four switches on its console, replaced the screen. Then she planted herself in front of her patient and said, "Now you have complete privacy, so far as *my* equipment is concerned. Sir."

"Thank you."

"I am not supposed to cut the voice monitors except on

18

Doctor's orders. But you had privacy *anyhow*. I am as bound to respect a patient's privacy as a doctor is, I *never* listen to sickroom conversation. I don't even hear it! Sir."

"Get your feathers down. If you weren't listening, how did you know we were discussing the matter?"

"Oh! Because my name was mentioned. Hearing my name triggers me to listen. It's a conditioned reflex. Though I don't suppose you believe me?"

"On the contrary, I do. Nurse—please switch on whatever you switched off. Then bear in mind that I *must* talk privately . . . and I'll remember not to mention your name. But I'm glad to know that I can reach you so promptly. To a man in my condition that is a comfort."

"Uh—very well, sir."

"And I want to thank you for putting up with my quirks. And bad temper."

She almost smiled. "Oh, you're not so difficult, sir. I once put in two years in an N.P. hospital."

Smith looked startled, then grinned. "*Touché!* Was that where you acquired your hatred for bedpans?"

"It was indeed! Now if you will excuse me, sir—"

When she was gone, Salomon said, "You really think she won't listen?"

"Of course she will, she can't help it, she's already triggered and will be trying too hard not to listen. But she's proud, Jake, and I would rather depend on pride than gadgetry. Okay, I'm getting tired, so here it is in a lump. I want to buy a body. A young one."

Eunice Branca barely showed reaction; Jake Salomon's features dropped into the mask he used for poker and district attorneys. Presently Eunice said, "Am I to record, sir?"

"No. Oh, hell, yes. Tell that sewing machine to make one copy for each of us and wipe the tape. File mine in my destruct file; file yours in your destruct file—and, Jake, hide your copy in the file you use to outwit the Infernal Revenue Service."

"I'll file it in the still safer place I use for guilty clients. Johann, anything you say to me is privileged but I am bound to point out that the Canons forbid me to advise a

19

client in how to break the law, or to permit a client to discuss such intention. As for Eunice, anything you say to her or in her presence is *not* privileged."

"Oh, come off it, you old shyster; you've advised me in how to break the law twice a week for years. As for Eunice, nobody can get anything out of her short of all-out brainwash."

"I didn't say I always followed the Canons; I merely told you what they called for. I won't deny that my professional ethics have a little stretch in them—but I won't be party to anything smelling of bodysnatching, kidnapping, or congress with slavery. Any self-respecting prostitute—meaning me—has limits."

"Spare me the sermon, Jake; what I want is both moral and ethical. I need your help to see that all of it is legal—utterly legal, can't cut corners on this!—and practical."

"I hope so."

"I *know* so. I said I wanted to *buy* a body—legally. That rules out bodysnatching, kidnapping, and slavery. I want to make a legal purchase."

"You can't."

"Why not? Take this body," Smith said, pointing to his chest, "it's not worth much even as manure; nevertheless I can will it to a medical school. You know I can, you okayed it."

"Oh. Let's get our terms straight. In the United States there can be no chattel ownership of a human being. Thirteenth Amendment. Therefore your body is not your property because you can't sell it. But a cadaver *is* property—usually of the estate of the deceased . . . although a cadaver is not often treated the way other chattels are treated. But it is indeed property. If you want to buy a cadaver, it can be arranged—but who were you calling a ghoul earlier?"

"What is a cadaver, Jake?"

"Eh? A dead body, usually of a human. So says Webster. The legal definition is more complicated but comes to the same thing."

20

"It's that 'more complicated' aspect I'm getting at. Okay, once it is dead, it is property and maybe we can buy it. But what is 'death,' Jake, and when does it take place? Never mind Webster; what is the *law*?"

"Oh. Law is what the Supreme Court says it is. Fortunately this point was nailed down in the seventies—'Estate of Henry M. Parsons v. Rhode Island.' For years, many centuries, a man was dead when his heart quit beating. Then for about a century he was dead when a licensed M.D. examined him for heart condition action and respiration and certified that he was dead—and sometimes that turned out grisly, as doctors do make mistakes. And then along came the first heart transplant and oh, mother, what a legal snarl *that* stirred up!

"But the Parsons case settled it; a man is dead when all brain activity has stopped, permanently."

"And what does that mean?" Smith persisted.

"The Court declined to define it. But in application—look, Johann, I'm a corporation lawyer, not a specialist in medical jurisprudence nor in forensic medicine—and I would have to research before I—"

"Okay, so you're not God. You can revise your remarks later. What do you know *now*?"

"When the exact moment of death is important, as it sometimes is in estate cases, as it often is in accident, manslaughter, and murder cases, as it always is in an organ, transplant case, some doctor determines that the brain has quit and isn't going to start up again. They use various tests and talk about 'irreversible coma' and 'complete absence of brain wave activity' and 'cortical damage beyond possibility of repair' but it all comes down to some M.D. laying his reputation and license on the line to certify that this brain is dead and won't come alive again. Heart and lungs are now irrelevant; they are classed with hands and feet and gonads and other parts that a man can do without or have replaced. It's the brain that counts. Plus a doctor's opinion about the brain. In transplant cases there are almost always at least two doctors in no way connected with the operation and probably a coroner as well. Not

21

because the Supreme Court requires it—in fact only a few of the fifty-four states have legislated in re thanatotic requirements—but—"

"Just a moment, Mr. Salomon—that odd word. My typewriter has placed a query after it." Eunice kept her hand over the "Hold" light.

"How did your typer spell it?"

"T-H-A-N-A-T-O-T-I-C."

"Smart machine. It's the technical adjective referring to death. From the Greek god Thanatos, Death."

"Half a second while I tell it so." Eunice touched the "Memory" switch with her other hand, whispered briefly, then said, "It feels better if I reassure it at once. Go ahead." She lifted her hand from the "Hold" light.

"Eunice, are you under the impression that that machine is alive?"

She blushed, then touched "Erase" and covered "Hold." "No, Mr. Salomon. But it does behave better with me than with any other operator. It can get downright sulky if it doesn't like the way it is handled."

"I can testify to that," Smith agreed. "If Eunice takes a day off, her relief had better fetch her own gadgets, or fall back on shorthand. Listen, dear, knock off the chatter. Talk with Jake about the care and feeding of machines some other time; great-grandfather wants to go to bed."

"Yes, sir." She lifted her hand.

"Johann, I was saying that in transplant cases the medical profession has set up tight rules or customs, both to protect themselves from criminal and civil actions and also, I am sure, to forestall restrictive legislation. They have to get that heart out while it's still alive and nevertheless protect themselves from indictments for murder, cum multimillion-dollar damage suits. So they spread the responsibility thin and back each other up."

"Yes," agreed Smith. "Jake, you haven't told me a thing I didn't know—but you have relieved my mind by confirming facts and law. Now I *know* it can be done. Okay, I want a healthy body between ages twenty and forty, still warm, heart still working and no other damage too difficult to repair . . . but with the brain legally dead,

22

dead, *dead*. I want to buy that cadaver and have *this* brain—mine—transplanted into it."

Eunice held perfectly still. Jake blinked. "When do you want this body? Later today?"

"Oh, next Wednesday ought to be soon enough. Garcia says he can keep me going."

"I suggest later today. And get you a new brain at the same time—that one has quit functioning."

"Knock it off, Jake; I'm serious. My body is falling to pieces. But my mind is clear and my memory isn't bad—ask me yesterday's closing prices on every stock we are interested in. I can still do logarithmic calculations without tables; I check myself every day. Because I *know* how far gone I am. Look at me—worth so many megabucks that it's silly to count them. But with a body held together with Scotch tape and string—I ought to be in a museum.

"Now all my life I've heard 'You can't take it with you.' Well, eight months ago when they tied me down with all this undignified plumbing and wiring, having nothing better to do I started thinking about that old saw. I decided that, if I couldn't take it with me, I wasn't going to go!"

"Humph! 'You'll go when the wagon comes.'"

"Perhaps. But I'm going to spend as much as necessary of that silly stack of dollars to try to beat the game. Will you help?"

"Johann, if you were talking about a routine heart transplant, I would say 'Good luck and God bless you!' But a *brain* transplant—have you any idea what that entails?"

"No, and neither do you. But I know more about it than *you* do; I've had endless time to read up. No need to tell me that no successful transplant of a human brain has ever been made; I know it. No need to tell me that the Chinese have tried it several times and failed—although they have three basket cases still alive if my informants are correct."

"Do you want to be a basket case?"

"No. But there are two chimpanzees climbing trees and eating bananas this very day—and each has the brain the other one started with."

"Oho! That Australian."

23

"Dr. Lindsay Boyle. He's the surgeon I must have."

"Boyle. There was a scandal, wasn't there? They ran him out of Australia."

"So they did, Jake. Ever hear of professional jealousy? Most neurosurgeons are wedded to the notion that a brain transplant is too complicated. But if you dig into it, you will find the same opinions expressed fifty years ago about heart transplants. If you ask neurosurgeons about those chimpanzees, the kindest thing any of them will say is that it's a fake—even though there are motion pictures of both operations. Or they talk about the many failures Boyle had *before* he learned how. Jake, they hate him so much they ran him out of his home country when he was about to try it on a human being. Why, those bastards—excuse me, Eunice."

"My machine is instructed to spell that word as 'scoundrel,' Mr. Smith."

"Thank you, Eunice."

"Where is he now, Johann?"

"In Buenos Aires."

"Can you travel that far?"

"Oh, no! Well, perhaps I could, in a plane big enough for these mechanical monstrosities they use to keep me alive. But first we need that body. And the best possible medical center for computer-assisted surgery. And a support team of surgeons. And all the rest. Say Johns Hopkins. Or Stanford Medical Center."

"I venture to say that neither one will permit this unfrocked surgeon to operate."

"Jake, Jake, of course they will. Don't you know how to bribe a university?"

"I've never tried it."

"You do it with really *big* chunks of money, openly, with an academic procession to give it dignity. But first you find out what they want—football stands, or a particle accelerator, or an endowed chair. But the key is plenty of money. From my point of view it is better to be alive and young again, and broke, than it is to be the richest corpse in Forest Lawn." Smith smiled. "It would be exhilarating to be young—and broke. So don't spare the shekels.

24

"I know you can set it up for Boyle; it's just a question of whom to bribe and how—in the words of Bill Gresham, a man I knew a long time ago: 'Find out what he wants—he'll geek!'

"But the toughest problem involves no bribery but simply a willingness to spend money. Locating that warm body. Jake, in this country over ninety thousand people per year are killed in traffic accidents alone—call it two hundred and fifty each day—and a lot of those victims die of skull injuries. A fair percentage are between twenty and forty years old and in good health aside from a broken skull and a ruined brain. The problem is to find one while the body is still alive, then keep it alive and rush it to surgery."

"With wives and relatives and cops and lawyers chasing along behind."

"Certainly. If money and organization weren't used beforehand. Finders' fees—call them something else. Life-support teams and copters equipped for them always standing by, near the worst concentrations of dangerous traffic. Contributions to highway patrol relief funds, thousands of release forms ready to sign, lavish payment to the estate of the deceased—oh, at least a million dollars. Oh, yes, nearly forgot—I've got an odd blood type and any transplant is more likely to take if they don't have to fiddle with swapping blood. There are only about a million people in this country with blood matching mine. Not an impossible number when you cut it down still further by age span—twenty to forty—and good health. Call it three hundred thousand, tops. Jake, if we ran big newspaper ads and bought prime time on video, how many of those people could we flush out of the bushes? If we dangled a million dollars as bait? One megabuck in escrow with Chase Manhattan Bank for the estate of the accident victim whose body is used? With a retainer to any prospective donor and his spouse who will sign up in advance."

"Johann, I'm durned if I know. But I would hate to be married to a woman who could collect a million dollars by 'accidentally' hitting me in the head with a hammer."

"Details, Jake. Write it so that no one can murder and

25

benefit by it—and suicide must be excluded, too; I don't want blood on my hands. The real problem is to locate healthy young people who have my blood type, and feed their names and addresses into a computer."

"Excuse me, Mr. Smith, but have you thought of consulting the National Rare Blood Club?"

"Be darned! I *am* growing senile. No, I hadn't, Eunice—and how do you happen to know about it?"

"I'm a member, sir."

"Then you're a donor, dear?" Smith sounded pleased and impressed.

"Yes, sir. Type AB-Negative."

"Be darned twice. Used to be a donor myself—until they told me I was too old, long before you were born. And your type—AB-Negative."

"I thought you must be, sir, when you mentioned the number. So small. Only about a third of one percent of us in the population. My husband is AB-Negative, too, and a donor. You see—well, I met Joe early one morning when we were both called to give blood to a newborn baby and its mother."

"Well, hooray for Joe Branca! I knew he was smart—he grabbed you, didn't he? I had not known that he was an Angel of Mercy as well. Tell you what, dear—when you get home tonight, tell Joe that all he has to do is to dive into a dry swimming pool . . . and you'll be not only the prettiest widow in town—but the richest."

"Boss, you have a nasty sense of humor. I wouldn't swap Joe for any million dollars—money won't keep you warm on a cold night."

"As I know to my sorrow, dear. Jake, can my will be broken?"

"Any will can be broken. But I don't think yours will be. I tried to build fail-safes into it."

"Suppose I make a new will along the same general lines but with some changes—would it stand up?"

"No."

"Why not?"

"You said it yourself. Senility. Any time a rich man dies at an advanced age with a new will anyone with an interest

26

in breaking it—your granddaughters, I mean—will try to break it, alleging senility and undue influence. I think they would succeed."

"Darn. I want to put Eunice down for a million so she won't be tempted to kill her AB-Negative husband."

"Boss, you're making fun of me again. Nasty fun."

"Eunice, I told you that I do not joke about money. How do we handle it, Jake? Since I'm too senile to make a will."

"Well, the simplest way would be an insurance policy with a paid-up single premium . . . which would cost, in view of your age and health, slightly more than a million, I surmise. But she would get it even if your will was broken."

"Mr. Salomon, don't listen to him!"

"Johann, do you want that million to revert to you if by any long chance you outlive Eunice?"

"Mmm . . . no, if it did, a judge might decide to look at the matter—and God himself doesn't know what a judge will do these days. Make the Red Cross the residuary. No, make it the National Rare Blood Club."

"Very well."

"Get it paid up first thing in the morning. No, do it *tonight*; I may not live till morning. Get an underwriter—Jack Towers, maybe—get Jefferson Billings to open that pawnshop of his and get a certified check. Use my power of attorney, not your own money, or you might be stuck for it. Get the signature of a responsible officer of the insurance company; then you can go to bed."

"Yes, Great Spirit. I'll vary that; I'm a better lawyer than you are. But the policy will be in force before night—with *your* money, not mine. Eunice, be careful not to kick those hoses and wires as you go out. But tomorrow you needn't be careful—as long as you don't get caught."

She sniffed. "You each have a nasty sense of humor! Boss, I'm going to erase this. I don't *want* a million dollars. Not from Joe dying, not from you dying."

"If you don't want it, Eunice," her employer said gently, "You can step aside and let the Rare Blood Club have it."

"Uh . . . Mr. Salomon, is that correct?"

"Yes, Eunice. But money is nice to have, especially when you don't have it. Your husband might be annoyed if you turned down a million dollars."

"Uh—" Mrs. Branca shut up.

"Take care of it, Jake. While thinking about how to buy a warm body. And how to get Boyle here and get him whatever permission he needs to do surgery in this country. And so forth. And tell—no, I'll tell her. Miss MacIntosh!"

"Yes, Mr. Smith?" came a voice from the bed console.

"Get your team in; I want to go to bed."

"Yes, sir. I'll tell Dr. Garcia."

Jake stood up. "Good day, Johann. You're a crazy fool."

"Probably. But I do have fun with my money."

"So you do. Eunice, may I run you home?"

"Oh, no, sir, thank you. My Gadabout is in the basement."

"Eunice," said her boss, "can't you see that the old goat *wants* to take you home? So be gracious. One of my guards will take your Gadabout home."

"Uh . . . thank you, Mr. Salomon. I accept. Get a good night's sleep, Boss." They started to leave.

"Wait, Eunice," Smith commanded. "Hold that pose. Jake, pipe those gams! Eunice, that's obsolete slang meaning that you have pretty legs."

"So you have told me before, sir—and so my husband often tells me. Boss you're a dirty old man."

He cackled. "So I am, my dear . . . and have been since I was six, I'm happy to say."

28

2

Mr. Salomon helped her into her cloak, rode down with her to the basement, waved his guards aside and handed her into his car. Shotgun locked them in, got in by driver-guard and locked that compartment. As she sat down Mrs. Branca said, "Oh, how *big!* Mr. Salomon, I knew a Rolls was roomy—but I've never been in one before."

"A Rolls only by courtesy, my dear—body by Skoda, power plant by Imperial Atomics, then Rolls-Royce pretties it and backs it with their reputation and service. You should have seen a Rolls fifty years ago, before gasoline engines were outlawed. There was a dream car!"

"This one is dreamy enough. Why, my little Gadabout would fit inside this compartment."

A voice from the ceiling said, "Orders, sir?"

Mr. Salomon touched a switch. "One moment, Rockford." He lifted his hand. "Where do you live, Eunice? Or the coordinates of wherever you want to go?"

"Oh. I'll go home. North one one eight, west thirty-seven, then up to level nineteen—though I doubt that this enormous car will fit into the vehicle lift."

"If not, Rocky and his partner will escort you up the passenger lift and to your door."

"That's nice. Joe doesn't want me to ride passenger lifts by myself."

"Joe is right. So we'll deliver you like a courier letter. Eunice, are you in a hurry?"

"Me? Joe expects me when I get there, Mr. Smith's

29

working hours being so irregular now. Today I'm quite early."

"Good." Mr. Salomon again touched the intercom switch. "Rockford, we're going to kill some time. Uh, Mrs. Branca, what zone for those coordinates? Eighteen something?"

"Nineteen-B, sir."

"Find a cruising circle near nineteen-B; I'll give you coordinates later."

"Very good, sir."

Salomon went on to Eunice. "This compartment is soundproof unless I thumb this switch; they can talk to me but can't hear us. Which is good as I want to discuss things with you and make phone calls about that insurance policy."

"Oh! Surely that was a joke?"

"Joke, eh? Mrs. Branca, I have been working for Johann Smith for twenty-six years, the last fifteen with his affairs as my sole practice. Today he made me de-facto chairman of his industrial empire. Yet if I failed to carry out his orders about that insurance policy—tomorrow I would be out of a job."

"Oh, surely not! He depends on you."

"He depends on me as long as he can depend on me and not one minute longer. That policy must be written tonight. I thought you had quit fretting when you learned that you could step aside for the Rare Blood Club?"

"Well, yes. Except that I'm afraid I might get greedy and take it. When the time comes."

"And why not? The Rare Blood Club has done nothing for him; you have done much."

"I'm well paid."

"Listen, you silly child, don't be a silly child. He wanted *you* to have a million dollars in his will. And he wanted you to know it so that he could enjoy seeing your face. I pointed out that it is too late to change his will. Even this insurance gimmick is chancy if his natural heirs get a look at the books and discover it—which I shall try to prevent—as a judge might decide it was just a dodge—as it is—and require the insurance company to pay it to his

30

estate. Which is where the Rare Blood Club comes in handy; they would probably fight it and win, if you cut them in for half.

"But there are other ways. Suppose you knew nothing about this and were invited to the reading of his will and discovered that your deceased employer had bequeathed you a lifetime income 'in grateful appreciation of long and faithful service.' Would you turn it down?"

"Uh—" she said, and stopped.

"'Uh,'" he repeated. "Exactly 'uh.' Of course you wouldn't turn it down. He'd be gone and you'd be out of a job and there would be no reason to refuse it. So, instead of a lump sum so big it embarrasses you, I'm going to write a policy that sets up a trust to pay you an annuity." He paused to think. "A safe return, after taxes, on a trust is about four percent. What would you say to around seven hundred and fifty a week? Would that upset you?"

"Well . . . no. I understand seven hundred and fifty dollars much better than I understand a million."

"The beauty of it is that we can use the principal to insure against inflation—and you can still leave that million, or more, to the Rare Blood Club when your own Black Camel kneels."

"Really? How wonderful! I never will understand high finance."

"That's because most people think of money as something to pay the rent. But a money man thinks of money in terms of what he can do with it. Never mind, I'll fix it so that all you need to do is spend it. I'll use a Canadian insurance company and a Canadian bank, as each will be stuffy about letting a U.S. court look at its records. In case his granddaughters find out what I've done, I mean."

"Oh. Mr. Salomon, shouldn't this money go to them?"

"Again, don't be silly. They are harpies. Snapping turtles. And had nothing to do with making this money. Do you know anything about Johann's family? Outlived three wives—and his fourth married him for his money and it cost him millions to get shut of her. His first wife gave him a son and died in doing so—then Johann's son was killed

31

trying to capture a worthless hill. Two more wives, two divorces, a daughter by each of those two wives resulting in a total of four granddaughters—and those ex-wives and their daughters are all dead, and their four carnivorous descendants have been waiting for Johann to die and sore at him because he hasn't."

Salomon grinned. "They're in for a shock. I wrote his will so as to give them small lifetime incomes—and chop them off with a minimal dollar if they contest. Now excuse me; I must make phone calls, then take you home and run over to Canada and nail this down."

"Yes, sir. Do you mind if I take off my cloak? It's rather warm."'

"Want the cooling turned up?"

"Only if you are too warm. But this cloak is heavier than it looks."

"I noticed it was heavy. Body armor?"

"Yes, sir. I'm out by myself quite a lot."

"No wonder you're too warm. Take it off. Take off anything you wish to."

She grinned at him. "I wonder if you are a dirty old man, too. For another million?"

"Not a durned dime! Shut up, child, and let me phone."

"Yes, sir." Mrs. Branca wiggled out of her cloak, then raised the leg rest on her side, stretched out, and relaxed.

Such a strange day! . . . am I really going to be rich? . . . doesn't seem real . . . well, I'm not going to spend a dime —or let Joe spend it—unless it's safe in the bank . . . learned that the hard way first year we were married . . . some men understand money—such as Mr. Salomon, or Boss—and some don't, such as Joe . . . but as sweet a husband as a girl could wish . . . as long as I never again let him share a joint account . . .

Dear Joe! . . . those *are* pretty 'gams' if you do say so as shouldn't, you bitch . . . 'Bitch—' . . . how quaint Boss is with his old-fashioned taboos . . . always necessary not to shock him—not too much, that is; Boss enjoys a slight flavor of shock, like a whiff of garlic . . . especially necessary not to annoy him with language everybody uses nowadays . . . Joe is good for a girl, never have to be care-

32

ful around him . . . except about money—

Wonder what Joe would think if he could see me locked in this luxurious vault with this old goat? . . . probably be amused but best not to tell him, dearie; men's minds don't work the way ours do, men are not logical . . . wrong to think of Mr. Salomon as an 'old goat' though; he certainly has not acted like one . . . you had to reach for that provocative remark, didn't you, dear? . . . just to see what he would say . . . and found out! . . . got squelched—

Is he too old? . . . hell, no, dear, the way they hike 'em up with hormones a man is never 'too old' until he's too feeble to move . . . the way Boss is . . . not that Boss ever made the faintest pass even years back when he was still in fair shape . . .

Did Boss really expect to regain his youth by transplanting his brain? . . . arms and legs and kidneys and even hearts, sure, sure—but a brain? . . .

Salomon switched off the telephone. "Done," he announced. "All but signing papers, which I'll do in Toronto this evening."

"I'm sorry to be so much trouble, sir."

"My pleasure."

"I do appreciate it. And I must think about how to thank Boss—didn't thank him today but didn't think he meant it."

"Don't thank him."

"Oh, but I must. But I don't know how. How does one thank a man for a million dollars? And not seem insincere?"

"Hmm! There are ways. But, in this case, don't. My dear, you delighted Johann when you showed no trace of gratitude; I know him. Too many people have thanked him in the past . . . then figured him as an easy mark and tried to bleed him again. Then tried to knife him when he turned out not to be. So don't thank him. Sweet talk he does not believe; he figures it's always aimed at his money. I notice you're spunky with him."

"I have to be, sir, or he tromps on me. He had me in tears a couple of times—years back—before I found out he wanted me to stand up to him."

"You see? The old tyrant is making bets with himself as

33

to whether you'll come trotting in tomorrow and lick his hand like a dog. So don't even mention it. Tell me about yourself, Eunice—age, how long you've been married, and how often, number of children, childhood diseases, why you aren't on video, what your husband does, how you got to be Johann's secretary, number of arrests and for what— Or tell me to go to hell; you are entitled to privacy. But I would like to know you better; we are going to be working together from here on."

"I don't mind answering"—(I'll tell just want I want to tell!)—"but does this work both ways?" She stopped to let down the leg rest, straightened up. "Do I quiz you the same way?"

He chuckled. "Certainly. I may take the Fifth. Or lie."

"I could lie, too, sir. But I don't need to. I'm twenty-eight and married once and still am. No children—no children *yet*; I'm licensed for three. As for my job—well, I won a beauty contest at eighteen, the sort that offers a one-year contract making appearances around your home state, plus a video test with an option for a seven-year contract—"

"And they didn't pick up your option. I'm astonished."

"Not that, sir. Instead I took stock of myself—and quit. Winning that state contest and then losing the national contest made me realize how many pretty girls there are. Too many. And some things I heard from them about what you have to go through to get into video and stay there . . . well, I didn't want it that much. And went back to school and took an associate's degree in secretarial electronics, with a minor in computer language and cybernetics, and went looking for a job." (And I'm not going to tell you how I got through school!) "And eventually filled in as Mrs. Bierman's secretary while her regular secretary had a baby . . . then she didn't come back and I stayed on . . . and when Mrs. Bierman retired, Boss let me fill in. And kept me on. So here I am—a very lucky girl."

"A very smart girl. But I'm sure your looks had much to do with Johann's decision to keep you on."

"I know they did," she answered quietly. "But he would not have kept me had I not been able to do his work. I

34

know how I look but I'm not conceited about it; appearance is a matter of heredity."

"So it is," he agreed, "but there are impressive data to show that beautiful women are, on the average, more intelligent than homely ones."

"Oh, I don't think so! Take Mrs. Bierman—downright homely. But she was terribly smart."

"I said 'On the average,' " he repeated. "What is 'Beauty'? A lady hippopotamus must look beautiful to her boy friend, or we would run out of hippopotamuses—potami—in one generation. What we think of as 'Physical beauty' is almost certainly a tag for a complex of useful survival characteristics. Smartness—intelligence—among them. Do you think that a male hippopotamus would regard *you* as beautiful?"

She giggled. "Not likely!"

"You see? In reality you're no prettier than a female hippopotamus; you are simply an inherited complex of survival characteristics useful to your species."

"I suppose so." (Humph! Give me one opening and I'll *show* you what I am.)

"But since Johann—and I—are of your species, what that means to us is 'Beauty.' Which Johann has always appreciated."

"I know he does," she said quietly. She straightened her scarlet-covered leg in full extension and looked at it. "I dress this way to amuse Boss. When I first went to work for Smith Enterprises I wore as little as the other girls in the outer offices—you know, skin paint and not much else. Then when I went to work for Mrs. Bierman I started dressing quite modestly because she did—covered up all over, I mean, like Nurse MacIntosh—not even a see-through. Uncomfortable. I went on dressing that way when Mrs. Bierman left. Until one morning I had only one such outfit—I wore disposables, cheaper than having them cleaned—and spilled coffee down the front and was caught with nothing to wear.

"And no time to buy anything for I was more afraid of being late—you know how impatient Mr. Smith is—than I was that he might disapprove of my dress. Or lack of it. So

35

I gritted my teeth and got out an office-girl bikini and asked Joe to paint me and hurry it up! Joe's an artist, did I say?"

"I don't believe so."

"He is. He does my skin painting, even styles my face. But I was late anyhow that morning as Joe really is an artist and refused to let it go with just spraying me the background color. The two-piece was white with assorted sizes of big blue polka dots . . . and Joe insisted on continuing the pattern all over me, with me cussing and telling him to hurry and him insisting on painting just one more big polka dot. I was so late that I cut through an Abandoned Area I ordinarily cirled around."

"Eunice, you should *never* go into an Abandoned Area. God God, child, even the police don't risk it other than in a car as well armored as this one. You could be mugged, raped, and murdered and no one would ever know."

"Yes, sir. But I was scared of losing my job. I tried to explain to Boss why I was late, and he told me to shut up and go to work. Nevertheless he was unusually mellow that day. The next day I wore the sort of full cover-up I have been wearing—and he was downright mean all day. Mr. Salomon, I don't have to be slapped in the face with a wet fish; from then on I quit trying to look like a nun, and dressed and painted to enhance what I've got, as effectively as possible."

"It's effective. But, dear, you should be more careful. It's all very well to wear sexy clothes for Johann; that's charity, the old wretch can't get much pleasure out of life and is no threat to you, the shape he is in."

"He never was a threat, sir. In all the years I've worked for Mr. Smith he has never so much as touched my hand. He just makes flattering remarks about each new getup—sometimes quite salty and then I sass him and threaten to tell my husband, which makes him cackle. All innocent as Sunday School."

"I'm sure it is. But you must be more careful going to and from work. I don't mean just stay out of Abandoned Zones. Dressed the way you dress and looking as you do, you are in danger anywhere. Don't you *realize* it? Doesn't your husband know it?"

"Oh. I'm careful, sir; I know what can happen, I see the news. But I'm not afraid. I'm carrying three unregistered illegal weapons—and know how to use them. Boss got them for me and had his gaurds train me."

"Hmm. As an officer of the Court I should report you. As a human being who knows what a deadly jungle this city is, I applaud your good sense. If you really do know how to use them. If you have the courage to use them promptly and effectively. If, having defended yourself, you're smart enough to get away fast and say nothing to cops. That's a lot of 'ifs,' dear."

"Truly, I'm not afraid. Uh, if you were my attorney, anything I told you would be privileged, would it not?"

"Yes. Are you asking me to be your attorney?"

"Uh . . . yes, sir."

"Very well, I am. Privileged. Go ahead."

"Well, one night I had to go out on a blood-donor call. By myself, Joe wasn't home. Didn't worry me, I've made donations at night many times and often alone. I keep my Gadabout in our flat and stay in it until I'm inside the hospital or whatever. But— Do you know that old, old hospital on the west side, Our Lady of Mercy?"

"I'm afraid not."

"No matter. It's old, built before the government gave up trying to guarantee safety in the streets. No vehicle lift, no indoor parking. Just a lot with a fence and a guard at the gate. Happened when I came out. This frog tried to hop me between the parked cars. Don't know whether he was after my purse. Or me. Didn't wait to find out—don't even know if it was a man, could have been a woman—"

"Unlikely."

"As may be. Stun bomb in his face with my left hand as I zapped with my right and didn't wait to see if he was dead. Buzzed out of there and straight home. Never told the police, never told Joe, never told *anybody* until just now." (But it took a triple dose of Narcotol to stop your shakes,

37

didn't it, dearie—oh, shut up, that's not the point.)

"So you're a brave girl and can shoot if you have to. But you are a silly girl, too, and very lucky. Hmm. Johann has an armored car much like this and two shifts of guards to go with it."

"Of course he has guards, sir, but I know nothing about his cars."

"He has a Rolls-Skoda. Eunice, we are no longer going to depend on how fast you are with weapons. You can sell your Gadabout or plant flowers in it; from here on you'll have mobile guards and an armored car. Always."

Mrs. Branca looked startled. "But, Mr. Salomon! Even with my new salary I couldn't begin to—"

"Switch off, dear. You know that Johann will never again ride in a car. Chances are he will never leave that room. But he still owns his personal defense car; he still keeps a double crew, two drivers, two Shotguns—and maybe they run an errand once a week. Eating their heads off and playing pinochle the rest of the time. Tomorrow morning my car will pick you up; tomorrow afternoon your own car—Johann's—will take you home. And will be on call for you at all other times, too."

"I'm not sure Boss is going to like this."

"Forget it. I'm going to chew him out for letting you take risks. If he gives me any back talk, he'll find I have enough chips to hire you away from him. Be sensible, Eunice; this doesn't cost him a dollar; it's a business expense that he is already incurring. Change of subject. What do you think of his plans for this soi-disant 'warm body'?"

"Is a brain transplant possible? Or is he grabbing at a straw? I know he's not happy tied down to all that horrid machinery—goodness. I've been combing the shops for the naughtiest styles I can find but it gets harder and harder to get a smile out of him. Is it practical, this scheme?"

"That's beside the point, dear; he's ordered it and we are going to deliver. This Rare Blood Club—does it have all the AB-Negatives?"

"Heavens, no. The last club report showed less than four thousand AB-Negs enrolled out of a nationwide probability of about million."

38

"Too bad. What do you think of his notion of page ads and prime time on video?"

"It would cost a dreadful lot of money. But I suppose he can afford it."

"Certainly. But it stinks."

"Sir?"

"Eunice, if this transplant is to take place, there must be *no* publicity. Do you remember the fuss when they started freezing people? No, you're too young. It touched a bare nerve which set off loud howls, and the practice was very nearly prohibited—on the theory that, since most people can't afford it, no one should be allowed to have it. The Peepul, bless 'em—our country has at times been a democracy, an oligarchy, a dictatorship, a republic, a socialism, and mixtures of all of those, without changing its basic constitution, and now we are a de-facto anarchy under an elected dictator even though we still have laws and legislatures and Congress. But through all of this that bare nerve has always been exposed: the idea that if everyone can't have something, then no one should have it. So what will happen when one of the richest men in the country advertises that he wants to buy another man's living body—just to save his own stinking, selfish life?"

"I don't think Boss is all that bad. If you make allowances for his illness, he's rather sweet."

"Beside the point. That bare nerve will jump like an ulcerated tooth. Preachers will denounce him and bills will be submitted in legislatures and the A.M.A. will order its members to have nothing to with it and Congress might even pass a law against it. Oh, the Supreme Court would find such a law unconstitutional I think—but by then Johann would be long dead. So no publicity. Does the Rare Blood Club know who these other AB-Negatives are who are not members?"

"I don't know. I don't think so."

"We'll check. I would hazard that at least eighty percent of the people in this country have had their blood typed at some time. Does blood type ever change?"

"Oh, no, never. That's why we rares—that's what we call ourselves—are so in demand."

39

"Good. Almost all of the population who have been typed have the fact listed in computers somewhere, and with computers so interlinked today it is a matter of what questions to ask and how and where—and I don't know how, but I know the firm to hire for it. We progress, my dear. I'll get that started and off-load the details onto you, and then get other phases started and leave you to check on them while I go to South America and see this butcher Boyle. And—"

"Mr. Salomon! Bad turf coming up."

Salomon thumbed his intercom. "Roger." He added, "Damn them. Those two beauties *like* to go through Abandoned Areas. They hope somebody will shoot so that they will have legal excuse to shoot back. I'm sorry, my dear. With you aboard I should have given orders to stay out of A.A.s no matter what."

"It's my fault," Mrs. Branca said meekly. "I should have told you that it is almost impossible to circle near Nineteen-B without crossing a bad zone. I have to detour way around to reach Boss's house. But we're safe inside, are we not?"

"Oh, yes. If we're hit, this old tank has to be prettied up, that's all. But I should not have to tell them. Rockford isn't so bad; he's just a Syndicate punk, an enforcer who took a fall. But Charlie—the one riding Shotgun—is mean. An XYZ. Committed his first murder at eleven. He—" Steel shutters slid up around them and covered the bulletproof glass. "We must be entering the A.A."

Inside lights came on as shutters darkened windows. Mrs. Branca said, "You make it sound as if we were in more danger from your mobiles than we are from the bad zone."

He shook his head. "Not at all, my dear. Oh, I concede that any rational society would have liquidated them—but since we don't have capital punishment I make use of their flaws. Both are on probation paroled to me, and they *like* their jobs. Plus some other safe—" The *rap-rap-rap!* of an automatic weapon stitched the length of the car.

In that closed space the din was ear-splitting. Mrs. Branca gasped and clutched at her host. A single

40

explosion, still louder, went *POUNGK!* She buried her face in his shoulder, clung harder. "*Got 'im!*" a voice yelped. The lights went out.

"They got us?" she asked, her voice muffled by the ruffles of his shirt.

"No. no." He patted her and put his right arm firmly around her. "Charlie got *them*. Or thinks he did. That last was our turret gun. You're safe, dear."

"But the lights went out."

"Sometimes happens. The concussion. I'll find the switch for the emergency lights." He started to take his arms from around her.

"Oh, no! Just hold me, please—I don't mind the dark. Feel safer in it—if you hold me."

"As you wish, my dear." He settled himself more comfortably, and closer.

Presently he said softly, "My goodness, what a snuggly baby you are."

"You're pretty snuggly yourself . . . Mr. Salomon."

"Can't you say 'Jake'? Try it."

" 'Jake.' Yes, Jake. Your arms are so strong. How old are you, Jake?"

"Seventy-one."

"I can't believe it. You seem ever so much younger."

"Old enough to be your grandfather, little snuggle puppy. I simply look younger . . . in the dark. But one year into borrowed time according to the Bible."

"I won't let you talk that way; you're *young!* Let's not talk at all, Jake. Dear Jake."

"Sweet Eunice."

Some minutes later the driver's voice announced, "All clear, sir," as the shutters started sliding down—and Mrs. Branca hastily disentangled herself from her host.

She giggled nervously. "My goodness!"

"Don't fret. It's one-way glass."

"That's a comfort. Just the same, that light is like a dash of cold water."

"Um, yes. Breaks the mood. Just when I was feeling young."

"But you *are* young—Mr. Salomon."

41

"Jake."

" 'Jake.' Years don't count, Jake. Goodness me, I got skin paint all over your shirt ruffles."

"Fair enough, I mussed your hair."

"My hair I can comb. But what will your wife say when she sees that shirt?"

"She'll ask why I didn't take it off. Eunice dear, I have no wife. Years ago she turned me in on a newer model."

"A woman of poor taste. You're a classic, Jake—and classics improve with age. Does my hair look better now?"

"Lovely. Perfect."

"I'm almost tempted to ask to have us driven back into that bad zone so you can muss it again."

"I'm more than 'almost tempted.' But I had better take you home—unless you want to go with me over into Canada? Back by midnight, probably."

"I want to and I can't, really I can't. So take me home. But let me sit close, and put your arm around me but don't muss my hair this time."

"I shall be careful." He gave his driver the coordinates of Mrs. Branca's flat, then added, "And get there without going through any more Abandoned Areas, you trigger-happy bandits!"

"Very good, Mr. Salomon."

They rode in silence; then Mrs. Branca said, "Jake . . . you were feeling quite young, just before we were interrupted."

"I'm sure you know it."

"Yes. I was ready to let you, and you know that, too. Jake? Would you like a skin pic of me? A good one, not one taken by that snoopy character who charges so much."

"Will your husband take one? Can you sneak me a copy?"

"No huhu, Jake dear, I have dozens of skin pix—I was once a beauty contestant, remember? You are welcome to one . . . if you'll keep your mouth shut about it."

"Privileged communication. Your secrets are always safe with your attorney."

"What do you like? Artistic? Or sexy?"

"Uh . . . what a choice to have to make!"

42

"Mmm, a pic can be both. I'm thinking of one of me in a shower, hair soaked, wet all over, not a speck of body paint, not even face makeup, not even—well, you'll see. Is that on your wave length?"

"I'll howl like a wolf!"

"You shall have it. Quick change of subject; we're almost there. Jake? Does Boss stand any chance with this brain transplant thing?"

"I'm not a medical man. In my lay opinion—none."

"So I thought. Then he doesn't have long to live whether he has the operation or not. Jake, I'm going to make still greater effort to dress even naughtier for him, as long as he lasts."

"Eunice, you are a sweet girl. There is nothing nicer you could do for him. Much better than saying thanks for this trust fund."

"I wasn't thinking about that ridiculous million dollars, Jake; I was thinking about *Boss*. Feeling sorry for him. I'll go shopping tonight for something *really* exotic—or if I can't find a novel exotic, then a simple skintight see-through . . . passé but always effective with the right paint job underneath—Joe is good at that. And—well, if I'm going to have guards now, some days I may wear nothing but paint—stilt heels to make my legs look even better—yes, I know they're pretty!—heels, a nylon minimum-gee, and paint."

"And perfume."

"Boss can't smell, Jake. All gone."

"I still have my sense of smell."

"Oh. All right. I'll wear perfume for you. And paint for Boss. I've never tried anything that extreme at work . . . but now that we no longer work at his offices—no longer see many people—and I can keep a semi-see-through smock around, just in case—I might as well see if Boss likes it. Joe will enjoy thinking up provocative designs, likes to paint me, and is not jealous of Boss, feels sorry for the poor old man just as I do. And it is *so* hard to find novelty in exotic clothes. Even though I shop at least one night a week."

"Eunice."

"Yes, sir. Yes, Jake."

"Don't shop tonight. That's an order—from your boss by virtue of the power of attorney I hold."

"Yes, Jake. May one ask why?"

"You can wear a paint-only job tomorrow if you wish—this car and my guards will deliver you like crown jewels. But I need the car tonight. Starting tomorrow you'll have Johann's car and guards, and you will *always* use them for shopping. And everything."

"Yes, sir," she said meekly.

"But you are mistaken about Johann not having long to live. His problem is that he has *too* long to live."

"I don't understand."

"He's trapped, dear. He's fallen into the clutches of the medical profession and they won't *let* him die. Once he allowed them to harness him into that life-support gear he lost his last chance. Have you noticed that his meals are served without a knife? Nor even a fork? Just a plastic spoon."

"But his hands tremble so. I sometimes feed him as he hates to have nurses 'messing around' as he calls it."

"Think about it, dear. They have made it impossible for him to do anything but stay alive. A machine. A weary machine that hurts all the time. Eunice, this brain transplant is just a way for Johann to outsmart his doctors. A fancy way to commit suicide."

"No!"

"Yes. They've taken the simple ways away from him, so he's had to think up a fancy one. You and I are going to help him do it, exactly the way he wants it done. We seem to have arrived. Don't cry, damn it; your husband will want to know why and you must *not* tell him. Do you feel like kissing me good-bye?"

"Oh, please do!"

"Stop the tears and turn up your pretty face. they'll be unlocking us in a moment or two."

Presently she whispered, "That was as good a kiss as the very first one, Jake . . . and I no longer feel like crying. But I heard them unlock us."

"They'll wait until I unlock from inside. May I go up the

44

lift with you and see you to your door?"

"Nnn . . . I can explain your guards but would have trouble explaining why the firm's chief counsel bothers to do so. Joe isn't jealous of Boss—but might be of you. I don't want him to be . . . especially when I came so close to giving him reason to be."

"We could correct that near miss."

"Could be, dear Jake. My Iowa-farm-girl morals don't seem very strong today—I think I've been corrupted by a million dollars and a Rolls-Royce . . . and a city slicker. Let me go, dear."

3

The guards escorted her up and to her door in respectful silence. Mrs. Branca looked with new interest at "Charlie," the Shotgun—wondered how a mousy, fatherly little man could be as vicious as Jake seemed to know that he was.

They "stood sideboy" as she spoke to her door's lock, then waited until her husband unbolted it. As the door opened Rockford saluted and said, "Oh-nine-forty, Miss—we'll be waiting right here."

"Thank you, Rockford. Good night. Good night, Charlie."

Joe Branca waited until he had thrown the bolts and reset the alarm before he spoke. "What t'hell happen? An' where you trap uniform apes?"

"Don't I get a kiss first? Surely I'm not all that late? It's not yet eighteen."

"Talk, woman. Other ape shows back two hours with your jitterbuggy—tha's okay; your boss's butler phoned." He took off her cloak and kissed her. "So where you been, dizzy baggage? Missed you."

"That's the nicest thing I've heard all day. That you've missed me."

"Walking the ceiling! What happen?"

"Were you worried? Oh, dear!"

"Not worried, Smith's door flunky said you been sent on errand an 'ud come home in a Brink's. So knew you safe. Just torched it took so long when call made spec you'd short it. Rozzer?"

"Roz. Simple, though. Boss sent me with his Best Boy—Jake Salomon, you know."

"Fixer. Roz."

"Mr. Salomon took me in his car to his office to work on things Boss wanted at once—you know how right-now Boss is and worse since he's been wired down."

"Poor old muck should take the Big One. Pitiful."

"Don't say that, dear. I cry when I think about it."

"You're a slob, Sis. But me, too."

"That's why I love you, dear. Anyhow a longish job and Mr. Salomon had his guards take me home—and they drove through Bird's Nest turf and we got fired on. Chopped all down one side."

"*Huh*? Doom?"

"Not even grief. Fun."

"Like what inside?"

"Teribly noisy. But exciting. Made me horny."

"Everything makes you horny, Tits." He grinned and mussed her hair. "You're home and no aches, what counts. So peel. Inspiration eating me, whole day. Walking the ceiling!"

"Which sort of inspiration, dearest?" she asked while sliding the half-sweater off her right shoulder and peeling it down her arm. "And have you eaten? If you start painting, you won't stop to eat."

"Ate some. Too high on inspiration. Big, big! I'll flash a pack for you. Chicken? Spaghetti? Pizza?"

"Anything. I'd better eat if it's that sort of inspiration." She kicked off her sandals, pushed down the panty-ruffle, sat on the floor to slide off the single tight attached to it. "Am I going to pose for a painting or are you going to paint on me and mug it?"

"Both. Tha's the grabber. A Nova."

She laid her dress carefully aside, rocked forward into Lotus seat. "I don't roz it. 'Both?' "

"Both. You'll see." He looked down, ran his eyes over her, smiled. "And both sorts inspiration."

"Well! Happy-making!"

"Not too hungry? Can wait."

"Beloved man, when was I ever that hungry? Never

48

mind the bed; just grab a pillow and come here!"

Shortly Mrs. Branca was thinking happily how lucky it was that she had not let dear Jake go ahead—the sweet thing would have been a disappointment compared with what she had at home . . . yet he had got her wonderfully primed for *this*. Really, it was best to be a faithful wife. Usually. What a wonderful, extraordinary day! Should she tell Joe about her big pay raise? No hurry. Couldn't tell him *anything* else. Too bad. Then she quit thinking coherently.

Sometime later she opened her eyes and smiled up at him. "Thank you, Beloved."

"Good vibes?"

"Just what Eunice needed. At times like this I'm convinced that you're Michelangelo."

He shook his head. "Not old Mike. Boys his jolly. Picasso maybe."

She hugged him. "Anyone you want to be, darling, as long as you go on being mine. All right. I'll pose now, and eat at the breaks."

"Forgot. Letter from Mama. Read?"

"Certainly, darling. Let me up and find it."

He fetched it, still unopened. She sat up and glanced through it to see how much editing it would require. Uh huh, just as you expected, dearie, the periodic threat to come pay us "a nice long visit." Well, she knew how to deal with *that*. Out! Because Joe did not know how to refuse his mother anything. That one visit had been one too many—yet that had been when they had had two rooms, before she had found this wonderful one-big-everything studio room for Joe. Let that clinging old bag move in? No more jolly romps on the floor? No, Mama Branca, I will *not* let you ruin our happy nest with your smothering presence. You stay where you are and live on Welfare . . . and I'll send you a check from time to time and let you think it's a present from Joe. But that's *all*!

"Anything?"

"The usual, dearest. Her stomach still bothers her but the priest sent her to another doctor and she's doing better, she says. But let me start at the beginning. 'My darling Baby

49

Boy, Not much news since last time Mama wrote but if I don't write I don't never get a letter back. Tell Eunice to write a longer letter this time and tell me everything that's happened to you; a mother worries so. Eunice is a very nice girl even though I do think you would be better off with a nice girl of your own religion—' "

"Enough."

"Be tolerant, Joe. She's your mother. I don't mind and I will take time—tomorrow—to write her a long letter. I'll send it by Mercury in the company pouch so that she will be sure to get it; Boss doesn't mind. All right, I'll skip the rest of that; we know what she thinks of Protestants. Or ex-Protestants. I wonder what she would think if she heard us chanting 'Om Mani Padme—' "

"Kark her drawers."

"Oh, Joe!" She skipped, including the self-invitation. " 'Angela is going to have another baby. The Visitor is sore at her but I gave the Visitor a piece of my mind and I guess that learned her not to mistreat decent people. I can't see why they can't just leave us alone. What's wrong with having a baby?' Which of your sisters is Angela, Joe?"

"Third one. Visitor's right. Mama's wrong. Don't read all, Tits. Just read and tell."

"Yes, dear. Nothing more, really, just gossip about neighbors, remarks about the weather. The actual news is that your mother's stomach is better and Angela is pregnant. Give me a moment to shower this red and black off—Boss liked the combo, by the way—and I'll be ready to be painted or to pose or whatever. You can flash a pizza for me while I get clean and I'll gnaw it between times. And, dear? I shouldn't pose later than midnight and I'd be awfully pleased if you would get up when I do tomorrow—rather early, I'm afraid. But you can go back to bed."

"So?"

"For Boss, dearest. To cheer him up." She explained her idea of full-paint costume alternated with erotic styles.

He shrugged. "Glad to. Why gee-string? Silly. Old man dying, let him look. Can't hurt."

"Because, dear. Boss prides himself on being 'modern'
50

and 'keeping up with the times.' But the truth is he formed his ideas so long ago that nakedness wasn't just uncommon, it was a sin. He thinks I'm a nice girl from so far back in the cornstalks that I've never been touched by changes. As long as I wear a minimum-gee—and paint and shoes—I'm dressed, not naked. By his 'modern' standards, I mean. A nice girl pretending to be naughty to amuse him. Which he likes."

He shook his head. "No roz."

"Oh, but you do, dear. Symbolism, as you have explained to me about art. But it has to be *Boss's* symbols. Nudity doesn't mean a thing to our generation. But it does to Boss. If I leave off that scrap of nylon, then by his symbols I'm not just a sweet girl, naughty-but-nice; I'm a whore."

"Whores okay. Angela one."

(A clumsy one, she said under her breath.) "Sure they are. But not to Boss. The hard part is to guess what his symbols are. I'm twenty-eight and he's over ninety and I can't possibly roz his mind. If I push it too far, he might be angry—even very angry; he might fire me. Then what would we do? We'd have to give up this lovely studio."

Still in Lotus, she looked around. Yes, lovely. Aside from the Gadabout parked near the door and the bed in the corner all the rest was the colorul clutter of an artist's studio, always changing and always the same. The steel grid over the high north windows made a pretty pattern—and was so strong that she never worried. She felt warm and safe and happy here.

"Eunice my darling—"

She was startled. Joe used short-talk so habitually that she was always surprised when he chose to shift idiom, even though he could use formal English as well as she could—well, almost, she corrected . . . but he was quite grammatical for a man who had had only a high school practical curriculum. "Yes, dearest?"

"I roz it perfectly. Wasn't sure you did. Just testing, Beautiful. Not ninety myself but any artist understands figleaf symbol. Could happen you crowd Mr. Smith's symbols too hard, don' know. But we'll do it. Figleaf so

51

that his mind can lie to itself—'No, no, mustn't touch; Mama spank'—then I paint you like sex crime looking for spot marked 'X.' "

"Oh, good!"

"But never worry about job. Sure, this pad is righteous, good north light, I like it. But we lose it, who cares? Broke don't scare me."

(It scares *me*, dear!) "I love you, darling."

"But we do it for nice old boy dying, not to save studio. Understand?"

"Roz indeed! Joe, you're the nicest husband a girl ever had."

He did not answer and got a pained scowl, which she recognized as birth pangs of creativity. So she kept still. Presently he sighed. "Down off ceiling. Problem what to do for Boss solves inspiration that put me up there. Tomorrow you're a mermaid."

"All right."

"And tonight. Upper body seagreen with rosy glow showing through on lips and cheeks and nipples. Lower body golden fish scales blending at waist. Undersea background with sunlight filtering down. Traditional seabottom symbols, romantic. But upside down."

She hesitated. "So?" (Hard to know when to ask, when to keep quiet, when Joe was creating.)

He smiled. "Fool-the-eye. You're swimming. Diving straight down to bottom, back arched, hair streaming, toes pointed—main light dapple-scrimmed for water. Beautiful. But can't wire you, even if had wires—no way to hide harness, and hair would hang down and buttocks and breasts would sag—"

"My breasts don't sag!"

"Chill it, Jill. You got beautiful breasts and you know I know. But masses of flesh sag and artist sees it. Everybody sees, just don' realize. Something wrong, don' know why. Eye not fooled. Has to be real dive, or it's fake. Bad art."

"Well," she said doubtfully, "if you borrowed a stepladder and dragged the mattress under your background, I suppose I could dive off and roll out and not hurt myself. I guess."

"I *don't* guess! Break pretty neck, little stupid. Dive *up*. Not down."

"Huh?"

"I *said*. Background upside down. So jump straight up in air. Like going for hot return in volley ball. I shoot stereo stop-action, a thousandth. Shoot six, seven, eight, nine times till just right. Turn pic upside down—lovely mermaid diving for sea bottom."

"Oh. Yes, I'm stupid."

"Not stupid, just not artist." He started scowling again; she kept quiet. "Too much for one night. Tomorrow paint background, tonight paint you for drill. Then maybe stereo-mug some jumps against any background, more drill. Bed early, up early—paint you again for Boss."

"Fine," she agreed. "But why paint me twice, dear, if I'm to be a mermaid for Boss tomorrow? If you set up the cot for me and I slept alone, I wouldn't disturb paint job much. Then you could touch it up in the morning. Not get up as early."

He shook his head. "Won't paint quite same way for Boss. But won't let you sleep in paint anyhow."

"My skin won't break out."

"No, my darling. Your skin don' break out because I don' paint you too much, or too often, or let paint stay on too long—and always damn sure you get it all off, then oil you. But you see, I see, everybody see what happen to girls who paint too much. Pimples, blackheads, itching, scratching—ugly. Sure, we'll paint you for Boss from ears to toes—but not too often and scrub you minute you're home. That's official."

"Yes, sir."

"So scrub jet and scarlet off, while I flash pizza."

A few minutes later she shut off the shower and called out through the door of the bath unit: "What did you say?"

"Forgot. Big Sam stopped by. Pizza ready."

"Cut me a chunk, that's a dear. What did he want? Money?"

"No. Well, I let him have a fin. But stopped to invite us. Sunday. All day meditation. Gigi's pad."

She stepped out into the room, till toweling. "All day,

53

huh? Just us four? Or his whole class?"

"Neither. A Seven Circle."

"Swinging?"

"Suppose so. Didn't say."

"Swinging." She sighed. "Darling, I don't mind you lending him a five you'll never see. But Big Sam is no guru, he's just a stud. And a bliffy."

"Big Sam and Gigi share what they got, Eunice. And nobody has to swing. Ever."

"Theoretically, yes. But the only good way to break a Circle is never to join it. Especially a Seven Circle. Did you promise? I can grit my teeth and smile if I have to."

"No. Told him had to see you, tell him tomorrow."

"Well? What do you want me to say, dearest?"

"I'll tell him No."

"Dearest, I don't think you answered me. Is there some special reason you want us in this Seven? An art critic perhaps? Or a dealer? If it's Gigi you have on your mind, why not ask her to model some daytime while I'm working? She'd be up here at once, her tail quivering—I've seen her eyeing you."

He shook his head and grinned. "Nyet, Yvette. Believe, lass—I stalled Big Sam because possible *you* wanted to join in. But Big Sam chills me too—bad aura."

"Oh, I'm so relieved! I'll swing, darling; I promised you that when I asked you to marry me. And I have, the few times you've wanted to. And most were fun and only one struck me as boring. But I like to size up the players."

"Grab pizza, climb throne. Paint legs while you eat."

"Yes, darling." She mounted the model's throne with a wedge of pizza in each hand; there followed a long period broken only by sounds of chomping, and of low profanity that punctuated his alternating pleasure and exasperation. Neither noticed either; Joe Branca was deep in the euphoria of creation, his wife was immersed in the warm glow of being cherished.

At last he said, "Down," and offered his hand.

"May I look?"

"No. Ribs and tits now. Don' raise arms yet. Want to study them."

54

"As if you didn't know every wrinkle."

"Shut up. What to think about how to paint 'em in the morning." Presently he said, "Been thinking maybe you crowd Boss too hard with only a gee-panty. Solved now."

"So?"

"Da. Paint a bra on you."

"But wouldn't that spoil it, dear? Mermaids don't wear bras."

"Was problem. Bad empathy. So use sea shells. Flat curved kind with nubbly backs. You know."

"Sorry but I don't, dear. Sea shells are scarce in Iowa."

"No matter. Sea shells fix bad empathy, symbols all match." He grinned. "Pretty one, I'll paint sea-shell bra cups so fool-the-eye that Boss won' know for sure. He'll spend day trying to see whether is real bra or just paint. If he breaks down and asks—I win."

She gurgled happily. "Joe, you're a genuis!"

As Dr. Boyle came out of the operating theater Mr. Salomon stood up. "Doctor!"

Boyle checked his impatient strides. "Oh. You again. Go to hell."

"No doubt I will. But wait a moment, Doctor."

The surgeon answered with controlled fury: "Listen, chum—I've been operating eleven hours with one short break. By now I hate everybody, especially you. So let me be."

"I thought perhaps you could use a drink."

The surgeon suddenly smiled. "Where's the nearest pub?"

"About twenty yards from here. In my car. Parked on this floor. Stocked with Australian beer, both cold and room temperature. And other things. Whisky. Gin. Name it."

"My word, you Yahnk barstahds do know how. Right. But I must change first." Again he turned away.

Salomon again stopped him. "Doctor, I took the liberty of having your street clothes packed into your bag and placed in my car. So let's have that drink at once."

Boyle shook his head and grinned. "You do take liberties—too right. Very well, if you can stand the stink, I'll tub and change at my hotel. 'Lay on, MacDuff!' "

Salomon let it go at that until they were locked into his car and he had poured beer for them—the authentic kangaroo kick for the surgeon, a much weaker American brew for himself; he had tangled with Australian beer in his youth and was wary. The big car started smoothly and continued so; Rockford had been warned that drinking might take place in the passenger compartment.

Salomon waited until his guest had half a glass down him and had sighed in relief. "Doctor, how did it go?"

"Eh? Smoothly. We had planned it, we rehearsed it, we did it. How else? That's a good team you got for me."

"I take it you are saying the operation was successful?"

" '—but the patient died.' That's the rest of the old saw."

Jacob Salomon felt a wave of sorrow and relief. He sighed and answered, "Well, I expected it. Thank you, Doctor. I know you tried."

"Slow down! I don't mean that *this* patient died; I merely completed the cliché. The operation went exactly as planned; the patient was in satisfactory shape when I relinquished control to the support team."

"Then you expect him to live?"

" 'It,' not 'he,' That thing back there is not a human being and may never be. It won't die, it *can't*—unless one of your courts gives permission to switch off the machinery. That body is young and healthy; with the support it is receiving it can stay alive—as protoplasm, not as a human being—for any length of time. Years. And the brain was alive when I left; it was continuing to show strong alpha-wave response. It should stay alive, too; it is receiving blood supply from that healthy body. But whether that brain and that body will ever marry into a living human being—what church do you attend?"

"I don't."

"Too bad, I was about to suggest that you ring up God and ask *Him,* as *I* do not know. Since I saved the retinas and the inner ears—first surgeon ever to do that, by the bye, even though they call me a quack—it might be able to see and hear. Possibly. If the spinal cord fuses, it might regain some motor control, even be able to dispense with some of the artificial support. But I tell you the stark truth, Counselor, the most likely outcome is that that brain will

58

never again be in touch with the outside world in any fashion."

"I hope your misgivings are unfounded," Salomon said mildly. "Your contingent fee depended on your achieving sight, hearing, and speech, at a minimum."

"In a pig's arse."

"I'm not authorized to pay it otherwise. Sorry."

"Wrong. There was mention of a bonus, a ridiculously large sum—which I ignored. Look, cobber, you shysters are allowed to work on contingent fees; we butchers have other rules. My *fee* is for operating. I operated. Finis. I'm an ethical surgeon, no matter what the barstahds say about me."

"Which reminds me—" Salomon took an envelope from his pocket. "Here's your fee."

The surgeon pocketed it. Salomon said, "Aren't you going to check it?"

"Why should I? Either I was paid in full. Or I sue. Either way, I couldn't care less. Not now."

"More beer?" Salomon opened another bottle of Down-Under dynamite. "You are paid. In full, in gold, in Switzerland—that envelope contains a note advising you of your account number. Plus an acknowledgment that we pay your expenses, all fees of assisting teams, all computer time, all hospital charges, whatever. But I hope, later, to pay that 'ridiculous' bonus, as you called it."

"Oh, I won't turn down a gift; research is expensive—and I do want to go on; I would like to be a respectable paragraph in medical histories . . . instead of being sneered at as a charlatan."

"No doubt. Not quite my own reason."

Boyle took a swig of beer and blinked thoughtfully. "I suppose I've been a stinker again. Sorry—I always come out of surgery in a vile mood. I forgot he is your friend."

Salomon again felt that bittersweet wave of relief and sorrow. He answered carefully, "No, Johann Smith is not my friend."

"So? I had an impression that he was."

"Mr. Smith has no friends. I am a lawyer in his hire. As

59

such, he is entitled to my loyalty."

"I see. I'm glad you aren't emotionally involved, as the prognosis on a brain transplant is never good—as I know better than anyone." Boyle added thoughtfully, "It might work this time. It was a good tissue match, surprisingly good in view of the wide difference between donor and recipient. And identical blood type, that helps. We might luck it. Even disparity in skulls turned out to be no problem once I could see that brain."

"Then why are you gloomy?"

"Do you know how many millions of nerve connections are involved? Think I could do them all in eleven hours? Or eleven thousand hours? We don't try; we just work on the nerves of the head, then butt the raw ends of two spinal cords together—and sit back and spin our prayer wheels. Maybe they fuse, maybe they don't—and no one knows why."

"So I understood. What I don't understand is how those millions of connections can ever take place. Yet apparently you were successful with two chimpanzees."

"Bloody! I *was* successful. Sorry. The human nervous system is infinitely inventive in defending itself. Instead of reconnecting old connections it finds new paths—if it can—and learns to use them. Do you know the psych lab experiment with inverting spectacles?"

"I'm afraid not."

"Some student has inverting lenses taped to his eyes. For a day or two he sees everything upside down, has to be led by the hand, fed, escorted to the jakes. Then rather suddenly he sees everything right side up again; the brain has switched a few hundred thousand connections and is now interpreting the new data successfully. At this point we remove the spectacles from the volunteer chump—and now his bare eyes see the world upside down. So he goes through it a second time—and *again* the brain finds new paths and eventually the images flip over again and he sees the world normally.

"Something somewhat analogous to that happened to my two prize chimps. Abélard and Héloïse. Nothing at first, thought I had still another failure. Then they started to

60

twitch and we had to restrain them to keep them from hurting themselves—motor action but no control. Like a very young baby. But in time the brains learned to manage their new bodies. Don't ask me how; I'm a surgeon and won't guess—ask a psychologist, they love to guess. Or ask a priest; you'll get as good an answer and maybe better. Say, isn't your driver chap taking us around the barn? My hotel was only five minutes from the medical center."

"I must now admit to having taken another liberty, Doctor. Your luggage was packed, your hotel bill has been paid, and all your things were moved to my guest room."

"My word. Why?"

"Better security."

"That hotel seemed secure to me. Armed guards on every door, more armed men operating the lifts—I could not get in or out without showing my I.D. at least thrice. Reminded me of the army. Hadn't realized what an armed camp the States are. Isn't it rather a nuisance?"

"Yes. But one grows used to it. Your hotel is safe enough, physically. But the press are onto us now and they can get inside. And so can the police."

Boyle looked troubled but not panicky. "Legal complications? You assured me that all that sort of thing had been taken care of."

"I did. It has. The donor was married, as I told you, and by great luck husband and wife had given pre-consent. We had a good many thousands of that blood type quietly signed up—and paid retainers—but we couldn't predict that one would be accidentally killed in time; the statistical projection did not favor it. But one of them was indeed killed and there were no complications—no insuperable ones," Salomon corrected, thinking of a bag of well-worn Federal Reserve notes, "and a court permitted it as 'useful and necessary research.' Nevertheless the press will stir up a storm and some other court may decide to look into it. Doctor, I can put you in Canada in an hour, anywhere on this planet in a day—even on the Moon without much delay. If you so choose."

"Hmm. Wouldn't mind going to the Moon, I've never been there. You say my clothes are in your guest room?"

"Yes. And you are most welcome."

"Is there a tub of hot water nearby?"

"Oh, certainly."

"Then I'll ask for another beer and that hot tub and about ten hours' sleep. I've been arrested before. Doesn't worry me."

5

Johann Sebastian Bach Smith was somewhere else. Where, he did not know, nor care, nor wonder . . . did not know that he was himself, was not aware of himself nor of anything, was not aware that he was not aware.

Then slowly, over eons, he came up from the nothingness of total anesthesia, surfaced into dreaming. The dreams went on for unmeasured time, endlessly . . . Mrs. Schmidt, can Yonny come out and play . . . Wuxtra! Horrible atrocities in Belgium, read all about it! . . . Johann, don't *ever* walk in like that without knocking, you bad, *bad* boy . . . under a cabbage leaf . . . more margin before the market opens tomorrow . . . like hell a cabbage leaf; it comes out of her belly button Yoho you don't know nothing . . . Johnny you know it's not nice to do that and what if my father came downstairs . . . a pretty girl is like a melody . . . hey get a load of that not a damn thing on her boobs . . . sergeant I volunteered once and that's enough for a lifetime . . . Our Father Which art in Heaven hallowed be thy Name of the game is look out for yourself Smith old Buddy you co-signed the note and I have other fish to Friday at the latest and that's a promise Johann darling I don't know how you could even bring yourself to think such a thing of your own wife is a man's responsibility Mr. Smith and I'm sure the court will agree that four thousand per monthlies is a very modest girl would never do such a thing Schmidt and if I ever catch you hanging around my daughter again I'll shoot the whole works they're not worth the paper they're printed on Johann I don't know what your father will say when he gets home on the range where the deer and antelope play square with me and you'll get a fair shake it, girlie, shake it, shake it twice is regulation

63

shake it thrice pudding with creamed in her coffin my head off and her old man heard us and that queered it not queer Johann just curious you understand me old body boy I aint got no body and no body works very long for some body else if he expects to get ahead in the world o' business girl has got just as much right to be treated like a lady as any body seen my girl's best friend is her cherish as long as you both shall live right and work hard and pay your bills of lading son goes down and the stars come out of my room at once my husband would kill me and the neighbors are always snooping where did you leave your bicycle would pay for itself in no time Pop if I get this paper rout and in full retreat as we go to press me closer Johnny you're so huge national debt will never be paid off and all our companies' policies must be in inflation so borrow now and pay later than you think I'm that sort of a girl simply because I let you go on to college to be a teacher son but now I see by the dawn's early warning system is useless gentlemen without second-strike capabilities of sustained growth when treated last time so it's your treat this time you treat me nice and I treat you nice you-nice Eunice *Eunice*! where did that girl go I've lost Rome and I've lost Gaul but worst of all I've lost Eunice somebody find Eunice . . . coming Boss . . . where have you been right here all along Boss—

His dreams went on endlessly in full stereo—sound, sight, odor, touch—and always surrealistic, which he never noticed. They flowed through him, or he through them, with perfect logic. To him.

Meanwhile the world flowed on around him—and forgot him. The attempt at transplanting a living brain offered opportunity for much loose talk by video commentators, plus guest "experts" who were encouraged to add their own mixture of prejudice, speculation, and bias in the name of "science." A judge in need of publicity issued a warrant for the arrest of "Dr. Lyndon Doyle" (*sic*) but Dr. Lindsay Boyle was outside of jurisidiction before the warrant was signed and long before the name was straightened out. A famous and very stylish evangelist prepared a sermon denoucning the transplant, using as a text "Vanity of Vanities."

But on the third day a spectacular and unusually bloody political assassination crowded Johann Smith out of the news and the evangelist found that he could use the sermon by changing a few sentences—which he did, understanding instinctively the American lust for the blood of the mighty.

As usual, the unlicensed birth rate exceeded the licensed rate while the abortion rate exceeded both. Upjohn International declared an extra dividend. The backing and filling for the upcoming Presidential campaign speeded up with a joint announcement by the national committees of the two conservative parties, the SDS and the PLA, that they would hold their conventions together (while preserving mutual autonomy) for the (unannounced but understood) purpose of reelecting the incumbent. The chairman of the extreme left-wing Constitutional Liberation Rally denounced it as a typical crypto-fascist capitalistic plot, and predicted a November victory for Constitutional freedom. The splinter parties, Democratic, Socialist, and Republican, met quietly (few members and almost no delegates under sixty-five) and stole away without causing more than a ripple in the news.

In the Middle East an earthquake killed nine thousand people in three minutes and brought close the ever-present possiblity of war through disturbing the balance of terror. The Sino-American Lunar Commission announced that the Lunar Colonies were now 87% self-sufficient in proteins and carbohydrates, and raised the subsidized out-migration quota but again refused to relax the literacy requirement.

Johann Sebastian Bach Smith dreamed on.

After an unmeasured time (how measure a dream?) Smith woke enough to be aware of himself—the reflexive self-awareness of waking as contrasted with the unquestioning and unexplicit self-experience of dreaming. He knew who he was, Johann Sebastian Bach Smith, a very old man—not a baby, not a boy, not any of his younger selves—and was aware of his sensory surroundings, which

65

were zero: darkness, silence, absence of any physical sensation, not even pressure, touch, kinesthesia.

He wondered if the operation had started, and what it would feel like when he died. He did not worry about pain; he had been assured that the brain itself had no pain receptors and that he was being anesthetized solely to keep him quiet and unworried while the job was done—besides, pain had not worried Smith in years; it was his constant companion, almost an old friend.

Presently he went back to sleep and to more dreams, unaware that his brain-wave pattern was being monitored and had caused great excitement when change in rhythm and peak had shown that the patient was awake.

Again he was awake and this time gave thought to the possibility that this nothingness was death. He considered the idea without panic, having come to terms with death more than a half century earlier. If this was death, it was neither the Heaven he had been promised as a child nor the Hell he had long since ceased to believe in, nor even the total lack of *self* he had come to expect—it was just one damn big bore.

He slept again, unaware that the physician in charge of his life-support team had decided that the patient had been awake long enough and had slowed his breathing and made a slight change in his blood chemistry.

He woke again and tried to take stock of the situation. If he was dead—and there seemed no longer reason to doubt it—what did he have left and how could he cut his losses? Assets: none. Correction: one asset, memory. He had a recent memory-of-a-memory, vague and undefined, of confused and crazy dreams—probably from anesthesia and no use to him—plus other memories older but much sharper of being (or having been) Johann Smith. Well, Johann you old bastard, if you and me are going to have to spend all eternity locked in this limbo we had better get to work on total recall of everything we ever did.

Everything? Or concentrate on the good parts? No, a stew had to have salt or it was too bland. Try to remember all of it. If we have all eternity with nothing to play but this one rerun, we're going to want to have *all* of it on tap . . .

as even the best parts may get boring after a few thousand times.

Still, it wouldn't hurt to concentrate—just for practice—on some exceptionally pleasant memory. So what'll it be, partner? There are only four top subjects, the rest are sideshows: money, sex, war, and death. So which do we choose? *Right!* You're correct, Eunice; I'm a dirty old man and my only regret (and a sharp one!) is that I didn't find you forty or fifty years back. When you were not yet a gleam in your father's eye, more's the pity. Tell me, girl, were those sea-shell doodads a brassière or just paint on your pretty skin? Euchered myself on that one—should have asked and let you sass me. So tell great-grandpappy. Give me a phone call and tell me. Sorry, I can't tell you the wave length, dear; it's unlisted.

Golly, you looked cute!

Let's try another one—no chance that I'll forget you, Eunice my dear, but I never laid a finger on you, damn it. Let's go way, way back to one we *did* lay a finger on. Our very first piece? No, you mucked that up pretty badly, you clumsy lout. The second one? Ah, yes, she was the cat's pajamas! Mrs. Wicklund. First name? Did I ever know her first name? Certainly I never called her by it, not then or later. Even though she let me come back for more. *Let* me? Encouraged me, set it up.

Let's see, I was fourteen, fourteen and a half, and she must have been . . . thirty-five? I remember her mentioning that she had been married fifteen years, so call it thirty-five at a guess. No matter, it was the first time I ever encountered a female who wanted it, managed to let me know that she wanted it, then without any bobbles could take charge of a lanky, too-eager, almost-virgin boy, steady him, lead him through it, make him enjoy it, let him know *she* enjoyed it—make him feel good about it afterwards.

God bless your generous soul, Mrs. Wicklund! If you are lost somewhere in this darkness—for you must have died many years sooner than I did—I hope you remember me and are as happy in remembering me as I am in remembering you.

All the details now— Your flat was right under ours.

Cold windy afternoon and you gave me a quarter (big money then, a dime was standard) for going to the grocery for you. For what? How good is your memory, you horny old goat? Correction: horny old 'ghost.' What have I got left to be horny with? Never mind, I *am*—it's up *here*, Doc. Half a pound of sliced boiled ham, a sack of russet potatoes, a dozen ranch eggs (seven cents a dozen then—my God!), a ten-cent loaf of Holsum bread and—something else. Oh, yes, a spool of sixty white cotton thread at the notions shop next to Mr. Gilmore's drugstore. Mrs. Baum's shop—two sons, one killed in War One and the other made a name for himself in electronics. But let's get back to *you*, Mrs. Wicklund.

You heard me bring my bike into the hallway and opened your door, and I carried your groceries on through to your kitchen. You paid me and offered me hot cocoa and—why wasn't I nervous about Mama? Pop at work and Mr. Wicklund, too; that figured—but where was Mama? Oh, yes, her Sewing Circle afternoon.

So while I drank cocoa and was being polite, you cranked your Victrola and put on a record—uh. "Margie," it was, and you asked me if I knew how to dance. You taught me to dance all right—on the sofa.

A life-support technician studied an oscilloscope, noted an increase in brain activity, concluded that the patient might be frightened and decided to tranquilize. Johann Smith slipped gently into sleep without knowing it—to the scratchy strains of a mechanical phonograph. He was "fox-trotting," so she told him. He did not care what it was called; his arm was around her waist, hers was around his neck, her warm clean odor was sweet in his nostrils. Presently she seduced him.

After a long, ecstatic, and utterly satisfying time he said, "Eunice honey, I didn't know you could fox-trot."

She smiled into his eyes. "You never asked me, Boss. Can you reach past me and shut off the Victrola?"

"Sure, Mrs. Wicklund."

6

Johann Smith became aware that this limbo was no longer featureless—head resting on something, mouth unpleasantly dry and felt crowded, as if with the sort of junk a dental surgeon inflicts on his victims. There was still total blackness but not quite dead silence. A sucking noise—

Any sensation was most welcome. Johann shouted, "Hey! *I lived through it!*"

Two rooms away the monitoring technician on watch jumped up so fast he knocked over his chair. "Patient's trying to articulate! Get Dr. Brenner!"

Brenner answered quietly over the voice monitor. "I'm with the patient, Cliff. Get a team in here. And notify Dr. Hedrick and Dr. Garcia."

"Right away!"

Johann said, "Hey, damn it! Isn't *anybody* here?" The words came out as incoherent grunts.

The Doctor touched a wand speaker to the patient's teeth, held the microphone hooked to it against his own throat. "Mr. Smith, do you hear me?"

The patient mumbled again, louder and more forcefully. The Doctor answered, "Mr. Smith, I'm sorry but I cannot understand you. If you hear me, make one sound. Any sort but just one."

The patient grunted once.

"Good, wonderful—you can hear me. All right, one sound by itself means Yes; two sounds mean No. If you understand me, answer with two sounds. Two grunts."

Smith grunted twice.

"Good, now we can talk. One sound for Yes, two for No. Do you hurt?"

Two grunts—"Uh . . . ko!"

"Fine! Now we try something else. Your ears are covered and completely soundproofed; my voice is reaching your inner ears through your teeth and upper jawbone. I'm going to remove part of the covering on your left ear and speak to you that way. The sounds may be painfully loud at first, so I will start with whispers. Understand me?"

One grunt—

Smith felt gentle firmness as something pulled loose. "Do you still hear me?"

"Uh . . . ko—"

"Now do you hear me?"

"Uh . . . *ko* . ah . ee . . oh . . ce . . . oo . . ow!"

"I think that was a sentence. Don't try to talk yet. Just one grunt, or two."

Johann said, "Of course I can't talk, you damned idiot! Take this junk out of my mouth!" The vowels came through fairly clearly; consonants were distorted or missing.

"Doctor, how the patient can talk with all that gear in the way?"

Brenner said quietly, "Shut up, Nurse. Mr. Smith, we have an aspirator down your throat to keep you from choking on phlegm, drowning in your own saliva. I can't remove it yet, so try to be patient. Besides that, your eyes are masked. Your eye specialist will decide when that comes off. I can't—I'm the life-support specialist on duty at the moment, not the physician managing your case; that's Dr. Hedrick assisted by Dr. Garcia. I can't do much more than I have till one of them gets here. Are you comfortable? One grunt or two."

One grunt—

"Good. I'll stay here with you. And talk to you if you want me to. Do you?"

One grunt—

70

"Okay, I will. You can talk with more than a Yes or No any time you wish. By spelling. I'll recite the alphabet, slowly, and you stop me with one grunt when I reach a letter you want. And so on for the next letter, until it's spelled out. It's slow . . . but neither one of us is going anywhere. Want to try it?"

One grunt—

"Good. I've had lots of practice at it; I've been on many a life-support watch in which the patient could not talk but was awake and perfectly rational. As you are," the Doctor added, lying hopefully, one eye on the master oscilloscope. "But bored, of course. Very bored—that's the worst part for a patient in life-support; he's bored silly, yet we can't let him sleep all the time; it's not good for him and sometimes we need his cooperation. All right, any time you want to spell anything, give three distinct grunts and I'll prove I know my abc's."

Three grunts—

"A . . b . . c . . d . . e . . f—" Johann grunted at "r."

" 'R'?" Dr. Brenner repeated. "Don't bother to answer if I'm right. Okay, first letter is 'r.' A . . b . . c . . d . .—"

The message read: "Right ear."

"Do you want the plug removed from your right ear?"

One grunt—

Carefully the Doctor removed it. "Testing," he said. "Cincinnati, sixty-six, Susannah. Are you hearing with both ears? Does my voice seem to move from side to side?"

One grunt, followed by three grunts—

"Okay, spelled message. A . . b . . c—"

Shortly the Doctor said, " 'Nobody'? Is that the first word of your message?"

Double grunt—

"All right, I'll try again. A . . b—" He was interrupted by a series of grunts, and stopped. "You don't want me to spell again . . . yet 'Nobody' is not the first word of your message. But I would have sworn that I got it right. 'Nobody—' Uh . . . hey! 'No . . . body'—two words?"

One emphatic grunt—

"Are you trying to tell me that you feel as if you had no body? Can't feel it?"

71

Grunt—

"Oh! Of course you can't feel it; you haven't finished healing. But honestly," the Doctor went on, lying with the skill of long practice, "your progress has been amazingly fast. Both speech and hearing so soon, that's wonderfully encouraging. In fact you've just won a bet for me. Five hundred," he went on, still lying, "and at that I demanded more than twice the recovery time you've shown. And now I'm going to double my winnings by putting them back and betting that you'll have full recovery of the use of your whole body in no longer time. Because this is a wonderfully healthy body you have even though you can't feel it yet. Marvelous repair factor."

Triple grunt— Then the spelled message was: "How long?"

"How long since your operation? Or how long until you get the use of your whole body?"

Dr. Brenner was saved by the bell. He stopped reciting the alphabet and said, "Half a moment, Mr. Smith; Dr. Hedrick has arrived, I must report. Nurse will stay with you—just let the patient rest, Nurse; this has been tiring."

Outside the door Dr. Brenner stopped the case-managing physician, saying, "Dr. Hedrick, one moment before you go in. You've checked the remotes?"

"Certainly. Awake-normal, apparently."

"And rational, in my opinion. I have removed the central stopples from both ear pads and we have been talking, spell-and-grunt, killing time until you—"

"I heard you on monitor, assumed you must have opened the ears. You take a lot on yourself, Doctor."

Dr. Brenner stiffened, then answered coldly, "Doctor—your patient, conceded. But I was here alone and had to use my own judgment. If you wish me to leave the case, you have only to say so."

"Don't be so damned touchy, young man. Now let's go in and see the patient. Our patient."

"Yes, sir."

They went inside. Dr. Hedrick said, "I'm Dr. Hedrick, Mr. Smith, physician in charge of your case. Congratulations! Welcome back to our weary world. This is a triumph for everyone—and vindication for a great man, Dr. Boyle."

Three grunts—

"You wish to spell a message?"

One grunt—

"If you will wait a moment, we will remove some items from your mouth and you can talk instead." (With great good luck, Hedrick amended to himself—but I never expected the case to progress even this far. That arrogant butcher really *is* a great man. To my surprise.) "Would that suit you?"

An emphatic grunt—

"Good. Hand aspiration, Dr. Brenner. Adjust those lights, Nurse. Monitor watch! Find out what's keeping Dr. Feinstein."

Johann Smith felt hands working rapidly but gently, then Dr. Hedrick said, "Let me check, Doctor. Very well, remove the jaw wedges. Mr. Smith, we will have to aspirate every few moments—I'd rather not have to force you to cough up fluid. Or go after it the hard way. But you may talk if you wish."

"Aye-*gah*-aye-*hay*-dih!"

"Slowly, slowly. You're having to learn to talk all over again, like a baby. That same remark now—but slowly and carefully."

"By . . . *God* . . . I . . . *made* . . . it!"

"You surely did. The first man in history to have his brain moved into a new body—and lived through it. And you will go on living. This is a fine body. Healthy."

"But . can't . peal—feel—a damn . . *thing* . from . chin . down."

"Lucky you," said the Doctor. "Because we've got you restrained all over against the day—soon, I hope"—but never, more likely, he added to himself—"when you will start feeling your entire new body. When that day comes, you may jerk uncontrollably—if we didn't have you restrained. Then you'll have to go to work and learn to control your body. Like a new baby. Practice. Possibly long and tedious practice."

"How . . . long?"

73

"I don't know. Dr. Boyle's chimps made it rather quickly, I understand. But it might take you as long as it takes a baby to learn to walk. But why worry about that now? You're got a new body, good for many, many years—why, you might be the first human being to live two hundred years. So don't be in a hurry. Now rest, please—I've got to examine you. Chin screen, Nurse."

"The patient's eyes are covered, Doctor."

"Ah, yes, so they are. Mr. Smith, when Dr. Feinstein arrives, we will see if he wants to expose your eyes to light today. In the meantime—uncover the patient, Nurse."

Uncovered, the new body was still mostly covered. A plastic corset "iron lung" encased the torso from chin to pubis; arms and legs were strapped and the straps cushioned; urethral and anal catheters were in place and secured; two blood vessels were in use, one for nourishment, the other for monitoring; four others were prepared for use but currently stopped off. Wires were here and there. The body inside this dismal mess could have been one that Michelangelo would have treasured but the assemblage of artifact and protoplasm could seem beautiful only to a medical specialist.

Dr. Hedrick seemed pleased. He took a stylus from his pocket, suddenly scratched the sole of the right foot—got the reflex he expected, got no response from Johann Smith, also as expected.

"Dr. Hedrick?" came a voice from the bed console.

"Yes."

"Dr. Feinstein is operating."

"Very well." He indicated to a nurse that he wanted the body covered. "Did you hear that, Mr. Smith? Your ophthalmologist is in surgery, can't see you today. Just as well, as you have had enough for one day. It's time for you to sleep."

"No. You . . do . . it. My : . eyes."

"No. We wait for Dr. Feinstein."

"No! You . are . in . charge."

"So I am and your eyes won't be touched until your specialist is present."

"Damn . . you. Get . . Jake . . Sal . o . mon!"

"Mr. Salomon is in Europe, will be notified that you are awake, and he may possibly be here tomorrow. I couldn't say. In the meantime I want you to rest. Sleep."

"Won't!"

"Ah, but you will." Dr. Hedrick pointed to Dr. Brenner, nodded. "As you pointed out, I am in charge. Want to know why I am certain you will sleep? Because we are slowing your breathing rate and introducing into your bloodstream a harmless drug that will insure that you *do* sleep. So good night, Mr. Smith, and again—my congratulations."

"Damn . . your . . . ins— . insuffera—" Johann Smith slept.

Once he half roused. "Eunice?" (Right here, Boss. Go back to sleep.) He slept on.

7

"Hi, Jake!"

"Hello, Johann. How do you feel?"

"Mean as a fox with its tail in a trap except when these tyrants dope me with something that makes me sweetness-and-light in spite of myself. Where the hell have you been? Why didn't you come when I sent for you?"

"On vacation. First decent vacation I've had in fifteen years. Any objections?"

"Get your feathers down. You do have a nice tan. And taken off a little weight, too, I think. Okay, okay—though I don't mind saying I was disappointed that you didn't trot back for a day or two at least when I woke up. Hurt my feelings."

"Humph! You have no feelings. Never did."

"Now, Jake—I do so have feelings, just never was one for showing them. But, damn it, I *needed* you."

The lawyer shook his head. "You didn't need me. I know why you thought you did. You wanted me to interfere with Dr. Hedrick's management of your case. Which I would not have done. So I extended my vacation to avoid useless argument."

Johann grinned at him. "Always the sly one, Jake. Okay, I've never been one to fret about yesterday's trouble. But now that you're back—well, Hedrick's a good doctor . . . but he's highhanded with me when it's not necessary. So we'll change that. I'll tell you what I want and you tell

77

Hedrick—and if he balks, you can let him know that he is not indispensable."

"No."

"What do you mean, 'No'?"

"I mean *No*. Johann, you still require constant medical attention. I haven't interfered with Dr. Hedrick up to now and the results have been good. I won't interfere now."

"Oh, for Pete's sake, Jake. Sure, sure, you have my interests at heart. But you don't understand the situation. I'm no longer in a critical condition; I'm convalescent. Look, here's late news, important. Know what I did this morning during physiotherapy? Moved my right index finger. On *purpose*, Jake. Know what that means?"

"Means you can bid in an auction. Or signal a waiter."

"Crab apples. Wiggled my toes a little, too. Jake, in a week I'll be *walking*, unassisted. Why, I spend thirty minutes each day now without this lung thing, this corset . . . and when they put it back on me, it's simply set to assist, if necessary. But despite all this wonderful progress, I'm still treated like a wired-up laboratory monkey. Allowed to stay awake only a short time each day—hell, they even shave me while I'm asleep and God alone knows what else; I don't. I'm strapped down every minute that at least six people don't have their hands on me for physio. If you don't believe me, lift the sheet and take a look. I'm a prisoner. In my own house."

Salomon didn't move. "I believe you."

"Move that chair around so that I can see you better. They've even got my head clamped—now I ask you, is *that* necessary?"

"No opinion. Ask your doctor." Salomon stayed where he was.

"I asked *you* . . . because I'm fed up with his top-sergeant behavior."

"And I declined to express an opinion in a field in which I have no competence. Johann, you're getting well, that's evident. But only a fool replaces a quarterback who is winning. *I* never thought you would live through the operation. I don't think you did, either."

"Well . . . truthfully, I didn't. I was betting my

78

life—literally—on a long gamble. But I won."

"Then why don't you try being grateful?—*instead of behaving like a spoiled child!*"

"Temper, Jake, temper—why, you sound like *me.*"

"God knows I don't want to sound like *you.* But I mean it. Show gratitude. Praise the Lord—and Dr. Hedrick."

"And Dr. Boyle, Jake. Yes, I *am* grateful, truly I am. I've been snatched back from the edge of death—and now have every reason to expect a wonderful new life—and all I risked was a few more weeks of a life that had grown intolerable." Johann smiled. "I can't express how grateful I am, there are no words. My eyes are twenty/twenty again and I'm seeing shades of color I had forgotten existed. I can hear high notes I haven't heard in years. I get 'em to play symphonies for me and I can follow the piccolo clear up to the roof. And the violins. I can hear all sorts of high sounds now, higher than ever—even my new voice sounds high; he must have been a tenor. And I can *smell,* Jake—and I lost my last trace of a sense of smell years ago. Nurse, walk past me and let me smell you."

The nurse, a pretty redhead, smiled, said nothing, did not move from the bed's console.

Johann went on, "I'm even allowed to eat now, once a day—eat and swallow, I mean, not a blasted tube. Jake, did you know that Cream o' Wheat tastes better than filet mignon? It can. Hell, *everything* tastes good now; I had forgotten what fun it is to eat. Jake, it's so grand to be alive—in this body—that I can't wait to go out in the country and walk in fields and climb a hill and look at trees and watch birds. And clouds. Sunbathe. Ice-skate, maybe. Square-dance. Ever square-dance, Jake?"

"I used to be good at it. No time for it, late years."

"I never had time for it even when I was young. I'm going to *take* time, now. Reminds me, who's minding the store?"

"Teal, of course. He wants to see you."

"You see him, I'm too busy learning to use my new body. And enjoying it. Do I have any money left? Not that I give a hoot."

"You want the ungarnished truth?"

"You can't scare me, Jake. If I have to sell this house to pay off this gang of jailers, it won't worry me. Might be fun. I can tell you this: I'll never be on Welfare. I'll get by—always have, always will."

"Brace yourself. You're worth more than ever."

"Huh? Oh, what a shame! When I was just beginning to enjoy being broke."

"Hypocrite."

"Not at all, Jake. I—"

"Hypocrite, I said. Oh, hush up. Your fortune had already reached the takeoff point, where it can't possibly be spent no matter how you try; it just keeps growing. I didn't even spend all your income on this operation and all that went with it. However, you no longer control Smith Enterprises."

"So?"

"Yes. I encouraged Teal to borrow money and buy some of your voting shares; it gave him incentive in 'minding the store.' And it looked better. Also, as de-facto chairman of the board, I thought it would look better if I owned a bigger block, too, so I traded you some blue chips and tax-exempts for some of your senior-corporation voting stock. At present two of us—you and I, or you and Teal—hold voting control. But no one of us. However, I'll trade back any time you want to resume control."

"God forbid!"

"We'll leave the matter open, Johann. I was not trying to take advantage of your illness."

"No, Jake. If I don't have controlling interest, I don't have even a moral responsibility to look out for the company. I'll resign as chairman of the board—and you can be chairman, or Teal, or you can put it up for grabs."

"Wait till you're well."

"Okay but I shan't change my mind. But now about that other matter—Uh, Nurse, don't you have to go empty something, or wash your hands, or check the roof to see if it's on tight? I want private conversation with my lawyer."

She smiled and shook her head. "No, sir. You know I can't leave the room even a moment without being relieved. But I'm authorized by Dr. Hedrick to do this, sir:

I can shut off the voice monitor to the remotes, then go over in that far corner and watch video with the sound turned up high so that you'll be certain I can't hear you. Dr. Hedrick said you might want privacy in speaking with Mr. Salomon."

"Well! The old bug—bug-hunter is human after all. You do that, Nurse."

Shortly, Johann was able to say quietly, "You saw that, Jake? God knows there could be no harm in you alone watching me a few minutes—you could call for help if I choked or something. Anyhow, any trouble would show on their dials. But, no they chaperon me every second and won't agree to the most harmless request. Look, very quietly now—do you have a pocket mirror on you?"

"Eh? Never carried one in my life."

"A pity. Well, have one on you next time you're in to see me. Tomorrow, I hope. Jake, Hedrick is a good doctor, conceded—but he won't tell me *anything*. Just this week I asked him whose body this had been—and he wasn't even polite enough to lie; he just told me that it was none of my business."

"It isn't."

"Huh?"

"Remember the contract I worked out? It said—"

"Never read it. Your pidgin."

"I told you; you didn't listen. Donor's privacy to be respected unless donor specifically grants permission to breach it . . . and even then his estate must confirm after death. In this case neither proviso was met. So you can never be told."

"Oh, rats. I can find out, once I'm up and and around. I would never publicize it; I just want to know."

"No doubt you will find out. But *I* won't be a party to breaching a contract with the dead."

"Hmm. Jake, you're a stiff-necked old bastard; it wouldn't do any harm. All right, all right. But get me that mirror. Look, you can get me one now. Go into my bathroom, usual excuse, and look around. Search. Four or five small mirrors in there, drawers and such—or were the last time I was on my feet. Almost certainly still are. Just don't let a nurse see it. In your pocket. Or under your jacket."

"Why don't you simply ask for one?"

"Because they won't let me have one, Jake. You may think I'm paranoid but I *am* being persecuted by this high-and-mighty doctor. Won't let me see my new face in a mirror. Okay, it's probably scarred; I don't care. Won't let me look at myself *at all*. When they work on me they put up a chin screen; I haven't even seen my hands. Would you believe it, I don't even know what *color* I am. Am I a soul? Or a honk? Or something else? It's maddening."

"Johann, it might be literally maddening for you to see yourself. Before you have your strength back."

"What? Oh, be your age, Jake; you know me better than that. If I'm the ugliest thing since wart hogs and covered with purple stripes, I can take it." Johann grinned. "I was ugly as sin before the operation; any change for the worse can't be great. But I tell you no lie, old friend; if they keep treating me like a retarded child, they really *will* drive me off the rails."

Salomon sighed. "I'm sorry to have to tell you this, Johann, but it is no news to me that they won't let you see yourself in a mirror—"

"What?"

"Steady down. I've discussed it with Dr. Hedrick and with the psychiatrist working with him. They are of the opinion that you could suffer a severe emotional shock—one that might give you a grave setback, even (as you say) 'drive you off the rails'—if you see your new self before you are fully well and strong."

Johann Smith did not answer at once. Then he said quietly, "Pig whistle. I *know* I'm physically something else now. What harm do they think it could do me?"

"The psychiatrist mentioned the possibility of a split personality."

"Move around and look me in the eyes. Jake Salomon, do you believe that?"

"My opinion is neither relevant nor competent. I am *not* going to buck your physicians. Nor help you to outwit them."

"So that's how the wind sets. Jake . . . I am sorry to be forced to say this—but you are not the only lawyer in this city."

"So I know. I am sorry—truly sorry!—to be forced to say *this*, Johann—but I am the only lawyer you can turn to."

"*What do you mean?*"

"Johann, you are now a ward of the Court. I am your guardian."

Johann Smith was slow to answer, then barely whispered: "Conspiracy. I never thought it of you, Jake."

"Johann, Johann!"

"Do you mean to keep me locked up forever? If not, what's the price to turn me loose? Is the Judge in on it? And Hedrick?"

Salomon controlled himself. "Please, Johann, let me speak. I'm going to pretend that you never said what you did say . . . and I'll have a transcript of the proceedings brought here for you to see. Hell, I'll have the Judge himself fetch them. But you've got to listen."

"I'm listening. How can I help listening?—I'm a prisoner."

"Johann, you will cease being a ward as soon as you are able to appear in court—in person—and convince the Judge—Judge McCampbell, it is, an honest man as you know—convince McCampbell that you are no longer *non compos mentis*. He took the step reluctantly—and I had to fight to be named your guardian, as I was not the petitioner."

"So? And who asked to have me committed?"

"Johanna Darlington Seward, *et aliae*—meaning your other three granddaughters, too."

"I see," Johann said slowly. "Jake, I owe you an apology."

Salomon snorted. "For what? How can you do or say anything calling for an apology when you are legally *non compos mentis?*"

"Whew! Hand me the traditional piece of snuff; that was razor sharp. Dear little Johanna—I should have drowned her at birth. Her mother, my daughter Evelyn, used to shove her into my lap and remind me that she was my namesake. Jake, the only thing that brat ever did for me was to pee on my trousers—on purpose. So June and Marla and Elinor are in it, too. Not surprising."

"Johann, they darn near made it. I had to resort to everything short of treason to get it into Judge McCampbell's court. Even then, only the fact that I have held your general power of attorney for an unbroken fifteen years kept the Court from naming Mrs. Seward as guardian and conservator. That and one other thing."

"What other thing?"

"Their stupidity. If they had shot for guardianship right off, they might have made it. Instead their first move was to try to have you declared legally dead."

"Well! Jake, do you suppose—later—that I can cut them out of my will entirely?"

"You can do better than that; you can outlive them. Now."

"Mmm, yes, I suppose I can. I will! It'll be a pleasure."

"That move wasn't serious, just stupid. Stupid lawyer. Took four days for the expert witnesses to unwind, took the Court four minutes to rule in accordance with 'Estate of Parsons v. Rhode Island.' Hoped I had seen the last of them then; that diploma-mill shyster seemed pretty cowed. Then Parkinson got into it . . . and *his* lawyer is *not* stupid."

" 'Parkinson'? Our boy Parky, our idiot ex-director?"

"The same."

"Hmm. Von Ritter was right; it doesn't pay to humiliate a man. But how could Parky show an interest?"

"He didn't. That Parkinson put them up to it is simply a conclusion but a firm one—Parkinson's mother-in-law's lawyer and Parkinson himself present every day in court, a happy spectator. Johann, I didn't dare ask that the matter be continued during your recovery; our own expert witnesses were unwilling to testify that you would ever be yourself again, able to manage your own affairs. So we stipulated your temporary lack of competence—surprised 'em, caught 'em unprepared—and I had our attorney move that I be appointed your guardian pro tem. Made it. But Johann, as soon as this was in the wind I started shuffling stock around. For several weeks Teal held a big chunk of your voting stock—Teal is okay; you made a good choice—Teal held all of your stock that I now hold, using money I lent him. An open transaction that could be verified, none of this 'ten dollars and other valuable considerations' dodge. During that period, your stock that I had sold to Teal using my money, plus Teal's stock that he already had, plus what I have long held, was voting control . . . because I knew that if I lost, the next day Parkinson would show up with proxies for your stock—signed by your granddaughters—and demand a stockholders' meeting and kick me out of the chair and fire Teal as president. Yet I didn't dare buy stock from you myself—or I would go into court as an interested party and the other side might sniff it. It was touch-and-go for a while, Johann."

"Well, I'm glad we're out of the woods. Parky."

"We aren't. Other actions coming up, none of which you need worry about today."

"Jake, I'm not going to worry about *anything*. I'm going to think about birds and bees and fleecy clouds and enjoy the wonderful taste of Cream o' Wheat. And prunes, strained prunes fixed baby-style. I'm just glad to know that my oldest friend didn't knife me while I was unconscious and sorry as hell I thought so even for a moment. Oh, I still think you're a timid, gutless, stinking sissy not to help me out on this mirror nonsense but we'll argue that another day. I can wait if I have to; I see why you don't want to buck a psychiatrist if I have to go into court when I'm up and convince Judge McCampbell that I can still hit the floor with my hat."

"I'm glad to hear it. And I'm glad to see that you are getting well, Johann. I'm certain you are since you are again, or still, the same stinking bad-tempered, unreasonable old scoundrel you always were."

Johann chuckled. "Thanks, Jake—and I see that *you* are in good health, too. May we never see the day we talk sweet to each other. What else is now? Oh, yes! Where in hell is my secretary? Eunice, I mean. There is not a one of this gang of kidnappers around me who ever knew her . . .

85

and they show no interest in trying to find her. Oh, Garcia knew her by sight—but he says that he doesn't know where she is and claims he's too busy to run errands. Told me to ask you."

"Oh." Salomon hesitated. "Do you know her address?"

"Eh? Somewhere at the north end of town. I suppose my accountant has it. Wait a moment! You took her home once, I remember clearly."

"So I did. It was indeed somewhere in the north end. But those rabbit warrens all look alike. My guards may know. Hold it—*your* mobile guards escorted her for several months, right up to the time you went in for surgery. Have you asked them?"

"Hell, Jake, I haven't been allowed to see *anyone*. I don't even know that they are still working for me."

"I'm fairly sure they still were when I left for Europe. But, Johann, while we can ask them, I doubt if it will do any good."

"Why not?"

"Because I *did* see Eunice just before your operation. She was interested—she was fond of you, Johann, much more so than you deserved—"

"Conceded! Make it march."

"Well, she didn't mention specific plans but I don't think she intended to stay in secretarial work. Hell, man, none of us expected that you would ever *need* a secretary again. I would happily have hired her myself; she is a good secretary. But—"

"I'm sure you would, you old goat. But surely you let her know that she could stay on my payroll forever? Well, until I died, at least."

"She knew that. But she is a proud girl, Johann. Not a parasite. I'll make an effort to find her. However, if I don't, there are many good secretaries. I'll find one for you. That's a promise."

"Look, I don't want another secretary; I want Eunice Branca."

"I meant—"

"I know what you meant. You'd find me some old witch who does perfect work but is no fun to look at or have

86

around . . . while you've probably got Eunice stashed away in your office."

Salomon said slowly, "Johann, I swear by all that's holy that I do not have her in my office nor anywhere."

"Then she *did* turn you down. Jake, I trust you with my life and all my worldly goods. But I don't trust you or any man not to steal a perfect secretary if he can."

"Nolo contendere. I did offer her a job anytime she wanted it. She did not accept."

"So we find her. *You* find her."

Salomon sighed. "What clues can you give me? Her husband, perhaps? Isn't he an artist?"

"I suppose you could call him that. Look, Jake, don't hold this against Eunice—but *I* would call him a gigolo. But I'm old-fashioned. I had to get a report when she married him. He was clean, no reason to lose the best secretary a man ever had just because she chose to marry him. Yes, he was an artist, one who didn't sell much; she supported him. That was *her* business; Branca was all right— didn't use drugs, didn't even drink. But he wasn't up to her. Illiterate. Surely I know how common that is today; I'm not prejudiced, I've got illiterates right in this house—and only God and Accounting know how many are working for Smith Enterprises. Branca may never have attended a school in which reading is taught. But I can give you one lead—if Eunice is not working as a secretary—easy to check through Social Security—and if they aren't on the Welfare rolls—she won't be, he might be—then check model agencies, video, artists, photographers, et cetera. For *both* of them. For he was as handsome as Eunice was beautiful; the snoopshot with the security report made that plain."

"Very well, Johann; I'll get a skiptrace firm on it."

"Hell, put a regiment of detectives on it!"

"But suppose they dropped out? People do."

Johann sniffed. "Perhaps he would, I would lay any amount that she never would. But if necessary, I want every Abandoned Area in this city combed."

"Expensive. You send a private detective into an A.A. and the premium on his life goes sky high."

"Didn't you tell me that I have more money than I know what to do with?"

"True. But I don't relish hiring a man for hazardous work even if he wants the job. But we're borrowing trouble; it may take nothing more than getting Accounting to dig out that address. Or do a back check on a Social Security number with the customary small bribe. I'll let you know."

Salomon stood up to leave. Smith said, "Hold it. Will I see you tomorrow? And will you phone in a report—tell Hedrick or the physician on watch; they won't let me talk on the phone—phone a report each day? Till you find her?"

"Every day, Johann."

"Thanks, Jake. You'll make Eagle Scout yet. Tell nursy she can come out of the corner now. They're probably waiting to slip me my Mickey Finn—this is the longest they've let me stay awake so far."

Two rooms away Salomon stopped to speak to Dr. Hedrick. The physician looked at him. "Rough," he stated.

"Quite. Doctor, how long do you expect to keep your patient from using a mirror?"

"Hard to say. Progress has been rapid lately . . . but Smith still has very imperfect control of the new body. Plus tingling and itching and numbness—all to be expected—and imaginary pains. Psychosomatic, rather; they are real to the patient. Counselor, if you expect me to have my patient ready for a competency hearing any time soon, emotional shocks must be delayed as long as possible. That's my opinion, though of course I am strongly influenced by Dr. Rosenthal's judgment. Besides imperfect body control, our patient is weak and emotionally extremely unstable."

"So I am aware."

"Mr. Salomon, you look as if you needed another tranquilizer. May I?"

Salomon grudged a smile. "Only if it involves grain alcohol."

88

Hedrick chuckled. "Will you settle for some bottled in Scotland?"

"Yes! No water. Well, just a touch."

"I'll dispense the drug, you add water to taste. I'll prescribe for myself, too—I also find this case a bit trying. Even though we are making medical history."

8

Dr. Garcia rubbed Jake Salomon's arm where he had just injected him. "Now wait three minutes. With a tenth cc. of 'Tranquille' in you, you could attend your own hanging in a calm mood."

"Thank you, Doctor. Dr. Hedrick, what's bothering Johann now? Your message was not specific."

Hedrick shook his head. "The patient won't talk to us. Simply demands to see you."

"Uh . . . he has found out? Or, rather, if he has, what then?"

Hedrick turned to his colleague. "Dr. Garcia?"

"You know my opinion, Doctor. Your patient has recovered, is simply weak from being too long in bed. There is no longer any excuse—any *medical* excuse—for restraints."

"Dr. Rosenthal?"

The psychiatrist shrugged. "The human mind is a weird and wonderful thing—and the longer I study it the less I'm sure about anything concerning it. But I agree with Dr. Garcia on one point: You can't keep a patient tied down forever."

Hedrick said, "I'm afraid that's it, Counselor."

Salomon sighed. "And I've been appointed a volunteer."

"Any of us will go in with you if you wish, sir. But the patient flatly refuses to talk to *us*. We'll be standing by, ready to move fast if a crisis develops."

"The dummy-switches dodge again?"

"Oh, certainly. And this time the nurse has been instructed to get out if you tell her to. *You*, not the patient. But don't worry; I'll be watching and listening by closed-circuit video; Dr. Garcia and Dr. Rosenthal will watch the monitor scopes."

"I'm not worrying, that drug must have hit me. Okay, I'll go in—and if I have to ride the tiger, I'll hang onto its ears."

Johann Smith said, "Jake! Where the hell have you been? You've come to see me just *once* in the past three weeks. Once! Damn you."

"I've been working. Which is more than you can say."

"You think so, eh? Physiotherapy is damned hard work, harder than you ever do, you shyster—and I have to go through it seven days a week."

"My heart bleeds, Johann—want a chit to see the Chaplain? I was laid up sick for ten days—which I'm sure Hedrick told you—and I still don't feel chipper, so move over, you lazy bastard, and let me stretch out. Damn it, Johann, I'm not as young as I used to be; I can't jump through hoops every time you snap your fingers."

"Now, now, Jake, don't take that line with me. I'm sorry you were ill. I told 'em to send you flowers. Did you get them?"

"Yes. Thank you."

"That's odd, I didn't send any. Caught you, didn't I? Jake, I never intend to overwork a man—but, damn it, when he's on my payroll, I expect to hear from him occasionally. And see him."

"I'm not on your payroll."

"Huh? What nonsense is this?"

"When the Court appointed me your guardian pro tem and conservator, McCampbell awarded me a token fee of ten dollars a month. That's all I am allowed to accept from you—and I haven't collected it."

Johann looked incredulous. "Well, we'll change that in a hurry! You get word to Judge McCampbell that I said—"

"Stow it, Johann. It was part of the deal to shut up your granddaughters. Now what is eating you? Mrs. Branca? You've had a report each day—negative. I fetched a

92

briefcase stuffed with detailed reports—all negative but showing what has been done. Want to read 'em? I see you have a reading machine now."

"Read negative reports? Jake, don't be silly. Yes, I'm fretted about Eunice—damn it, even if she didn't want to work for me any longer, you'd think she would have paid me the minimum courtesy of a sickroom visit. But that's not what is on my mind—not why I sent for you, I mean. Nurse!"

"Yes, sir?"

"Switch off the voice monitors; then go hide your head in the idiot box. Pick any program as long as it's loud; I want privacy."

"Yes, sir." She stood up and switched off the dummy switches.

"Nurse."

"Yes, Mr. Salomon?"

"Ask Dr. Hedrick if we can have full privacy. I don't think Mr. Smith is going to swing from the chandelier simply because I don't have a nursing degree."

"Mr. Salomon, Dr. Hedrick says that we are doing so well"—she smiled brightly—"aren't we, Mr. Smith?—that if you wanted to talk privately, I could leave. Just push this red button when you want me." She smiled again and left.

Johann said, "Well, that's a surprise!"

"Why so? You're getting well, Hedrick says so."

"Hmm. 'I fear the Greeks, even bearing gifts.' Jake, come close, I want to whisper . . . because I wouldn't put it past 'em to have a spare microphone tucked away somewhere."

"Paranoia, you old fool. Why would Hedrick bother to listen to our conversation?"

" 'Young fool,' please—I'm young again. Paranoid, possibly. Anyhow I don't want anybody to hear this but you. Because if I'm mistaken, it won't sound good to have this repeated in court in a competency hearing. So lean close and listen hard. Jake . . . *I'm almost certain this new body of mine is female!*"

Jake Salomon's ears started to buzz and he was glad that Garcia had given him that shot. "So? Interesting idea. If

93

'true, what are you going to do? Take it back to the complaint desk and demand another one?"

"Oh, don't talk like a fool, Jake. Whatever body I have now, I'm stuck with—and if it's female, well, it'll seem odd but half the human race manages to bear up under it; I guess I can. But don't you *see*? If my notion is correct, that's why they've taken such great care not to let me see myself. Afraid I would jump my cams, no doubt." Johann chuckled. "I'm tougher than that. Shucks, they haven't even let *you* see anything you could spot as female—sheet over my whole body, not even my arms in sight, and enough gear hooked to me to clutter up any lines of figure. Towel over my scalp—I suppose the hair is growing back, or such. If I'm horsefaced enough, you couldn't tell my sex just from my face. My new face."

"Perhaps. It's an interesting theory. How did you reach it?"

"Oh, a number of things. Especially the fact that, even though I now can use my hands and arms, they won't let me. Except during controlled physiotherapy. Can't *touch* myself, I mean; they strap me down again at once, with an excuse about 'spastic muscle action' and so forth. Which I did have at first and don't have now. But never mind. This is the first time there hasn't been a nurse in the room. So find out. Lift the sheet and look! Tell me, Jake, *am I male or female*? Hurry—she might come back."

Salomon sat still. "Johann."

"What, Jake? Hurry up, man!"

"You're female."

Johann Smith was silent several moments, then said. "Well, it's a relief to be sure. At least I'm not crazy. I 'female' and 'crazy' aren't synonyms. Well, Jake? How di it happen?"

"I've known it all along, Johann. It's been a strain on m to see you and not let on. For you are correct; your doctor were afraid that you might not take it well. While you wer still weak."

"They don't know me very well—it's not half th surprise it was to me when—at about six, it was—I foun out that girls really *are* different from boys. Little girl dow
94

the block, it was. Showed me. But how did it happen, Jake? It wasn't what I signed up for."

"Oh, but it was."

"Eh?"

"No instruction you gave said one word about race or sex. You specified 'healthy,' and around twenty to forty years old, and with AB-Negative blood. Nothing else."

Johann blinked. "Yes. But it never occurred to me that they might put me into a woman's body."

"Why not? They put women's hearts into male bodies and vice versa every day."

"True. I'm simply saying that I never thought about it. But even if I had, I don't think I would have risked cutting my chances in half by making such a restriction. As may be, I've never been one to cry over spilt milk. Well, now that I know, there's no reason to continue that silly business about 'no mirrors.' Will you step out and tell that stubborn doctor that I want to see myself at once and no more nonsense? If necessary, knock his ears in."

"I'll see, Johann." Salmon buzzed for the nurse, then went out. He was gone five minutes, returned with Drs. Hedrick, Garcia, and Rosenthal, and a second nurse, who was carrying a large hand mirror.

Hedrick said, "How do you feel, Miss Smith?"

She smiled wryly. "So it's 'Miss' Smith now, is it? Much better, thank you; my mind is at ease. You could have told me weeks ago; I am not as unstable as you think."

"That is possible, Miss Smith, but I am bound to do what I think is best for my patient."

"No criticism, none. But now that the cat is out of the bag, please ask the nurse to show me what I look like. I'm curious."

"Certainly, Miss Smith."

Dr. Garcia waved the nurse at the console aside and sat down; Hedrick stationed himself on one side of the bed, Rosenthal on the other. Only then did Hedrick take the mirror from the nurse, hold it to let his patient see herself in it.

Johann Smith looked at her new face first with intense interest, then with unbelief—then her features broke in

95

horror. "Oh, my God! Dear God, what have they done to us? Jake! You *knew!*"

The lawyer's face was working in the convulsions of a strong man trying not to weep. "Yes, I knew, Johann. That's why I couldn't find her for you—*because she was here all along.* Right here—and I had . . . to *talk* to her!" He gave up and sobbed.

"Jake, how could you let them do it? Eunice, oh Eunice my darling, forgive me—*I didn't know!*" Her sobs echoed his, an octave higher.

Hedrick snapped, "Dr. Garcia!"

"Started, Doctor!"

"Dr. Rosenthal, take care of Mr. Salomon. Nurse, help him, he's about to fall! Damn it, where's that aspirator?"

Five minutes later the room was quiet. The patient had been forced into sedated sleep. Dr. Hedrick satisfied himself that Miss Smith was safe and turned the bedside watch over to Dr. Garcia. Hedrick then left the sickroom.

He found Mr. Salomon stretched out on a couch at the remote watch station; Dr. Rosenthal was seated by the couch, a stethoscope around his neck. Hedrick cocked an eyebrow at the psychiatrist, who mouthed soundlessly, "Okay," then added aloud, "Perhaps you will check me."

"Very well, Doctor." Hedrick sat down where Rosenthal had been, hitched the chair closer, took Salomon's wrist and felt his pulse. "How do you feel?"

"I'm okay," Salomon said gruffly. "Sorry I made a fool of myself. How is *she?*"

"Sleeping. You were fond of her."

"We *both* were fond of her. Doctor, she was an angel."

"Go ahead and cry. Tears are lubricant for the soul. Males would be better off if they cried as easily as women do. Eh, Rosenthal?"

"Correct, Doctor. Cultures in which men cry easily have little need of my specialty." He smiled. "Mr. Salomon, you're in good hands so I'll run along—got to shrink a few heads for my collection. Unless you need me, Doctor?"

"Run along, Rosy. You might be here in the morning when we wake the patient. Say ten o'clock."

"Good-bye, Dr. Rosenthal. Thank you. Thank you for everything."

"No huhu, Counselor. Don't let that veterinarian sell you any flea powder." He left.

"Dr. Salomon," said Hedrick, "this big castle is loaded with beds. What do you say to sacking out in one, then about twenty-one or -two o'clock I can give you a pill guaranteed to slug you for eight hours of dreamless sleep?"

"I'm okay, really I am."

"If you say so. I can't force treatment on you. But as another human being who has come to know you fairly well—and admire you—I must admit that I am more worried about *you* than I am about my patient. You referred to her as an 'angel'—by which you meant the donor, not Miss Smith."

"Eh? Yes, of course. Eunice Branca." Salomon's features contorted momentarily.

"I never knew her and I've had little experience with angels; doctors don't see people at their best. But her body would do credit to an angel; I have never seen a healthier one. Twenty-eight years old by the records, physiologically perhaps five years younger. She—Miss Smith I now mean, Miss Johann Smith—can take a severe shock and bounce out of it; she has that superb young body to sustain her. But you have had much the same shock and—forgive me—are no longer young. If you won't sleep here —best—"

"I don't want to sleep *here!*"

"Very well. Second best would be for you to permit me to check your heart and lungs and blood pressure. If I don't like what I find, then I want you to rest while I send for your physician."

"He doesn't make house calls."

Hedrick grunted. "Then he's not a physician; physicians go where they are needed. A most unprofessional remark as we are expected to pretend that any M.D. with a license is a dedicated saint with the wisdom of Jove—even when we know he is a bungler whose dedication is to the Internal Revenue Service. Don't quote me; they might lift my union card. Now about that checkup? Do you want it?"

"Uh, yes. Please. And I'll take that pill if you'll let me take it home. Don't ordinarily use such—but tonight is a special case."

"Good. If you'll slip off your shirt—"

While he worked the physician said quietly, "Mr. Salomon, I don't have Dr. Rosenthal's training. But if it will do you any good to talk, I can listen. This has been on your mind, I know. I think your worst hurdle is past—letting Johann Smith know that he is now 'Miss' Smith, plus the still worse shock of seeing him —her—discover that she now inhabits his former secretary's body. So you are past that crisis. If there is more it would help to get off your mind, feel free to talk. In my profession as in yours, such talk is privileged."

"I don't mind talking about Eunice. But I don't know what to say."

"Well, you might tell me how such a lovely girl got killed. Never knew the donor's name until you told me. There was a privacy restriction. So we don't ask—as long as the donation is properly certified."

"Yes, there was such restriction. We'll never know why but I suspect that the child—woman, I mean, and a very competent one—but I thought of her as a child, being so much older than she was. I think Eunice had a romantic notion that she could give her body to her boss if she no longer needed it and not let him find out. Ridiculous, but it fitted her sweet nature. I had to tell *you,* once it looked as if old Johann might live through it. Because I knew he would blow his wig. And he did."

"A *very* good thing you told me, Counselor. I think—and Dr. Rosenthal thinks—that we would never have pulled this patient through if we hadn't taken extraordinary precautions to keep her from knowing her sex. In view of the patient's relation to the donor. Close, that is."

"Close. Close for both of us. Doctor, I am not exaggerating—if I had been as little as twice Eunice's age—and she not married—I would have done my damnedest to marry her. And the same, I feel certain, goes for old Johann. So I knew what a shock it would be to

98

him—worse than simply learning that she had been killed."

"Car accident?"

"Nothing so innocent. Killed by a mugger. Psychopath probably but the point is immaterial as Johann's mobile guards caught him almost in the act and killed him. That's how she was saved—her body was saved, I mean—because they rushed her to a hospital hoping to save her." Jake Salomon sighed. "It does help to talk."

"Good. How did Johann Smith's guards happen to be so Johnny-on-the-spot, yet not quite?"

"Oh. The poor darling tried to save ten minutes. She was a blood donor—AB-Negative, and—"

"*Oh!* Now I know why 'Miss' Smith has seemed vaguely familiar. I saw her once, I'm now certain, giving blood to a patient I had been called in to support. A lovely girl, with a warm disposition, friendly, who dressed in, um, exotic styles."

"Erotic styles you mean, let's not use euphemisms. Yes, Eunice did. She knew she was beautiful and did not mind sharing her beauty. Played up to it."

"I wish I had known her."

"I wish you had, Doctor; your life would have been richer thereby. If she had a call to give blood, Johann's guards were under orders to drive her. Protect her. Pick her up at her door, escort her to the car, deliver her, wait for her. But this was an emergency and she lives —lived—nineteen levels up in one of those beehives in the north end. Vehicle lift, sure—but not able to lift the sort of armor Johann owned. Owns. So the poor darling decided to save ten minutes and used the passenger elevator without waiting for escort. And that's where she was jumped. Killed."

"A pity. I suppose she didn't know that we can always stretch a patient an extra ten minutes if we know a donor is on the way."

"Maybe she did, maybe she didn't—but it is characteristic of Eunice Branca that she tried to hurry."

"A pity. You can put your shirt on. How old did you say you were?"

"I didn't say. Seventy-two is staring me in the face."

"I'm amazed. You seem to be younger—internally I mean, not necessarily your face—"

"So I'm ugly. I know it."

"I think 'distinguished' is the accepted term. You seem much younger, physiologically. Say twenty years."

"So I take my hormones."

"I'm not sure you need them. Go home if you wish. Or stay. If you stay, I'd like to put a monitor on your heart. Professional interest." (And to make damn sure you don't conk out, old fellow—sometimes a heart stops for no good reason, after a shock such as you have had.)

"Uh . . . I *am* tired. Could I skip dinner and go straight to bed? With maybe a twelve-hour dose instead of eight?"

"No trouble."

Soon Jake Salomon was in bed and asleep. Hedrick ate, looked in on his patient, left orders with the night watch to call him if the displays exceeded certain tolerances, went to bed and to sleep; he never needed the drugs he prescribed.

Despite sedation, Johann Smith's dreams were troubled. Once the old man in the borrowed skull muttered, "Eunice?" (I'm here, Boss. Go back to sleep.) "All right, my dear. Just wanted to know where you'd gone." (Quit fretting, Boss. I'm *here*.) Johann smiled in his sleep and then slept quietly, no more bad dreams.

9

The morning nurse bustled in with a tray. "Good morning, Miss Smith! How are we today?"

"I don't know how you are, but I'm hungry."

"Good! Hot oatmeal this morning, dear, and orange juice and a boiled egg—and we'll soak a little toast in egg so that it will go down easily. I'm going to tilt the bed up a touch."

"Mrs. Sloan—"

"Yes? Let me tuck the napkin under your chin."

"Stop that, or I'll tell you where to tuck it! Uncover me and unstrap me; I'm going to feed myself." (Boss, don't be rude to her. She's trying to help you.) (*Eunice?*) (Of course, dear—didn't I promise I wouldn't leave again?) (But—) (Shush, she's talking.)

"Now, Miss Smith, you *know* I can't do that. Please, dear. Doesn't this smell good?"

"Uh . . . I suppose you can't unstrap me without Dr. Hedrick's permission. I'm sorry I snapped at you." (That's better, Boss!) "But don't try to feed me, please don't. Instead please find Dr. Hedrick and tell him I'm being difficult again. You might also tell him that, if he doesn't want to go along with my unreasonable demands, he had better try to reach Mr. Salomon. Because if anyone tries to put food in my mouth while my hands are strapped, I'll do my best to spit it on the ceiling." (Is that better, Eunice?) (Some, Boss. Say ten percent.) (Uh, darn, I don't have any *practice* in being a lady.) (I'll teach you, Boss.) (Eunice, are you really there, dear? Or have I come unstuck just as they thought I would?) (Discuss it later, Boss dear—you're going to have to face the doctor right away . . . and *don't* mention *me* . . . or you know what'll happen. They'll *never* unstrap our wrists. You know that, don't you.) (Of course I do! Think I'm crazy?) (Irrelevant and immaterial as Jake would say. The point is never to let Dr. Hedrick—or *anybody*—guess that I'm here . . . or they'll be *certain* you're crazy. Now I'm going to shut up.) (Don't go 'way!) (Boss, I'll *never* go away; I'll just keep quiet. You and I had better talk mostly when others aren't around. Unless I see you about to make a mistake.) (Going to nag me, huh?) Johann heard her merry giggle. (Haven't I always, Boss? Watch it; here come the cops.)

Dr. Hedrick came in, followed by Dr. Garcia. "Good morning, Miss Smith."

"Good morning, gentlemen."

"Nurse says that you would like to try feeding yourself."

"That's true but that's not all of it. I want these straps and clamps removed, all of them."

"Letting you feed yourself is no problem. It's a good idea, good practice. As for the rest— That calls for thought."

"Doctor, the masquerade is over. If you can't see your way clear to remove all restraints from my body, then forget about breakfast; I won't starve. Get my lawyer instead."

"As it happens, Mr. Salomon is in the house—"

"Then get him!"

"Just a moment, please." Dr. Hedrick glanced at Dr. Garcia, who had seated himself at the console; Dr. Garcia nodded. "Miss Smith, would you agree to a reasonable compromise? Or at least listen?"

"I'll listen. But—" (Shut up, Boss!) "I'll listen, Doctor."

"Mr. Salomon is, as you know, an elderly man, and he had a trying day yesterday. I persuaded him to stay overnight, and rest. I'm told that he is just getting up; he has not had breakfast. I have and so has Dr. Garcia—but so long ago that we could use a bit of brunch. Now I can unstrap your arms, let you feed yourself— But unstrapping

102

your pelvis . . . well, as you must have guessed, there is some odd plumbing down there and other things. Takes time to unhitch everything.

"So here is my thought. You can invite Mr. Salomon to join you for breakfast . . . and you could invite us, too, for that bit of brunch—and we four can talk over what needs to be done next. I shall follow the wishes of your guar—your lawyer. Or let him select another physician and withdraw, if I find that I must."

"My guardian," Johann said quietly. "We'll do whatever my guardian requires. But I hope he does not decide to replace you, Dr. Hedrick. I have been a difficult patient and I'm sorry. I know what a miraculous job you have done on me . . . and I am grateful."

"Thank you, Miss Smith."

"I would be delighted to have you three gentlemen join me for brunch . . . if you will be so kind as to unstrap my arms."

(Boss!) (What's biting you, little one? I thought I was being a perfect lady?) (You are—*but don't you dare let gentlemen in here to eat with us until we're made pretty!* Not a speck of makeup, and our hair must be a mess. Horrid!) (But look, dear, it's just Jake and our doctors.) (It's the principle of the thing. I know more about being a girl than you do—well, don't I? When did I *ever* come to work with my face stark naked and my hair in rats? Why, I often got up much earlier than I had to, just to make sure that I was as pretty as possible, just for you. Didn't I? Did I not?)

"A pain, Miss Smith?"

"Eh? I mean, 'Oh?' Sorry, Doctor, just thinking. If I am to have gentlemen guests for breakfast, shouldn't I start practicing how to be a lady? It's new to me, you know. Do I have any makeup on?"

Hedrick looked startled. "Do you mean lipstick?"

"Whatever it is that ladies put on their faces; I'm sure it's always more than lipstick. And my hair should be brushed. Or do I have hair?"

"Why, certainly you have. Still short but a fine, healthy growth."

103

"That's a relief. I thought possibly I had a plastic skull and would have to wear wigs."

"There was some prosthetic restoration. But Dr. Boyle managed to save the scalp and you'll never notice the prosthesis." Hedrick smiled briefly. "Tougher than natural bone. With good blood supply to your scalp and normal hair—just hasn't grown out very far."

"I'm relieved. Dandruff?"

"Haven't noticed any."

"We won't worry about it this morning. Doctor, I'd like to be made up to look like a lady ready to receive guests. If you'll have one of the servants take in a cup of coffee and some orange juice to Mr. Salomon along with our invitation to breakfast, I'm sure he won't mind waiting." (How'm I doing, Eunice?) (Fine, old dear!)

Dr. Hedrick looked puzzled. "Miss Smith, when I set up a support team, I try to anticipate every possible emergency, supplies, drugs, and so forth. This is the first time I've been asked to produce lipstick. And cosmetics."

"Oh. But you're not being asked to, Doctor. The ladies' powder room on the first floor is stocked with all shades of lipstick and many cosmetics. Should be. Was. Should still be, or someone will hear about it. And one of the nurses can help me. That pretty redhead— Minnie? Ginny? Miss Gersten, I mean. She must know quite a lot about cosmetics." (She does—that red hair came out of a bottle, Boss.) (Meeow! Shut up, pussy cat.) (Wasn't being catty, Boss. She does well, in spite of those godawful uniforms.)

"Winifred Gersten," said Dr. Garcia. "Nurse, find Winnie. And take that tray out; it's cold."

Forty minutes later Miss Johann Smith was ready to receive. Her hair was fluffed, her face had been made up with restrained boldness by the red-haired nurse, and the result as shown in a mirror had been approved by the second voice inside Smith—grudgingly, it seemed to Johann—(I can do better. It'll do for now.)

The bed had been contoured to let her sit up and from somewhere a smart bed jacket had been produced, one that matched her eyes. Best of all, her hands and arms were free.

104

Johann found that her hands were trembling. She attributed it to excitement and decided that, if she had trouble controlling a fork, she would stick to things that would not slop on her jacket—besides, she was not hungry now. Too excited.

(Steady down, Boss darling. Leave the eating to me.)

(But—)

(No 'buts.' I've been feeding that face for years. The body remembers, Boss. You talk to the gentlemen; I'll handle the calories. Now let's shut up; they're arriving.)

"May we come in?"

"Do, gentlemen, please. Good morning, Jake. I hope you had a good night's rest." (Put out your hand to him, Boss.)

"Slept like a child."

"Good. So did I." Johann extended her left arm and hand, that being the side the lawyer was on. "Look, Jake! Hands!"

Salomon took her hand, bowed over it—hesitated and then touched it to his lips. Johann was so amazed that the hand was almost snatched back. (Good God! What does Jake think I am? A pansy?) (He thinks you're a beautiful girl. You are. I should know. Look, Boss, we must talk about Jake—later. Say hello to your shrink.)

Dr. Rosenthal was saying, "I'm a party-crasher. May I come in, Miss Smith?"

"You're most welcome. Someone is going to have to assure these other gentlemen that I don't have termites in the attic; I'm depending on you, Doctor."

The psychiatrist smiled down at her. "That is an appeal hard to resist. I must say your improvement since yesterday is astounding. You're looking lovely—Miss Smith."

Johann smiled and gave him her hand. Dr. Rosenthal bowed over it and kissed it—not a quick and frightened peck such as Salomon had given it, but a kiss that was soft and warm and unhurriedly sensuous. Johann felt a tingle run up her arm. (Hey, what is this?) (Stay off his couch, Boss. He's a wolf—I can tell.)

When he straightened up he held her hand a moment

105

longer than necessary, smiled again, then moved away. Johann thought of asking him if that was his standard way of treating patients, decided not to—but felt slightly annoyed that the other two doctors had not offered the same homage. Yonny Schmidt had been born at a time and place where hand-kissing was unheard of; Johann Smith had never taken it up; Miss Johann Smith was discovering that the silly custom was habit-forming. She felt flustered.

She was saved by another voice from the door, that of her butler. "May we serve now, Miss Smith?"

"Cunningham! It's good to see you. Yes, you may serve." Johann wondered who had given instructions to make the meal formal?

The butler stared over her head and said tonelessly, "Thank you, Miss." Johann was startled. The butler, like all the male household staff (and some of the females), was sudden death armed or unarmed; his manner alone could intimidate news snoops. (The poor man is scared!) (Of course. So calm him down, Boss.)

"But first come here, Cunningham."

"Yes, Miss." Her household chief walked carefully toward her, stopped a very respectful distance away.

"Oh, do come closer. Look at me. Right at me, don't turn your eyes away. Cunningham, the way I look is a shock to you. Isn't it?"

Cunningham swallowed without speaking; his Adam's apple bobbed.

"Oh, come now," Johann said firmly. "Of course it is. But if it upsets you, think what a shock it is to *me*. Until yesterday I didn't even *know* that I had been turned into a woman. I'll have to get used to it and so will you. Just remember this: Underneath I am the same cantankerous, unreasonable, unappreciative old scoundrel who hired you as a guard-footman nineteen years ago. I'll go on expecting perfect service, notice it as little, and remember to say 'Thank you' as seldom. Do we understand each other?"

The butler barely smiled. "Yes, sir—I mean 'Yes, Miss'."

"You meant 'Yes, sir' but you're going to have to learn to call me 'Yes, Miss' and I'm going to have to learn to expect it. We old dogs must learn new tricks. How's Mrs. Cunningham's lumbago?"

"Some better, she says. Thank you, Miss."

"Good. Tell Mary I asked. You may serve."

The brunch was almost merry. Johann tasted the wine when Cunningham offered a sample, approved it but declined a glass herself. She barely touched it to her tongue but the flavor spread like strong brandy and she had been startled almost into choking by the vibrant wonder of its bouquet. Yet the bottle she recognized as that of an adequate but not spectacular Chablis. She played safe with orange juice.

Table talk was lively and directed mostly at the hostess with no reference to her status as a patient. The men seemed to vie for her attention—and Johann found that she enjoyed it. She laughed frequently, answered their sallies, and felt witty herself.

But she could see that Jake was not eating much and looked at her all the time except when she looked back . . . at which his gaze wavered and shifted. Poor Jake. (Eunice, what are we going to do about Jake?) (Later, Boss—one thing at a time.)

She was startled again when Cunningham came to remove her plate from her lap table—startled to see that scrambled eggs and two rolls had disappeared as well as orange juice, half a glass of milk, and one of three link sausages. "Coffee, Miss?"

"I don't know. Dr. Hedrick, am I allowed coffee?"

"Miss Smith, now that you can eat sitting up, there is no reason why you should not eat or drink anything you want."

"Then I'll celebrate. The first coffee I've been permitted in ten years—Demi-tasse for me, Cunningham, but man-size cups for the gentlemen. And Cunningham?—is there any Mumm ninety-seven on ice?"

"Certainly, Miss."

"Serve it." She raised her voice a little. "Any sissies who won't drink champagne this early in the day may sneak out quietly."

No one left. When glasses were filled and bubbles were

chasing up their stems, Dr. Hedrick stood up. "Gentlemen, a toast—" He waited until they were standing. Johann raised her glass with them.

But did not drink: the toast was "To our lovely and gracious hostess—long may she live!"

"Amen!" "Cheers!"—and the tinkle of breaking glass.

Johann felt tears, ignored them. "Thank you, gentlemen. Cunningham, fresh glasses."

When they were filled she said, "Gentlemen, I ask for another standing toast"—she waited, then went on—"this should be to Dr. Boyle . . . and to you, Jake old friend, without whose loyal help I would not be here . . . and certainly to you, Dr. Hedrick, and to all the doctors who have helped you and helped Dr. Boyle . . . and to all the patient nurses I have snapped at. But those can wait. I ask you to drink"—her tears were falling and her voice was almost a whisper—"to the memory of the sweetest, loveliest, and most gallant girl I have ever known . . . Eunice Branca."

The toast was drunk in silence. Then Jake Salomon slowly crumpled into his chair and covered his face with his hands.

Dr. Hedrick jumped to help him, Dr. Garcia was quick on the other side. Johann stared in helpless distress. (Oh, I should have known better! But I meant it, darling, I meant every word.) (I know you did, Boss, and I appreciate it. But it's all right. Jake has got to admit that I'm dead. And so do you.) (Are you dead, Eunice? *Are you?*) (Don't worry over a word, Boss. I'm here and I won't leave you ever. I promised you. Have you ever known me to break my word?) (No, never.) (So believe me this time. But we've got to take care of Jake.) (How, dearest girl?) (When the time comes, you'll know. Talk later, when we're alone.)

Dr. Rosenthal was leaning over her. "Are you all right, my dear?"

"I'm okay—just terribly sorry about Mr. Salomon. Is *he* all right?"

"He will be shortly. Miss Smith, don't worry about Mr. Salomon. Yes, you brought on another catharsis—which he needed, or he would not have had it. As for his physical well-being, he's in Dr. Hedrick's hands . . . and Curt Hedrick hasn't lost a patient he reached in time since he started practicing his specialty. Your house is loaded with everything Dr. Hedrick could possibly need . . . and Mr. Salomon isn't even ill; he simply needs to lie down, plus a happy drug."

Dr. Rosenthal sat with her while the room was cleared of dishes, brunch table, dining chairs, etc. Dr. Hedrick returned with Dr. Garcia. Johann again asked, "How is he?"

"Half asleep. Slightly ashamed of being a 'spectacle' and a 'nuisance'—his terms. But only slightly as what I gave him doesn't permit such self-hate very long. How are *you*?"

"She's ready to go six rounds," Rosenthal assured him.

"'So the scopes say. We might as well get on with our conference, Miss Smith. I discussed all that I am going to say with Mr. Salomon while you were getting pretty before brunch, and it has his approval. I am withdrawing from your case."

"Oh, Dr. Hedrick! *No!*"

"Yes. Dear lady, ain't nobody going away mad. This means that you are well. *Well.* Oh, still weak, still in need of care. But I'm not deserting you. I'm turning you over to Dr. Garcia."

She looked at Dr. Garcia, who nodded. "Nothing to worry about, Miss Smith."

"But—Dr. Hedrick, you will come back and see me? Won't you?"

"Delighted to. But not very soon, I'm afraid. You see— Well, there is an interesting transplant case which has been hanging fire. A radical one, the heart and both lungs. Now they are ready to start surgery. I received a call before you were awake, asking if I would be available. I said that I would have to call back—and after I saw you I did call and said that I could do it. After consulting Dr. Garcia, of course, and notifying Mr. Salomon." He smiled quickly. "So, if you will excuse me, I'll leave."

Johann sighed and reached out her hand. "Since you must."

Hedrick took her hand, bent over it; Dr. Rosenthal said

lazily, "Aren't you going to scrub first, Doctor?"

Hedrick said, "You go to hell, Rosy!" and kissed her hand. It seemed to Johann that Dr. Hedrick stretched it at least twice as long as Dr. Rosenthal's earlier effort. She felt goose pimples on her arm and a most curious feeling at her middle—yes, she decided, if one had to be a woman, this was a custom to be encouraged.

(Going to lay him, boss?) (Eunice!) (Oh, piffle, Boss. We're Siamese twins now and should be honest with each other. *You* wanted to lay *me* for years. But couldn't. You knew you wanted to, I knew it too; we just never talked about it. Now you still can't. But you can lay *him* if you want to . . . and it's the best way to say 'Thank you.' But watch it. dearie. Do it here, not where you might get caught. He has a jealous wife; he has all the signs.) (Eunice, I'm not going to discuss such a ridiculous idea! I'm surprised at you. You, a nice girl—and married yourself.) (Wups, dearie! I'm not married. 'Until death do us part' is the limit . . . and I'm a ghost. 'Minds me, though—my husband—erase and correct; my widower, Joe Branca. Got to talk about *him*, too. Doc's turning to go. So wet your lips and smile, if you have it even faintly on your mind. And you *have*.)

Miss Smith wet her lips and smiled. "Adios, Doctor, not good-bye. Hurry back. When you can." (You're learning, dearie, you're learning.)

Dr. Garcia said, "Miss Smith—"

"Oh. Yes, Doctor?"

"If you're ready, I'll get nurses in and we'll unharness you and several other things. You can have a general anesthetic if you wish. I suggest locals, with a chin screen to keep you from seeing how I'm bungling it. With something you want to read projected, and some music."

"Music would be nice. But I won't read, I'm too interested. Locals, then. Or nothing, pain doesn't upset me."

"But it upsets me, so we'll use local anesthesia."

For an hour and more she listened to a tape of evergreens, from classic rock she had never grown used to clear back to folk music popular before Johann Schmidt

110

was born. Mostly she enjoyed lazily the sensuous pleasure of feeling her body being touched and handled and manipulated. Not only was it wonderful to *have* a body after days of complete paralysis from the neck down (plus fear of being forever a basket case, a fear Johann had never fully admitted) but also, most important, this body felt everything so sensitively—just to be touched was pleasure.

Not much like that old wreck you discarded! For the past ten, fifteen years that body's sole virtue had been that it still ran. It reminded her of a fifth-hand Model-T Ford that he and four other young cake-eaters had bought for seventy dollars in Baltimore and had driven half across the continent—no lights, no brakes (the reverse had to serve), no driving licenses (unheard of), no instruments, no nothing. But the tough and ugly little touring car had chugged along on three cylinders (not always the same three) at an (estimated) top speed of twenty-five miles an hour. They had stopped now and then to throw water on the spokes to keep them from falling out.

Somewhere on a dirt road in Missouri it had coughed and quit, and smell had traced the trouble to the wiring. Yonny had fixed it—wrapped the burned insulation with toilet paper, tied it with string . . . cranked the heap and it had started at once and chugged along as before.

She wondered where the sturdy old junkpile had wound up? And what had become of her male body? Johann's will had left it to a medical school—but since Johann hadn't died, quite, that will did not control. Had they pickled it? Or swept it out with the trash? Must ask.

Several times she felt pulling sensations that should have hurt but did not and once a sharp pain which she ignored. There were odors, sour-sweet and nauseating; she thought of suggesting that the air system be turned up, then decided to mind her own business. Presently the odors were gone and she became aware that she was being given a bed bath; then sheets and pad were being changed.

The chin screen was removed; the top part of the fresh bottom sheet was whisked into place by two nurses while a third lifted Miss Smith's shoulders. Two nurses left the room, carrying a hamper between them. "There," said Dr.

Garcia. "That wasn't so bad, was it?"

"Not at all. I feel grand." She wiggled her toes, opened and closed her thighs. "Grand! Now I'm *me* all over—free! Doctor? Since I'm no longer wired for sight and sound, not to mention plumbing, do we need this fancy hospital bed? I would stop feeling like an invalid sooner if I had my own bed."

"Mmm . . . must you rush it? This bed is the right height for nurses to work on you—back rubs and such—and it has side rails which can be raised when you sleep. Miss Smith, every nurse's nightmare is the thought of a patient falling out of bed."

"Well! What do you think I am? A baby?"

"Yes, Miss, that's what I think you are. A baby getting acquainted with its body. Babies can fall. But I don't intend to let you fall. Either out of bed, or in learning to walk. Or in taking a tub bath, which you will be demanding almost at once."

(Play it cool, Boss!) "Doctor, I will follow your orders. But my own bed has its points. It will contour, just touch a button. And it has hydraulic lift. Raises as high as this one or higher—but will also lower till it's hardly more than a mattress on the floor, ten inches high. Will this one do that?"

"Mmm, no."

"I *did* fall out of bed, ten years back. It shook me up so, that I ordered this special bed. Back when I was still walking I used to raise it to the easiest height—about at my hips—to get into it. Then lower it all the way down to sleep."

"Mmm . . . maybe we can make a deal. Will you promise me *always* to lower the bed once you get into it? Even if you don't intend to sleep."

She smiled. "Signed and witnessed and with posted performance bond."

"I don't think we need to go that far. Miss Smith, we no longer need to monitor you the forty-'leven way we've been doing. But I want a continuous check on heart action and respiration until you are living a normal life. That's the main reason I need this life-support bed. But if you will let

112

me fasten to your skin, anywhere on your ribs, a little pickup-transmitter weighing a half ounce and no bigger than an alloy dollar, we don't need this fancy bed. It's comfortable, you'll forget it's on you. You can bathe with it in place—waterproof and sticks like a poor relation."

She smiled. "Start sticking!"

"I'll fetch it. And have the nurses swap beds."

"Oh, the nurses can't move my bed. It takes big huskies and a power dolly. Tell Cunningham. But no rush. Speaking of nurses—Winnie, don't you need to wash your hands or something? I want to talk to my doctor."

The redhead smiled at her. "Dear, I've heard everything. Don't mind me."

"Look, Winnie, you did a lovely job on my face when I did not know how. But that's the point, dear. Outside I'm a woman. But up here back of my eyes is still a crabby old man who is far too shy—chicken, I mean—too chicken to discuss intimate matters with a pretty girl present. And I *must*."

"Miss Gersten, go to the watch station and take a break. I'll call you."

"Yes, Doctor."

One she was gone Johann said, "You're durn sure all the mikes are dead?"

"We're private, Miss Smith."

"Call me 'Johann,' Doc; this has got to be a man-to-man—and embarrasses me even discussing it with a man. All right, first question: Did I come sick—menstruate—in the last few days?"

Garcia looked surprised. "You twigged? Yes, you are just over your period; we removed a tampon while we were working on you and it was not necessary to replace it. But where did I miss? I thought I had anticipated it and had bolshoi painkiller in you in time. You felt cramps?"

"Not a twinge. But things didn't *feel* right . . . and that's when I started getting suspicious about my sex." She looked thoughtful. "Perhaps it was the tampons—I felt something odd down there—and now the feeling is no longer there."

"Might have been that. I would have used napkin pads,

113

usual hospital practice. But there were just too many bells and whistles—plumbing I mean—in the way. I didn't think you would notice a tampon placed while you were sedated. Contrary to popular belief there is almost no sensation inside a vagina."

"So? There damn well is in *mine!* I just didn't know what the sensation was."

"Well, the matter has never come up before; your case is unique. Was that all that was troubling you, Miss—sorry! 'Johann.' "

"No. This new body of mine— Has it had a whatchamacallit, a female examination?"

"Oh, certainly. Dr. Kystra, best G-Y-N man in town. Done while you were paralyzed, checked again after your spinal cord fused but done while you were in deep sedation. All okay."

"I want a full report. Damn it, Doc, I'm in charge of this body now . . . and I know as little about how to be female as my Grossmutter knew about aircraft. Nothing, that is."

"I can get the report out of file if you want it—"

"I do!"

"—but I can tell it in terms you are more likely to understand. Shall I?"

"Go ahead."

"You have a normal female body, physiological age circa twenty-five—calendar age somewhat older, I understand. Breasts normal virginal—which doesn't mean your body is virgo intacta; it isn't. Just means you haven't suckled a child. No trace of abdominal surgery, from which I conclude that your appendix is in place and your tubes are intact—"

"Meaning I could get pregnant."

"—the latter opinion having been confirmed by insufflation while you were paralyzed. You not only *could* get pregnant; you *will*. Unless you live an absolutely chaste life—and even if you plan to, I would still recommend precautionary contraception—say six-month implants in one buttock. The best-laid plans of mice and men, you know. And women. Especially women. Since you are Rh-negative, about six-sevenths of the male population could

114

give you a damaged or stillborn child. We can prevent that if we know it in time, but an unexpected pregnancy can turn out tragically. So don't let it be unexpected. Plan it. In the meantime use contraception."

"Doc, what makes you so damn sure I'll get pregnant? Even if I get married—which I do not plan on—hell, I've had only hours to get used to the notion of being female; I certainly haven't had time to consider being *actively* female. But even so, as the old gal said, 'Shucks, honey, hundreds and hundreds of times ain't nothing happen a-tall.' "

"If you adjust normally to being a young female, you *will* be active about it, that's why. Or you will eventually wind up on Dr. Rosenthal's confession couch or some emotional equivalent such as joining a nunnery. Johann, your new body has a normal female hormonal balance; you had better plan accordingly. Even getting your tubes cut is no answer; you might come down with the emotional never-get-overs through regretting it. As for what the old gal said, it doesn't apply. Because of that child you've already had."

"*What?*" (Boss, why didn't you mind your own business? I could have told you all of this you need to know.) (Shut up, Eunice.)

Garcia looked surprised. "You didn't know? I had assumed that, since this body was that of your secretary, you knew that she had had a child. Or children."

"Not only didn't know it, I don't believe it." Surely the security investigation would have turned up such an obvious fact . . . and God knows Eunice had never been out of his sight since then long enough to bear a child.

"I'm afraid you will have to believe it, uh, Johann. Striations called stretch marks on belly and buttocks—hardly noticeable unless your skin is tanned and then easily concealed by cosmetics. But present. Not definitive, as a woman, or even a male, can get stretch marks from obesity. But characteristic. But the thing that nails it down is that the cervix of the virgin womb does *not* look like that of a woman who has borne a child. The difference is so marked that a layman can spot it. I have

115

seen yours. Q.E.D. Could be photographed if you doubt me."

(Drop it, Boss!)

"Oh, I believe you, now that you've explained it."

"A comparison photo might be a good idea. Make you more careful. I was not implying any criticism of Mrs. Branca; I was simply warning you that the baby-baking apparatus you inherited from her is in prime shape and ready to be triggered each lunar month. Say about ten days from now."

"I'll be careful."

"Want a lecture on contraception?"

"No." Johann smiled wryly. "Apparently I have at least a week before I need a chastity girdle."

"Approximately, by statistics. But, uh, Johann. No, 'Miss' Smith—do you know the technical term we physicians use to describe girls who depend on rhythm?"

"No. What?"

"We call them 'mothers.' "

"Oh. *Oh!*"

"So don't wait too long. Next question?"

"Uh . . . no more today, Doctor; I need to digest what you've told me. Thank you."

"Not at all, Miss Smith. Shall I have them switch beds now?"

"I'll send for Cunningham later; I'd like to rest. Doctor? Could you stick that dingus on my ribs? Then have the nurses stay out a couple of hours?"

"Certainly. If you'll let me raise the safety rails, as this bed is *not* only ten inches from the floor."

"Oh, of course."

10

(Well, Eunice?) (So you want to hear about my little bastard? Boss, you're a dirty old man.) (Sweetheart, I don't want to hear anything you don't want to tell. You could have quintuplets by a Barbary ape and it wouldn't affect how I feel about you.) (Mealymouthed old hypocrite. You're dying of curiosity.) (I am like hell 'dying of curiosity.' It's your business and yours alone.) (Oh, don't be so mean, Boss. My business *is* your business. How else? Seeing the close relationship we have . . . and which I *like*, if there is any doubt in your dirty old mind. You brought me back to life . . . when I was as dead as folk songs. And now I'm happy. So coax me a little, I'll give.) (All right, dearest—how in the world did you manage to have a baby? When did you find *time*? Your snoopsheet traced you clear back through high school.)

(Boss, did that security report mention the high school semester I lost from rheumatic fever?) (Let me think. Yes, it did.) (Misspelling. Spell it 'romantic' fever. I was fifteen and a cheerleader. Our basketball team won the regional conference . . . and I felt so good, I got knocked up.) (Eunice, 'knocked up' is not an expression a lady uses.) (Oh, Boss, sometimes you make me sick. By your rules I'm not a lady and never was—and I've got as much right to be inside this skull as you have and maybe more—so you haven't any business trying to force me to talk the way your mother did. Not when I no longer have Joe to turn to when I get tired of your prissy ways.)

(I'm sorry, Eunice.)

('Sall right, Boss. I love you. But you and I are cuddled up pretty close; we ought to relax and enjoy it. I can teach you a lot about how to be female, if you'll let me. But right now you listen. Don't interrupt.) The ghost voice started reciting a string of monosyllables, all of them taboo in the faraway days of Johann's youth.

(Eunice! Please, darling, it doesn't become you.)

(Pipe down, Boss. I'm going to finish this even if you blow every fuse.) The recitation went on—

(That does it, I guess—those are the words I had tagged in my mind never to use in your presence. Now tell me—was there even *one* you didn't understand?)

(That's not the point. A person should not use language which offends others.)

(I never did, Boss. In public. But I'm home now—or thought I was. Do you want me to go away again?)

(No, no, no! Uh, you were away?) (I certainly was, Boss. Dead, I suppose. But I'm here now and I want to stay. If you'll let me. If I can relax and be happy and not have to be on guard all the time for fear of offending you. I can't see why a Latin polysyllable makes me more a lady than a monosyllable with the same meaning. You and I think with the same brain—yours—eat with the same mouth—mine, or used to be—and pee through the same hole. So why shouldn't we share the same vocabulary? Speaking of peeing—oh, pardon me, sir, I meant to say 'micturition'—)

(None of your sarcasm, girl!)

(Just who are you calling a 'girl,' girlie? Feel yourself, go ahead and feel. Some knockers, eh, Boss?—and how you used to stare at them, you horny old goat. Made me tingle. But I was saying, speaking of micturition, that we are going to have to ring for a bedpan fairly soon, now that we no longer are rigged with plumbing . . . and there is no way for me to leave the room while you pee. I don't dare leave it's *dark* out there and I might not find my way back. So it' either get used to such things—or send me away forever—or bust your nice new bladder.)

118

(Okay, Eunice, you've made your point.)

(Have I offended you again, Boss?)

(Eunice, you have *never* offended me. Sometimes you have startled me, sometimes you have surprised me and often delighted me. But you have *never* offended me. Not even with that list of blunt words.)

(Well . . . as I saw it, if you already knew them, you couldn't really be offended; if you didn't understand them, then you couldn't *possibly* be offended.)

(All right, dear. I'll quit trying to correct your speech. But for the record—I used all those words long before your mother was born. Possibly before your grandmother was born.) (Grandma is sixty-eight). (Learned 'em all and used them with relish long before your grandmother was born—with relish because they were sinful, then. I take it they aren't, to you kids now.)

(No, they're just words. Short-talk.)

(Not short-talk, as they were used before video corrupted the language. Except—What was that one word? 'Frimp'?)

(Oh. Shouldn't have included that one, Boss; it's not a classic word. Current slang, swing talk. It's a general verb, one which includes every possible way to copulate—) (Pfui! You youngsters. When I was a kid, we had at least two dozen words meaning 'frimp,' some new, some old besides the standard taboo words for it.) (You didn't let me finish, Boss.—every possible way to hook up two or more bodies—any number—of any sex, or combinations of all six sexes, and including far-out variations that would shock you right out of this bed. But swing is a today scene, so it's not surprising you hadn't heard the word 'frimp' before.)

(Oh, I'd heard it. I have news for you, infant.)

(Yes, sir? I mean 'Yes, Miss Smith,' dearie. *'Miss'* Smith—what a giggle I got when I first heard it. But it's nice, since it means both of us. Say, Rosy is all right, isn't he? Puts more into hand-kissing than some studs do into a romp on the pad.) (Sweetheart, you not only have a dirty mind—but it veers.) (How can I help having a dirty mind when it's actually *yours*, Boss—I'm hip deep in the stuff.) (Shut up, Eunice; it's my turn. The swing scene is nothing new. The Greeks had a word for it. So did the Romans. And so on through history. The orgy was relished in Victorian England. It was far from unknown in my youth in the heart of the Bible Belt, even though it was dangerous in those days. Eunice, as long as we are trying to get easy with each other, let me say this: Anything you've ever seen, or tried, or heard of, I did, or had done to me, before your grandmother was born—and if I liked it, I did it again and again and *again*. No matter how risky.)

The second voice was silent a moment. (Maybe we simply start younger today. Less risk and fewer rules.)

(Beg to doubt.)

(Oh, I'm sure we do. I told you how young I was when I got caught. Fifteen. And I started a year younger.)

(Eunice my love, the main difference between the young and the old, the cause of the so-called Generation Gap—a gap in understanding that has existed throughout all time—is that the young simply cannot believe that the old ever really were young . . . whereas to an old person his youth is something that happened just last week, and it annoys the hell out of him when someone in effect denies that this old duffer ever *owned* a youth.)

(Boss?) The thought was gentle and soft.

(Yes, dearest?)

(Boss, I always knew you were young underneath, behind all those horrid liver spots—knew it when I was alive, I mean . . . and wished dreadfully that you weren't old and sick in your body. It hurt me so, to see you hurt. Sometimes I went home and cried. Especially when it made you cross and you would say something you didn't mean and then be sorry. I *wanted* you to get well . . . and knew you couldn't. I was one of the first to sign up—Joe and I both—as soon as word reached us through the Rare Blood Club. Couldn't do it sooner or you might have found out—and forbidden me to.)

(Eunice, Eunice!)

(Don't you believe me?)

(Yes, darling, yes . . . but you're making us cry.)

(So blow your nose, Boss, and stop it. Because everything turned out *all right*. Look, you wanted to hear

120

about my little bastard—will that take your mind off troubles we no longer have?)

(Uh . . . only if you want to, Eunice. My love. My only love.)

(I made it plain that I *wanted* to tell you, didn't I? I'll tell all—and that'll take a long time!—if you want to hear. If you won't be shocked. Say 'Please,' Boss—because the details of my sex life ought to help you in handling your own sex life. *Our* sex life, that is. Or did you mean that stuff you were shoveling at Dr. Garcia about not being 'actively female'?)

(Uh . . . I don't know, Eunice, I haven't been a woman long enough to know *what* I want. Shucks, darling, instead of thinking like a girl I'm still ogling girls. That little redheaded nurse, for example.)

(So I noticed.)

(Was that sarcasm? Or jealousy?)

(What? I do not intend to be sarcastic, Boss dear; I don't want us ever to be nasty with each other. And jealousy is just a word in the dictionary to me. I simply meant that, when Winnie was making up our face and you were sneaking a peek down the neck of her smock every time she leaned over, I was staring as hard as you were. No bra. Cute ones, aren't they? Winnie is female and knows it. If you were male in your body as well as in your head, I wouldn't trust her as far as I could throw a bed.)

(I thought you said you weren't jealous?)

(I'm not. I merely meant that Winnie would trip you and beat you to the floor. But I was not criticizing her. I've nothing against girls. A girl can be quite a blast.)

Johann was slow in answering. (Eunice, uh, were you implying that you have—used to have—relations with other, uh—)

(Oh, Boss, don't be so early-twentieth-century; we've turned the corner on the twenty-first. Tell it bang. Do you mean 'Am I a Lez?' Homosexual?)

(No, not at all! Well, perhaps I did mean that in a way. At least I wanted you to clear up what you meant. As it didn't seem possible. You were married and—or was your marriage just a cover-up? I suppose—)

121

(Quit supposing, dear. Bang. I was not homosexual and neither is Joe. Joe is a tomcat always ready to yowl, and wonderful at it. Except when he's painting; then he forgets everything else. But 'homosexual' isn't a word that bothers anyone my age, either the word or the fact. And why not, with the Government practically subsidizing it with propaganda about too many babies that starts in kindergarten? If I had taken the Bilitis pledge, I would never have had that phony 'rheumatic fever.' But, while girls are cuddly and I've never had any inhibitions about them, I was—*always*—far too interested in boys to live on Gay Street. But which team are you on, Boss? One minute you're telling me how you drool over Winnie, the next minute you seem upset that I drooled, too. So what are you going to do with us, dear? Left-handed? Right-handed? Both hands? Or no hands at all? I guess I could stand anything but the last. Do I have a vote?)

(Why, of course you do.)

(I wonder, Boss. You sputtered when I suggested that you could thank Doc Hedrick in bed . . . and sparked some more at the notion of going to bed with a girl. Sure you're not planning on sewing it up?)

(Oh, Eunice, don't talk silly! Beloved, happy as I am that we are together, that 'Generation Gap' is still there. My fault this time, as I have a lifelong habit of being careful in what I say to a woman, even one I am in bed with—)

(You're certainly in bed with *me!*)

(I certainly am. And I'm finding it ever harder to be flatly truthful with you—'tell it bang' as you say—than it is to adjust to being female. But before Dr. Hedrick brought up the matter I saw the implications—and complications—and consequences—of being female . . . and young . . . and rich.)

('Rich.' I hadn't thought about *that* one.)

(Eunice beloved, we're going to *have* to think about it. Of course we're going to be 'actively female'—)

(*Hooray!*)

(Quiet, dear. If we were poor, the simplest thing would be to ask your Joe to take us back. If he would have us. But

122

we *aren't* poor; we're embarrassingly rich—and a fortune is harder to get rid of than it is to accumulate. Believe me. When I was about seventy-five, I tried to unload my wealth while I was still living so that it would not go to my granddaughters. But to give away money without wasting most of it in the process is as difficult as getting the genie back into the bottle. So I gave up and simply arranged my will to keep most of it out of the hands of my alleged descendants.)

('Alleged'?)

(Alleged. Eunice, my first wife was a sweet girl, much like yourself, I think. But the poor dear died in childbirth—bearing my one son, also dead for many years now. Agnes had made me promise to marry again and I did, almost at once. One daughter from that marriage and her mother divorced me before the child was a year old. I married a third time—again one daughter, again a divorce. I never knew my daughters well and outlived both of them and their mothers. But—Eunice, you're a rare-blood yourself; do you know how blood types are inherited?)

(Not really.)

(Thought you might. Being mathematically inclined, the first time I laid eyes on an inheritance chart for blood types I understood it as well as I understand the multiplication tables. Having lost my first wife to childbirth, with both my second and third wives I made certain that donors were at hand before they went into delivery rooms. Second wife was type A, third was type B—years later I learned that both my putative daughters were type O.)

(I think I missed something, Boss.)

(Eunice, it is impossible for a type-AB father to sire type-O children. Now wait—I did *not* hold it against my daughters; it was none of their doing. I would have loved Evelyn and Roberta—tried to, wanted to—but their mothers kept me away from them and turned them against me. Neither girl had any use for me . . . until it turned out that I was going to dispose of a lot of money someday—and then the switch from honest dislike to phony 'affection' was nauseating. I feel no obligation to my granddaughters since in fact they are *not* my granddaughters. Well? What do you think?)

(Uh—Boss, I don't see any need to comment.)

(So? Who was it not five minutes ago was saying that we ought to be absolutely frank with each other?)

(Well . . . I don't disagree with your conclusion, Boss, just with how you reached it. I don't see that heredity should enter into it. Seems to me you are resenting something that happened a long time ago—and that's not good. Not good for you, Boss.)

(Child, you don't know what you're talking about.)

(Maybe not.)

(No 'maybes' about it. A baby is a baby. Babies are to love and take care of and that's what this whole bloody mess is about, else none of it makes sense. Eunice, I told you that my first wife was something like you. Agnes was my Annabel Lee and we loved with a love that was more than a love and I had her for only a year—then she died giving me my son. Then I loved *him* just as much. When he was killed something died inside me . . . and I made a foolish fourth marriage hoping to bring it alive again by having another son. But I was lucky that time—no children and it merely cost me a chunk of money to get shut of it.)

(I'm sorry, Boss.)

(Nothing to be sorry about now. But I was telling you something else—Eunice, when we're up and around, remind me to dig into my jewelry case and show you my son's 'dog tag'—all that I have left of him.)

(If you want to. But isn't that morbid, dear? Look forward, not back.)

(Depends on how you look back. I don't grieve over him; I'm proud of him. He died honorably, fighting for his country. But that military dog tag shows his blood type. Type O.)

(Oh.)

(Yes, I said 'O'. So my son was no more my physical descendant than were my daughters. Didn't keep me from loving him.)

(Yes, but—you learned it from his identification tag? After he was dead?)

(Like hell I did. I knew it the day he was born; I had

124

suspected that he might not be mine from the time Agnes turned out to be pregnant—and I accepted it. Eunice, I wore horns with dignity and always kept suspicions to myself. Just as well—as all my wives contributed to my cornute state. Horns? Branching antlers! The husband who expects anything else is riding for a fall. But I never had illusions about it, so it never took me by surprise. No reason why it should, as I got the best parts of my own training from married women, starting clear back in my early teens. I think that happens in every generation. But horns make a man's head ache only when he's stupid enough to believe that *his* wife is different—when all the evidence he has accumulated should cause him to assume the exact opposite.)

(Boss, you think *all* women are like that?)

(Oh, no! In my youth I knew many married couples in which both bride and groom—to the best of my knowledge and belief—went to the altar virgin and stayed faithful a lifetime. There may be couples like that among you kids today.)

(Some, I think. But you couldn't prove it by me.)

(Nor by me. Nor by all the kinseys who ever collected statistics. Eunice, sex is the one subject *everybody* lies about. But what I was saying is this: A man who takes his fun where he finds it, then marries and expects his wife to be different, is a fool. I wasn't that sort of fool. Let me tell you about Agnes.

(Agnes was an angel—with round heels. That's obsolete slang which means what it sounds like. I don't think Agnes ever hated anyone in her short life and she loved as easily as she breathed. She—Eunice, you said you had started young?)

(Fourteen, Boss. Precocious slut, huh?)

(Precocious possibly, a slut never. Nor was my angel Agnes ever a slut and she happily gave away her virginity—so she told me—at twelve. I—)

('Twelve!')

(Surprised, dear? That Generation Gap again; your generation thinks it invented sex. Agnes was precocious; sixteen was fairly young in those days, from what a male could guess about it—not much!—and seventeen or eighteen was more common. I think. Actually encountering female virginity and being *certain* of it—well, I'm no expert. But Agnes wasn't hanging up a record even for those days; I recall a girl in my grammar school who was 'putting out,' as kids called it then, at eleven—and getting away with it cold, teacher's pet and butter wouldn't melt in her mouth and winning pins for Sunday School attendance.

(My darling Agnes was like that except that Agnes's goodness wasn't pretense; she was good all the way through. She simply didn't see anything sinful about sex.)

(Boss, sex is *not* sinful.)

(Did I *ever* say it was? However, in those days I felt guilty about it, until Agnes cured me of such nonsense. She was sixteen and I was twenty and her father was a prof at the cow college I went to and I was invited to their house for dinner one Sunday night—and our first time happened on their living room sofa so fast it startled me, scared me some.)

(What frightened you, dear? Her parents?)

(Well, yes. Just upstairs and probably not asleep. Agnes being so young herself—age of consent was eighteen then and while I don't recall ever letting it stop me, boys were jumpy about it. And that night I wasn't prepared, not having expected it.)

(Prepared how, Boss?)

(Contraception. I had a year to go to get my degree, and no money and no job lined up, and having to get married wasn't something I relished.)

(But contraception is a *girl's* responsibility, Boss. That's why I felt so silly when I got caught. I wouldn't have dreamed of asking a boy to marry me on that account—even if I had been certain which boy. Once I knew I was caught I gritted my teeth and told my parents and took my scolding—Daddy was going to have to pay my fine; I was not yet licensed. Grim—but no talk of getting married. I wasn't asked who did it and never volunteered an opinion.)

(Didn't you have an opinion, Eunice?)

(Well . . . just an opinion. Let me tell it bang. Our basketball team and us three girl cheerleaders were all in the same hotel, with the coach and the girls' phys-ed teacher riding herd on us. Only they didn't; they went out on the town. So we gathered to celebrate in the suite the boys were in. Somebody had lettuce. Marijuana. I took two puffs and didn't like it—and went back to gin and ginger ale which tasted better and was almost as new to me. Didn't have any intention of swinging; it wasn't the smart scene at our school and I had a steady I was faithful to—well, usually—who wasn't on the trip. But when the head cheerleader took her clothes off—well, there it was. So I counted days in my mind and decided I was safe by two days and peeled down, last of the three to do so. Nobody made me do it, Boss, no slightest flavor of rape. So how could I blame the boys?

(Only it turned out I didn't have two days leeway and by the middle of January I was fairly certain. Then I was certain. Then my parents were certain—and I was sent south to stay with an aunt while I recovered from rheumatic fever I never had. And recovered two hundred sixty-nine days after that championship game, barely in time to enter school in the fall. And graduated with my class.)

(But your *baby*, Eunice? Boy? Girl? How old now? Twelve? And where is the child?)

(Boss, I don't know. I signed an adoption waiver so that Daddy would get his money back if somebody with a baby license came along. Boss, is that fair? Five thousand dollars was a lot of money to my father—yet anyone on Welfare gets off free, or can even demand a free abortion. I can't see it.)

(You changed the subject, dear. Your baby?)

(Oh. They told me it was born dead. But I hear they usually say that if a girl signs the papers and somebody is waiting for it.)

(We can find out. If your baby didn't live, then the fine was never levied. Didn't your father tell you?)

(I never asked. It was a touchy subject, Boss. It was

'rheumatic fever,' never an unlicensed baby. Just as well, I guess, as when I turned eighteen, I was licensed for three with no questions raised.)

(Eunice, no matter what cover-up was used, if your baby is living, we can find it!)

The second voice did not answer. Johann persisted. (Well, Eunice?)

(Boss . . . it's better to let the dead past bury its dead.)

(You don't want children, Eunice?)

(That wasn't what I said. You said it didn't matter that your son wasn't really yours. I think you were right. But doesn't it cut both ways? If there is a child somewhere, almost thirteen now—we're strangers. I'm not the mother who loved it and brought it up; I'm nobody. *Really* nobody—you forget that I was killed.)

(Eunice! Oh, darling!)

(You see? If we found that boy, or girl, we couldn't admit that I'm still alive—alive again, I mean—inside your head. That's the thing we don't *dare* admit . . . or back they come with those horrid straps and we'll *never* be free.) She sighed. (But I wish I could have had *your* baby. You were telling me about Agnes, dearest. Tell me more. Am I really somewhat like her?)

(Very much like her, Eunice. Oh, I don't mean she looked like you. But if I believed in reincarnation—I don't—I would be tempted to think that you were Agnes, come back to me.)

(Maybe I am. Why don't you believe in it, Boss?)

(Uh . . . do you?)

(No. I mean I *didn't* believe in it, even though most of our friends did. I couldn't see any reason to believe either way, so I kept my mouth shut. But, Boss, it gives one a different viewpoint to have been killed . . . and then turn out not to stay dead. Dearest Boss—you think I'm a figment of your imagination, don't you?)

Johann did not answer. The voice went on: (Don't be afraid to admit it, Boss; you won't offend me. *I* know I'm *me*. I don't need proof. But you do. You need to know. Admit it, darling. Be open with me.)

She sighed again. (Eunice, I do need to know. But—if

128

I'm crazy—if you are just my own mind talking back to me—I'd rather not know it. Darling, forgive me . . . but I was relieved when you told me that you didn't want us to try to find your baby.)

(I knew you were relieved . . . and I knew why. Boss, don't be so right-now. We have all the time in the world, so relax and be happy. Proof will turn up—something I know and that you couldn't possibly know except through me. And that will be that, and you will be as certain as I am.)

She nodded to herself. (That makes sense, Eunice—and it sounds like the scoldings you used to give me when I got fretful. You used to mother me.)

(I'm going to go right on mothering you, and scolding you when you need it—and loving you all the time, Boss. But there is one thing there is some hurry about.)

(What?)

(That bedpan. Unless you want us to have a childish accident.)

(Oh, damn!)

(Relax, Boss. Get used to it.)

(Damnation, I do *not* want to be placed on a bedpan by a nurse like a baby being put to potty. You know what'll happen? Nothing! I'll clamp down and not be able to do it. Eunice, there's my bathroom through that door—can't we ask to be helped into there . . . and left in private?)

(Boss, you know what would happen. You ring for the nurse and tell her. She'll try to argue you out of it. Then she'll go find Dr. Garcia. He'll show up and argue, too. If you're stubborn, he'll get Jake. By the time Jake shows up, we've wet the bed.)

(Eunice, you're infuriating. All right, let's ring for that goddam pan.)

(Hold it, Boss. Can we get this side rail down?)

(Huh?)

(If we can, what's stopping us from going to the bathroom without asking?)

(But, Eunice—I haven't walked in more than a year!)

(That was before you got this secondhand, good-as-new, factory-reconditioned, female body, Boss.)

(You think we can walk?)

(Let's find out. If standing up makes us dizzy, we can hang onto the bed and ease down to the floor. I'm *certain* we can crawl, Boss.)

(Let's do it!)

(Let's see how this side rail works.)

Johann found the guard rails baffling. There seemed to be no way for a person in the bed to let them down. Not surprising, she told herself; if these bars were meant to protect a befuddled patient, then proper design called for it to be impossible for a patient to remove them. (Eunice, we're going to have to ring for the nurse. Damn!) (Don't give up, Boss. Maybe it's a button on the console. If we scrooch around till our head is at the foot, I think we can reach the console.)

So Johann pulled up her knees and twisted and switched ends—and was surprised and delighted at how limber her new body was. Then she stretched her right arm through the bars at the foot of the bed, could not quite reach the console—and cussed, and then discovered how the side rails locked—two simple catches, one for each side, at the foot of the bed below the springs, out of reach (no doubt the designer thought) of any patient ill enough to need the side rails.

She thumbed open the leftside catch; the rail, counterweighted, pushed down easily. She giggled. (How're we doing, partner?) (Fine so far, Boss. Hang onto the end of the bed while we get our feet down. Keel over and they'll put us in a wet pack—so hang on!)

Johann got her feet to the floor, stood trembling while she clung to the bed. (Dizzy.) (Of course. It will go away. Steady down, dear. Boss, I think we could walk . . . but let's play safe and crawl. If we get dizzy again and take a dive on the rug, Winnie will be in here like a shot—and from then on they'll feed us through the bars. What do you think?) (I think we had better reach that pot pronto before we have to blame it on the cat. We crawl.)

Getting to the floor was no problem; crawling was another matter, she caught her knees on the hospital gown. So she sat up—Johann discovered that her new body folded easily and naturally into a contortion young Johann

130

had found difficult at twelve.

She did not stop to wonder. The bed jacket was no trouble; it fastened in front with a magnostrip, she shrugged it off and laid it aside. But the hospital gown fastened in back. (Stickstrip?) (Just a tie-tie. Feels like a bow knot. Careful, Boss, don't snarl it.)

The gown joined the jacket. Unencumbered now, Johann resumed crawling. The bath-dressing room door snapped out of her way and she reached her objective.

Presently she sighed in relief. (I feel better.) (That makes two of us. Want to try walking back? As far as we have something to grab onto? Or clear to the bed if we whistle a chair and have it roll in front of us.) (I'm game.)

Johann found that she was not unsteady on her feet—walking was easier than it had been for twenty years. Nevertheless she stayed close to the walls, the bathroom having been equipped years ago with grab rails for a frail old man grimly afraid of falling. It took her close to a tall three-way mirror in the dressing room end. She stopped.

Then she stepped into the central spot and looked at herself. (My God, Eunice, but you're beautiful!)

(My God, but we're a sloppy bitch! Boss, look at those toenails! Claws. Talons. And, oh dear, my breasts sag! And my belly is positively flabby.)

(Beautiful. Utterly gorgeous. Eunice beloved, I always wanted to see you stark naked. And now I do.)

(So you do. I wish I had had time to get looking nice before you saw me. Hair a mess. And—yes, I thought so. We stink.) (Hey!) (Sorry, hit the panic button by mistake. Boss, we're going to have a hot, soapy bath before we get back into that bed. That's straight from Washington. We can't do much about flab in one day—but we can get clean.) She turned and inspected her buttocks. (Oh, dear! A broad should be broad—but not *that* broad.) (Eunice, that's the prettiest fanny in the state. In the whole country.) (Used to be, maybe. And it's going to be again and that's a promise, Boss. Tomorrow morning we start systematic exercise. Tighten up everything.) (Okay, if you say so—though I still say you're the most gorgeously beautiful thing I ever saw in my life. Uh, Eunice? That mermaid

131

getup you wore once—You were wearing a trick bra with it . . . weren't you?)

She giggled. (Heavens, no. Just me, Boss. And paint. But my breasts were firm as rocks then; Joe had something to work with. I guess that's the nakedest you've ever seen me.)

(What do you think I'm staring at *now*, Beautiful?)

(Oh, I meant back before I was killed. When I was your 'nice' girl who didn't dare let you see me as naked as I knew you would like, you dirty old man. Although you *could* have seen me naked—and much more beautiful—any time you had gotten up the nerve to ask.)

(I'm going to spend hours every day standing right here and staring.)

(No reason why you shouldn't, dear; it's your body now. But let's put an exercise mat on the floor and get in that toning up at the same time. Most exercises can be done better with the aid of a full-length mirror. I think we—)

The door snapped open. "*Miss Smith!*"

Johann started with surprise, then answered savagely, "Miss Gersten, what the devil do you mean by bursting into my bath without knocking?"

The nurse ignored the outburst, hurried to her patient, put an arm around her. "Lean on my shoulder, let's get you back into bed. Oh, dear, I don't know what Dr. Garcia will say! He'll kill me—are you all right?" Johann saw that the little nurse was about to cry.

"Of course I'm all right." Johann tried to shrug off the arm, found that the girl was stronger than she looked. "You didn't answer."

The nurse did cry then. "Oh, please, dear, don't argue with me! Let's get you into bed before you hurt yourself. Maybe Dr. Garcia won't be quite so angry."

Seeing that the younger woman was most unprofessionally disturbed, Johann let herself be urged out into the bedroom and to the bed. The little redhead caught her breath. "There! Now if you'll hold tight around my neck, I can get your legs up—you bad, bad girl! To worry me so!"

Johann did not cooperate. "Winnie."

"Yes, dear? Oh, do let me get you into bed! Doctor will be terribly angry."

"Not so fast. If you're planning on telling teacher, go do it. I can hang onto the bed, I won't fall."

The nurse looked desperate. "Are you trying to get me fired, Miss? Maybe blacklisted? What have I ever done to you?"

"Winnie dear."

"Yes?"

"You aren't going to say a word to Dr. Garcia." Johann slid an arm around the redhead's waist. "Are you?"

The nurse looked flustered but did not pull away. "Well, I should. I'm supposed to report everything."

"But you aren't going to. And I'm not going to tell him, either. Tight secret, just you and me. And no huhu for anyone."

"Well . . . I won't if you won't."

"Promise?"

"I promise."

Johann kissed her. Winnie did not dodge but seemed startled and somewhat timid. Then she caught her breath and her lips opened and the kiss progressed rapidly.

The nurse pulled her mouth free and said huskily, "I could get fired almost as quickly for *this*." She did not say what "this" was. She ignored the fact that Johann's free hand was cupping one of her breasts.

"So we'll stop and I'll get into bed—no, don't help me; I don't need it."

Johann proved it by doing it. The nurse pulled the sheet over her, at once resumed her professional *persona*. "Now let's put our clothes back on, shall we?" She stooped to retrieve them. "What a naughty girl, throwing her clothes on the floor. And giving me such a fright."

"Stuff 'em in the hamper. I'm not going to wear them."

"Now, now, dear. You needn't wear the jacket. Just the gown. Or do you want a fresh one?"

"Winnie, I'm not going to wear those silly angel robes ever again, so chuck it. You can hang up the jacket. But I won't wear a hospital gown. I'll stay raw."

"Dr. Garcia—"

"Quit threatening me with Dr. Garcia. We're past that. Aren't we?"

The nurse bit her lip. "Well . . . yes."

"It's none of his business if I sleep raw. And I shall, until something more appropriate can be bought for me. Or—Do you sleep in the house? Maybe you could lend me a nightie. A girl-type nightgown."

"Well, yes, I sleep here. But I can't lend you a gown because, well—I sleep raw myself."

"Sensible."

"But there are nightgowns and negligees and things right here. In your dressing room."

"Be damned. Who ordered them?"

"I don't know, Miss Smith. They were brought in and stored there when, well, when it became clear that you were going to need them."

"Good planning. Uh, do you know if they're my size? Whatever that size is, I don't know myself."

"Oh, yes! I helped measure you."

"More good planning. Find me the most feminine nightgown in there—I might as well practice."

"Glad to." The nurse left the bedroom.

(Butch.) (Oh, nonsense, Eunice. Sure, she's a cute little trick . . . but I simply suddenly realized what treatment she would respond to. Had to dig back into my memory; I'm out of practice.) ('Butch' I said. You enjoyed it.) (Didn't *you* enjoy it?) (Sure I did. She kisses like don't-stop. But I'm not a hypocrite about it. *Who* was shocked when I said girls could be a blast? You, you dirty old hypocrite. And butch.)

(Eunice, you are out of your frimping mind. I've had most of a century to appreciate girls; do you expect me to change overnight? The time I'll feel like a queer is the first time some *man* kisses us. I'll probably faint.) (Poor Boss! Doesn't know whether he's A.C. or D.C. Never mind, dear, Eunice will coach you—as I *do* know how to kiss a man.)

(I imagine you do.) (Was there salt in that one? Never mind, I know how. *He* faints. Boss, you claimed you had done everything. *Every*thing?) (See here, little snoopy, I am

134

not going to give you any excuse to call me both 'butch' and 'pansy' in the same sentence. You can have my memoirs later. But, Eunice, speaking of 'butch,' is that what Winnie is? She certainly responded.) (More 'sweetheart' than 'butch' is my guess, though she may stroll both sides of Gay Street. But if you were asking 'Is she a Lez?' then I would bet anything she's not. Ambi, sure, but *much* more interested in men. Haven't you watched her? Sparks.)

Winnie returned with a nightgown in each hand. "I think these two are the prettiest, Miss Smith. I thought—"

"Winnie."

"Yes, Miss Smith?"

"No 'Miss Smith.' I mean you are not to call me 'Miss Smith.' Not after kissing me. Or did I get the message wrong?" (Butch.) (Shut up, Eunice. She's going to help us.)

The nurse said nothing, blushed.

Johann said gently, "That's answer enough, dear. So call me—no, damn it, I don't want you to call me 'Johann.' I need a new name. Winnie dear, what girl's name is closest to 'Johann'?"

"Uh, 'Johanna.' "

"Mmmm, yes. But there is already a 'Johanna' in my family. Got another?"

"Well . . . if you called yourself 'Joan' and gave it the two-syllable pronounciation, it would be almost like 'Johann' except for the 'J' instead of the 'Y' sound."

"Perfect! You've named me. I think that makes you my godmother. Do you mind being godmother to an old, old man who has just been reborn as a woman?"

Winnie smiled. "I'm flattered."

"So call me 'Joan,' not 'Miss Smith.' Uh, I need a middle name. 'Eunice.' " (Why, Boss, now *I'm* flattered.) (Yes, beloved. Now shut up.) " 'Joan Eunice Smith.' Winnie, do you know why that's my middle name?"

The nurse said slowly, "I'm not supposed to know."

"Then you do know. It's for the sweet and gracious lady who gave me this wonderful body—and I hope she can hear me wherever she is." (I *can*, Boss!) "Put down those gowns and come here and name me with my new name.

135

Name me formally, for it's all the christening I will ever have. Then seal it."

Almost timidly the little redhead came close to the bed, bent over her patient. She said softly, "I name thee 'Joan Eunice' "—and kissed her.

Perhaps Winnie intended to make it a formal peck; Joan Eunice did not let it be. Both women were leaking tears before it was over.

Joan patted the nurse's cheek and let her straighten up. "Thank you, dear. I'm Joan now. Joan Eunice. Hand me a tissue and you need one, too." (How was that one, Eunice?) (Butch, your technique is improving. I felt that one clear down in our toes.) (Who the hell are you calling 'Butch,' Butch? My name is Joan Eunice.) (No, you're Joan and *I* am Eunice and collectively we're Joan Eunice . . . and I've never had a nicer present, Boss. Joan. And I know you're not a butch but you had better cool it with our godmother. Unless you mean business.)

"Which gown do you like . . . Joan?"

"Winnie, I don't know first verse about women's clothes. What do you think?"

"Well . . . this Cretan design is rather extreme. But you have the figure to justify it." (No, Boss! Take the one with the high neckline.) (Eunice, I thought you were proud of our bumps? They don't really sag.) (It's not that at all. Trust me, Joan; I know what I'm doing.)

"You may be right, Winnie. But it may not be the right gown for doctors and lawyers. I had better start easy, with the high neckline. Help me, please."

While they were getting Joan into a nightgown she asked, "Winnie? How did you happen to burst in on me?"

"What? Why, the displays of course. Both your heart rate and respiration were way up. Exercise. So I rushed in to check—and sure enough, my bad girl had managed to get out of bed. Oh, how you frightened me, dear!"

"Winnie, there's a hole in that story I could throw a dog through."

The nurse stiffened. "What do you mean—Joan?"

"My heart rate and respiration must have climbed a good ten minutes before you came in."

136

"Oh, dear! You won't tell on me? You promised."

"I did and so did you. Winnie with the sweet mouth, from now on neither of us is ever going to tell Dr. Garcia a durn thing unless *we* think he needs to know it. You and I, dear. Solid. Now tell me what happened."

"Uh . . . oh, this is silly. Whoever is on watch at the remotes isn't supposed to take his eyes off the displays even a moment. But you were doing so nicely . . . and Mrs. Sloan was taking a nap—which she needed, poor dear—and Dr. Garcia had gone to check on Mr. Salomon . . . and he takes a grim view of being sent for unless the patient needs him . . . and the washroom is just down the hall from the displays—"

"I get it. We had the same urge at the same time. Right?"

Winnie blushed again. "I deserve to be fired. I know better than to take any chance with a patient. Patients do the darnedest things."

"You aren't ever going to be fired, you're going to be here long after Dr. Garcia leaves. If you'll stay. How do I look?"

"Simply lovely. I wouldn't have guessed it but I do think this gown does more for you than that Cretan number." (What did I tell you, Boss?) "But I'm going to put more lipstick on you. It's all gone."

"Now how in the world did *that* happen?"

Winnie giggled. "Don't ask *me*. But guess maybe I'll put on some myself before Doctor sees us. Joan? Is it all right for me to call you 'Miss Joan' when Dr. Garcia is around? He's terribly strict."

"Tell him to go soak his head. Sho', sho', honey, if it makes you feel easier. But I'm 'Joan' when he's not around. You're my coach. You're going to make a lady out of me." (That's *my* job, Boss. And a tough one, I can see.) (So you need help with it. Don't joggle my elbow; Winnie is our secret weapon.) (Okay. But this weapon might explode.) (Look, infant, I learned to cope with women long before your grandmother was born.)

"I'll be glad to help, any way I can . . . Joan dear."

"Then you can start by convincing dear Doctor that I'm

137

well enough for a tub bath. I stink. Ladies ought not to stink."

"Why, you had a bed bath not two hours ago!"

"I need more than a bed bath and you know it. Sell him the idea that you can help me into and out of the tub and keep me from falling. If you have trouble with him, fetch him in and I'll throw a tantrum. If he gives us grief, I'll make him scrub my back." Joan grinned. "So get lipstick on us; then go find him."

(Joan Boss honey, see what I mean about the high neckline job? See what it does for us?) (I know that I feel somewhat more covered up. But only somewhat. Eunice, those breast panels are wicked.) (Oh, fuff, they're not even transparent, just translucent. But that's why this nightgown is so much sexier than the Cretan one. Men always mistake bare skin for sexiness. A typical male mistake.) (Maybe so, but I have never in my long life complained about bare skin.) (I won't argue, Joan, but I'm going to pick out our clothes. Until you start thinking like a woman. But I had a specific reason for picking the gown which is —superficially—more modest. So that we will have it on when Jake comes in.)

(Eunice, Jake has probably gone home. He's had a rough time.)

(So he has and what do you think I'm talking about? He's still in the house; he would not leave without saying good-bye.)

(Oh, nonsense, Jake and I aren't that formal.)

(Boss, Jake is a gentleman to his fingertips. He might feel free to duck out without formality in dealing with his old friend Johann Smith—but not with a lady. 'Johann' is one thing, 'Joan Eunice' is another matter.)

(But he knows I'm Johann.)

(So? Then why did he kiss our hand? Joan, I'm going to have to watch you every second; you don't know anything about men.)

(I spent almost a century being one.)

138

(Irrelevant. Hush up; he may be here any time, I've got to tell this bang. Joan, the last few months before I was killed I was Jake's mistress.)

(How was the old goat?)

(Is *that* all you have to say?)

(Eunice, you think I know nothing about men. Possibly true, in one sense. But *I* can teach *you* about men—from the inside—the way you can teach me about men from the outside. Jake is tough. Yet I saw him collapse twice in grief over you. Understandable that your death would upset him some. Understandable that it was a strain on him to help out in the masquerade of not letting me know that I had inherited your lovely body. Nevertheless you were just a girl he had known through business, one who helped him with my affairs. Not one he knew intimately. Yet this tough old lawyer collapsed twice. Over you. So he *must* have known you far better than anyone guessed. How? And *where*? Only one answer. In bed.)

(Not always in bed, you dirty old man with a girl's name. In bed, certainly. But lots of other places, too. In his car. In *your* car. Several times in this house—)

(Be damned! Then all my servants know it, too.)

(I doubt if they suspect. We used your study to work—and did work—and Cunningham didn't let us be disturbed any more than he would have disturbed you and me. You asked a rude question, you'll get a blunt answer. The old goat was *good*. And quite daring in grabbing every chance. We hardly missed a day up to the time I was killed.)

(A couple of j.d.'s, you two. Well, 'My hat's off to the Duke.')

(Jealous, Boss?)

(No, envious. I wouldn't have been up to it the first day I laid eyes on you. Impossible. And now still more impossible. Just envious. The old goat.)

(Not impossible, Joan.)

(Eh?)

(I was shocked when I saw Jake. My death must have

139

hurt him terribly. I know it did, he loved me. But we can pull him out of it, Joan, you and I—only this time we won't use your study.)

(*What?* Why, that's *incest!*)

(Don't be ridiculous, dear. I was no relation to Jake and I don't think you are, either.)

(I mean it would *feel* like incest. Jake? *Jake?* Eunice, when I admitted that I supposed that I would— eventually—be 'actively female,' I didn't have *Jake* in mind.)

(I did.)

(Then get it out of your mind! Forget it. Dr. Hedrick if you want to—at least I'll try to cooperate—after I get used to being female. Your former husband, Joe, I owe that to you—)

(Not Joe.)

(Why not? You spoke highly of him in that respect, and I always thought you thought well of him in other respects. Not urging you—hell, I can't think about sex other than abstractly about *any* man; I'm not yet reoriented. But I had already decided to go along with your need for Joe.)

(Boss, I *can't.* Not with Joe. Because he *was* my husband. To him, I'd be a zombie. A walking corpse. I doubt if he would touch us . . . and if he did, I'd be terribly tempted to tell him. Tell him I'm still here. Can't. I know it.)

(And *I* can't make it with Jake. It's the same with Jake, too, you know. A walking corpse.)

(Not quite the same. Surely, he knows we're a patchwork, your brain and my body. But he loved us both. He's loved you much longer than he's loved me. While Joe doesn't even know you.)

(*Jake* loved *me?* Eunice, you're out of your mind!)

(Impossible, dear; I don't have one to be out of. Why do you think Jake put up with your bad temper? Not for money; he's rich, even though he's not as rich as you are. Why is he still around at all? For *me?* He would have avoided seeing *me*—this body—had it been possible; it hurts him. He stuck because *you* needed him. Look, dear—Joan, I mean—Joan, this is your big sister Eunice
140

talking, you listen to her. Be nice to Jake. Be a sweet girl to Jake. Then let things run easy. I'm not asking you to do anything you don't want to do—heavens, no! Jake would spot it if you forced yourself; he's no fool about women. Just be sweet. Don't be Johann, be Joan. Be little and feminine and let him take care of you.)

(Well—I'll try. Jake is going to think I'm off my rocker.)

(He's going to think you're a darling girl. It's possible he'd rather be your father than what he was to me. If so, we'll be good and let him baby us.)

She sighed. (I'll try, Eunice. But I don't know. Jake!)

(That's my good girl, Joan. Be helpless and female; Jake will do the rest.)

Dr. Garcia bustled in, came straight to the bed. "What's this about a tub bath? I thought I made it plain that you weren't to rush things."

(Don't let him argue, Joan!) (Watch me trip him!) "Oh Doctor, you startled me so!"

"Eh? How?"

"Bursting in on me without warning. Is that nice?"

Garcia looked baffled. "Miss Smith, I've been here more than a year and I've always entered this room without ceremony. Am I to understand that you find it offensive? After all this time?"

"That's not the point, Doctor. When you first came here you were attending a helpless old man. Then you were helping Dr. Hedrick with a female patient who was paralyzed, and unconscious most of the time—and I do appreciate the care you gave that helpless patient, for I am she. But things change. I am now having to learn to be a woman and, if possible, a lady. It's not easy. Won't you help me by showing me the formal courtesies you show other ladies?"

Garcia reddened slightly. "A doctor doesn't have time for formalities."

(Slug him again, dearie! He's still twitching.) (I shall!) "Doctor, if I were in danger, I would expect you to rush in without buzzing; I depend on you. But you came in to tell me I can't have a bath—surely not an emergency. I'm not

141

asking much—just asking you to think of this room, not as an old man's sickroom, but as a lady's boudoir. To help me. Please?"

Dr. Garcia said stiffly, "Very well, Miss Smith. I shall remember."

"Thank you, sir. By the way, my name is 'Joan Smith' now; I can't go on being 'Johann.' You might call me 'Miss Joan' to help me get used to it. Or simply 'Joan,' as I don't want to be unnecessarily formal with my doctor, truly I don't. Just that little touch of formality that I need as training in learning how to be my new self. Will you call me 'Joan'?"

He grudged a smile. "All right—Joan."

She gave him Eunice's best you-wonderful-man smile. "That sounds nice. And you *are* welcome any time, Doctor, either professionally or just to visit. Which I hope you will do. Just have the nurse make sure I'm ready to receive a gentleman. Things. You know." She raised herself on an elbow and looked at him, acutely aware of her "modest" nightgown. "Such as lipstick." She wet her lips. "Odd to have to wear it. Is it on properly? Does it look right?"

"You look lovely!"

(Cancel and erase—change 'butch' to 'tart.' You're a natural-born tart, dearie. Where's your beat?) (Stow it, sister tart; I haven't finished hustling him.) "Why, thank you sir! Now tell me why I can't have a hot, soapy, tub bath so that I will *feel* lovely, too. I'll follow your orders, Doctor, but I would like to understand them. Can you tell me without using a lot of long medical words?"

"Well— Joan, my objection is to the tub itself. People are forever breaking legs or cracking skulls through slipping in bathtubs. And you haven't even learned to stand up, much less walk."

"True." Joan threw the sheet back, dropped her feet over the edge of the bed, sat up—controlled a slight dizziness and smiled. "Let's see if I can. Will you help me, Doctor? Arm around me perhaps?"

"Lie down!"

142

"Must I? I feel fine. Is there a stool? My feet don't touch the floor."

"Miss Sm— Joan, damn it, so help me I'm going to quit this business and buy a junkyard! Lie down while I call a nurse. Then we'll get on each side of you and let you stand up. When you find out how weak and dizzy you are, I'll expect you to go back to bed and stay there."

"Yes, Doctor," she said meekly, and lay down.

Winnie answered the summons. "You rang, Doctor?"

"We're going to try a practice walk. Help me get the patient up. You take her left side."

"Yes, sir."

With too much help Joan got out of bed, stood up. The room wobbled a little but she steadied herself on Winnie while letting her arm be feather-light on the Doctor's shoulder.

"How do you feel?"

"Fine. We should have music; I feel like dancing."

"Feel like it if you wish, don't try it. Slow march now and short steps." They walked toward the door, while Joan relished the thick pile of the rug against her bare feet. Walking was fun; *everything* was fun! (Eunice my love, do you realize what a perfect body this is?) (It's way out of shape. But two weeks' hard work and we'll have it tuned up.) (Oh, pooh, I never felt this good even as a child.) (You'll see, Boss. Say a vertical split with our hair sweeping the floor, then hold it through ten controlled breaths—and come out of it with a slow walkover and melt on down into a full Lotus with never a hurried movement. Just wait.) (You think we'll be able to do that? I was clumsy even as a boy.) (No huhu. The body remembers, dear.)

They stopped. "Now turn around slowly, and head for your bed."

"Doctor? Now that I'm up, why not head me straight for that soap and water?"

"Aren't you tired?"

"Not a bit. I didn't lean on you, did I? I thought I had been promised a real bath as soon as I was able to walk.

143

Must I stand on my hands as well? Back away and I'll try."
She let go of his arm.

The Doctor promptly put his arm around her waist. "No nonsense! Nurse, that tub has grab rails; make her use them."

"Yes, Doctor."

"If this patient falls, you had better head for Canada —you can find the shortest route by following me. If you're fast enough."

"Winnie won't let me fall," Joan said warmly while warmly leaning into his arm. "But if you're worried, you can come in and help. Scrub my back."

He snorted. "Ten minutes ago you bawled me out merely for walking into your bedroom unannounced."

"And if you do it again, I shall again. That's social; this is professional. Doctor, I'm well aware that you've seen my new body—professionally—many times. One more time won't kill me." She wiggled slightly in his arm.

"Scrubbing a patient's back is *not* part of my professional duties. Lukewarm tub, Nurse, and don't let her stay in too long."

Once inside the bathroom and the door shut Joan threw her arms around her nurse and giggled. "Honey, did you see his face?"

Winnie shook her head. "Joan, you don't need me to coach you in how to be female. You already know."

"Oh, but I *do* need you, dear. Because I *don't* know. I simply used on dear Doctor things that used to fluster me when I was his age—and male." She giggled again. "For a second I thought he was going to take my dare and scrub my back." (And *I* thought you were going to lay him, right on the rug.) (Oh, be quiet, Eunice; I didn't even pinch him.) Joan let go of Winnie, stepped back, and started to skin the gown over her head. "Now for a bath. Oh boy!"

"Joan! *Please* hold onto something. Doctor might show up any second."

"Oh, pooh, he wouldn't dare. Never again." Joan turned and touched the latch switch. "Now he can't, so quit fretting."

"You mustn't lock the door. Hospital baths are never locked."

"This isn't a hospital and I'll lock my bathroom door whenever I like and if Dr. Garcia finds out I've locked it the only way he *can*—by trying to walk in—and dares to mention it, I'll scream my head off to Jake Salomon and there'll be a change in doctors. Winnie dear, I wasn't a cranky old man more years than I care to think about without learning how to get my own way. I just have to use different weapons now. Want to peel off that uniform and hang it in the dressing room? I not only may splash you but this end is going to fill up with steam."

"No, Joan—lukewarm tub. You heard him."

"I heard him and it's going to be the temperature *I* like and that's another thing he'll never know and you know that I'm lively as a frog and not the weak kitten he insists on thinking I am; a hot tub won't hurt me. If you want to get your uniform clammy, that's your business. Better yet, climb into the tub with me. It's big, and short as I am now, I might slide under and drown, alone."

"I shouldn't," Winnie said slowly.

"Isn't that a horrid thought? Patient faints in tub and drowns before nurse can reach her. Not good enough for flash news but they might mention it on the late-late-late early news."

"Joan! You're teasing me." (You sure are, Boss. Erase and correct again—Both tart *and* butch.) (Fiddlesticks, Eunice. That's a big enough tub for all three of us.)

Winnie bit her lip and slowly unfastened her smock. Joan turned away and started filling the tub, adjusted the temperature, and avoided watching her.

An hour later Joan was seated in an easy chair, with her feet on a stool. To the nightgown had been added a filmy negligee and a pair of high-heeled boudoir pumps. Her hair had been arranged, her face had been most carefully made up, and she was lavishly scented with a cologne labeled "April Mist" but which deserved the title of "Criminal Assault." Her toenails were trimmed, not to Eunice's satisfaction but well enough for the time being. Best of all, she was enjoying the euphoria of a woman who is utterly clean, scented and powdered, and dressed attractively.

Beds had been switched, the room no longer held any flavor of sickroom, and Joan found that this greatly increased her feeling of well-being. Eunice's stenodesk had been restored to its usual spot beyond Johann's baby grand piano, Joan having learned that it was in her study where it had last been used, and had told Cunningham to have it brought in. It did not fit the room—but it fitted her notion of what the room should be; it was homey, it belonged.

She was alone, Winnie having gone to invite Mr. Salomon to dine with his hostess-ward. Joan sighed with satisfaction. (Feel better, hon? I do.) (Heavens, yes. But why did you lose your nerve?) (Oh, piffle, Eunice! I never intended to seduce her.) (Liar. Hypocrite. Dirty old man. You had her all set. Then you went chicken. I've met men like you before, dearie—talk a good game, then lose their nerve in the clutch. Cowardly Casanovas. Pfui!)

(Nonsense! You don't shoot ducks on water. If I ever make a real pass at her—I'm not saying I will but I admit she's a cuddlesome little bundle—) (She is indeed!) (Oh, shut up! If I ever do, I'll give her a sporting chance—not grab her when she dasn't scream.) ('Sporting chance' my tired back. Listen to your big sister, Joan—sex isn't a sport, it's a way to be happy. There is *nothing* more exasperating to a woman than to be ready to give in—then have the matter dropped. You'll find out. You'll cry in your pillow and hate every man alive. Till the next time, that is.)

(Eunice? You've never had that sort of turn-down, have you? I don't believe it.) (Happens to every woman, Joan. Men are sissies, if we women weren't so willing, if we didn't just plain lead 'em by the hand, the race would die out.)

(Uh—You know more about a woman than I do—) (Lots more!) (—so let's talk about specifics. We're clean now and I know we're pretty; I checked us in the big glass and you agreed. But it isn't the job you used to turn out. I don't mean body paint, wouldn't be appropriate now anyhow. But what does it take? Just that 'tuning up'? Exercise?)

(More than that, Boss—although exercise is essential. You're talking about a professional job?) (Yes. The works.) (Well, I used to do myself—but I had had lots of practice, plus expert help from Joe. But let's say you want the best and don't care what it costs—) (Certainly! What's money? I can't get rid of it.) (All right, say you retain Helena Rubinstein, Limited, or some other top glamour shop. Say you phone and tell them to send a full team. They would send an art director—male, but he may not be all that male and he's seen more female bodies unmade-up than an undertaker—and he doesn't touch you; he's too high up. He creates. And bosses. Won't look at you until several others get you ready. Mmmm, bath girl, masseuse, manicurist, pedicurist, coiffeuse, depilatrix, parfumiste, face and skin team of at least four, costume designer, highlight and accent specialist, and assistants for all of these if you expect the job done in less than all day. If you put a time limit on it, the price goes up—and if you don't, the price goes up.)

(Say that again?)

(It's like taxes. Any way you play it the price goes up. Boss, we don't need them. With what I know and the chassis we have to work with and a good lady's maid, you can be as glamorous as you like. I don't know where you would find a creative paint man equal to Joe; nevertheless there are good ones for hire. We can shop the market, we'll find one.)

(Eunice, I had no idea that being a woman was so complicated.)

(Relax, Boss. Being a woman is easier than being a man—and *lots* more fun. I'm going to teach you to be a twenty-first-century woman—and I'd be pleased if you would teach me how it was to be a twentieth-century man, and we'll close that silly 'Generation Gap.' Understand each other as well as loving each other.)

(Beloved.)

(I think you're pretty nice, too, you cranky old bastard. With your brain and my body, we make a fine team. We'll get by.) (I'm sure we will, darling.) (We will. The first thing we need is a *good* lady's maid—scarce as whales in Kansas. We'll probably have to train one. Then lose her as soon as she's worth anything.) (Eunice, do we need a maid? You used to do yourself.) (I did, and kept house for Joe, and was your secretary and worked any hours you wanted me. But you're not used to that, Boss. You had a valet.) (Yes, of course. But I was very old and didn't have time to waste on such things. Eunice, one of the worst parts about getting old is that the days get shorter while the demands on your time increase. I didn't want a valet; I was forced into it. Didn't enjoy being dependent on a secretary, either—until *you* came along.)

(Dear Boss. Joan, we *will* need a maid. But not a secretary until you're active in business again—) (Won't be!) (We'll see. You may have to be. But may not need a secretary unless you get pushed for time. I can handle it. And thanks for having Betsy brought in; it makes me feel at home to see her again. My stenodesk, I mean. Pet name.)

('Betsy,' huh? I always thought of it as 'the Octopus.')

149

(Why, what a nasty name to apply to a nice, respectable, well-behaved machine! Boss, I'm not sure I'm speaking to you. I'm glad Betsy isn't switched on; if she had heard that, her feelings would be hurt.)

(Eunice, don't be silly. I wonder what's keeping Jake?)

(Probably cutting his toenails. Lesson number two in how to be a woman: Men are almost always late but you never, never, never notice it—because they pride themselves on promptness. Boss, you didn't quite promise Winnie to stay in this chair—when she gave you strict orders.) (Of course not. Because it might not suit me. And it doesn't; I want to try the eighty-eight. Eunice, two gets you seven it hasn't been kept in tune—and I gave Cunningham orders about both pianos, this baby and the concert grand downstairs, not five years ago. So let's see.)

She stood up, did not notice that high heels gave her no trouble, and glided gracefully over to the little piano, sat down and opened it—let the first bars of Dvorak's Slavonic Dance # 10 run through her mind, then started to play—
—and achieved a clash of noise.

"What the hell!" She looked at the keyboard, then hit middle C with her right forefinger. It sounded okay—and so did the C an octave below it. Several one- and two-finger experiments convinced her that the piano was not at fault. Yet to strike a single chord required studying the keyboard, then carefully positioning each finger by sight.

Presently she managed a slow, uneven, faulty version of "Chopsticks" by watching the keyboard and controlling her hands so hard they trembled. She quit before reaching its undistinguished coda and crashed the keys with both hands. (There go ten years of piano lessons!) (What did you expect, Boss? I was never much good even with a guitar.) (Well, I'm glad Mama didn't hear that—she always wanted me to be a concert pianist. Eunice, why the devil didn't you study piano as a kid?) (Because I was too busy studying boys! A much more rewarding subject. Joan, if you want to play the piano again, we can learn. But we'll have to start almost from scratch. It's in your head, I know; I could hear it. But to get from there down into our hands—*my* hands, dear—will probably take more patient work than slimming our hips.)

(Doesn't matter, not really.) She got up from the piano bench. (Boss. Just a sec. While we're here, let's warm up Betsy and give her a check run.) (Huh? I know nothing about a stenodesk. It'll be worse than the piano.) (We'll see.)

She moved over and sat down at the stenodesk. (Well, Eunice? Which way to the Egress?) (Relax, Boss. The body remembers. Just say 'Dictation, Eunice,' then recite something you know. Think about what you're dictating.)

(Okay.) "Dictation, Eunice. 'Four score and seven years ago our fathers brought forth on this continent a new nation, conceived in liberty, and dedicated to the proposition. . . .' "

Deftly her hands touched the switches, swiveled the microphone in time to catch the first word, required the machine to listen & hold while she inserted punctuation, used erase & correct when the machine spelled "fourth" rather than "forth"—all without hurrying.

She stopped and looked at the result. (Be durned! *How*, Eunice?) (Don't ask, dear—or we might get fouled up in the dilemma of the centipede. But Betsy is purring like a kitten; she's glad I'm back.) (Well, so am I. Uh, Eunice, this machine—Betsy, I mean—has access to the Congressional Library St. Louis Annex, does it not? —she not?) (Certainly. Hooked into the Interlibrary Net, rather, though you can restrict a query to one library.)

(Better query just one. I want to find out what is known about memory and how it works.) (All right. I'm interested, too; I think my memory is spotty. Can't be sure. But on a search-of-literature it's best to let Betsy handle it through preprograms—ask for references, followed by abstracts, followed by items selected from abstracts . . . else, on a generalized question like that, thousands of books would be transmitted and poor Betsy would gulp them down until she was constipated, and stop and not do anything until her temporary memory was erased.)

(You know how, I don't. Uh, stick in a restriction not to bother with behaviorist theories. I know all about Pavlov and his robots I care to know, namely, that every time a

151

dog salivates a behaviorist psychologist has to ring a bell.)

(All right. Boss? Can we spend a little more money?) (Go ahead, buy the Pyramids. What do you want, dearest?) (Let's have a Triple-A-One snoop search run on me. Eunice Branca, I mean—the 'me' that used to be.) (Why, beloved? If you've been selling government secrets, they can't touch you now.) (Because. It might fill some of those holes I think I have in my memory . . . and it might turn up something you've heard from me since I came back but which was not in the security report you got on me originally. Then you would *know*, dear . . . and could stop worrying that I may be only a figment of your imagination.)

(Eunice, if I'm crazy, the only thing that worries me is that some damned shrink might cure me. Then you would go away.)

(That's sweet of you, Boss. But I won't go away; I promised.)

(And even if I *am* crazy, it just makes me fit that much better into the present world. Eunice, don't you remember *anything* between being killed and waking up here?)

The inner voice was silent a moment. (Not really. There were dreams and I think you were in them. But there was one that does not seem like a dream; it seems as real as this room. But if I tell you, you'll think *I* am crazy.) (If so, it doesn't detract from your charm, dear.) (All right but don't laugh. Joan, while I was away, I was in this—place. There was an old, old Man with a long white beard. He had a great big book. He looked at it, then He looked at me and said, 'Daughter, you've been a naughty girl. But not too naughty, so I'm going to give you a second chance.')

(A dream, Eunice. Anthropomorphism, straight out of your childhood Sunday School.) (Maybe, Boss. But here I am and I *do* have a second chance.)

(Yes, but God didn't give it to you. Eunice my own, I don't believe in God nor Devil.)

(Well . . . you haven't been dead—and *I* have. Truly I don't know what I believe; I guess I wasn't dead long enough to find out. But do you mind if we pray occasionally?"

152

(Jesus H. Christ!)

(Stop that, Joan! Or I'll use every one of those words you consider 'unladylike.' It's not much to ask.)

(I'm henpecked. Okay. If it's a beautiful church, with good music, and the sermon isn't over ten minutes.) (Oh, I didn't mean in a *church*. Can't stand 'em. Filled with bad vibrations. I mean pray by ourselves, Joan. I'll teach you.)

(Oh. All right. Now?)

(No, I want to get these search orders in. You think about something else; I don't want centipede trouble—think about Winnie all slickery with soapsuds.) (A pious thought. Much better than prayer.) (Dirty old man. How do *you* know—I'll bet you've never prayed in your life.) (Oh, yes, I have, dearest—but God had gone fishing.) (So think about Winnie.)

She was busy for several minutes. Then she patted the machine affectionately and switched it off. (Well, did you?) (Did I what?) (Did you think about Winnie? Lecher.) (I took advantage of the unusual peace and quiet to contemplate the wonders of the universe.) (So?) (I thought about Winnie.) (I know you did; I was right with you. Joan, for a girl who is, in one sense at least, a virgin, you have an unusually low and vivid imagination.) (Aw, shucks, I'll bet you say that to all the girls.) (The stark truth, Joan sweet—with your imagination I can hardly wait for you to start us on that 'actively female' career. In all the wrestling I've done I've never had a man—or a girl—grab me the way you were thinking about.) (Oh. Learned that one from a respectable housewife, clear back in my teens. A most charming lady.) (Hmm! Perhaps I was born too late for the real action.) (So I've been trying to tell you. Did you get those orders in?) (Certainly, Boss, when did I ever miss? Let's get back to our chair; our back is tired.)

Joan Eunice negotiated the thirty feet back to her chair without remembering that she had kicked off her pumps to handle the lower controls of the stenodesk more easily; the rug simply felt good to her bare feet. Then she did notice as she sat down in the big easy chair and folded her legs in the awkward, elegant, and surprisingly comfortable Lotus position. But it did not seem worthwhile to go get them.

The door buzzer sounded. "It's me, Winnie."

"Come in, dear."

The nurse entered. "Mr. Salomon asked me to tell you that he will be in to see you in a few minutes. But he can't stay for dinner."

"He'll stay. Come here and kiss me. What did you tell Cunningham?"

"Dinner for two, in here, just as you said—to be served when you rang. But Mr. Salomon seemed quite firm about leaving."

"I still say he'll stay. But if he doesn't, you come eat dinner with me. Would you fetch my pumps? Over there on the floor beyond the piano."

The nurse looked, fetched the pumps, stood over Joan Eunice, and sighed. "Joan, I don't know what to do about you. You've been a bad girl again. Why didn't you ring?"

"Don't scold me, dear. Here, sit on the stool and lean against my knees and talk. There. Now tell me— By any chance were you ever a lady's maid before you took nurse's training?"

"No. Why?"

"You did such a fine job of taking care of me in the bath and getting me pretty. Well, it was just a thought. I don't suppose a nurse—a professional woman—would consider a job as a maid. No matter how high the salary. But Dr. Garcia is going to insist that I have a nurse after he leaves. I don't need a nurse and you know it. But dear Doctor will insist. I *do* need a maid; I won't be able to dress myself at first—women's clothes are so different. Not to mention knowing nothing about makeup. Or buying women's clothes. What are you paid now, Winnie?"

The nurse told her.

"Goodness! No wonder they're always saying there's a shortage of nurses. I can't hire an in-house guard at that price. What would you think of staying on as my nurse—but actually doing things for me that a maid would do and I don't know how to do—at three times your present salary? With whatever you wish paid in cash so that you won't have to report it?"

154

The redhead looked thoughtful. "How would you want me to dress, Joan?"

"That's up to you. Your white nurse's uniform, if you prefer it—since you'll be my nurse in Dr. Garcia's eyes. Or what you wish. There's a bedroom through that door where my valet used to sleep. With a nice bath—and another room beyond it which we can redo as your living room. Redecorate all three rooms to suit your taste. Your private apartment."

(Boss, what was that about not shooting ducks on water?) (Stuff it, Eunice. If she takes the bait, it's better than hiring some illit and having to train her—and then have her steal the jewelry and drop out about the time she's some use.) (Oh, I see advantages. But you place Winnie one unlocked door away and she'll be in bed with you before you can say 'Sappho.' *You* may not want men in our life—but *I* do.) (Oh, nonsense! She's already thinking about the money. If she takes the job, she'll be more standoffish—she'll start calling us 'Miss' again.)

"Miss Joan? It'll really be my *own* apartment? I can entertain?"

"Of course, dear. Private. Oh, Cunningham's staff will clean and so forth, any service you want. Breakfast tray, whatever. Or never enter it if you prefer it that way."

"It sounds heavenly. I'm sharing a room with two other girls . . . at a rent that's horrid because it's inside an enclave. Safe—but I never have any *privacy*."

"Winnie. Look at me, dear, and lay it on the line. The bed in there now is, I believe, a single. Would you like to have it replaced with a big, big double bed?"

The girl blushed. "Uh, it would be nice."

"So stop blushing. I won't know you have a visitor unless you tell me; that door is soundproof. Of course visitors have to be identified and checked for weapons, just as visitors to an enclave have to be—but that simply means you must vouch for a visitor to my chief guard the first visit. But I won't know it unless you choose to tell me. The in-house staff all have visitors. But security is my chief guard's worry, not mine."

"But he does have to show his I.D.?"

"You still would have to vouch for him to Chief O'Neil but— Hold the countdown. Did you mean he would rather *not* show an I.D.? Is he married, or something?"

Winnie blushed again, did not answer. Joan Eunice went on, "Nobody's business, dear. This is a private home, not a government compound. You vouch for him, that's enough. Chief O'Neil doesn't trust I.D.s; they're often faked. But he has a photographic eye. Are you going to stay with me? As nurse in residence, or lady's companion, or social secretary, or whatever you want to call it."

"Lady's maid. If I'm to be your maid, Miss Joan, I'd rather that your staff knew it and no pretense. And dress as your maid. What sort of uniform? Traditional? Or Acapulco? Or something in between?"

"Oh, not traditional, surely; you have such pretty legs. All-out Acapulco, if you like."

Winnie looked pleased. "I might go all out. A girl gets tired of these white coveralls." (Joan! Tell her not to use an all-out Acapulco paint job. Bad for her skin.)

"Suit yourself, dear. But don't use a lot of paint. Bad for your skin."

"Oh, I know! I'm a real redhead, you probably noticed. I can't even sunbathe. I was thinking of a little black frill skirt with a white lace apron about the size of a saucer. Little perky maid's cap, white on a black ribbon. Cling-On cups, in black. Transparent? Or opaque?"

"Whichever suits you, Winnie. High heels?"

"Uh, translucent, I guess, like the panels in that nightie. High heels, certainly, or the effect is lost—I can wear real stilts if I'm barefooted most of the time. Then just enough paint for accent. There are lovely decals that go on in no time and come right off with cold cream. Butterflies and flowers and things. Cheap, too. Everything I mentioned I can buy in disposables. I'll look like a proper lady's maid, yet not spend more time getting dressed than I do in pulling on this smock and tights."

"You'll look cute, dear. Going to dress up in a maid's outfit and model it for your friend?"

Winnie started to blush again, then grinned. "I certainly

am! And let him take it off me, too!" (Cheers!) (Eunice, you have a one-track mind.) (You should know, dearie—it's *your* mind.)

A few moments later Winnie announced Mr. Salomon, then left. The lawyer came toward Joan solemnly, took the hand she extended and bowed over it. "How are you feeling?" he asked.

"Disappointed," Joan answered soberly. "Because my oldest and dearest friend hasn't time to dine with me my first day up. But physically I feel fine. Weak, but that's to be expected."

"Sure you're not overdoing?"

"I'm sure. My respiration and heartbeat are being telemetered—if I weren't all right, someone would come in and order me to bed. Truly, I'm all right, Jake—and I won't get strong unless I *do* stay out of bed. But how about *you*, old friend? I have been terribly worried."

"Oh, I'm all right. Just made a fool of myself, Johann."

"You did not make a fool of yourself . . . and I feel certain Eunice knows it, Jake." (Watch it, Boss!) (Pipe down.) "You could have paid her no finer tribute than those honest tears." Joan found her own tears starting; she encouraged them while ignoring them. "She was a sweet and gallant lady, Jake, and it touched me more than I can say to learn that you appreciated her wonderful qualities as much as I did. Jake—please sit down, if only for a moment. There is something I *must* ask you."

"Well . . . all right. Can't stay long."

"Whistle that chair closer, and face me. Uh, a glass of sherry? Doctor says I may have it—and I find that I need it. That Spanish cocktail sherry, dry as your wit. Will you do me the honor of pouring for us?"

Joan waited until the lawyer had filled their glasses, and had seated himself. She raised her glass and at the same time raised her chest, letting those "wicked" panels do their best. "A toast, Jake—no, don't get up. The same toast, Jake—always the same toast from now on whenever you and I drink together . . . but silently." She took a sip and put her glass down. "Jake—"

"Yes . . . Johann?"

" 'Joan,' please—I can't be 'Johann' any longer. Jake, you know that I never expected to live through any such operation? It was a—device. A legal device."

"Yes, Joha— Yes, Joan, I knew. That's why I helped."

"I knew. The most generous act of friendship I have ever known. What is it the Japanese name it?—the friend who helps, when it is necessary to die. Never mind. Jake, look me in the eye. Do you know, deep in your heart, that I would rather be dead . . . than to have lived through it by this incredible circumstance? Be alive . . . at *her* expense? Do you *know* that, Jake? Or must I live still another life, hating myself?"

Salomon raised his eyes, met hers firmly. "Yes—Joan. I know it. It was no fault of yours . . . you must not hate yourself. Uh . . . *Eunice wouldn't want you to!*"

"I know! Weep, dear Jake; don't hold back your tears—see, I am not holding back mine. Just try not to go to pieces, or I will, too. Jake, each of us would happily have died rather than let this happen. I am as certain of it about you as I hope you are about me. I don't think I could stand it if you had not reassured me. Look at me—a lovely body and young—yet I am almost ninety-five years old and have not one friend left alive . . . but you."

"You'll make more friends."

"I wonder if I can. The span is great, perhaps too great. I feel as the Wandering Jew must have felt, alive beyond his allotted time. His name—Aha—something. My memory is not as good as this young body. But I can't forget one question which I *must* ask. Jake, is there any possibility that Eunice's husband had something to do with her death? That prize I put up, that blood money—*did i tempt him?*"

(Boss, Boss, you're way off base. I know!) (Sorry beloved, more sorry than I can say. But I must have *proof.* "Jake? *Did I entice a murder?*"

The lawyer shook his head. "I'm astounded. But o course you don't know the circumstances. You entice *nothing.* I wrote that offer most carefully. Were there an guilt I would share it. There was none."

158

"How do you *know?*" (Drop it, Boss. Please!)

"Mr. Branca was in Philadelphia, visiting his mother." (You see, Boss?) "I had to find him to get the post-death ratification. Took three days, while both of you were kept ready for surgery. Joe Branca didn't know she was dead. Hell of a job even to find him. Three long days."

" 'Three days.' Why wasn't I told!"

"And *waste* Eunice's death? Are you crazy? You were unconscious; Garcia put you under as soon as I notified him that a body was going to be ready. Then that dreadful wait. I need *your* forgiveness, too, for—Joan—no, 'Johann!' I hated you . . . for being alive when *she* was dead. But I pushed on—for *her* sake. Oh, I got over it, it was a sick hate. I knew better."

"Do you hate me now?"

"Eh?" Salomon looked at her, in sorrow. "No. You are not only my old friend, who has always been honest and decent under his crusty exterior—whose virtues outweighed his faults." Salomon managed to smile. "Though sometimes just barely. But also you are the only tie I have left to her."

"Yes. You may find me better-tempered now, Jake. It's easier to smile, easier to be patient, then it was in that old wreck of a body I had. But, Jake, about Joe Branca. All right, he was in Philadelphia. But could he have *arranged* it?"

"No."

"You're certain?"

"Certain. Joha—Joan, it's that million dollars that worries you, fear that it might have started a chain of events. When they located Joe Branca, I had to jet there and get that piece of paper. He was dazed. Couldn't believe it. But accepted the fact. But *not* the money. I couldn't get him to sign the post-death authorization without first preparing another document, waiving the money. The escrow trustee—Chase Manhattan—was instructed by Joe to pay it to the Rare Blood Club—his idea—as a memorial to Eunice Evans Branca." (Oh, Boss! I'm crying.) (We all are.) (But, Boss—Joe must be starving.) (We'll take care of it.)

159

She sighed. "I'll be damned."

"Perhaps. And perhaps myself. But I don't think Joe Branca will be. He's an unworldly man—Joan. From a slum family. A flower in the muck. I couldn't even get him to accept a lesser sum. He insisted on paying for witnessing and notarizing his mark, and the tax stamp on the assignment—and it took almost every dime he could dig up. He just shook his head and said, 'Broke don't scare me.' "

"Jake, we must take care of him."

"I don't think you can, Joan. In his own odd way he is as proud as she was. But I did one thing. In searching for him I had to get a court order to open their studio —indispensable it turned out, as an old letter from his mother gave us the clue that located him. But I learned that the rent was almost due . . . the corporation's rent agent wanted to know how soon the lease was going to lapse—he assumed that, with *her* dead, the rent would not be paid. So I covered the matter for the moment; then when I got back, I bought the lease. As long as Joe chooses to stay, he won't be asked for rent. Then I checked around and located her bank account and arranged with a friendly judge to let me guarantee the matter and had it assigned to Joe without bothering him with legal formalities. The little dear was smart about money—a nice sum, enough to keep him eating a couple of years, I think." (All gone in a couple of months, *I* think. Boss, Joe doesn't understand money. A bank account isn't real, to him.) (Don't worry, darling. Jake and I will handle it.)

She sighed. "I feel reassured, Jake. But distressed about her husband. We must look into it. If he's that unworldly, then there must be some way to subsidize him without his knowing it."

"All right, Joan, we will try. But Joe Branca taught me—at my age!—that there are things money cannot buy. Not if the prospective seller is indifferent to money."

"Will you have more sherry? And may I have another drop? If you can't stay, I think I'll ask to be put to bed and right to sleep. Skip dinner."

"Oh, but you must eat, Joan. For your strength. Look, if I stay, will you eat?"

She gave him Eunice's best sun-coming-up smile. "Yes! Yes, Jake dear! Thank you."

Dinner was informal, service only by Cunningham and two assistants. Joan did her best to simulate a charming, gracious hostess—while trying not to appear greedy; everything tasted so *wonderful!* But she waited until coffee had been served and Jake had refused a perfecto and accepted a glass of port, and she then could say, "Thank you, Cunningham, that will be all," before returning to personal matters.

Once they were alone she said, "Jake, when will I be up for a competency hearing?"

"Eh? Any time you feel well enough. Are you in a hurry?"

"No. I would be utterly content to be your ward the rest of my life."

Her lawyer smiled slightly. "Joan, by the actuarial tables you now have a life expectancy of about sixty years; mine is more like ten or twelve."

"Well . . . that's hard to answer. But will you go on as before as my de-facto manager? Or am I asking too much?"

Salomon studied his glass. "Joan . . . once the court dissolves this guardian-and-ward relationship, there is no reason why you should not manage your affairs."

(Joan! Change the subject; he's trying to leave us!) (So I know! Keep quiet!) (Tell him your middle name!) "Jake. Jake dear . . . look at me. Look hard and keep on looking. That's better. Jake—is it that you would rather *not* see me . . . as I am now?

The lawyer said nothing. She went on, "Isn't it better to get used to what *is* . . . than to run away from it? Wouldn't she—Eunice—want you to stay?" (Keep slugging, Sis—he *wants* to stay.)

"It isn't that simple . . . Joan."

"Nothing ever is. But I don't think you *can* run away

161

from it any more than I can—for I won't stop *being* what I am—her body, my mind—and you will always know it. All you accomplish by leaving is to deprive me of my one friend and the only man on earth I trust utterly. What does it take to change my name?"

"Eh?"

"Just what I said. I changed my surname from 'Schmidt' to 'Smith' when I enlisted on December eighth nineteen-forty-one simply by spelling it that way to a recruiting sergeant. No one has bothered me about it since. This time perhaps it must be formal, considering the thousands of places where my signature appears. It is technically a sex-change case, is it not? A court takes judicial notice, or some such, and it's made a matter of record?"

Salomon slipped into his professional *persona* and relaxed. "Yes, of course; I had not thought about *that* aspect—too many other details on my mind. Joan, your earlier name change was legal—although informal—because any person is free to call himself by any name, without permission of a court, as long as there is no criminal intent—to defraud, deceive, evade responsibility, avoid taxes, whatever. You can call yourself 'Joan'—or 'Johann'—or 'Miniver Cheevy'—and that is your name, as long as your purpose is innocent. And pronounce it as you like. Knew of a case once of a man who spelled his name 'Zaustinski' and pronounced it 'Jones' and went to the trouble of publishing the odd pronunciation as a legal notice—although he did not have to; a name may be pronounced in any fashion its owner chooses."

"Why did he do it, Jake?"

"His grandmother's will required him to change his name in order to inherit—but did not specify how he must pronounce it. Joan, in your case a formal change of name is advisable, but it might be best to wait until you are no longer my ward. But de facto your new name is already what you say it is."

"Then my name is now—'Joan Eunice Smith.' "

Salomon knocked over his glass of port. He made quite a busyness of mopping it up. Joan said, "Jake, let it be, no importance. I did not mean to shock you. But don't you

162

see the necessity? It's a tribute to *her*, a public acknowledgment of my debt to her. Since I can never pay it, I want to publish it, place it on the wall for all to see, like a Chinese man's debt to his tong. Besides that, ninety-five percent of me *is* Eunice . . . and only five percent is old Johann now named 'Joan' and even that fraction no one can see, only surgeons have seen it. Last but by no means least—Jake dear, look at me—if you ever forget that fraction and call me 'Eunice,' it won't matter; it's my name. And if you *intentionally* call me 'Eunice,' it *will* matter, for I shall be pleased and flattered. And any time it suits you to call me 'Joan Eunice,' it will make me happy, as I will be *certain* you have done it intentionally—and accepted me as I am."

"Very well . . . Joan Eunice."

She smiled. "Thank you, Jake. I feel happier than I have felt since I first knew. I hope you do."

"Um. Yes. I think so. It's a good change—Joan Eunice."

"Did you get wine on your clothes? If so, let Cunningham see to it. Jake, is there any reason for you to go clear out to Safe Harbor tonight? I'm sure Cunningham can find you clean socks or whatever."

"Goodness, Joan—Joan Eunice—I've been here two nights already."

"Do you think three will wear out your welcome? You can't wear it out."

"And the drive isn't that far, as I placed my house for sale with the enclave trustees months ago. I have rooms at the Gibraltar Club now. Good service, central location, none of the fiddlin' worries of a householder."

"I see your point. Hmm, must remember to resign from the Gib myself." She smiled. "They'll never let me past the ladies' lounge—now."

The lawyer said dryly, "I took the liberty of withdrawing you from membership shortly after I became your guardian—Joan Eunice."

She laughed in delight. "And me a founding member! This is delicious—souls and honks and thirds all welcome . . . but females are second-class citizens. Jake dear, I'm going to have to get used to a lot of things."

"I suppose so—Joan Eunice."

"So I'll need you more than ever. Where have you been sleeping?"

"The Brown Room."

"Cunningham must be slipping. He should have put you in the Green Suite."

"Well . . . the Green Suite has been used for hospital equipment and supplies. I authorized it."

"Then you can just unauthorize it, as that is *your* suite. They can store that stuff somewhere else. Or remove it, as little of it will be needed from now on."

"Hedrick had most of it removed the middle of the day."

"All right, you stay in the Brown Room tonight; then tomorrow Cunningham can get the Green Suite in shape for you."

"Joan Eunice, what leads you to think I'm moving in here? I'm not."

"I didn't say you were. I said that the Green Suite is yours. Whether you stay a night or a year. Yours without invitation, yours to come and go without bothering to say hello or good-bye. Although I hope it will suit you to say hello to me frequently. Is Hubert, my former valet, still around?"

"Yes. He's tended me the last two nights."

"From now on he'll tend the Green Suite and take care of you whenever you honor us with your presence. Jake, you had better move some clothes here."

"Damn it— Pardon me, Joan Eunice."

"For saying 'Damn it'? It's a strange day when my oldest friend must curb his language in my presence. Jake, I've heard you use language that would blister paint at forty yards—and *at* me, not merely in my presence."

"True. But I must now remember that you are a lady, Joan Eunice."

"Please yourself. I'm going to have more trouble learning to be a lady than you will have in remembering that I am supposed to be one. If you slip, ignore it—for you know that I never took a back seat to any muleskinner in other days. You were saying?"

"Well, I was saying, 'Damn it, we must remember your reputation'—Joan Eunice."

"My *what*? My reputation as a *woman*? I doubt if I have one—other than as a sideshow freak. Doesn't worry me."

"You're not in the news, Joan Eunice, since shortly after the operation. Oh, you will be again when we go into court . . . and perhaps sooner, when someone in your household staff or Dr. Hedrick's staff spills the fact of your recovery."

"So I'll be a sideshow freak again and who cares? A nine-day wonder lasts only a couple of days now; they wear out faster than they did when I was a kid. Jake, I haven't worried about what anyone said about me for over half a century. The image our P.R. men built up was for the company, not for me personally. As for Mrs. Grundy—I think she's dead. The present generation does not care about her opinion—a change for the better in a world otherwise deteriorating. I doubt if Eunice ever heard of Mrs. Grundy." (Sure have, Boss. My fourth-grade teacher. Used to shack with the vice-principal until his wife found out. We kids giggled over it—but *you* would have liked her . . . you dirty old darling. Keep working on Jake, dear—time to back away closer.) (Who's driving this car?) (I am.)

Mr. Salomon said thoughtfully, "I think you are right about this younger generation, Joan Eunice. Only people my age and older give such matters a thought. But *you* know that I should not live under your roof now. And so do I."

"Jake, I am not trying to force you. Nor am I trying to compromise you—"

"Eh? *Me?* It's *your* reputation I am thinking of. With your servants, at least."

(Why, the old hypocrite. Ask him about the time he crowded me into a cloak closet with Cunningham almost breathing down our necks. Go on, I dare you. Oh, he's a one, that one—courage under fire.) "Jake, that is sweet of you but I don't give a triple damn how my servants gossip in the kitchen. But I am able to protect *you* from gossip, sir. I have acquired the most conventional of Victorian chaperonage—a respectable lady's maid. She'll sleep just through that door, where Hubert used to sleep. If it frets

165

you, she can always be present when you and I are together." (Hey, what is this? Trying to get Winnie into the act? She might go for it—Jake won't. Watch it, dear.) (Quit kibitzing, Eunice.)

The lawyer raised his brows. "You've hired a maid already? Surprising. Though you never were one to dillydally. Or did you shift around part of your in-house staff?"

"Some of both, Jake. I anticipated that Dr. Garcia will insist on my having a trained nurse . . . so I persuaded one of the nurses to stay on, in both capacities. Winnie. You've seen her, the little redhead."

"Possibly I have."

('Possibly' he says. *All* you men are hypocrites. If he hasn't patted her butt, he's thought about it.)

"I'm lucky to get her. Intelligent. Educated. Able to teach me things I must know and, being a nurse, used to caring for people even more than a maid does. I used the usual argument—money—but I was careful to respect her professional pride; she'll still be my nurse, she'll lady's-maid me as a friendly favor. I think she may be in bed. But she would get up and chaperon us if asked. Shall I send for her?"

"What? Oh, don't be silly, Joan Eunice. You're making a mountain of a molehill."

"It seemed to me that you were, Jake. I do feel defenseless as a woman . . . even though I was far more vulnerable as a sick old man than I am now in this strong young body. But I feel *safe* with you present—and not at all safe when you are away. Jake, I can't urge you to live here . . . but can't you see what a favor it would be to me? As well as— How many rooms do you have at the Gib?"

"Two. Adequate for my needs."

"The rooms there aren't large . . . whereas the living room of the Green Suite is as large as this room. We could cut a door from it into the upstairs library and it could be your study. Move anything into it you need for my affairs or your own—plenty of room for files or books. Jake, don't need this big mausoleum any more than you need your house. But if I tried to sell it, I couldn't get ten percent

166

of what it cost; I built it during the worst of the Riot Years and the cost doesn't show; it's a prettied-up fortress, stronger than police barracks. Well, we may have such years again; I may yet be glad I spared no expense. In the meantime it's big and safe and comfortable, and you might as well use it. When you wish, I mean, especially when you work on my affairs."

"Well, I have been working on some of your affairs here in the house. Uh, Joan Eunice, as your guardian, I had to take over management of your household."

"Hasn't Cunningham saved you from such picayune worries? I must speak to him."

"Well . . . yes, he has and I've let him go on as before; I've made no changes. But I have had to look over the household books and authorize charges and confound it, they're stealing you blind. Cunningham especially."

"Good!"

"What's good about it?"

"Jake, you told me that it was impossible to spend my income. If my butler is black-marketing two-thirds of what he buys for me and pocketing the proceeds—and he always has—then he's anxious to keep his job. Which means that he has to please *me*. Jake, can you think of a cheaper way to buy the nearest thing to loyalty that can be bought? Let him steal. Do not bind the mouths of the kine who tread the grain. The good horse must always get his lump of sugar."

"Bad precedent. Corrupts the country."

"The country *is* corrupt. But 'it is the only game in town'; we have no choice. The problem is always how to live in a decadent society. Jake, I want you to live here. I hope you will live here. It will make me feel happy and *safe* for you to be under the same roof. But don't worry about my reputation—and Winnie is here to protect yours. Most certainly don't think about such trivia as household expenses; just close your eyes and sign. But don't hesitate to chew out Cunningham if the service is less than perfect; that's the price he must pay for the privilege of swindling me. By the way, my chief guard steals, too; I think he has a fifty-fifty split with Cunningham. I've never tried to find

167

out the arrangement; it would embarrass them."

Salomon smiled. "Joan Eunice, for a young—and beautiful—woman, you sound remarkably like a cynical old man I used to know."

"Do I, Jake dear? I must learn not to sound that way. I must now leave the 'cynical old man' things to you and try to behave like a lady. If I can. But please don't disrupt a smooth household by trying to reform it—or it will wind up like a reform administration: less efficient and still more expensive. Didn't your servants steal from you?"

The lawyer looked sheepish. "Well . . . yes. But I had the best cook in Safe Harbor enclave. If I had fired her, I might have wound up with one just as expensive—who put sugar in gravy. I think I was groused that they were stealing from you—when you were helpless. But I didn't want to tamper with your household while there was any chance that you might recover. Wanted to hand it back as it was. And I have. Or shall."

"Thank you, Jake. At the moment, while I may not yet be a lady, I feel not at all like a cynical old man. I find that I feel like a woman who has been ill and is not yet fully recovered. I had best go to bed. Will you help me?"

"Uh, I'll call the nurse."

"Jake, Jake—this is the body I have; we must quit being jumpy about it. Here, lend me your arm. I can stand if you'll help me . . . and walk to the bed if you'll let me lean on you."

Salomon gave up, offered her both hands to help her out of the chair, steadied her with his arm to the bed. Joan Eunice got into it quickly, slid her negligee off as she slid under the sheet. "Thank you, Jake."

"My pleasure—Joan Eunice."

"Will you have breakfast with me? Or lunch if you want to sleep late?"

"Uh . . . lunch."

"I'm looking forward to it." She put out her hand. He took it, bowed over it—hesitated only slightly and kissed it firmly.

Joan Eunice kept his hand and pulled. "Come closer,

Jake dear." She reached up, took his face between her palms. "You loved her."

"Yes."

"I loved her."

"I know."

"Say my name. My new name."

"Joan—Joan Eunice."

"Thank you, Jake." Unhurriedly, she pulled his face down, kissed him softly on the lips. "Good night, dear friend."

"Good night—Joan Eunice." He left quickly.

(Joan you bitch, you're pushing him too hard.) (I am *not!*) (The hell you aren't. For a second I thought you were going to drag him right into bed.) (Ridiculous!) (And you're pushing yourself too hard, too.) (Eunice, quit crabbing. I could have backed out up to the last split second. I found that I did not mind it. After all, there are *many* cultures in which men kiss men, as a gesture of friendship.)

(In case you haven't noticed, you are no longer a man—you're a mixed-up chick.) (I've noticed. Look, snoopy, it was a necessary symbol. I had to show Jake that he could touch me, even kiss me good-night . . . and not have it be tragic. And it wasn't. Reminded me of my father kissing me good-night . . . which he did until I was a big boy.)

(Well . . . perhaps Jake is going to settle for being fatherly. But don't count on it, Joan. Let me warn you, Sis— Jake can kiss *much* better than that. He can kiss so well that your insides melt down, starting at your belly button and spreading in all directions.) (A possibility. A remote one. Now will you shut up, and let us sleep? I really *am* tired.) (Love me, Boss?) (I've never stopped loving you dear—and never will.) (Me, too—and wish I could kiss you good-night. Sleep, Boss—everything's going to be all right.)

Before she could get to sleep, Winifred came in, in robe and slippers. "Miss Joan?" she said softly.

"Yes, dear? Put the floor lights on."

"Mr. Salomon said that you had gone to bed—"

"And you look as if you had. Did he wake you?"

"Oh, no. I was chatting with Mrs. Sloan; she's on watch. But Dr. Garcia left word that your bed was to be all the way down—and I see that it isn't. How do I put it down?"

"I do it myself, right from the bed—down, like that—or back up, like that. I wasn't asleep yet. It's all right, I'll put it all the way down before you leave . . . and you can tell Doctor that I was a good girl."

"Fine! You can have this capsule if you want it. You don't have to take it, Mrs. Sloan says that Doctor says."

"I'll take it; I want to go right to sleep. If you'll hand me the water there . . . and kiss me good-night. If you won't, I'll sulk and ring for Mrs. Sloan and ask *her* to kiss me good-night."

The little nurse grinned. "I'll force myself."

Winifred left about sixty seconds later. (Well, Eunice? How did that one stack up?) (Quite well, Butch. Say eighty percent as well as Jake can do.) (You're teasing.) (You'll find out. Winnie is sweet—but Jake has had years more practice. I'm not chucking asparagus at Winnie. I thought you were going to drag her right in with us.) (With Mrs. Sloan outside and watching our heart rate? What do you think I am? A fool?) (Yes.) (Oh, go to sleep!)

Peace Negotiations, both in Paris and in Montevideo, continued as before. Fighting continued on a token basis, and the dead did not complain. Harvard's new president was dismissed by the student government, which then adjourned without appointing a successor. The Secretary of H.E.W. announced a plan to increase the water content of San Francisco Bay to 37%; the Rivers & Harbors Commission denied that H.E.W. had jurisdiction. In Alma-Ata a Morale Corps sergeant gave birth to a healthy two-headed boy by Caesarean section; it was watched worldwide and on Luna, via satellite, to a specially arranged chorus of the Thoughts of Chairman Lu. In Washington the I.R.S., acting under Budget Executive Order (Emergency) of '87, announced an additional temporary surtax of 7%. In Miami Miss Universe (Miss Ghana—42-22-38), speaking through her press secretary & interpreter, revealed that she intended to be the first starship commander and had been studying neo-Einsteinian ballistics under hypnosis for two years. The General Secretary of the People's Fraternal Society of Cosmonauts, Astronauts, & Space Engineers (A.F.L.-C.I.O.) wondered publicly as to Miss Universe's ability to do simple arithmetic with her shoes on. Madam President of the Federated Women's Clubs of the World stated that the Honorable Secretary was a counterrevolutionary rat-fink and a typical example of male arrogance. In Los Angeles smog deaths were down 3% under emergency pollution-abatement measures and a brisk west wind.

In a big, ugly, ornate, old house Miss Joan Eunice Smith sat in Lotus on a mat in her dressing room near a large mirror and facing her nurse-companion-maid, also in Lotus. "Comfortable, Winnie dear?"

"Very."

"I think you're even more limber than I am. All right, let's get into the mood for exercise. You start it."

"All right. But, Miss Joan? What does it *mean*? Oh, I like it; it's very relaxing. But *what* jewel in *what* lotus, and *why*?"

"It means nothing. And everything. If you must have words, it means peace and love and understanding and anything that you think of as good. But it's not for thinking, dear; it's for *being*. Let yourself be open to it, don't think. Don't even try not to think. *Be*."

"All right."

"Start us. Remember the breathing. I'll get in step."

"Om Mani Padme Hum."

(Om Mani Padme Hum. See that aura round her, Boss? She must have had *quite* a night.) (Shut up, Eunice; these prayers were *your* idea.) "Om Mani Padme Hum."

"Om Mani Padme Hum." (Om Mani Padme Hum.) "Om Mani Padme Hum." "Om Mani..........."

(That's enough, Joan.) (So short, beloved? Clock says only twenty minutes.) (I use a different clock. We're warm all through, we're ready.. Winnie is more than ready; you'll have to call her back.)

"Om Mani Padme Hum. Winifred. Winnie darling, hear me. The sun is rising and so must we."

The little redhead was still perfectly in Lotus, soles of her feet turned upward on her thighs, hands in her lap, palms upward. She was still intoning, with her breathing paced exactly with her prayers. But her eyes had turned up; only the whites showed. "Come back, Winnie. Time."

The girl's eyes turned down to normal; she looked

172

puzzled, then smiled. "Already? Seems like only a moment. I must have fallen asleep."

"Happens. Are you ready? Warm and loose and your muscles soft as cotton?"

"Uh . . . yes, I am."

"Then let's try some singles." Joan Eunice flowed upward from the mat like a flower unfolding and was standing. "You criticize me and I'll criticize you. Then we can have companion exercises for dessert." Joan looked at herself in the long glass. "I think my belly is firmer every day. I keep telling myself."

"It's perfect and you know it." The redhead got up more slowly, caught herself in a yawn.

"Still sleepy, dear? No pleasant dreams last night?"

The girl barely blushed, then shrugged and smiled. "Pleasant all right but not enough hours. I hope we didn't disturb you."

"Didn't hear a sound. Wouldn't have guessed if you hadn't told me when you came in to kiss me good-night. Dear, if you're short on sleep, maybe you'd rather just criticize."

"Oh, no, I'm getting more out of our exercises than you are—don't want to miss a day. But—yes, I'm short on sleep. Paul— Oh, dear! But I didn't say his last name."

"Didn't hear you, I was rubbing my ears."

"Fibber. He didn't leave until half past two. So I did lose sleep. Not that I minded!"

"I'm sure you didn't. Winnie dear, I did *not* mean to snoop. Oh, normal curiosity—being a virgin myself."

The nurse looked startled, said, "But—" and shut up.

Joan Eunice smiled. "Sho', sho', hon, I know what that 'But' means. Mrs. Branca was married . . . and Johann Smith was married four times, not to mention jumping out of windows. But Joan Eunice is a virgin—dig me, doll baby?"

"Well, looked at that way—"

"Only way I *can* look at it. So I'm curious as a Girl Scout. But telling me would still leave me knowing nothing, even if you wanted to tell, which I'm sure you don't.

Someday—no hurry—I suppose I'll find out for myself. So don't you dare blush again and let's get on with our exercises. I'll run through the Tortoise variations and you push me if I need it."

After an hour of twisting and stretching and posing Joan Eunice said, "Enough. Much more and we'd be sweating instead of glowing. Ready for gruesome twosomes?"

The high note of the outer door sounded in the bath-dressing room. "Damn," said Joan. "I mean a ladylike 'darn.' Damn. Into your tights, dear, and I'll drop your smock over your head. Tell 'em 'No ice today.' "

"Right away." Dressed in seconds, the girl left.

(How'd we look today, Eunice? Tits beginning to suit you?) (We're more than halfway there, Joan; in anotl... week you can cut the time down.) (Not anxious to; it's the most fun of the day . . . except when our lord and guardian deigns to dine with us. Tell me, hon—have you been fretting about those negative reports?) (No, *you* have been fretting; they were what I expected. Nobody knows how memory works except that everyone is sure he knows and thinks all the others are fools.) (I've been thinking about those flatworms. If you can chop up a trained flatworm and feed it to another flatworm and then the second one seems to remember what the first one learned, then—) (Boss! I keep telling you, I am *not* a flatworm! I told you a long time ago that the body remembers, and—let's table it; here comes the fuzz.)

"Miss Joan, it's Dr. Garcia and Mr. Salomon."

"Oh. Well, I'm not going to dress; we've still to finish. Grab me a negligee—not that plate-glass job. The London Fog is suitable, don't you think?"

"I guess. Makes you look only half naked instead of bare."

"Who taught me to dress that way, winsome Winnie?" (I did.) (Sure, Eunice—but she thinks she bosses me. I'm her good baby who always does what Mama says . . . until we get dear Doctor out of our hair.) "Please tell the gentlemen that I will be right out."

Miss Smith stopped to apply lipstick, decided that her face could get along with no other renewals, took a brush-comb and teased her too-short locks into fluffiness, stepped into stilt-high mules, put on the negligee and looked at herself in the long glass.

She decided that the selective opacity of the robe was just right—except that the upper part was a little *too* modest. So she delayed long enough to apply lipstick to areolae.

Now satisfied with her appearance—(Boss, we look like a high-priced pooka.) (Very high-priced, I hope. Were you criticizing?) (Not at all, I was applauding.)—she went out into her boudoir. "Good morning, Doctor. Hi, Jake dear. Won't you sit down? Coffee? Or we can find some Old Kentucky Rat Poison, bottled in the barn."

"Coffee," agreed Salomon. "You look charming, my dear."

"Snake charming. I've been exercising and smell like a horse."

"Not more than a small pony. I'll turn up the ventilation. Joan Eunice, Dr. Garcia wants to check you over."

"Really? What's wrong? I feel fine. Aside from these cold prison bars all around me, and my head on a pillow of stone."

"Dr. Garcia thinks we can do something about those cold prison bars. Joan Eunice, we agreed that it was not smart to go into court until you were discharged as well in all respects. He thinks it may be possible, now."

"Oh. *Oh!* How about that platoon of psychiatrists?"

"We'll have them. We may never need them. But we'll be ready to offset their expert witnesses. You will have to put up with long searching interviews; our own experts must go into court prepared." (Prepared to justify their fancy fees. Don't worry, Boss; I'll hide under a rock whenever a shrink is around.)

"That's okay. I'm delighted that Dr. Garcia thinks I'm well. Shall we step into my dressing room, Doctor? Come along, Winnie. Jake, the Wall Street Journal is over there."

Once she was alone with her doctor and nurse Miss Smith said, "Well, Doctor? Shall I stretch out on the massage table?"

"No, this examination is pro forma, to allow me to log

175

that I gave you a physical on the day I discharged you. I'll listen with a stethoscope and make you say 'Ah!'—things like that. If you'll sit down at your dressing table and drop the top of your robe, please."

"Yes, sir."

She kept quiet while he passed the stethoscope here and there, coughed when she was told to, inhaled sharply and sighed noisily as directed. Once she said, "Wups! Sorry, I'm ticklish," and asked, "What does that tell you?"

"Just palpating for lumps. Again, pro forma—although it's been some time since this was done." (Enjoying it, kiddo?) (Maybe you are, Eunice; I'm not. I'd rather be approached more romantic-like.) (Don't kid your grandmother; you enjoy it.)

The doctor stepped back and looked at her thoughtfully. Joan Eunice said, "Anything more, sir? G-Y-N?"

"Not unless you ask for it. Trouble?"

"Not a bit. I feel healthy enough to whup a grizzly bear."

"And you check out that healthy, too. Nevertheless your case worries me."

"Why, Doctor?"

"Because your case is unique. I know almost as little about it as you do. Joan, when you left this house—as Mr. Smith—I never expected to see you alive again. When you were brought back, I did not expect you to regain consciousness. When you regained consciousness, I felt sorry for you . . . as I never expected you to be other than paralyzed from the neck down. Yet here you are, well and healthy. Apparently."

"Why only 'apparently,' Doctor?"

"I don't know. We know little enough about any transplant—and nothing about a brain transplant other than what we have learned from you. Joan, for the past two weeks there has been no reason—other than caution—why you needed more supervision than any other young woman in good health. Say Winifred here, for example."

He shrugged. "Of the two you seem to be somewhat more ruggedly healthy than she is. Nevertheless I would bet that Winifred, barring accidents, will live out her normal span . . . whereas you don't fit any curve; you're

176

unique. Please, I'm not trying to frighten you, but only a fool makes predictions based on ignorance; I am not that sort of fool."

"Doctor," she answered calmly, "you're saying that this body could reject the brain—or vice versa, it's the same thing. Or that I could drop dead, heart failure, for no defined reason. I know it; I read a great deal on transplants, while I was still Johann Smith. I am not afraid. If it happens—well, I've had a wonderful vacation from old age, with its pain and boredom." She smiled happily. "It's been like dying and going to Heaven—and even a few weeks of Heaven can be eternity."

"I'm glad you accept it so philosophically."

"Not 'philosophically,' Doctor. With wonder and joy and reaching out greedily for every golden second!"

"Well . . . I'm pleased that Winifred is going to stay with you and I hope that you will keep her a long time—"

"As long as she will stay! Always, I hope."

"—because, otherwise, I would worry. But Winnie can do in an emergency anything I could do, and she'll have everything here with which to do it—and she knows and I want you to know that I will get here fast if she sends for me. All right, my dear, let's get that transmitter off you; you won't be monitored any longer. Nurse. Rubbing alcohol, and cotton."

"Yes, Doctor." Winifred went past the massage table, reached into a cupboard.

Dr. Garcia detached the tiny transmitter. "Slight erythema, and a faint circle of mechanical dermatitis. With your amazing repair factor I'm betting you won't be able to find where it's been by tomorrow. But I'm going to miss my morning movie."

"Sir?"

"I don't suppose anyone has told you but I have watched the monitors every morning, while you exercised . . . waiting for your heart to pound. Or your respiration to warn me. Nothing. Never anything abnormal, I mean; I could tell that you were exercising. Very mild exercise, I concluded."

"Why, yes, I suppose so. Yoga."

177

"Well! I would not class yoga as 'mild.' If we mean the same thing."

"I meant that yoga isn't a hundred-yard dash, or weight lifting. But I—well, both of us—have been doing the classic poses. Except the headstands; I'm not foolish, I know I have a Sears-Roebuck skull."

"I wouldn't have let her, Doctor! But she never tried one; truly she didn't."

"Doctor, I haven't been building muscles for show; I am simply trying to get perfect control over my new—wonderful!—body. Here, let me show you."

Joan stood up, letting the negligee fall, stood on the floor six inches from the exercise mat—shifted her weight onto her left foot, brought her right leg up behind her in perfect extension while she leaned slowly forward . . . deep . . . deeper . . . until she clasped her left ankle with both hands and pressed her cheek against her shin, with her right leg arrow straight above her in a perfect split.

She held it for three controlled breaths, then dropped her hands flat to the floor, slowly lifted her left leg, balancing it against the right, until she was holding a hand stand, legs together, back arched, toes pointed.

Again slowly she let her limbs sink like drooping petals until they touched the mat—let the Arch sink into the Wheel, melted still farther into the Diamond pose, knees and elbows touching mat and floor—held it—let it roll slowly forward into Lotus. "Om Mani Padme Hum." (Om Mani Padme Hum. Pick up your check at the gate, girl; we won't need to shoot this scene over.) (Thanks, Eunice. But I had a good guru, Guru.) (De nada, Chela.)

Dr. Garcia was applauding. "Terrific! Unbelievable. Like everything else about this case. Winnie! Can you do that?"

Joan flowed upward, was standing. "Sure she can! Skin 'em off, dear, and show Doctor."

The nurse blushed deeply. "No, I can't. Don't believe her, Doctor; I'm just learning."

"Oh, fuff. I have to steady her only a little. Come back in two weeks, Doctor, and she'll do it by herself. It's not hard—just takes angleworms in your ancestry."

178

"Which you seem to have. But, if Winnie didn't teach you, where did *you* learn it, Joan?"

(Oh, oh! Watch it, Boss—he smells a mouse.)

"How old are you, Doctor?"

"Eh? Thirty-seven."

"I learned it about forty years before you were born. But didn't have time to keep it up," she went on. "Then for many years didn't have the physique even to try. But it all came back so easily that I am forced to assume that Mrs. Branca was better at it than I was even as a limber kid." (Let's see him check *that*, sweetheart.) (Never make a lie too complicated, Boss.) (Look, infant, I was lying with a straight face when your grandmother was in rompers. Erase and correct—your great-grandmother.)

"Well . . . I'm going to write it up as part of your final physical—if I can figure out how to describe it. Your robe, Joan?"

"Thank you." She took it and held it, instead of presenting her back for him to put it on her. "Doctor, Mr. Salomon will be settling your fees and expenses. But, to show my great appreciation, I want to add something."

He shook his head. "A doctor should not accept more than his fee . . . and, I assure you, mine are high."

"Nevertheless I want to." She dropped the robe. "Winnie, turn your back, dear." She went straight into his startled arms, put up her face to be kissed.

He hesitated about one heartbeat, then put his arms around her and kissed her. Joan sighed softly, her lips came open, and she flowed more closely against him.

(Don't faint! Let's not miss *any* of this.) (Don't bother me, Eunice; I'm *busy!*)

The Doctor broke from it, caught his breath, and looked at her soberly. Then he reached down, recovered her robe and held it. Joan let him put it on her, then said, "Thank you, Doctor." She turned and smiled.

"Um. I think I can honestly report that you are in excellent physical condition. Mr. Salomon is waiting."

"Please tell him I'll be out in a moment."

Joan waited until the door closed. Then she went into Winifred's arms and giggled against her shoulder. "Winnie, did you turn your back? Didn't you peek a little? I hope."

"I turned my back. But I had a full view in the mirror. *Whew!*"

"Whew twice. So *that's* what it feels like. Honey, I don't feel nearly so virginal now."

"Is he good? It looked like it."

"I don't know. I have no way to judge. Dear darling Jake kisses me; you've seen him—but just 'uncle' sort of pecks. And you kiss me—and *yours* aren't pecks. But you're a girl and smaller than I am. Doctor is the first man who has really kissed me . . . and it made me feel so little and helpless that I darn near dragged him down onto the mat. You've never kissed him?"

"*Him?* Joan honey, if I told any of the nurses about this, I would not be believed. Dr. Garcia doesn't even pat bottoms; he just growls."

"He patted my bottom. I think he did. Things were fuzzy right then."

"I *know* he did. I saw it and didn't believe it. Joan? You wouldn't have made me skin down. Would you?"

"Why not? I was."

"Yes, but you're a patient. I'm a nurse, I'm supposed to be a robot and a chaperon."

"Only we know you're not. Don't we?"

"Well . . . anyhow I can't do that one; it's much too hard."

"I told him to come back in two weeks and you'd be able to. Shall I remind him?"

"Oh, Joan! You're teasing me again." The redhead added thoughtfully, "Do you really think I could, by myself, in only two more weeks?"

"I know you can. But not in clothes, not even tights. So if you are going to blush and go chicken, I had better not remind dear Doctor."

"Uh . . . that did look like quite a kiss. But Paul wouldn't like it."

"Wouldn't like what? Your demonstrating precision body control to a doctor? Or kissing a doctor? Or what the kiss might lead to? And how is Paul to know if you don't tell him?" (Boss, you are corrupting the youth of the land.)

(Egg feathers, Eunice. Either Paul won't marry her . . . or he's married and can't. Either way he's got no business monopolizing her. As you pointed out, sex is not a sport, it's for being happy.)

"Uh . . . Doctor wouldn't kiss me, anyway. He doesn't even know I'm female."

"Never believe it. You are and he's not stupid. He'll kiss you if I suggest that it's the applause expected for a perfect performance. You've got two weeks to make up your mind, and right now I've got to go see dear Jake."

"—having business before this Honorable Court draw nigh!" —"May it please the Court, while Petitioners are ready to proceed, may they respectfully invite to the Court's attention that no proper foundation has been laid. This matter relates to the competency of Johann Sebastian Bach Smith, grandfather of the four Petitioners . . . and Counsel is not aware that he is in court."

"*Order!* There will be order in the court—*at once*. Or the room will be cleared. Counsel, are you suggesting that Miss Smith—this young lady at whom I am pointing—is *not* Johann Sebastian Bach Smith?"

"Counsel suggests nothing, Your Honor. I merely note that we have nothing in the record to show that the person at whom the Court pointed *is* Johann Sebastian Bach Smith—and that the question of competency cannot be considered until proof of identity is indubitably established."

"Is Counsel attempting to instruct this Court in the law?"

"Oh, not at all!"

"It sounded like that. May I remind Counsel that this Court sits today in equity, not in law—and that the procedures are what the Court says they are."

"Most certainly, Your Honor. I regret if I inadvertently sounded otherwise."

"You were one-sixteenth of an inch from contempt, and don't let it happen again."

"Yes, Your Honor."

"........as I am sick and tired of the behavior of about fifty percent of the spectators and at least ninety percent of the press, I order the Bailiff to clear the room. Use a platoon, Evelyn, and clear these cattle out of the chutes promptly—and if that fancy video equipment is damaged in the process, we won't worry about it.

"Counsels, Petitioners, Guardian, and Ward—putative ward, let the record show—will adjourn to my chambers while we get this silly hassle cleared up."

"Jake, this is fun! If I'm not *me*, then I'm flat broke and footloose. You'll have to marry me—to keep me off Welfare."

"Johann, shut up that drivel. This·is serious."

"Jake, I refuse to see doom. If I'm not me, then I'm dead and it would be worth being broke to hear my will read and see the faces of my loving descendants when they discover that they wind up with trivial incomes that aren't even tax-free. Jake, every rich man wants to hear his will read—and I may get the chance."

"Hmm. Under the theory they seem to be following, Eunice is entitled to hear your will read—remember that paragraph about 'all persons not specifically named who are in my personal and private employ at the time of my demise—' "

"Can't say that I do, but if you put it in, it's there."

"It's there. If you're not Johann, then you have to be Eunice. It's an 'either-or' " (Nope! It's *both*.) (Eunice, this is going to be fun?) (I think so, too, Boss.)

The part of his chambers selected by Judge McCampbell was a comfortable lounge. Once in it he looked around.

"Mmm . . . Jake, Ned, Miss Smith, Alec, Mrs. Seward, Mrs. Frabish, you're Mrs. Crampton, aren't you?—Mrs. Lopez. Parkinson, how the devil did you get in here?"

"Amicus curiae, Your Honor."

"You're no friend of this Court and you don't belong here."

"But—"

"Will you walk or would you rather be thrown out?"

Parkinson elected to walk. When the door sealed behind him, the Judge said, "Sperling, set that thing so I can record when I feel like it, then you can leave. Alec, you look as if you were all set to object."

"Me? Oh, not at all, Judge."

"Good. Because we're going to cut through the fog on this silly business. Who needs a fog cutter?" The Judge stepped to a corner bar. "Alec? Gin and tonic as usual?"

"Thanks, Judge."

"I'm forgetting the ladies. Mrs. Seward? Something with alcohol? Or coffee? This machine will make tea, too, if I can remember which buttons to push. And how about your sister? And your cousins? Miss Smith? I recall what you used to order at the Gib some years back. Are your tastes the same now?"

(Watch it, Boss! It's loaded.) (Relax, Eunice.) "Judge, with a new body my tastes have changed in some respects. But I remember fondly Glen Grant on the rocks—back before my doctors put a stop to it. But I haven't tasted anything with that much authority since those days, and, since this is a competency hearing, I'll settle for coffee. Or a Coke, if you can twist its tail for that."

The Judge rubbed his nose and looked thoughtful. "I'm not sure it's a competency hearing until we settle this matter of identity. Jake could have told you about Glen Grant. The idea of Johann Smith ordering a Coke shakes me."

Joan smiled at him. "I know—hardly seems in character. My doctors made me quit carbonated drinks long before they made me give up whisky. Back about the time you entered law school. If I'm Johann Smith, that is. If I'm not, I'll ask to be excused—as in that case I'm not a ward of the Court and shouldn't be here. Isn't that correct?"

McCampbell looked still more thoughtful. "Jake, do you want to caution your client? No, not your 'client,' your—no, not that either. Blessed if I know what you are; that's what we've got to find out. Young lady, sit down and I'll fetch you a Coke. Alec, get drink orders from your four ladies and serve them. Jake, you and Ned serve yourselves—Alec and I have a date with some fish in Nova Scotia tomorrow morning and I'll be switched if I'll keep

185

fish waiting over a surprise turn in this hearing. Alec, confound your Irish soul, are you seriously questioning the identity of this young lady?"

"Well—Judge, are you going to talk about contempt if I suggest that your question is not properly put?"

McCampbell sighed. "Young lady, pay no attention to him. He was my roommate in college and gives me a bad time whenever he comes into my court. Someday I'm going to give him thirty days to think it over—and about four-thirty tomorrow morning I'm going to trip him into some very cold water. Accidentally."

"Do that, Mac, and I'll sue. In Canada."

"I know he was your roommate, Judge; you were both 'Big Greens'—Dartmouth seventy-eight, was it not? Why not let him ask me questions and find out for himself who I am?"

Mrs. Seward said shrilly, "That's not the way to go about it! First you must take the fingerprints of that—that *impostor*—and—"

"*Mrs. Seward!*"

"Yes, Judge? I was just going to say—"

"*Shut up!*"

Mrs. Seward shut up. Judge McCampbell went on, "Madam, simply because it suits me to be informal in my chambers do not think that this is not a court in session or that I would not find you in contempt. I would enjoy it. Alec, you had better convince her of that."

"Yes, Your Honor. Mrs. Seward, any suggestions you have, you will make through *me*, not to the Court."

"But I was just going to say that—"

"Mrs. Seward, keep quiet! You're here only by courtesy of the Court until this matter of identity is cleared up. I'm sorry, Judge. I advised my clients that, at the most, this was a holding action. I know that Jake Salomon would not risk bringing a ringer—sorry, Miss Smith—a ringer into court."

"And I know it."

"But they insisted. If Mrs. Seward won't control herself, I'll have to ask your permission to withdraw from the case."

The Judge shook his head and grinned. "No, sirree,

186

Alec. You fetched them here, you're stuck with them—at least until Court adjourns. Jake? Is Ned still fronting for you? Or will you speak for yourself?"

"Oh, I think we can both speak up from time to time, without friction."

"Ned?"

"Of course, Judge. Jake can speak for himself and should. But I'm finding it interesting. Novel situation."

"Quite. Well, speak up if you have anything to contribute. Alec, I don't think we can get anywhere today. Do you?"

Alec Train stood mute. Joan said, "Why not, Judge? I'm here, I'm ready. Ask me anything. Bring out the rack and the thumbscrews—I'll talk."

The Judge again rubbed his nose. "Miss Smith, I sometimes think that my predecessors were overly hasty in letting such tools be abolished. I think I can settle to my own satisfaction whether or not you are the person known as Johann Sebastian Bach Smith, of this city and of Smith Enterprises, Limited. But it is not that simple. In an ordinary identity case Mrs. Seward's suggestion of fingerprints would be practical. But not in this case. Alec? Do Petitioners stipulate that the brain of their grandfather was transplanted into another body?"

Petitioners' counsel looked unhappy. "May it please the Court, I am under instructions not to stipulate anything of the sort."

"So? What's your theory?"

"Uh, 'Missing and presumed dead,' I suppose. We take the position that the burden of proof is on anyone who steps forward and claims to be Johann Sebastian Bach Smith."

"Jake?"

"I can't agree as to the burden of proof, Judge. But my client—my ward who is also my client, Johann Sebastian Bach Smith—is present in court and I am pointing at her. I know her to be that named individual. Both of us are ready to be questioned by the Court in any fashion in order to assure the Court as to her identity. I was about to say that both of us are willing to be questioned by anyone—but on

187

second thought I cannot concede that there is *any* interested party other than my client."

"Judge?"

"Yes, Miss Smith? Jake, do you want her to speak?"

"Oh, certainly. Anything."

"Go ahead, Miss Smith."

"Thank you. Judge, my granddaughters can ask me anything. I've known them since they were babies; if they try to trip me, I'll have them hanging on the ropes in two minutes. For example, Johanna—the one you called 'Mrs. Seward'—was hard to housebreak. On her eighth birthday—May fifteenth nineteen-sixty, the day the Paris Conference between Eisenhower and Khrushchev broke down—her mother, my daughter Evelyn, invited me over to see the little brat have her birthday cake, and Evelyn shoved Johanna into my lap and she cut loose—"

"I did no such thing!"

"Oh, yes, you did, Johanna. Evelyn snatched you off my lap and apologized and said that you had a bed-wetting problem. Can't say as to that—my daughter lied easily."

"Judge, are you going to sit there and let that—that *person*—insult the memory of my dead mother?"

"Mrs. Seward, your counsel cautioned you. If you don't heed his caution, this Court is capable of nailing you into a barrel and letting you speak only when I say to pull out the bung. Or some such. Squelch her, Alec. Suppress her the way they did in the trial in 'Alice in Wonderland'—which this is beginning to resemble. She's not a party to this; she is here only to give evidence in case the Court needs it. Miss Smith—"

"Yes, sir?"

"Your opinions as to the veracity of your putative descendants are not evidential. Can you think of anything that Johann Smith would know and that I would know or could check on—but which Jake Salomon could not possibly have briefed you on?"

"That's a tough one, Your Honor."

"So it is. But the alternative—today—is for me to assume that you are an imposter most carefully coached and then to question you endlessly in an attempt to trip

188

you. I don't want to do that . . . because final identification—now that the matter has been raised—will have to be by evidence as conclusive as fingerprints. You see that, don't you?"

"Yes, I see it but I don't quite see how." She smiled and spread her graceful hands. "My fingerprints—and everything about me that can be seen—are those of my donor."

"Yes, yes, surely—but there are more ways of killing a cat than buttering it with parsnips. Later."

"Harrumph!"

"Yes, Jake?"

"Judge, in the interests of my client I cannot concede that physical means of identifying this body are relevant. The question is: Is this the *individual* designated by Social Security number 551-20-0052 and known to the world as Johann Sebastian Bach Smith? I suggest that 'Estate of Henry M. Parsons v. Rhode Island,' while not on all fours, is relevant."

McCampbell said mildly, "Jake, you are much older than I am and I'm reasonably sure you know the law more thoroughly than I do. Nevertheless, here today, I am the Judge."

"Certainly, Your Honor! May it please the Court, I—"

"So quit being so damned respectful in my chambers. You sat on my orals and voted to pass me, so you must think I know some law. Of course the Parsons case is relevant; we'll get to it later. In the meantime I'm trying to find a basis for a pro-tem ruling. Well, Miss Smith?"

"Judge, I don't care whether I'm identified or not. In the words of a gallant gentleman: 'Broke don't scare me.' " She suddenly chuckled and glanced at her granddaughters. "May I tell you something funny—privately?"

"Mmm . . . I could clear the room of everyone but you and your counsel; nevertheless you had better save any jokes until after we adjourn."

"Yes, sir. May I address one irrelevant remark to my granddaughters?"

"Hmmph. I may strike it from the record. Go ahead."

"Thank you, Judge. Girls—Johanna, Marla, June,

Elinor—look at me. For thirty-odd years you have been waiting for me to die. Now you hope to prove that I am dead, else this silly business would never have come up. Girls, I hope you get away with it . . . for I can't wait to see your faces when my will is read." (You zapped 'em, Boss! *Look* at those expressions!) (I surely did, darling. Now shut up; we're not home free.)

"Your Honor—"

"Yes, Alec?"

"May I suggest that this is not relevant?"

Joan cut in. "But I *said* it would be irrelevant, Mr. Train. Just the same, they had better start thinking about how to break my will, instead of this nonsense." She added thoughtfully, "Perhaps I had better set up a lifetime trust that will make them slightly better off with me alive than dead . . . to protect myself against patricidal assassination. Judge, is 'patricidal' the right word? Now that I'm female?"

"Blessed if I know. Better make it 'avicidal'—no, 'avicide' already means the killing of birds and has nothing to do with 'avus.' Never mind, Miss Smith, take up such matters with your attorney and let us return to our muttons. Have you thought of anything which Jake Salomon could not have coached you on?"

"It's difficult. Jake has been handling my affairs for most of a generation. Mmm, Judge, will you shake hands with me?"

"Eh?"

"We had best do it under the table, or out of sight of anyone but Mr. Train."

Looking puzzled, the Judge went along with her request. Then he said, "Be damned! Excuse me. Miss Smith—shake hands with Alec."

Joan did so, letting her body cover it from spectators. Mr. Train looked surprised, whispered something to her which she answered in a whisper. (Boss, what was what?) (Greek. Tell you later, dear—though girls aren't supposed to know.)

McCampbell said, "Mr. Salomon could not have coached you?"

"Ask him. Jake was a Barb, not a Greek."

190

"Of course I was a Barb," Salomon growled. "I had no stomach for being the exhibit Jew in a chapter that did not want its charter lifted. What is this?"

Train said, "Well, it seems.that Miss Smith is a fraternity brother of the Judge and myself. Mmm . . . 'sister,' I suppose. Judge, it's easy to check this on both Johann Smith and Mr. Salomon. In the meantime I find it persuasive."

"Perhaps I can add to it," Joan said. "Mr. Train —Brother Alec—of course you should check on both Jake and myself. But look me up in our fraternal archives under 'Schmidt' rather than 'Smith' as I changed my name in forty-one. Which my granddaughters know. But you both know of our fraternal Distress Fund?"

"Yes."

"Certainly, Miss Smith."

"The fund did not exist when I was pledged—my senior year it was, after I made Phi Beta Kappa and because our local chapter needed a greasy grind and had an alumnus willing to pay for my initiation. The fund was started during World War Two; I helped augment it some years later and was one of its trustees from fifty-six until late in the eighties when I dropped most outside activities. Judge, you tapped the fund for fifteen hundred in the spring of seventy-eight."

"Eh? So I did. But I paid it back, eventually—then donated the same amount at a later time, according to our customs."

"I'm glad to hear it. The latter, I mean; you were off the hook before I resigned as a trustee. I was a hard-nosed trustee, Judge, and never okayed a loan until I was certain that it was a distress case and not just a convenience to a lazy undergraduate. Shall I relate the circumstances which caused me to okay your loan?"

The Judge blinked. "I would rather you did not, at least not now. Alec knows them."

"Yes," agreed Train. "Would have lent him the money myself if I had had it." (What is this, Boss?) (Case of 'rheumatic fever,' sweet.) (Abortion money?) (No, no—he married the girl—and here I am digging up the skeleton.)

191

(Bitch.) (No, Eunice—my granddaughters don't know what I'm talking about, nor does Jake.)

"I see no reason to discuss it," Miss Smith went on, "unless the Judge wants to question me privately—and if you do, Judge, do remind me to tell you a real giggle about the ancestries of my so loving granddaughters. Odd things happen even in the best families—and the Schmidt family was never one of the best. We're a vulgar lot, me and my descendants—our only claim to prominence is too much money."

"Later perhaps, Miss Smith. I am now ready to hand down a decision—temporary and conservative. Counsels?"

"Ready, Judge."

"Nothing to add, Your Honor."

McCampbell fitted his fingertips together. "Identity. It need not depend on fingerprints or retinal patterns or similar customary evidence. John Doe could lose both hands and both feet, have both eyes gouged out, be so scarred and damaged that even his dentist could not identify him—and he would still be John Doe, with the same Social Security number. Something like that happened to you, Miss Smith, assuming that you are indeed Johann Sebastian Bach Smith—though I am happy to see"—he smiled—"that no scars show.

"This Court finds persuasive the evidence of your identity brought out in this hearing. We assume, pro tem, that you are Johann Sebastian Bach Smith.

"However"—the Judge looked at Salomon—"we now get to the Parsons case. Inasmuch as the Supreme Court has ruled that the question of life or death resides in the brain and nowhere else, this Court now rules that identity must therefore reside in the brain and nowhere else. In the past it has never been necessary to decide this point; now it is necessary. We find that to rule in any other fashion would be inconsistent with the intent of the Supreme Court in 'Estate of Henry M. Parsons v. Rhode Island.' To rule in any other way would create chaos in future cases in any way similar to this one: Identity must lie in the brain.

"Now, Jake, I am in effect going to shove the burden of the proof over onto you and your client. At a later time you

192

must be prepared to prove beyond any possible doubt that Johann Sebastian Bach Smith's brain was removed from his body and transplanted into this body"—McCampbell pointed.

Jake nodded. "I realize that, Judge. A person who wants to cash a check must prove his identity—this is on all fours. But today we were taken by surprise."

"So was the Court—and, Alec, I'm going to take you by surprise someday . . . with something better than a pie bed or an exploding cigar. Damn it, you should have warned Court and Counsel."

"I apologize, Your Honor. I received my instructions quite late."

"You should have at once asked for a continuance, not let this hearing open. You know better. Never mind, the hearing has been instructive. Miss Smith—Miss Johann Sebastian Bach Smith subject to remarks above—you were made a ward of this Court and placed under the guardianship of Mr. Jacob Salomon for one reason alone: You were at the time not competent to manage your affairs by reason of post-operative incapacity. Let the record show that neither insanity in the legal sense nor mental illness in the medical sense had anything to do with it; you were in an extended condition of unconsciousness following surgery and that was all. You are no longer unconscious, you appear to be in good health, and the Court takes judicial notice that during this hearing you appeared always to be alert and clearheaded. Since the sole condition—unconsciousness—on which you were made a ward no longer obtains, you are now no longer a ward and Mr. Salomon is discharged of his guardianship—what's the trouble, Alec?"

"May it please the Court!—as Counsel for the Petitioners I must ask to have an objection entered into the record."

"On what grounds?"

"Why, lack of expert witnesses as to, uh, 'Miss Smith's' competence."

"Do you have expert witnesses ready to examine her?"

"Of course."

"Jake?"

"Certainly. Waiting on call."

"How many?"

"Harrumph! One more than Alec has, however many he qualifies."

"So I expected, and if we start qualifying expert witnesses now and let each one exercise his little ego, those fish in Nova Scotia would die of old age. Keep your shirt on, Alec. No expert witnesses were used to show this person's incompetence; the gross condition of unconsciousness was stipulated—and now no longer exists. Alec, your objection goes into the record but I am putting you on notice that your claim of need for expert witnesses lacks foundation—and this time the burden of proof is on *you*. Petitioners will have to show something more than great anxiety to get their hands on the large sums of money at stake in this matter. Every citizen, every person, is conditionally presumed to be competent—and that means *everyone*—you, me, Jake, Miss Smith, Petitioners, and the illiterate who fills that bar and cleans out the empties. This Court will not set the extremely bad precedent of allowing you, or anyone, to conduct a fishing expedition into the matter of a person's competency without proper foundation. However— Jake."

"Yes, Judge."

"We all know what this hearing is really about. Money. Lots of money. You might explain to Miss Smith that her competence may be challenged at some later time."

"We're prepared for it."

"While I've discharged you as her guardian, you will stay on as conservator of the property of Johann Sebastian Bach Smith pending positive proof of identity—and I do mean *positive*; you've got to trace Smith's brain into this body every step of the way. What was the name of that surgeon? Boyle? I suppose you'll need him. And several others. I'm not going to take anything for granted, nor permit any stipulations; there is too much at stake and I don't intend to be reversed. Alec, if you are going to challenge competency, you will have to wait until after that time and—if it's in my court—show foundation for such challenge. That satisfy you?"

"I guess it will have to."

"I guess so, too. Court's adjourned."

Mrs. Seward stood up, red-faced, and said to Alec Train, "*You're fired!*"

McCampbell said coldly, "Madam, consider yourself lucky that you saved that outburst until after Court adjourned. Now, get out of my chambers. You other three ladies may leave, too."

Johanna's sister June said as she stood up: "Judge, may I ask a question?"

"Certainly, Mrs. Frabish."

"You've turned this person loose—that's all right, I'm not criticizing. But are you leaving her in our grandfather's house? I think you ought to know that it is loaded, simply *loaded*, with valuable works of art. What is to keep \her from gutting it while we are proving that she *can't* be our grandfather?"

"Oh. Madam, Mr. Salomon knows the duties and responsibilities of a conservator. However—Jake, it would be prudent not to permit any objects of sentimental or artistic value to leave that house during this waiting period."

"No problem. Since I've had to manage the household, I've been staying there much of the time. But I'll have a word with Johann's chief guard."

"Judge, may I say something?"

"Certain, my— Miss Smith."

"I'd like protection against *them*. June doesn't know what objets d'art I own. Not one of them has been inside my house since it was built. During my long illness and confinement not one of them called on me or sent flowers or anything. And the same for my post-surgery convalescence—except that I learned that Johanna—Mrs. Seward—tried to crash in right after my operation. I don't trust them; I'd like the Court's protection."

"Jake?"

"I wasn't there but I heard it from Johann's chief guard."

"Mrs. Seward?"

She sniffed. "I had a perfect right! Next of kin."

"I think I understand it. All right, you four ladies—listen carefully, then leave. You will refrain from visiting the home or offices or other properties of Johann Sebastian Bach Smith. You will refrain from making any attempt to see or to speak with this young lady I have been addressing as 'Miss Smith.' If you need to communicate with her or with the Court's appointed conservator, Mr. Salomon, you will do so only through this Court or through your attorney, whoever he may be, to Mr. Salomon and *never* directly to Miss Smith. This is an order to all four of you and each of you will obey under pain of severe penalties for contempt. Do you understand? Are there any questions?"

McCampbell waited, then went on, "Very well. Now all four of you leave."

The Judge remained standing while they filed out. When the door sealed, he sighed. "Whew! Miss Smith—or should I say 'Brother Schmidt'?—will you have that Glen Grant on rocks now? Glenlivet actually, I don't have Glen Grant."

She smiled. "Truly, I haven't tried anything that potent on this new body. Jake and I should leave—you and Brother Alec have a date with a fish."

"Oh, do sit down. Alec has his gear in his car in the basement and my copter is picking us up from the roof in about an hour. Another Coke?"

"Is there sherry? I get a very pleasant buzz on just a glass of sherry—I conclude that my donor did not drink at all." (Almost never, Boss—and you're giving me a taste for the stuff.) (Quiet, darling—later.) (All right . . . but ask him about our *name*. Isn't Judgie Wudgie a darling? Wonder what he's like in bed?) (You and your one-track mind! I'll ask him about our name. Now shut up!)

"Sherry it shall be. Jake? Ned? Alec?"

196

"Judge, since Jake doesn't need me, I'll ask to be excused."

"Okay, Ned. Alec, serve yourself and take care of Jake; I want to stare at Brother Schmidt. I probably won't be seeing you again, Miss Smith. Your granddaughters are almost certain to try to move it into a higher court. That business of proving who you are by our fraternity grip—that tore it. All I could do today was to give you a little protection in the interim."

"Which I appreciated, sir. Here's an odd thing about this sex change. When I was an old man, frail and helpless, I was afraid of nothing. Now I'm young and healthy and strong. But female. To my surprise I find that I want to be protected."

Alec Train said over his shoulder from the bar, "I'll protect you, Brother Schmidt! Don't trust Brother McCampbell—he was the worst wolf in our chapter. Step aside, Brother Wolf—it's my turn to stare at our new brother."

"Boys, I am not a 'new brother,' I was pledged years before you were born. But I'm not surprised that you like to stare at me, as my donor—Jake, do they know?"

"It's not much of a secret, Johann. Judge McCampbell knows, I think Alec knows, too." (Joan, if he doesn't know, tell him. And don't forget our name!) (What do you think I'm leading up to?)

"All right. My donor, Eunice Branca, my former secretary and the sweetest, loveliest girl I've ever known, was not only a perfect secretary; she was a beauty contest winner not many years back. I know what a treasure I inherited from her. I don't wear her body with the charming grace she gave it—but I'm trying to learn." (You're learning, Boss.)

"It is the opinion of this Court that you have learned."

"Shut up, Mac. Brother Schmidt, I agree with him merely because he's right."

"Thank you both—on behalf of Eunice Branca. Jake? Now that Court has adjourned do I have to wear this Mother Hubbard? It's too warm."

"That's up to you. I suppose it depends on how much you have under it."

"Mmm . . . perhaps I'd better not. Minimum decency under the customs of today—but it would get a burlesque queen thirty days back when I was a youngster." (Exhibitionist. You're asking to be coaxed.) (Certainly. And who taught me? At least the bra isn't just paint, like that mermaid outfit *you* zapped *me* with.)

Alec Train said, "Brother Schmidt, in identity cases it is sometimes necessary to require the challenged individual to strip completely. Birthmarks and scars and such—tell her, Judge."

"Ignore him, Brother Schmidt. I wouldn't call that lovely Grecian robe a 'Mother Hubbard.' But I can see that it was intended for outdoors and I'll happily hang it up for you."

"Uh . . . oh, goodness, I'm having trouble shucking off my early-twentieth-century Puritanism. Jake has seen me in the nothing-much girls wear today, and he's seen Eunice in even less than I have on under this; Eunice wasn't shy about sharing her beauty." (You milked *that*, didn't you, dearie? Which one are you after?) (Shut up!) Joan ran a finger down the magnostrip, let the robe fall open; Alec Train hurried to claim it ahead of the Judge.

Then she posed. "See? This is almost the way Eunice Branca looked—except that she walked in glory, always . . . while I am an old man who is trying to learn to wear her body." Besides Eunice's body, Joan was wearing some of Winnie's clothes—black frill skirt, translucent black Cling On cups, six-inch Sticktite stilt sandals that left her pretty feet in view—no paint, just restrained enhancement with rouge and shadow.

She posed, they stared. Jake cleared his throat louder than usual. "Joan, had I known what you were wearing—not wearing, rather—under that robe, I would have advised you to keep it on."

"Oh, pooh, Jake, you wouldn't have scolded Eunice for dressing this way. But that brings up something I must ask. Judge, I can't go on being 'Johann Smith.' Will you let me change my name?"

"That's not properly put, Brother Schmidt. You can have any name you like. At most a court confirms it. You mean that you need a girl's name now. Helen, perhaps? Or Cleopatra?"

"Thank you—for Eunice." (Boss, find out if Judge is still married.) (Go back to sleep!) "Not either of those names. I want to be known as 'Joan'—for 'Johann'—'Joan . . . Eunice . . . Smith.' "

Judge McCampbell looked surprised, then smiled in approval. "A good choice. The flavor of your masculine name, plus, I assume, a tribute to your donor. But may I offer a word of advice? You can start calling yourself that today—"

"I already have."

"I noticed that Jake called you 'Joan.' But let it be a family name, and keep your masculine name at other times—use it to sign letters, checks, and so forth—until your identity has been finally established—in the Supreme Court if possible. Don't cloud the issue."

"I gave her the same advice," Salomon put in.

"I'm not surprised. Miss—Brother Schmidt, what do you want me to call you? In private."

"Why, either 'Joan' or 'Eunice.' Both by preference, as I do not want anyone ever to forget Eunice Branca. Me least of all—I want to be reminded of my benefactor. Benefactrix. But don't call me 'Miss' in private. Look, brothers, as 'Brother Schmidt' I am half a century older than you two . . . but as 'Joan Eunice' I am only a few weeks old. However, Eunice's body is that of a young woman, and that is what I am learning—must learn!—to be. You could have daughters my age. So please call me 'Joan Eunice' and save 'Miss Smith' for court appearances." She smiled. "Or 'Brother Schmidt' if you wish—although 'Yonny' was what I was called by our brothers in my chapter."

Alec said, "Joan Eunice Brother Yonny Schmidt, I'm pleased to call you whatever you like, and I don't have daughters your age and you make me feel younger just to look at you. But I'm not speaking for my roommate and I'd hate to tell you how old some of *his* offspring are; he was

199

the scourge of P.S. 238—stay away from him and let me protect you. And did I mention how happy I am that Mrs. Seward fired me? Brother Joan Eunice, I would never have been in this case other than as a favor to Parkinson's mother-in-law. But at first it did look like a straightforward case of protecting the interests of an invalid too ill to protect himself. Believe me."

"Don't listen to him," advised the Judge. "He's an ambulance chaser. I throw legitimate business his way just to protect the good name of our Brothers. But back to this matter of identity. Joan Eunice, I don't know how much law you know—"

"Just what has rubbed off in the course of a long and evil life. I depend on experts. Such as Jake."

"I see. Well, your granddaughters probably think it is wrong of me to help you establish your identity. It is not. True, in a civil suit or a criminal action a judge must be impartial. But such a matter as establishing identity is neither one, and there is no rule of law or equity which prohibits a court from being helpful. The situation is like that of a citizen who has lost his passport and appeals to his consul. The consul doesn't sit as a judge; he tries to get the mixup straightened out. So— Jake, you've been in the Law much longer than I have; do you want my opinions?"

"I am always most happy to have Judge McCampbell's opinions on any matter."

"I think I'll reconvene court and slam you for contempt. After I've finished this drink. All right, you're going to get 'em anyhow. Do you anticipate any difficulty in proving that the brain of Brother Schmidt was moved into the body of Eunice Branca?"

"None. A nuisance but no difficulty."

"Or in showing that this body—this lovely body—was once that of Eunice Branca?"

"Same answer."

"What evidence?"

"Police reports, photographs, hospital personnel, and so forth."

"Let's say it's my court. I'm going to make you go back and touch second at every opportunity. I intentionally got

200

into the record today that ruling based on 'Parsons' estate v. Rhode Island'; I think it's important—"

"So do I."

"Thank you. In following the principle that identity lies in the brain and nowhere else"—(We could tell him something, couldn't we, Boss?) (Yes, beloved—but we aren't going to!)—"I am going to be as tough as possible. No depositions when it is possible to bring the witness into court. Photographs and other records not only allowed but required—but the originals must be brought into court, not copies, and photographers or record keepers must appear and identify same, and the surgeons or others whose work appears in those films, photographs, or records must appear and confirm each record. Do you know if each body was fingerprinted just prior to surgery?"

"Not of my own knowledge. Damn it, I was taken by surprise today—and at the time of Eunice Branca's death I had other things worrying me."

Joan Eunice reached over and squeezed his hand.

Alec Train said, "I can help on that. When Parkinson brought Mrs. Seward to see me, I checked on that point at once. Prints were taken from both bodies—so I gave identity no further thought. That's why *I* was taken as much by surprise as you two. I don't know what chimney-corner lawyer put the idea in Mrs. Seward's head—Parkinson, probably; he's stayed at her elbow all through—but I received instructions just as court convened. I'm not spilling any privileged communication when I say that—nor do I know of any Canon which forbids me to say that I am damn sick of both Mrs. Seward and Parkinson."

"Hmm. Every possible bit of evidence," McCampbell went on. "You will have to trace that brain out of that body—Joan Eunice—no, Jake. Jake, do you know what became of Johann Smith's body?"

"That one I can answer. Here we have a unique case of a body becoming a chattel while the person who lived in it is still alive. I knew what Johann Smith—Joan Eunice, that is—had wanted done with it, as his will contains the standard 'donated for medical research' clause. But the will

201

did not control because Johann Smith was, and is, alive. The Medical Center asked what to do with it. I told them to hold it, in their morgue. I assume that it is still there."

Mr. Train said, "Counselor, I hope you're right. But unless that cadaver was nailed down, two gets you ten that some eager medical student has chopped it up."

The Judge said, "I'm afraid Alec could be right. Jake, it may be a matter of great urgency to perpetuate the evidence—*all* the evidence. Verb. sap. We all know how key evidence has a way of disappearing when big money is involved. And besides eager medical students—well, we all know that almost any illegal act is for sale at a price. Films and records can be stolen, others substituted, ostensibly respectable witnesses can be bribed. Let's speculate for a moment that Brother Schmidt is opposed by nameless dishonest persons, persons willing to bribe, suborn, and so forth. Such crime is not cheap. Does anyone have a guess as to how much money might be used to destroy or change the evidence?"

Jake said, "I won't guess. But in the case of four nameless females I can find out."

Joan said, "I can help a little on this. Marla and Elinor lost their father before they were of age and his estate wound up minus and no insurance to speak of. So I supported my daughter Roberta until she died and kept her kids in school until they flunked out, then continued to support them until each married—one of their grievances against me is that I stopped their allowances when they married. But I continued a credit watch on them, as I did not want any descendant of mine to become a charge on the taxpayers. Much the same with the other two girls except that Jim Darlington outlasted my daughter Evelyn, and both girls—Johanna and June—married while their parents were living. To put it briefly, unless one of them has come into some windfall, all four could not scrape together enough money to tackle any really expensive crime."

"I'm glad to hear it," said McCampbell. "Just the same, Jake, time is of the essence in preserving evidence—and I want you to know that this court will give you all possible legal help in protecting and perpetuating any evidence you dig up. Unh, Alec and I plan to be away four days—but I'll leave my emergency wavelength with Sperling and will bounce back here if you need me."

"Thank you, sir."

"Wait a minute," said Alec Train. "There *is* money in this case. Mac, you know how I am about fees."

"Yes. Larcenous."

"Ignore him, Brother Schmidt. I tailor my fees, all the way from zero up to outrageous. In this case I did not want the job, so I demanded an outrageous retainer against a, yes, larcenous per diem—and Parkinson paid without a quiver. Through Mrs. Seward but there was no question as to who called the tune. The question is: Will Parkinson go on paying . . . and is he willing to hire his friendly, neighborhood safecracker to go after some necessary link? I don't know—especially as it isn't his money, but his mother-in-law's."

"I don't know," answered Jake, "but I always assume that my opponent might cheat if I fail to cut the cards. I'm going after that evidence with all possible speed. Sorry, Joan, I should have anticipated this—I'm getting old." (He is *not*. Tell him so, Boss.)

Joan Eunice patted his hand. "Jake, you are *not* getting old and there was no reason to anticipate this. Gentlemen, let me say again, I don't care a whit if my granddaughters win. If they win, they lose—because if they prove me legally dead, I have cut them off with that shilling. And, thanks to Eunice Branca and Dr. Boyle and Jake Salomon, I'm young and healthy and enjoying life and not distressed at the idea of losing a fortune that has become a burden to me."

Alec Train said, "Brother Schmidt Joan Eunice honey, don't you realize that it is unAmurrican to talk that way about millions of dollars?"

She grinned at him. "Brother Alec, if I come out of this broke, I'll bet you a million dollars that I can net a million dollars after taxes in the next five years, starting from scratch. Jake, will you back my bet? Since it calls for me starting broke?"

"Certainly."

"Wait a minute!" Train protested. "I'm just a poor but honest lawyer. Will you make that bet fifty cents? Mac, will you lend me fifty cents?"

"Not without security. Joan Eunice, listen, please. I don't doubt that you are willing to tackle the world broke. But I know in my heart that you are indeed Brother Johann Schmidt . . . who okayed a loan to me when I really needed it. Old Eata Bita Pi didn't let me down . . . and I'm not going to let Brother Schmidt down."

"Thank you, Brother Mac."

Jake growled, "You frat house aristocrats made me sick when I was in college and I don't like it much better today. Judge, the only good reason for giving Joan Eunice a hand is because it's the fair thing to do. Not because she—he—okayed a loan years ago to some snot-nose fraternity brother."

"Counselor, your point is well taken. I think I can truthfully say that I have never allowed fraternal bonds—including Shriner, which you and I are—to affect my behavior on the bench—"

"The hell it hasn't, old buddy mine; you rule against me just for the hell of it. Ask anybody."

"Even when I've been forced to instruct this Irishman in the finer points of the law. I would have helped in this matter in any case; both as a citizen and as a ward of the Court Joan Eunice is entitled to any help a court can offer in establishing her identity. But I confess that my emotions were aroused by a circumstance that I did not dream existed. Not that Joan Eunice is my fraternity brother—that is simply a pleasing coincidence—but that she—he at that time—gave me a hand when it mattered. Uh"—he stared at his glass—"no need to go into details. You know them, Joan Eunice?"

"Yes."

"You can tell Jake later. Let me list the things I think are necessary in this case; both of you lawyers check me and I'm going to stick a fresh tape in this thing so that we can all have copies." He turned to his clerk's recording equipment. "That is I *think* I am going to.

Damn! Excuse me, Joan Eunice. I wonder if Sperling has gone home."

(Let's look at that thing, dear.) "I'm 'Brother Schmidt' any time you feel like swearing, Judge. May I look at your recorder? It's a bit like one I have at home."

"Go ahead. I sometimes wish we still used shorthand reporters."

"Thank you." (How about, Eunice?) (It's Betsy's idiot baby sister, no huhu. You whistle Yankee Doodle or think about Judgie Wudgie and don't bother me.) (Om Mani Padme Hum. Om Mani Padme Hum. Om Mani Padme—) (Got it, dearie.) "Recording with a fresh tape, Judge; set for three copies, and erase memory."

McCampbell said, "I'm amazed every time I find someone who understands machinery."

"I don't, really. But Eunice Branca taught me to run one somewhat like yours." (Boss, you're learning how to lie—just tell the truth but not all of it.) (Honey girl, I *invented* that way of lying way back when your great-grandmother was a virgin.)

"First, Eunice Branca's death must be established. As it was murder, we will assume extensive records with positive identification including fingerprints—and since they are police records, we must also assume that they are vulnerable to any determined and well-financed attempt to destroy or replace them. Then Mrs. Branca's body must be followed into surgery and positive identification of the body again established at that point. Johann Schmidt's body must also be followed to that point and positively identified just before surgery. Then we must be certain beyond any doubt that the brain was removed from the Schmidt body—Joan Eunice, this must be distressing to you. Would you like to retire to my washroom? There's a couch in there."

"Please go ahead, sir; I've learned to live with it." (Makes *me* feel like throwing up, Boss.) (Me, too, darling—but we aren't going to; we're going to look solemnly serene. Om Mani Padme Hum.) (Om Mani Padme Hum. Let's make a Lotus; this chair is big enough.) (Yes, darling. Om Mani Padme Hum.)

205

"—and finally, in court, we will take Joan Eunice's fingerprints, have them compared by experts with each earlier set, and thereby forge the final link. Joan Eunice, do I simply switch this off now?"

(After the three copies pop out, it will shut itself off.) "When the three copies pop out, it will erase and shut off. Jake, we're keeping these gentlemen from their fishing."

"Those fish aren't restless," the Judge assured her. "Just a moment." He stepped to his closed-circuit viewphone. "Evelyn."

"Yes, Judge."

"How are things outside? Quiet?"

"Judge, how did you guess? I've got three men in the infirmary and the building is buttoned up. You might take a look on three and four, and then play back the sixteen o'clock spot news."

"How badly were your men hurt?"

"Nothing serious. One with a lungful of sneeze gas when we had to clear the main entrance and seal the riot doors, one with a flesh wound on a cheekbone, and the third with cracked ribs. My guess is the newsies bought 'emselves a riot, as cameras were in position when the trouble started."

"I see. Are we going to need the Guard?"

"I wouldn't say so. The police have the streets around us pretty well patrolled and our own people are either staying overnight or being taken off the top by chopper. Message from Judge Anders—says there's no reason for you not to go fishing and he'll assume that he's presiding judge pro tem. He's staying in his chambers tonight."

"I'll call him and thank him. Off."

The Judge switched to view three, studied it. "Doesn't look too rough. Just the same they ought to tear this building down and build a stronger one farther from any Abandoned Area." He switched to view four. "Oh oh!"

The room filled with crowd roar, the screen showed a milling mob. Moving slowly through the crowd were two police Merrimac tanks, their loudspeakers monotonously repeating the warning-to-disperse. "Brother Schmidt, does your house have a copter landing?"

Joan shook her head. "No, it's designed so that a copter

206

can't land on it. It seemed the safer choice when it was built."

"Well . . . I could put you into any enclave by copter. Or you could stay here overnight."

Jake said, "Judge, my car is a Rolls-Skoda. We'll be all right."

"I can't force you to stay. But let's get a playback on the news and see what stirred up the lice." McCampbell punched the time in, then punched for playback.

"Headline of the Hour! Brain Transplant Fraud! Our earlier flash has been confirmed; the sensational brain transplant of Tycoon Johann Smith was a hoax. The question is: Did he die a natural death? Or was he murdered? The latter theory seems likely in view of today's bald-faced attempt to steal his enormous fortune through claiming in open court that his alleged former secretary, a woman of doubtful reputation going by the name of 'Blanca'—"

Salomon growled, "Judge, would you mind shutting off that damned rot?"

McCampbell switched it off. "Seems I started something. Can't say I'm sorry. I will *not* let my courtroom be turned into a circus."

Joan Eunice said meekly, "I'm sorry, Judge."

"Eh? Joan Eunice, you are not at fault. You were forced into court needlessly and against your will; you did nothing. As for me, I hold to the old-fashioned ideal that a courtroom is where the Sovereign is present in person, dispensing equity and justice to all . . . *not* bread-and-circuses for the rabble. As long as I'm on the bench I'll run it that way, no matter how many news snoops get sore or how many illits want a livelier show."

"I'm sorry your bailiffs were hurt."

"Well, so am I. But they aren't conscripts, they are career people who know it is hazardous. And they are necessary—if that bill ever passes to disarm bailiffs, that day I quit the bench . . . and the Law as well. Jake?"

"Yes, Mac?"

"You can risk your neck if you want to, but even a Rolls-Skoda is not a Merrimac. Enough people can tip it

207

over, then they can build a bonfire around it and roast you like chestnuts . . . and there are characters out there who would do it just for kicks. No, not a word out of you; I'm not going to let her leave this building in a ground car even if I have to reconvene court for three seconds and make her a ward again. She leaves by copter. The question is: Where does she go? You could sleep in my chambers, Joan Eunice; there is a buttery in the bar and the washroom is a complete bath and that couch opens into a bed. Lumpy, I'm afraid." (Ask Judgie Wudgie if *he* goes with the bed!) (I didn't hear you—and pipe down.)

"I was going to say," Jake said mildly, "that I have a house in Safe Harbor. Unstaffed and empty but it's a safe rendezvous. You could have your Chief Bailiff tell my driver and Shotgun to wait until this quiets down, then pick us up there—although I would bet on those boys to drive through any mob and not let the car be tipped; they're mean."

"No doubt. And wind up with a hit-and-run, too; we'll do it the easy way. Either of you want to use my washroom while I phone Evelyn and the roof?"

A few minutes later Jake and Joan were about to leave; the Judge's copter was waiting for them, he having brushed aside remarks about fish. Joan said, "Judge? I think you know I am grateful, but I would like to show my thanks by doing something—money, I mean—for those men who were hurt."

"No."

"Why not? Oh, I know it was not my fault but nevertheless they were hurt because of me. You know I can afford it."

"Because they are officers of the Court and I would have to treat it as constructive bribery. Tell her, Jake."

"He's correct, Joan—although he's being stuffy about it."

"Not too stuffy. Joan Eunice, there is an enclave home for dependents of police, bailiffs, firemen, and such, killed in line of duty. Jake can tell you about it. I would rather not hear what you do about it."

"I see." Joan ignored the fact that Jake was waiting with her robe, stepped closer to McCampbell, turned her face up, and put her arms around his neck. "Does this constitute bribery?"

"I think so," McCampbell answered, putting his arms around her. "But I won't analyze it."

"Of course it's bribery! Get away from him, Brother Schmidt! I handle his bribes."

"Shut up, you noisy Mick."

Joan turned her face just as her lips were about to touch McCampbell's. "You're next on my bribe list, Brother Alec."

"So get back into line! R.H.I.P." McCampbell stopped any further words from her; she let her lips come softly open, did not hurry him. (Whee . . . *ooo!* I thought so.) (Don't let me faint, Eunice.)

Some seconds later she opened her eyes, looked up into the Judge's face. "My goodness!" she said softly.

Alec Train tapped his shoulder. "Court's adjourned, Judge. Be elsewhere."

Joan gave the Judge a quick, possessive squeeze, untangled herself and went into his former roommate's arms, turned up her face. She was careful to make this kiss as long and as warm as the other. (*Unh!* What do you think, Eunice?) (They are both oral as hell and they kiss almost as well as Jake and if Jake weren't here they would have us down on the rug this instant—break it up, dear; you've kissed him as long as you did Judgie Wudgie and Jake is getting edgy.) (All right. Spoilsport.) (Not at all—but you don't know how to handle men without upsetting them. Break!)

A moment later Jake silently helped her into her street robe. She thanked him, clicked the magnostrip, arranged the shoulder drape, let the Judge hand her into his lift. They said good-bye, the lift closed. Alec Train turned to his friend:

"Mac, kissing Brother Schmidt is more emphatic than spreading most gals."

"Amen!"

"What would it be like to be married to her? And why is it that when the parade goes by I'm always out for a short beer?"

"The O.B. damaged your head with his forceps. That's why they had to make a lawyer out of you."

"How about yourself?"

"Oh, me, too—stipulated. I wasn't bright enough to be a lawyer; I had to wangle an appointment to the bench. Christ, what a chick!"

"Passed by acclamation. Mac, having kissed her, do you really think she can be old 'Sell 'em Johann,' the terrible-tempered tycoon?"

"Well . . . everything fits—and she did have the Grip."

"And the password; I checked. But, Mac, any of our brothers, even ones whose bias hardly extends to girls, would sell our secrets—what am I saying?—would *give* them to that one. If she kissed him."

"Stipulating that you are correct in your estimate of our brothers—and I agree—Joan Eunice can't have had much chance to subvert one of them. Jake has practically had her under house arrest, at my suggestion. And Jake himself—well, he sounded like a Barb, but you can check it in that bookcase, in 'Who's Who in Law.' "

"I don't think I can walk that far. But let's assume that old Johann was a brother—easy to check—and she did know all about the Distress Fund and the fact that you needed a loan our senior year."

"Yes. That's the convincer."

"No, it's not. I mean that *Johann* would have been just as susceptible. She was his secretary; it might have amused him to spill fraternal secrets to her—grip, password, even details about the fund."

"Oh, crap, you honkie bastard. Joan Eunice is just what she purports to be—an utterly delicious girl who has Johann's brain in her skull. Alec, I concede that Joan Eunice doesn't seem much like Johann Smith. But even you might be socially acceptable if that sponge between your ears were placed in the brainpan of a creature as delectable as she is." The Judge shook his head. "She's enough to make a queen switch from A.C. to D.C."

"Man, she really got to you, didn't she?"

"And *you*, my friend. *Who* said we needed a vacation from women? You, as I recall. But you drooled over her. You would give up boys for life if she were to phone and ask for you. Don't try to fool your roomie; I know you better than Ruth does."

"I won't argue. But you're at least as far down the Street as I am, Mac . . . and she affected you the same way. Uh, does Norma know how little fishing we plan to do?"

"Sure she suspects. But she's always been tolerant. Alec, how disappointed would you be if I called off our trip? Jake may need a friendly judge in a hurry. Especially if those vultures find a shyster unscrupulous enough to buy some direct action. I'd hate to be missing if Brother Schmidt needed me."

"My God, a soul with a soul. Oddly enough I was thinking the same thing. Can't let Brother Schmidt down. Mac, could it prejudice anything if I volunteered my services—free—to Jake? If this gets sticky, he's going to need to be several places at once. I could share the load."

"And share the wealth. It would give you an excuse to see Brother Schmidt again."

"Any law against taking a profit? But Jake does need help."

"And you're familiar with the case. Alec old dear, it's a noble thought. While you did represent the Petitioners, not only have they fired you, but this was never an adversary situation; theoretically those creeps are as anxious to arrive at the truth for the benefit of their beloved grandfather as Jake is. They don't dare admit that they are trying to grab his gelt."

"I wonder if Jake has a phone in that empty house he mentioned? If not, I can leave word at the Gibraltar Club—he has rooms there—and at Johann Smith's town house. And with Jake's answering service."

"Yes. But let the call be from me; it might speed the service. We'll stay and wait for it. Ruth's not expecting you, Norma is not expecting me; I'll have dinner sent up from the basement."

"Clear thinking. So fix fresh drinks while I put in those

calls. Hey! You can reach them in your copter."

"Only via the piloting circuit. Not private. Better we keep this *tight*. Alec, it is unlikely that Jake will have anything for you to do before morning. But he might—a trip to the coast or such. You could stay on call by spending the night here."

"Well!" Alec Train stopped with his hand near the phone. "Roomie, I thought that Brother Schmidt had driven all other thoughts out of your mind. Or did I misunderstand?"

"Let's phrase it this way: It would be pleasant to discuss Brother Schmidt in intimate detail with some sympathetic person who appreciates her as much as I do."

"In that case, mix those drinks and start a lukewarm shower. I'll join you as fast as I can."

14

Jake Salomon handed Joan Eunice into the Judge's copter, got in beside her and locked the door. Quickly they were airborne. The passenger compartment was separate from the pilot's space and well soundproofed; conversation was possible. But he said nothing and tended to keep his eyes away from her.

Joan let it go on only a short time. "Jake dear? Are you angry?"

"Eh? Heavens, no. What made you think so?"

"You seemed quite distant. I thought you might be annoyed with me for having kissed Judge McCampbell and dear Mr. Train."

"Your business."

"Oh, Jake. Please don't scold me even by your manner. I've had a difficult day, especially the time I had to spend with my goddam granddaughters. It hurts, Jake, to be hated. To know that someone wants you dead. Yet I had to try to appear serene and ladylike. Be a credit to Eunice. Jake, it isn't easy to be a lady—after almost a century of being male. Do you know how I manage it at all? I say to myself, 'What would Eunice do?'—then I try to do it. Kissing those sweet and helpful men— Jake, I'm not used to kissing men. You could have trained me but you won't give me more than a good-night peck. I said to myself, 'I must thank them—and what would Eunice do?' I decided that she would kiss them the best she knew how. So I tried, even though I don't know how. Well? Is that what Eunice would have done?"

"Well . . . yes, Eunice would have kissed them." (He knows darn well I would have, dear.) (I know. He's being difficult.) (So keep punching. Tell him how wonderful he is. Joan, men *always* believe it when you tell them they are wonderful.)

"Then I don't see why you are being cold with me, Jake. I thought you were truly wonderful all day long, the way you handled things and protected me. I wanted to kiss *you* for being so wonderful—and would have, and will!—if only you would let me. Was it because I didn't stop to put my robe on before I kissed them?"

"Well . . . it would have been more ladylike."

(Punch hard on this one, dearie—for Jake knows darn well that I spread skin on him the very first time I kissed him . . . and later I kissed him bare naked the first time it was safe to. He didn't fight—he was eager.) (I'll try.)

Miss Smith looked worried, which did not suit her features. "I suppose so. But I don't know *how* to be a lady, Jake; the rules have changed so much. Eunice often startled me by what she did and how she dressed—yet I am certain that she was always a perfect lady. Tell me this, Jake, honestly and candidly, and I'll treat your answer as Gospel and use it as a yardstick for future behavior—because I *do* want to be a credit to Eunice; I want 'Joan Eunice' to be the perfect lady that Eunice was. Under those exact circumstances and being just as anxious to show appreciation to two sweet and wonderfully helpful gentlemen . . . would Eunice have put this street robe on first? Or would she have spread her sweet skin on them and let them cuddle her a bit if they wanted to—and they wanted to, I'm sure you noticed. Think about it, Jake. You knew Eunice better than I did; we know that—so give me a straight answer, because I'm going to use it as a guide in trying to *be* Eunice. Would she have played safe? Or would she have given herself?"

Jake Salomon gave a sigh that was almost a groan. "Hell, you did *exactly* what Eunice would have done. That's what upset me."

Joan sighed. "Thank you, Jake, I feel better." She loosened her seat belt, moved closer to him, ran her thumb down the magnostrip of her robe. "Can't get this pesky thing off in here. Kiss me, Jake, kiss me better than they did. Kiss me and cuddle me and tell me that Eunice would be proud of me."

"Joan!"

"Don't shame me, Jake. I'm a girl now and I need to be kissed so hard we'll forget I kissed those other two. Call me 'Eunice,' dear; please do, it's my name and I want to hear you call me by it and tell me I'm a good girl."

He groaned. "Eunice!"

She turned her face up. "Kiss me, darling."

Trembling, he gave in.

The kiss went on and on. It took Joan only seconds to turn it from tender to rugged, nor did he hold back. (Eunice? I'm going to faint.) (I'm not going to let you, sweetheart; I've waited a *long* time for this!)

Eventually Jake broke, but she stayed close and he continued to hold her. She sighed and touched her hand to his face. "Thank you, Jake dear—for this, and for everything."

"Thank *you* . . . Eunice. Joan Eunice."

"Let me be 'Eunice' a while longer. Am I a good girl? Do I do credit to her?"

"Uh . . . yes!"

"I tried. Jake dear, do you believe in ghosts? I think Eunice must have been here with us. I couldn't have done that well without her help. It often seems so."

"Uh, it's an interesting thought." (Hmmph! We ought to tickle him for that. Joan, if you tickle him under his short ribs, he comes unstuck. Helpless.) (I'll remember. But not today.) "In any case, she would have been proud of you. You're a sweet girl."

"I mean to be. To you. I love you, Jake."

He hesitated only a heartbeat. "I love you—Eunice. And Joan Eunice."

"I'm glad you made it both of us. Jake dearest, you're going to have to marry me. You know that, don't you?"

"What? Oh, heavens, dear, don't be silly. I love
215

you—but there's too much age difference."

"What? Oh, fiddlesticks! I know I'm almost a quarter of a century older than you are. But it no longer shows. And you understand me and no other man possibly could."

"*Huh!* I mean *I* am too much older than *you.*"

(Joan, don't let him talk that way! Tell him men and liquor improve with age. Or some such. Anyhow, he was feeling quite young a few minutes ago—I noticed. Did you?) (Yes. Now quiet, please.)

"Jake, you are *not* old. Goodness, I know what '*old*' is! You're a classic, Jake—and classics improve with age. And . . . just minutes ago, you were feeling quite young. I noticed."

"Uh . . . possibly. But none of your sass—youngster."

She chuckled. "Jake, it's nice to be a girl to you. I won't argue, I'll wait. In time you will realize that you need me and I need you, and that no one else will do for either of us. Then you can make an honest woman of me."

"Harrumph! That might be more than I could manage, even with a marriage license."

"Rude darling. I can wait. You can't escape me, Jake. Eunice won't let you."

"Well . . . I'm durned if I'll argue; it would just make you stubborn. In either of your personae. My old friend Johann was as stubborn a man as I've ever met—and Eunice was just as stubborn in her own sweet way. And, dear, I never know which one you are. Sometimes I think you've acquired that split personality your doctors were afraid of."

(Get him off this subject!) (I will, dear—but not by being jumpy about it. Aren't we ever going to tell him?) (Yes, of course. But not soon, Joan. Not till we're in the clear. Remember those straps.) "Jake darling, I'm not surprised that you feel that way about me—because I do myself. Oh, nothing psychopathic, just the odd situation I am in. You've known me how long? A quarter of a century."

"Twenty-six years, pushing twenty-seven."

"Yes. And while I was never given to copping feels from female employees—would you say that 'horny old bastard' was an honest description of me?"

216

"I've never known your behavior toward women to be other than gentlemanly."

"Oh, come now, Jake! You're talking to Johann at the moment. Level with me."

Salomon grinned. "Johann, I think you were a horny old bastard right up to the day we took you in for surgery."

"That's better. Years after I was benched in the matter . . . first for social reasons, the fact that an old man looks a fool if he behaves like a young stud, and later through illness and physical incapacity—years after I was benched my interest in a pretty face or a pretty leg was unflagging. Then I acquired Eunice's healthy young body. Female. Look at me Jake. *Female.*"

"I've noticed!"

"Not the way *I* have! Even though you've kissed me—a real kiss and I loved it, dear—you can't have noticed the way *I* have been forced to. I'm cyclic now, Jake, ruled by the Moon; I've menstruated twice. Do you know what that means?"

"Eh? Natural phenomenon. Healthy."

"It means that the body controls the brain as much as the brain controls the body. I'm tempery and inclined to tears just before my period. My feelings, my emotions, even my thoughts are female—yet I have almost a century of male emotions and attitudes. Take my pretty little nurse-companion, Winnie—and would you *like* to take her?"

"Uh . . . damn you, Johann! She's a nice girl. Fifth Amendment."

"She is indeed a nice girl. But because I'm Eunice as well as Johann I know how she feels. She's as female as a cat in heat—and you're an old bull, Jake, and dominant, and if you *wanted* to take Winnie, she wouldn't put up more than token resistance."

"Joan Eunice, don't talk nonsense. I'm three times her age." (Boss, what are you getting at?) (I'm not sure but I'm getting there.) (Well, don't get Winnie knocked up on the way. I thought we were saving Jake for *us.*) (Don't be a pig, little piglet. Winnie's a nurse; she sees to her contras as carefully as she cleans her teeth.) "Jake dear, I'm not much older than Winnie in my body . . . and you've known and

217

loved this body, even though I have no memory of it. We know that Eunice was always a lady—so how did you ever manage to get started with her? Did you rape her?" (Hell, no, *I* raped *him*—but he was a pushover.)

"That's a most unfair question!"

"It's a very female question. Knowing you from many years of association—and knowing Eunice both from some years of association but most importantly from now having her body and glands and hormones and deepest emotions—I suspect that you were far too proud to make a pass at her so she found some way to make clear that you were welcome. Once you were *certain* that Eunice was not trying to make a fool of you—that settled it. Well? Am I right?" (If he says No, he's lying. It took five minutes, sister—and would have been all over in ten but we were interrupted. Had to wait till next day. Remember the mermaid getup? Had to scrub it off before I went home; Jake and I ruined it—and I had to tell Joe a sincere fib.) (Did he believe you?) (I think so. He was painting . . . which means he hardly notices anything else.)

"Jake, are you going to answer? Or let me draw my own conclusions—possibly mistaken?"

"I could answer that it's none of your business!"

"And you would be right and Johann apologizes. But *not* Eunice. Jake, that's what Eunice's body tells me must have happened. But I can't be certain and I do want to be like her and if that is *not* what she would have done because it is not what she did—then tell me. I'm not asking for intimate details." (Aw, get the juicy parts, dearie—I want to know how it seemed to *him*, every sweaty detail. I already know how it seemed to *me*—and I'll tell you.) (Don't be so right-now, darling—I'm trying to gentle him.)

"Joan Eunice—no, 'Eunice!' You always have had the damnedest way of getting your own way."

"Is that an answer, Jake? I don't have Eunice's memory." (Says who? Boss, I've figured out something—and it's not flatworms. Everyone has erasable memory and non-erasable memory, just like Betsy—and that non-erasable part is the *me* that's still here now that I'm dead. 'Soul' maybe. Names don't matter; it's that part

218

that's not just glands and plumbing.) (Save the philosophy until we're alone in bed tonight, Eunice; I'm trying to cope with a man—and it's heavy going.) (Do you think we're going to be *alone* in bed tonight? Want to bet?) (I don't know—and I'm scared.) (Don't be scared. When it happens, you recite the Money Hum and I'll drive. Once around the course and you'll be ready to solo. Except that I'll always be with you. Know sumpin, Boss honey? It's even nicer to *be* you than it was to be your secretary. Or will be, once we're back on ground rations.) (Huh?) (Soul talk, dear—means sex. I had it for fourteen years—and I'm *hungry*.) (I had it over five times that long—I'm at least five times as hungry.) (Could be—you're a horny bitch, Boss.)

Jake finally answered, "Joan, I don't think it's fair to Eunice's memory for me to tell tales about her—but I'll concede your point, assuming that you want to learn, for your own guidance, as much as possible about how she behaved. Eunice was honest and straightforward"—(I'm devious as a snake—but that's what I wanted Jake to believe.)—"and she apparently decided that she liked me that much . . . and made it easy for me. It was neither rape nor seduction." (It was both, but I did *not* want him to think so. He's a darling, Joan. When he's gentled enough—slip the bit into his mouth. But let him think he asked for it.) (I'll try. Meantime I'm still doing this emotional strip-down—and you listen instead of interrupting; you might learn something about *me*.) (I'll be good, Boss. Mostly.)

"I felt certain that it must have been that way, Jake—knowing you, knowing her. But that's only one side of me as I am now—the 'Eunice' side. The other side is Johann, with almost a century of male orientation. I told you I now understand Winnie, as a girl—because now I *am* a girl. But there is still Johann, alone with Winnie every day—and it's all I can manage to keep my hands off her." (Hmmph! You *don't* keep your hands off her.) (I said, Shut up! I haven't let it get past heavy cuddle. If you and I ever stroll Gay Street, you shameless mermaid, it will be dessert, not the pièce de résistance.) (That piece won't resist!) (Hush up!) "Do you understand, Jake? Old Johann—*me!*—thinks that Winnie is quite some dish."

"Well . . . I understand it—in Johann."

"I wonder if you would understand it in Eunice? Jake, how do you feel about homosexuality?"

"I don't feel anything about it. Never been interested."

"Not even curious? Jake, I'm a full generation older than you are. When I was a kid, homosexuality or 'perversion' as it was called, was hardly even a myth; I never heard of it until long after I was centered on girls. Oh, I don't mean there wasn't any; I know now that there was, lots of it. But it was spoken of seldom and kept under cover. When I was fifteen, a man made a pass at me—and I didn't know what he was after; he just scared me.

"Would a fifteen-year-old boy today be that innocent? You know he wouldn't be; there are books and magazines and pictures—and other boys—to make certain that he understands even if he doesn't join in. The Government just misses endorsing it as a way to hold down our outlandish overpopulation—would endorse it openly, I feel sure, if it were not that a large percentage disapprove of it publicly while practicing it in private. It reminds me of that weird period in my youth when people voted dry and drank wet and the bootlegger was more sought after than the black-market butcher is today. How long has it been since the last 'sex offense' was prosecuted?"

"Rape by violence is still prosecuted; I can't recall any others in the last twenty years. Blue laws about sex are dead letters; Supreme Court decisions have made them impossible to prosecute. Correction: Unlicensed pregnancy is a Federal offense under the 'General Welfare' clause . . . but I've often wondered what would happen if a case were ever allowed to reach the Supreme Court."

"That's the only 'sex crime' which was not a crime when I was a kid, Jake. But I was talking about the 'crime against nature' which is no longer a crime; it isn't even a peccadillo, it arouses less disapproval than smoking. However, by the time homosexuality was socially acceptable, my attitudes were long frozen. But I wonder what Eunice thought about it? Did you ever discuss it with her?"

Jake snorted. "Believe me, Johann—sorry, Joan Eunice—that was *not* a subject we had time for!"

"I suppose not. Nor did she discuss it with me." (Fibber!) "But she gave me a gentle reprimand about it once."

"So? How?"

"Oh, one day before I was bedfast, a messenger delivered something to my office. He was a real nancy-pants—lots of makeup, false eyelashes, curled hair, and waved his hips. A high, girlish lisp and oh so graceful in his gestures. After he was gone I made some intolerant remark and Eunice told me gently that, while she didn't find such one-way boys attractive, she didn't see anything wrong in a man loving man, or a woman loving a woman." (Hey! I don't remember any such conversation.) (So I'm a liar. But you *could* have said it—and I'm making a point.)

"Yes, that sounds like Eunice. She was tolerant of people's frailties."

"My point is that, Eunice being the age she was, she was certain to be indifferent to—perhaps I should say 'understanding about' what Johann thought of as 'perversities.' But here's what I'm getting at, Jake; I find Winnie sexually attractive. I also find Alec Train and Judge McCampbell sexually attractive. Startled me. And *you*—which did not startle me. But today was the first time I have been thoroughly kissed by very male men. And I *liked* it. Shook me." (How about dear Doctor?) (None of your lip, sweet lips—we don't tell Jake *that* one.)

Joan Eunice went on, "There is my dilemma. Which time am I being homosexual? With Winnie? Or with you three very male bulls?"

"Joan, you ask the damnedest questions."

"Because I'm in the damnedest situation a man ever found himself in. I'm not the ordinary sex change of a homo who gets surgery and hormone shots to tailor his male body into fake female. I'm not even a mixed-up XXY or an XYY. This body is a normal female XX. But the

221

brain in it has had a man's canalization and many years of enthusiastic male sex experience. So tell me, Jake, which time am I being normal, and which time perverse?"

"Uh . . . I'm forced to say that your female body controls."

"But *does* it? Psychologists claim that sexual desire and orgasm take place in the brain—*not* in the genitals. My *brain* is XY."

"I think you are trying to confuse the witness."

"No, Jake, I'm the one who is confused. But possibly not as confused as the young people today. You know they claim to have six sexes."

"Heard of it. Nonsense."

"Not entirely. I've been doing lots of reading during my de-facto house arrest, trying to find out *who* I am, *what* I am, *how* I should behave. They label these so-called sexes both by behavior and physiology, with a new school of psychology—when wasn't there a new one?—to account for them. The six are ortho-male, ortho-female, ambi-male, ambi-female, homo-male, homo-female—and some list a seventh, the solos or narcissists. Even an eighth, the non-sex, the neuters, both physical and psychological."

"And I say it's nonsense."

"I do, too, but not for the same reason. From my unique experience, embracing both physiological sexes directly and not by hearsay, I say there is just *one* sex. Sex. *SEX!* Some people have so little sexual drive that they might as well be neuters no matter whether they are concave or convex. Some people have very strong sexual natures—and again the shape of the body doesn't figure. Such as my former self, horny long after sex had abandoned me. Such as *you*, darling—taking a lovely young married woman less than half your age as your mistress. Such as Eunice—happily married at home, I think—"

"Yes, she was. I felt guilty about it."

"But not too guilty to share her riches. Jake, I wouldn't speak to you if you had scorned her. I was about to name Eunice as my third example of a person strongly sexed. Enough sexual drive in her body—I *know!*—for *anything.* Enough love in her heart—I feel certain—for any number

222

I *know* she loved me, even though she was too warmly empathic to mock me by offering me what I could not accept—and did give me, lavishly, the only thing I could accept—her beauty, for my eyes. Jake, I think Eunice was limited in her love only by time. She kept you happy—"

"She certainly did!"

"I'm just as certain she did so without depriving her husband. Jake, do you have reason to believe that she limited herself to you—and her husband?"

"Uh— Damn you, Johann! I don't *know*. But I don't think she had *time*. Uh, I used up all the sneak-out time she could manage."

(Look, Boss, I'll tell you about every time I struck a blow for equal rights. Don't pester Jake.) (You're missing the point, Eunice. I'm forcing Jake to move Saint Eunice off her pedestal—that's the *only* way we'll ever get him.)

"How do you know? Can you be sure she didn't tell you the same sort of little white lies she told her husband? For that matter, Jake, Joe may have been as proud of his antlers as an old buck deer—the percentage of husbands who are *pleased* by their wives' adulteries has been climbing steadily in this country at least since nineteen-fifty—see any of the kinseys. That he loved her we both are certain. That does not prove he tried to keep her in a cage. Or wanted to."

"Joan, I would just as lief you didn't run down Eunice to me."

"Jake darling! I am *not* running her down. I am trying to find out what you know about her, so that I can model myself more closely after her. I loved her—and love her still more today. But if you told me that you *knew* she was mistress to six other men, a whore on the side, and playing girl games in her spare time—well, I've never known you to lie to me, Jake, so I would try to go and do likewise. You haven't told me much but what you *have* told me confirms what I believed—that Eunice was a perfect lady, with enough love in her heart to love three men at once and give each of them exactly what he needed to make him happy." (Thank you, Boss. Shall I bow?) (Quiet, little darling.) "But not a wanton, never a slut, and—while she wasn't

223

prudish—I doubt if Winnie would have interested her."
(Now wait one frimping minute!) (I'm telling him what he
wants to hear, dear—if you want Winnie, we'll keep it out
of Jake's sight.) (*Who* wants Winnie? You dirty old man!)
(We *both* do—but it may be smart never to let it hatch.
Dearest, Winnie wouldn't look at us with a man around.)
(Want to bet?)

Joan sighed. "Jake, with my unique double inheritance it
would be easy for me to turn ambi-female. I'm not going
to, because I don't think Eunice would. With the deep
female drive this body has—bloodstream brimming with
hormones and gonads the size of gourds is the way it
feels—I could easily become 'No-Pants Smith, the Girl
Most Likely To.' Very easily—as Johann Smith was an old
vulgarian who regretted only the temptations he had been
forced to pass up. But I'm not going to do that, either, as
Eunice did not behave that way. But if I don't get married
fairly soon, I'm going to find it hard to stay off the tiles."

"Joan, I love you—but I am *not* going to marry you. It's
out of the question."

"Then you had better help my granddaughters to
swindle me."

"Eh? Why?"

"You know why. A multimillionaire who is young and
female stands as much chance of getting a good husband as
that well-known tissue-paper dog had of chasing that
asbestos cat through Hell. Lots of them in our
country—and all they ever got were Georgian princes,
riding masters, and other gigolos. I don't want one, won't
have one. I'd rather be broke, like Winnie, and take what
love I can find. Jake, besides the fact that you understand
me and no one else can, you'd still be in my top ten because
my money does not impress you. Quite aside from
wonderful fact that I love you and you love me, any
marriage broker would call us a perfect match."

"Hardly. There's still the matter of age—body ages.
Joan, a man who marries at my age isn't taking a wife, he's
indenturing a nurse."

"Oh, frog hair, Jake! You don't need one and I'll lay
even money that you'll stay strong and virile right through

my breeding period. But when you do need one I'll nurse you. In the meantime we'll sing 'September Song'—you lead, I'll harmonize."

"I sing bass. And I won't sing 'September Song.' "

"Jake? We could buy you a new body. When you need it."

"No, Joan. I've had a long run and a good one, most of it happy, all of it interesting. When my time comes, I'll go quietly. I won't make the mistake you did, I won't let myself fall into the hands of the medics, with their artificial kidneys and their dials and their plumbing. I'll die as my ancestors died."

She sighed. "And *you* called *me* stubborn. I've taken you up on a high mountain and shown you the kingdoms of the earth—and you tell me it's Los Angeles. All right, I'll quit pestering you—and humbly accept any love you can spare. Jake, will you take me out on the town and introduce me to eligible young men? You can spot a fortune hunter—I think Eunice may be too naïve, too inclined to think the best of people." (Rats, Boss, I bought me a gigolo with my eyes open . . . and, since I wasn't kidding myself, I bought top quality.) (I know you did, darling—but the Joe Brancas in this world are as scarce as the Jake Salomons.)

"Joan Eunice, if you want me to escort you, I'll be honored . . . and I'll try to keep pascoodnyaks away from you."

"I'll hold you to that, you not-so-very-old darling. Jake, I asked if you believed in ghosts. Do you have any religion?"

"Eh? None. My parents were Orthodox, I think you know. My Bar Mitzvah speech was so praised that I had to fight to study law instead of being trained as a rabbi. But I shook off all that before I entered college."

"Parallels me, somewhat. My grandparents came from the south of Germany, Catholic. So the priests had a crack at me first. Then we moved to the Middle West before I started school, and Papa, who was never devout, decided it would be better—better for business, maybe—to be a Baptist. So I got the Bible-Belt routine, with hellfire and damnation and my sins washed away with full immersion.

It was the Bible-Belt indoctrination that stuck, particularly the unconscious attitudes.

"But, consciously and intellectually, I shucked off all of it when I was fourteen—probably the only real intellectual feat of my life. I became an aggressive atheist—except at home—and scorned to believe in anything I could not bite. Then I backed away from that—atheism is as fanatic as any religion and it's not my nature to be fanatic—and became a relaxed agnostic, unsure of final answers but more patient. I stayed that way three-quarters of a century; I left religion to the shamans and ignored it."

"My own policy."

"Yes. But let me tell you something that happened while I was dead."

"What? You were never dead, Joan—Johann, damn it!—you were merely unconscious."

"I wasn't, eh? With no body, and my brain cut off from the world and me not even aware of myself? If that is not death, Jake, it is an unreasonable facsimile. I told you that I thought Eunice's spirit has often given me a hand."

"I heard you. I ignored it."

"You stiff-necked old bastard. I haven't taken up séances and such. But here is what happens. When I am in a quandary—often, these days—I ask myself, 'What would Eunice do?' That's all it takes, Jake; I know at once. No ectoplasm or voices from a medium—just instant knowledge *not* based on my own experience. Such as this afternoon when I decided in a split second to kiss Alec and Mac. No hesitation—you saw! That's *not* the way old Johann would behave . . . and yet you tell me I haven't missed behaving like Eunice even once. That's why it feels as if her sweet spirit were guiding me. Any comment?"

"Mmm . . . No. You do behave like her . . . other than when you tell me flatly that you're speaking as Johann. But I don't believe in ghosts. Johann, if I thought I had to go on being Jake Salomon throughout all eternity, I'd—well, I would register a complaint at the Main Office."

"Let me tell you what happened to *me* at the Main Office."

"Huh?"

"While I was dead, Jake. I was in this—place. There was a very old Man with a long white beard. He had a big book. He looked at me, then consulted His book, then looked back at me. He said, 'Son, you've been a bad boy. But not too bad, so I'm going to give you another chance. Do your best and don't worry; you'll have help.' What do you think, Jake?" (What is this, Boss? Did it happen to *you*, too?) (Eunice, if it happened to you, it happened to me; it's the same thing. And *you* are my help, beloved. My guardian angel.) (Oh, frimp you! I'm no angel, I'm *me*.) (A very earthy angel, beloved darling—just what I need.) (Love you, too, you dirty old man.)

Salomon answered slowly, "Anthropomorphism. Right out of your Bible-Belt Sunday school."

"Oh, certainly. It had to be in symbols I could understand. If I had been a creature from around Proxima Centauri, the old Man and the beard might have been a Thing with eight tentacles and faceted eyes. Cliché symbols are nothing against it; I've never thought it was a physical experience. Men live by symbols, Jake. That —symbolic—experience was as real to me as any physical experience. And allow me to point out that I *do* have a second chance and I *have*, and *am* having, lots of help—from you especially, from Mac and Alec, from doctors and nurses . . . and also from something inside that tells me instantly, in any difficult situation, exactly how Eunice would handle it. I don't say it's Eunice . . . but it's *not* Johann; he wouldn't know how. Well?"

Salomon sighed. "Of the inventing of gods there is no end. And almost always anthropomorphic. Joan, if you are going in for that sort of self-delusion, why not go whole hog and join a nunnery?"

"Because Eunice would not. Although she might enjoy revamping a monastery."

Jake chuckled. "She might, at that."

"Maybe I should try it—since you are so damn chinchy about making me an honest woman. More likely I'll change my name again and disappear and wind up in a crib in Bombay. Will you come visit me, Jake?"

"No. Too hot."

"Chinchy. Mean old Jake. You wouldn't refuse to go see Eunice because of heat."

"Eunice would never wind up in a crib."

"No, she wouldn't. So I have to go on being a lady even though it's quite a strain on old Johann."

"Poor you. All you have is youth, beauty, and half as much money as the I.R.S."

"And *you*, Jake. I could lose the rest and still be rich." (I was wondering if you would see that opening. Sister, you don't need my advice; I think I'll take a vacation.) (You promised to stay!) (Yes, Boss darling. I can't leave; we're Siamese twins. But even if I could, I'd stay because I want to.) (Eunice beloved, I have never been happier in my life.) Joan Eunice moved closer to Jake. "Jake dear, I have never been happier in my life."

A brassy voice from the cockpit said, "I am about to swing for landing. Please secure seat belts."

Salomon answered, "Seat belts fastened and now being tightened. Proceed with landing." To Joan he said, "Straighten up, Eunice—and do snap up that magno."

Joan Eunice pouted her lip and obeyed.

15

Security check took little time; Salomon was known to the enclave guards and the copter was expected. It was a short walk from the landing to Salomon's house but, as in all upper-class enclaves, inhabitants in sight outdoors pretended not to see them. The door opened to Jake's voice and again they were private.

Joan Eunice took off her street robe and handed it to Jake, saying, "May I look around? Jake, it's been years since I've been here; you've made changes."

"Some. Moved my personal gear to the Gib or to your house, not much left but furniture which I'll sell with the house. Oh, I keep some clothing and toilet articles here, and I can find us a drink and a tin of biscuits. Perhaps smoked oysters or caviar; we have to kill an hour or two. Or I could send out for dinner."

"Let me see what there is in your kitchen; I would enjoy playing housewife. And I do want to look around."

"Look all you like, but tell me what you want to drink. Joan, have you ever *been* in a kitchen?"

"None of your lip, lad; I'm a good cook. Mama taught me to make Apfelstrudel—dough you could read print through and so light it melted in your mouth—before you were born. Sherry, or a Dubonnet highball—no Schnaps, I'm not risking it yet."

"I'll stack my kosher cooking against your Bavarian

messes any day, girl. The Goyim can't cook the way the Chosen People can."

"Oh, pooh, you fake Jew. You haven't tasted my pot roast with noodles. I bached between wives—and cooks—and mistresses, and I always cooked. Jake, wouldn't it be fun to cook for each other and swap recipes? We could do it here. I don't dare enter my own kitchen; Della would faint."

"Might be fun. We can eat my cooking when your boasts don't pan out. Excuse me; I'll see what liquor there is."

Joan Eunice headed straight for the master bedroom. (Eunice, is *this* one of the places?) (Of course. See that sag in the bed? Boss, this is the only place we managed an all-night. Heavenly!) ('All night?' Then his mobiles do more than suspect; they know.) (Oh, they may suspect but it doesn't matter. Charlie isn't interested in women, and Rockford—well, he's on my team. He approves of anything immoral, illegal, or dishonest—and my conduct was all three, by his standards. He's an atavism. But the all-night—I doubt if they suspected. We used more fan-dancing to keep it out of their sight than Joe's sight—things involving two hired Brink's cars and a non-existent errand for you.) (How did you fan-dance it for Joe?) (Didn't. I thought up a story and told Jake I would use it—then told Joe that I had met a man I wanted to spend a night with . . . did he mind if I was away Friday night?)

(As simple as that?) (Yes, Boss. We both were free but we were careful never to hurt each other. Only a second-class contract—since I was licensed for children and Joe was not. Either of us could have registered a dissolution on three days' notice.)

(But what did Joe say?) (Nodded and went on painting. He kissed me good-bye and told me to have fun; Joe was always sweet. But he may not have missed me. He was painting from a new model, a beautiful boy who was a frimp type. Joe may have been changing his luck; he sometimes did.)

(And *you* didn't mind?)

(That beautiful boy? Boss, you've *got* to move into the twenty-first century, now that you're me. What possibl harm? I've told you and told you that Joe and I were *always* careful of each other's happiness; what more could I ask? Besides, I don't know that Joe had his eye on him other than as a model but—well, if they had invited me to move to Troy with them, I wouldn't have minded, for a night or two. I've always preferred older men—but the boy was pretty as a Palomino and clean as a sterilized cup; I wouldn't have found it boring. Plus the fact that a woman is flattered if two males like her enough to let her watch what *they* do.)

(Eunice my love, you continue to startle me. That angle I would never have thought of. Yes, I guess it would be a compliment, in a way. I think that men—even men today—are shyer about such things than women are.)

(Men are horribly shy, Boss—whereas women usually are not. We just pretend to be, when it's expected of us. Look, a woman is a belly with a time bomb inside, and women know it and can never get away from it. They either quit being shy—no matter how they behave to please men—or they go crazy; it's the choice we have to make. And high time *you* made that choice, dear. Accept your femaleness and live with it. Be happy.) (I think I have.) (You're coming along. But sometimes it feels like the bravado of a little boy who says, 'I am not either scared!' when he's ready to wet his pants, he's so frightened.) (Well, maybe. But I've got you holding my hand.) (Yes, dearest. Mama will take care of you.)

Joan went into Jake's bathroom, primarily to snoop. She had just found something she half expected to find—when she heard Jake's voice. "Hey! Where are you? Oh! Coming, or going? Fixed you Chablis over ice, best I could do."

"That'll do fine. Jake. Was this *hers*?" She held up a luxurious negligee—two ounces of cobweb.

Jake gulped. "Yes. Sorry."

"I'm not sorry." Suddenly Joan stripped off the Cling-Ons, shoved down her frill-skirt panties and stepped out of them, leaving her bare from sandals to eyebrows, put on the negligee. "Do I wear it the way she would? Wups, I wrapped it man-style." She rewrapped the lap-over to the left. "Do I do her justice?"

"Eunice! *Eunice!*"

She folded it back, let it slither to the floor, went into his arms, let him sob against her face: "That's enough, darling, Eunice doesn't want you to cry. Eunice wants you to be happy. Both Eunice and Joan Eunice. Hold me tight, Jake. We're lost and lonely—and all we have is each other." While she cuddled him and soothed him, she opened the zipdown of his shirt. (Eunice, I'm scared!) (Easy does it, dear. Chant the Money Hum to yourself; I've taken over. Om Mani Padme Hum.) (Om Mani Padme Hum. Om Mani—)

Joan was jerked out of it by the telephone signal. She pulled her mouth from Jake's and started to cry. "Oh, damn!"

Jake said huskily, "Ignore it. It's a mistake, no one knows I'm here."

"Uh—If we don't answer, they'll try again and interrupt us again. I'll take care of it, dear. Where is the pesky thing? Living room?"

"Yes, but there's an extension over there."

"Keep thinking nice thoughts." Joan hurried over, high heels tapping, stood close to the pickup so that only her face would be seen, flipped the switch—said in Eunice's most crisp secretarial voice: "Mr. Salomon's residence. Who is calling?"

The screen stayed blank. "Recorded. Urgent call for Counselor Salomon, third attempt."

"Urgency noted. Proceed. Who is calling?"

Another voice came on, screen still blank. "This is Mr. Salomon's answering service. Judge McCampbell has placed an urgent call. I told the Judge that the Counselor was more likely to be at his club or at the Johann Smith residence, but he insisted that I keep trying this code, too. Is he there?"

"One moment." Joan glanced back, noted with annoyance that Jake had closed his shirt and picked up her clothes. "I have Mr. Salomon. Can you reach Judge McCampbell? I will hold."

"Thank you. One moment."

Joan stepped still closer and tilted the pickup to make

232

certain that it caught only her face. Jake stepped up by her, handed her her clothes. She accepted them, did not put them on.

The screen lighted. "Jake, we— Hey! Brother Schmidt!"

"Alec! How nice!"

"Step back so I can see you, dear. Mac, don't shove," Train added as the Judge's face appeared by his in the screen. "Is Jake there?"

"Right beside me, boys."

"All I can see is his shirt. Stand on a box, honey, so that you're both on screen; this must be a four-way conference. Or back away."

"Here he is." Joan tilted the pickup higher, reluctantly pressed the cups to her breasts, stepped into her frill-skirt, wiggled it into place. Then she backed off. "Can you see me now?"

"Not well enough," the Judge's resonant baritone answered. "Jake, back off a little. Joan, you need a stool. Better yet, Jake, hold her up in your arms—you lucky man."

"What's the message, gentlemen? And, thank you Judge, for your flitter. We were delivered quickly and safely."

"De nada, compadre. Jake, my old roomie got a brilliant idea—no doubt through long association with me." The Judge explained what each was willing to do in order to speed confirmation of Joan's identity. "This can be our comm center. I am going to live in my chambers a few days—ready to issue a warrant, phone a judge in another jurisdiction or whatever. Then we'll rush it through my court and crowd them into an appeal—get this nailed down tight. Meanwhile Alec is your man Friday. Want him to go anywhere in a hurry? He's stupid but healthy, and losing a night's sleep to time-zone changes is good for him."

"Probably not before morning. But I'm relieved, gentlemen; I've been wondering how I could be everywhere I need to be. Since I'm retired from everything but Joan's personal affairs, I'm without staff—and I've been cudgeling my brain trying to think whom I could get who would be reliable and competent. As we all know, this is touchy."

233

"We know!" agreed Alec. "And we're going to fix those harpies—aren't we, Mac?"

"Yes—but legally and so that it cannot be reversed. Jake, you can reach us here—and don't hesitate to wake us if you decide you want Alec to catch a midnight liner. Where will you be? Your house?"

"Until my car arrives; then we'll be at Joan's. Or on our way. My answering service can flip you into my car's wavelength. It's a longish drive."

"We'll be in touch. Don't worry, Jake, and don't let Joan worry. We'll have her baptized before you can say 'missing heir.' "

"I'm not worried," said Joan, "but I feel like crying. Boys—Brothers—how can I thank you?"

"Shall we tell her, Mac? Would she blush? Thank *me*, that is, Brother Schmidt; don't thank Brother Mac; he's just doing his duty, what the taxpayers reluctantly pay him for. But you can thank *me*—I'm a volunteer."

"I'll thank you both, in whatever way you wish," Joan said simply.

"You heard that, Mac? Brother Schmidt committed herself—and you can't break a promise between Brothers, that's the old Bita Pi law. Brother Schmidt Joan Eunice honey, back off and let us see *all* of you. Jake, get out of pickup; you ruin the composition. Go have a beer. Take a nap."

"Ignore him, he's drunk." advised his former roommate.

"So's Mac, we've been working on it. But I'm not too drunk to hop a guided missile, Jake, if you say to."

"Jake," said the Judge, "this is getting out of hand. Not that I disagree with this low forehead's enthusiasm. Good night, sir. Good night, Joan. Off."

Joan Eunice flipped the switch, made certain that the screen was dead, started undressing.

"Joan. Stop that."

She went on removing her saucy, scanty clothing, heeled off her sandals, then stood facing him. "Jake, I refuse to be treated like a porcelain doll. You had me expecting to be treated as a woman."

He sighed. "I know. But the golden moment passed."

"Well . . . I'm not going to dress. You've seen this body many times, we both know—and I want us both to get easy about it. Actually I'm shy, Jake; I'm only weeks old, as a woman, and not used to it. But I want to get used to it. With you."

"Well— As you wish, dear; you know how beautiful I think you are. What shall we do? Read aloud to each other till my car arrives? Watch video?"

"Beast. If you were a gentleman you would at least take your clothes off. Instead you are a difficult, stubborn beast and I don't know why I love you. Except that Eunice loved you—*loves* you, wherever she is—so I have to love you. Jake, if you won't take me to bed, at least sit down in that big chair and let me crawl up into your lap. We can talk. We'll talk about Eunice."

He sighed. "Girl, you'll give me a heart attack yet. All right, come curl up in my lap. On one condition."

"Jake, I'm not sure I'll agree to any conditions. I'm in a very unstable state."

"You certainly are, dear. But it's *my* lap. No ticky, no washee."

"I should go back to the courthouse; I don't think Mac and Alec would insist on conditions. Might as well relax, Jake; I'm climbing into your lap with no more yatter. There! That's better. Arms around me, please."

"First the condition. That you not try to rape me in a chair—"

"Don't think I could."

"You'd be surprised what can be done in a chair, Joan."

"Would not, I've done 'em all. As Johann. But they require cooperation."

"Mmm, so they do. —and that, as soon as my car arrives, you dress at once and no nonsense, and we go home."

"All right—since you made that 'we.' I was afraid you were feeling ornery enough to send me home alone. In which case I was going to have Rockford and Charlie take me straight back to Alec and Mac. Aren't they delightful wolves, Jake? Hold me tight. The only way you can protect me from them is you-know-what."

"Hmm. Joan, can you keep a chuckle to yourself?"

"Well . . . I promise never to tell anyone but Eunice."

"Eh? Okay, I don't think you would break a promise made that way. But, let me add that if you did tell, it would hurt Alec and Mac both—and Eunice would not like that."

"No, Eunice certainly would not like that. Jake, you're going to be able to hogtie me with that phrase the rest of my life." (Don't fret, Boss honey. Any time Jake is wrong, I'll give you the ammo to change his tune.) "All right, I'll tell no one but Eunice—and the old Man with the long white beard next time I see Him."

"Safe enough. Okay, here's the chuckle. Your two charming wolves—and they *are* charming—are as gay as Julius Caesar."

"What? Jake, I have trouble believing that."

"I won't offer proof but I assure you that I know it beyond any reasonable doubt."

"But— Look, dear, I've *kissed* them. I may be an ersatz female . . . but not where it matters, and I *know* those kisses weren't phony. They were hot over me. Shucks, darling, I could tell it by Braille. Besides, they are married."

"I said, 'As gay as Julius Caesar,' dear—not Governor Arkham."

"Oh. Ambi gay, you mean. I still have trouble believing it. Doesn't it show at all? Even in a kiss?" (*I* spotted it, Joan, the potential at least. But they're still wolves . . . and we may be back there someday. To thank them.) (Eunice, is that the only way a female can thank a man?) (That's the only convincing way, twin. This is news?) (No, beloved—but it was possible that your generation had learned something mine had not. They haven't. Not in anythng you've told me. Just more open about it.)

"Joan, there is *no* way to spot it, if an ambi does not want it known. Either ambi, or clear over the line and no return. Look, when you were Johann, could you spot a virgin?"

"Jake, I'm not sure I ever met a virgin. But you have."

"You must mean someone we both know."

"Of course."

236

"Who? Winnie? Wouldn't have thought so. But she does blush easily."

"Not Winnie. If she is one, I didn't have her in mind." (You crawled out of that one!) (Winnie can tell her own secrets. Honey girl? Does Jake know about your baby?) (No, and we're not going to tell him!) (Didn't intend to, darling—just didn't want to be caught foolish.)

"Well, I can't guess. Who is this paragon?"

"Me."

"Uh— But—" Jake Salomon shut up.

"Sure, sure, dear—Johann was not, and Eunice was married. Not to mention an old wolf who tripped her." (I tripped him.) "But none of that applies to this new female in your lap. I'm a virgin. But would not have been, by now—I think—if that goddam phone hadn't sounded. Don Ameche should never have invented it."

"Who's he? Some Russian? Alexander Graham Bell invented the telephone."

"An obsolete joke, Jake—sorry. Ameche played Bell in a movie, oh, about the time you were three or four years old. But let's not talk about long-dead actors, nor my virginity that I can't get rid of; let's discuss Eunice." (My favorite subject!) "That overhead light is in my eyes; where can I squeeze it down? And will you keep your lap warm while I trot and do it?"

"I can do it from here. Is that better?"

"Oh, much! I want to see you, darling—but floor lights are enough. Now tell me about Eunice. I not only want to be like her in other ways . . . but I would like to learn to make love the way she did. As much as you'll tell me."

"Joan, you know I can't tell such things about a lady."

"But I *am* Eunice, Jake. I just don't have her memory. So I need help. Eunice loved you, and still loves you, I feel certain—and Joan Eunice loves you—with a love not at all like the fierce affection Johann always had for his one friend—Joan Eunice loves you with a love that comes also from Eunice's sweet body that I wear so proudly. So tell me about her. Was she as eager as I am?"

"Uh—" (Slide your hand inside his shirt, twin. Be careful not to tickle.) "Joan, Eunice was eager. I had trouble

237

believing it at first—me an old wreck and she so young and beautiful. But she managed to make me believe it."

"But you are *not* an old wreck, darling. You are in better shape than I was at your age. Oh, your face has character lines; it has a granite majesty that impresses everyone. But your body is as firm and trim as a man half your age. Muscly. And your skin is smooth and elastic, not that distressing crepelike texture I remember too well. Darling . . . even if you divorce me later, will you marry me soon enough to let me have your baby?" (Hon, you're knocking him out of the ring! That's one I never dared use.)

"Eunice! Joan Eunice."

"Oh, I don't mean soon enough for *you*—I mean soon enough for *me*. I may have fifteen more fertile years—but the sooner the better; a woman ought not to have her first baby at past forty. But *you* will be making babies as long as you live. How many children do you have, Jake beloved?"

"Three. You met two of them once. And four grandchildren."

"I don't mean those, I mean others. I'll bet you have at least a dozen more, here and there. You've been rich a long time; you could afford it. How many that you haven't mentioned?"

"Joan Eunice, that's snoopy."

"Yes, and no one has to answer that sort of question. But didn't Eunice ever ask?" (I did and I think he fibbed. I want to hear what he says *this* time.)

"Uh—"

"I won't tell anybody but Eunice. Not even the old Man with the book."

"You insidious little cuddle puppy. I think I have four more. Plus one by a married lady who may have been kidding me. Three I supported until they were on their own; the fourth—and that possible fifth—I couldn't even offer to. But they were never in want."

"How was it handled, dear? Three maiden ladies who moved elsewhere and became overnight widows?"

"Uh . . . only in one case. I offered to marry her—I was a grass widower then—but she elected not to, and did marry later and her husband adopted the child and I made

238

a cash settlement. The other similar case I was married but the settlement was just as amicable. The other two were married. Some grief about one—she was a compulsive confesser, from which the good Lord deliver me!—and her husband had to be soothed with mucho dinero. The last—well, her husband was sterile—mumps—and together they picked a father. Me. Startled the hell out of me. But he offered to put it in writing and did. I tore it up and settled it with a handshake." (This is *all* news to me, Joan. But I couldn't believe that such a virile and charming man had left no by-blows. Keep him talking.)

Jake grinned and caressed her sweet body. "That is the only one I'm certain about, as I have never insisted on blood tests if a lady accused me and I *could* have been the man. But in that case I am certain, as we took a holiday together, by sailboat, with her husband as nominal chaperonage. So that time it was I, at the right time and place. Then—" He paused. "Joan Eunice, I don't know whether Johann would have approved of the sequel, or not . . . but I don't want to shock the sweet girl you are now." (Honey, don't let him stop *there!*)

"Johann can't be shocked, Jake. If it's rough, I won't tell Eunice. But don't let me crowd you."

"Well . . . it wasn't rough, it was sweet. They didn't use me and drop me. I was welcome in their home thereafter . . . and in their bed."

"Three in a bed?"

"Uh . . . don't be nosy! Sometimes."

"But no more babies?"

"They were licensed for four and had them. But I think they picked a different father for each. I simply know that, in the several times I stayed in their home over about ten years, I never slept alone. I still get Christmas cards from them, each with a photograph of the family—and my daughter looks like her mother, not like me, thanks be to God. Joan, they were and are a respectable married couple, devout, and devoted to each other and to their children, and old-fashioned . . . except that, when they were faced with the need for a donor, they elected to pick donors themselves, then use the old-fashioned way rather than syringes and a clinical atmosphere."

"Uh . . . was she sweet in bed?"

"Quite. But unsophisticated. Not a patch on Eunice, if you were thinking about her."

"I was." (*I* was!)

"Eunice—Eunice was the most glorious thing that could happen to any man. Sweet as an angel, and as skilled—and as uninhibited!—as the most famous courtesan in history." (I'm *purring!*)

"Jake. I prefer the old-fashioned way, too."

"Yes?"

"You were sweet to all those ladies and you got two unmarried ones pregnant and I'm rich enough to get away with it and right now you are feeling young—I *know* you are! Will you pick me up and carry me over there? Or shall I walk?"

"Eunice."

"Let's both walk. But hurry."

"Yes. Yes, darling."

She jumped up, took his hand . . . as the house intercom sounded with: "Mr. Salomon! Rockford here. Your car is waiting."

Joan said, "Oh, my God!" and started to cry.

Jake put his arm around her and petted her. "I'm sorry, darling."

"Jake. Tell them to go get dinner. Tell them to be back in, uh, two hours."

"No, dear."

She stomped her bare foot. "Jake, I won't, I won't! This is unbearable."

He said quietly, "You promised. Look, darling, I'm not nineteen years old and able to perform in back seats of cars or on back porches with a party going on in the house. I have to have quiet and peace." (Don't believe him, dear! Though he might be scared off for a first time.)

Joan bawled and shook her head. He spoke loudly: "Rockford!"

"Yes, sir?"

"We'll be out in a moment or two. Keep the reactor warm."

He stepped to the wall and squeezed down the intercom to zero, then said gently, "Get dressed, dear."

"I won't! If we leave now, you'll have to stuff me into the car bare naked."

He sighed and picked her up; she stopped crying and looked suddenly happy.

The expression did not last. He turned her in his arms as he sat down on a straight chair, got a firm grip on her, and walloped her right buttock. She yelped. And struggled.

He got her more firmly, placing his right leg over both of hers, and applied his hand smartly to her left cheek. Then he alternated sides, stopping with ten. He set her on her feet and said, "Get dressed, dear. Quickly."

She stopped rubbing the punished area. "Yes, Jake."

Neither said another word until he had handed her into the car, climbed in after her, and they had been locked in. Then she said timidly, "Jake? Will you hold me?"

"Certainly, darling."

"May I take my robe off, please? Will you take it off me?"

With the robe out of the way she sighed and snuggled in. After a bit she whispered, "Jake darling? Why did you spank me?"

It was his turn to sigh. "You were being difficult . . . and it is the only thing I know of which will do a woman any good when a man can't do for her what she needs. And right then—I couldn't."

"I see. I think I do."

She remained quiet a while, enjoying his arms around her and breathing against his chest. Then she said, "Dear? Did you ever spank Eunice?"

"Once."

"For the same reason?"

"Not quite. Well, somewhat. She teased me into it." (I tickled him, dear. And got the surprise of my life.)

"Then I'm glad you spanked me, too. But I'll try not to tease you—though I'll never be the angel she was." (Fallen angel, Boss. And enjoyed it all, clear down to the Pit.)

"Jake?"

"Yes, Eunice?"

"I didn't really mind being spanked by you. Even when I was crying. But— Well, I'm padded now— Built to take a spanking. And when you are spanking me, you aren't ignoring me—and any attention is better than none. And besides—" She hesitated.

"Besides what, Eunice?"

"Well, I don't know—but I think it happened."

"What happened?"

"Female orgasm. Well, maybe. I don't know what one is supposed to feel like. But while I was crying and hurting; you have a heavy hand, sir—suddenly I felt very warm inside and something seemed to grow and explode—that's the best I can describe it. And I was ecstatically happy and didn't mind the last few wallops, hardly noticed them. Was that a female orgasm?"

"How would *I* know, dearest? Perhaps you'll be able to tell *me*. Later."

"Later tonight?"

"Uh, I think not, Eunice. It's late and we have had nothing to eat and I'm tired even if you aren't—"

"I am, rather. But happy."

"So tonight we'll rest. When it does happen—and I'm no longer fighting it—let's make the first time absolutely private and quiet. No phones and no servants and no distractions. After that—well, it might be target-of-oppor-tunity. But I'm not a kid. You know what I mean, darling; you've been old, too."

"Yes, dearest, *much* older than you are. Eunice can wait. Jake? What was this teasing Eunice did that was so bad it got her spanked?"

He suddenly grinned. "The little imp tickled me until I nearly went out of my mind. So I spanked her. But we were alone, and that ended satisfactorily. Quite."

"How?"

"How do you think? I excelled my usual mediocre performance, and Eunice—there aren't words for it, but she excelled her utter perfection, impossible as that sounds." (He darn near split me like a melon, twin—and I *wanted* him to!)

"So? Someday *I* will tickle you—and get spanked for it.

242

So take your vitamins, dear. Jake, you *enjoyed* spanking me. Didn't you?"

He was silent several moments. "I enjoyed it so much that I spanked you neither as hard nor as long as I wanted to. And started feeling 'young' as you put it—but knew that, if I didn't get you out of the house right then, you probably wouldn't leave at all. And I don't care to advertise it to servants."

"You had better marry me. So we can ignore servants."

"You had better shut up. You're still learning to be a girl, and I'm still learning how to handle you. You're Eunice—but you aren't Eunice. And we must clear up legal matters before we talk about such things."

"Old mean. Girl beater. Sadist. Hold me *tight*."

16

Jake escorted Joan Eunice to her boudoir. Winnie was waiting there—to Joan's annoyance as she thought it possible that Jake's stern character might slip if the upper house was quiet. But she did not show it. "Hi, Winnie!"

"Miss Joan! Are you all right? I've been so worried!"

"Of course I'm all right; Mr. Salomon was taking care of me. Why were you worried, dear?"

"Why, the dreadful things they've been saying about you in the news and there was a riot at the Hall of Justice; I saw it. And—"

"Winnie, Winnie! The idiot box is for idiots; why do you look at it? I was never in danger."

"But she has had a trying day, so you take good care of her, Winnie."

"Oh, I will, sir!"

"And I am tired, too, so I'll say good-night and go to bed. After I find a sandwich, perhaps."

"Hubert put a tray in your suite, sir."

"Hubert gets another merit badge. Though to tell the truth, Winnie, I've had a worrisome day myself, and it's left me with little appetite and jangled nerves. I may dine on a sleeping pill."

"Jake dear—"

"Yes, Eunice?"

"Don't take a pill. And do eat."

"But—"

"I know, I'm a bundle of nerves myself. But I know

what to do about it—and Winnie and I can soothe your nerves and restore your appetite and make you sleep like a baby."

He cocked one eyebrow, looked at Eunice, then at Winnie. "I think either of you could. But both?"

"Jake, you're a dirty-minded old man; you'll have Winnie blushing. But we can—can't we, Winnie? The Money Hum."

"Oh. Yes, we can, Mr. Salomon."

"Harrumph! Does it involve blood? Or broken bones?"

"Oh, no, sir! It's restful. Relaxing."

"I'll try anything once."

Joan said, "But you have to strip for it to—"

"I thought there was a catch."

"Oh, Jake. We'll let you sissy; you can wear shorts. We strip for it; the spiritual effect is better. It's the way we warm up for our exercises. Go undress; then put on shorts and a robe. We'll join you in the Green Suite. Right after it you're going to have a bite to eat and a tepid tub and straight to bed and right to sleep."

"Maybe I'd better bathe first. A day in court leaves me smelling like a skunk."

"You smell all right. Anyhow, Winnie and I have such control by now that we can decide not to be able to smell—or to hear a distracting noise, or anything—if we choose to."

"That's true, Mr. Salomon."

"Okay. Winnie, if she beats me, you protect me. Adios, dears."

"Five minutes, Jake."

As soon as they were alone Winifred said, "You're going to make me strip down bare? Again?"

"I didn't 'make' you strip the first time. And dear Doctor certainly did notice that you are a girl. Looked to me as if the kiss he gave you was better than the one he gave me. Stop blushing. Winnie, you can sissy, too, if you want to—but I *do* need you present. Or Jake will think I'm trying to make him."

"Oh, Mr. Salomon would never think that about *you.*"

"He's male. He's as male as dear Doctor. I need

chaperonage, as all I'm after is to help him sleep without pills. The poor dear has had a dreadful day. Winnie, he was wonderful in court; I'll tell you about it. Later. Let's get these duds off and grab negligees. Modest ones." Joan Eunice stopped suddenly. "Perhaps I've goofed. Winsome? Do you have a date?"

Miss Gersten blushed again. "Uh . . . not until later."

"Paul working late? Sorry—erase and correct. None of my business."

The little redhead continued to blush but she answered steadily, "My business is always your business, Miss Joan. Uh, I'm supposed to take care of you—and I do try! But you feel like a big sister to me."

"Thank you, sweet Winsome. But big sisters should not snoop."

"I've been meaning to tell you. Paul and I have split."

"Oh, I'm sorry!"

"I'm not. I don't think Paul ever meant to get a dissolution; he was stringing me. But—well, Bob isn't married. Not yet."

" 'Not yet.' Planning on getting married, dear?"

"Well . . . I don't think getting married is something one plans. It just happens. Like thunderstorms."

"You could be right. Sweet, whether it's getting married, or fun and happiness, I hope it's perfect for you. And 'Bob' is such a common name that I can't be tempted to guess. If I don't see him."

"You probably won't. He comes up the service lift and into my rooms from the back corridor—nobody sees him but the guard on duty. And they don't gossip."

"If any guard ever gossips about anything in this house, and I find it out, he'll be on Welfare so fast he'll be dizzy. Winnie, the rest of the staff can be human about it. But a guard is in a specially trusted position and must keep his mouth shut. Winnie, if you ever want to see Bob—or anyone—somewhere else, I'll have my mobile guards deliver you and pick you up, and even I won't know where."

"Uh . . . thank you. But this is the safest place for us—so few places are safe today. The most that can happen here is that Bob might be embarrassed. *I* wouldn't be embarrassed at all, I'm proud of him!"

"That's the way to feel, dear. As an ex-man I know that's the attitude a man values most in a woman. 'Proud of him.' But let's hurry; we're keeping Jake waiting. If you're going to wear pants, better find some with stretch in them. And thank you for lending me this outfit—turned out that, without the apron and cap, it was still most effective. I had the robe off a while. Tell you later."

In moments the girls were hurrying down the corridor to the Green Suite, each just in a negligee and barefooted. At the last instant Winifred had decided that, if her mistress was going to practice meditation in the correct uniform, she would also.

They found the counselor in a bathrobe, looking sheepish. Joan said, "I hope we haven't kept you waiting. Is your tub ready? If not, I'm willing to draw it before we start. Then into it and out, don't risk falling asleep. Then—"

"I cheated. I took a quick tub—tepid, as you specified—and ate a little, too."

"Good. Then we'll pop you straight into bed after this and kiss you good-night and you'll be asleep before we're out the door. Jake, this is the simplest of yoga, not exercise, just meditation. Controlled breathing, but the easiest sort. Inhale through one repetition of the prayer, hold it through one more. Exhale through one, hold through one, and repeat. All of us together, in a triangle. Can you sit in Lotus? Probably not unless you've practiced."

"Eunice—"

"Yes, Jake?"

"My father was a tailor. I was sitting in tailor's seat before I was eight. Will that do?"

"Certainly if you are comfortable. If not, any position that lets you relax. For you have to forget your body."

"Squatted in a tailor's position I can fall asleep. But what's this prayer?"

Joan Eunice slipped off her negligee, melted down onto the rug into meditation pose, soles upward on her thighs, palms upward in her lap. "It goes like this. Om Mani

Padme Hum." (Om Mani Padme Hum. I should have taught Jake this long ago.)

"I know the phrase. 'The Jewel in the Lotus.' But what does it mean to *you*, Joan Eunice?"

Winifred had followed Joan's example as quickly as she set it, was bare and in Lotus—and not blushing. She answered, "It means everything and nothing, Mr. Salomon. It is all the good things you know of—bravery and beauty and gentleness and not wanting what you can't have and being happy with what you do have and trees swaying in the wind and fat little babies gurgling when you tickle their feet and anything that makes life good. Love. It always means love. But you don't think about it, you don't think at all, you don't even try not to think. You chant the prayer and just *be*—until you find yourself floating, all warm and good and relaxed."

"Okay, I'll try." He took off his bathrobe, had under it boxer's shorts. "Joan Eunice, when did you take up yoga? Winnie teach you?"

"Oh, no!" said Winifred. "Miss Joan taught *me*—she's much farther along the Path than I am."

(Watch it, Boss!) (No huhu, Lulu.) "One learns many things, Jake—and loses them for lack of time. I used to play chess, yet I haven't set up a board for fifty years. But for longer than that I could no longer even attempt a Lotus seat . . . until Eunice gave me this wonderful young body which can do anything."(Which shell is the pea under, Eunice?) (It'll be under *you* if you relax too much; you should have emptied our bladder.) (Never fear, dear. I shan't go under, must watch Jake.) "Join us, Jake. You lead, Winnie; start as soon as Jake is in position."

Salomon started to sit on the floor, suddenly stopped and got out of his shorts. Joan was delighted, taking it as a sign that he had decided to give in to it all the way. But she did not let her serene expression change nor move her eyes. Winifred was staring at her navel; if she noticed it, she did not show it.

"Inhale," Winifred said softly. "Om Mani Padme Hum. Hold. Om Mani Padme Hum. Breath out. Om Mani Padme Hum. Hold......"

(Om Mani Padme Hum. Dig that clamdigger, dearie?)
(Shut up! You'll ruin the mood. Om Mani Padme Hum.)

"Om Mani Padme Hum!" said Salomon in a voice that would have graced a cathedral. "Om Mani Padme Hum!"

"Winnie darling," Joan said softly. "Let it fade and wake up wide. We're going to have to wake Jake."

The redhead's eyes fluttered, she whispered one more prayer and waited. "Jake darling," Joan said softly, "Eunice is calling. Wake just enough to let us help you into bed. Eunice is calling you back. Jake dearest."

"I hear you, Eunice."

"How do you feel?"

"Eh? Relaxed. Wonderful. Much rested but ready to sleep. Say, it *does* work. But it's just autohypnosis."

"Did I even hint that it was anything else? Jake, I don't expect to find God by staring into my belly button. But it does work . . . and it's better than forcing your body with drugs. Now let Winnie and me help you into bed."

"I can manage."

"Of course you can but I don't want the relaxation to wear off. Indulge me, Jake, let us baby you. Please."

He smiled and let them—slid onto the opened bed, let them cover him, smiled again when Joan Eunice gave him a motherly good-night kiss, seemed unsurprised when Winifred followed her mistress's example—turned on his side and was asleep as the girls left the room.

"Don't bother," Joan said as Winifred started to put on her negligee. "It's my house and no one comes upstairs after dinner unless sent for. Except Hubert and I assume that Jake sent him to bed, knowing that he was to be called on by two tarts in three quarter time and not much else." She slid an arm around the redhead's slender waist. "Winnie, much as I like to dress up—isn't it *nice* to wear just skin?"

"I like it. Indoors. Not outdoors, I sunburn so badly."

"What about at night? When I was a boy, ages and ages ago, it got unbearably hot in July and August where we lived—the sidewalks used to burn my bare feet. Houses

250

were bake ovens even at night—no air-conditioning. An electric fan was a luxury most people did not have. Nights when I couldn't sleep because of heat I used to sneak quiet as a mouse and bare as a frog out the back door, being oh so careful not to let my parents hear, and walk naked in the dark, with grass cool on my feet and the soft night breeze velvet on my skin. Heavenly!"

"It sounds heavenly. But I would be terrified of getting mugged."

"The word 'mug' hadn't been invented, much less any fear of it. I was a middle-aged man before I became wary of the dark." They turned into the master bedroom. "Kiss me good-night, Winsome, and go keep your date. Sleep late in the morning; I'm going to."

"Uh, my date isn't until after midnight. Aren't you going to tell me what happened today?"

"Why, of course, dear. Thought you might be in a hurry. Come take a bath with me?"

"If you want me to. I bathed after dinner."

"And you have your face on for your date. I bathed this morning but it seems a week ago. Sniff me and tell me how badly I stink."

"You smell all right. Luscious."

"Then I'll let it go with toothbrush and bidet and a swipe at my armpits; I'd rather go to bed."

"You haven't had dinner."

"Not all that hungry. Just happy. Is there milk in my bedroom fridge? Milk and crackers is all I want. Want to join me with a glass for yourself and get crumbs in bed and talk girl talk? Things I can't mention to dear Jake now that I'm a girl and not mean, old, cantankerous Johann."

"Joanie, I don't believe you ever were cantankerous."

"Oh, yes, I was, hon. I hurt most of the time and was depressed all of the time and wasn't fit to live with. But Joan Eunice is never depressed; her bowels are too regular. Scrounge us two glasses of milk and a box of crackers while I take a pretend bath. Don't go downstairs; there will be something over there in the iron rations. Fig newtons, maybe, or vanilla wafers."

Soon they were sitting, munching, in the big bed while Joan Eunice gave an edited account of the day: "—so we visited in Judge Mac's chambers and let the car go ahead, as Judge Mac the sweet darling wouldn't hear of my leaving through the streets. Even though the phony riot was over. Then we switched from copter to car at Safe Harbor and came home." (Protecting her 'innocence,' twin?) (Not bloody likely. Protecting Jake's reputation.)

"But the best part of the day was when I took off that street robe and let 'em look at the Acapulco outfit you dressed me in. Made 'em go ape, dear."

" 'Ape?' "

"Out-of-date slang. They dropped one wing and ran in circles, like a rooster about to tread a strange hen."

"It wasn't the outfit, it was you."

"Both. Eunice Branca had a heavenly body and I'm doing my best to justify it. With your help. As may be, both those darling men kissed me the nearest thing to rape I've encountered."

"Better than Dr. Garcia?"

"I don't think Dr. Garcia gave me his all-out best. I think he was inhibited by surprise and by the presence of a redheaded nurse I could name. But these two weren't inhibited and had a couple of drinks in them and each was going his darnedest to do better than the other one. *Whew!* Winnie, I do not exaggerate—if Jake hadn't been there, I think they would have had me down on the rug for a gang bang in two seconds."

"Uh . . . would you have struggled?" (Going to be truthful, tart?) (Who taught me to be a tart? Any reason not to tell her, Eunice?) (None. Except that she's likely to rape you herself.) (Oh, pooh, she's just killing time till her date.) (Don't say I didn't warn you.)

"Winnie, if I were a real lady, I would be horrified. But I won't pretend with my chum. I don't know much about being female but I seem to have strong instincts. Cross my heart, if either of those sweet men had given me a gentle shove, I would have landed on that rug with my legs open and eyes closed. Gang bang? By then I felt ready to take on a regiment."

Winifred said thoughtfully, "It happened to me once."

"A *regiment*?"

"No. A gang bang."

"Well, let's shoo the crumbs out of bed and squeeze down the lights and snuggle and you tell big sister. Were they mean to you?"

"Not really. Oh, dear, I'm blushing already. Turn off everything but one floor light and let me tell it against your neck."

"That better?"

"Yes."

"Now tell Mama."

"Uh, it was the night I graduated from training. I wasn't a virgin—I'm not sure there was a virgin in my class. But this was something else. Some interns gave a party for some of us. That was fine and I expected one of them to get me alone. Interns are the horniest people and a girl didn't accept a date with one unless she meant business. But the party was loads of champagne and no food. Joan, I had never had champagne before."

"Oho! I can write the ending."

"Well . . . champagne doesn't *taste* strong. I sopped up a lot of it.

"Then I was in bed and it was happening. Wasn't surprised and tried to cooperate. But things were vague. I noticed that he wasn't dark-haired after all; he had hair as red as mine. When I had been certain that he was dark-haired and had a mustache. When I noticed later that he was almost bald, I realized that something odd was going on. Joan, there were seven interns at that party. I think all of them had me before morning. I don't know how many times. I knew what was happening after thick, curly red hair was replaced by mostly bald. But I didn't try to stop it. Uh . . . I didn't *want* it to stop. A nympho, huh?"

"I don't know, dear, but that's the way I felt this afternoon. Wanted it to happen at last, wanted it to go on happening—and *I* don't even know what it feels like. Go on."

"Well, it did go on. I got up once and went to the bathroom and noticed in the mirror that I didn't have a stitch on and couldn't remember having undressed. Didn't seem to matter. I went back to bed, and found that I was feeling lonely; the party seemed to have stopped.

"Only it hadn't. A man came in and I managed to focus my eyes and said, 'Oh, Ted! Come here'. And he did and we did, and it was worse than ever.

"I woke up about noon with a dreadful hangover. Managed to sit up and here were my clothes, neatly folded on a chair, and on the bedside table a tray with a thermos of coffee and some Danish pastry and a glass with a note by it. It read: 'Drink this before you eat. You'll need it. Chubby.' Chubby was the one who was almost bald."

"A gentleman. Aside from his taste for mass rape."

"Chubby was always nice. But if anybody had told me that I would ever be in bed with Chubby, I would have laughed in her face."

"Were you ever again?"

"Oh, yes. I really did appreciate the thoughtful little breakfast and especially the hangover cure. It put me back together. Not good enough to go on watch but good enough to get dressed and back to my room."

"Were you all right? I mean, uh, not caught or anything?"

"Not even sore. Not anything. Wasn't my time, even if I hadn't been protected with an implant, which I was. And one nice thing about going to bed with interns, almost no chance of picking up an infection. No, I was lucky all the way, Joan. Oh, no doubt the story went the rounds—but I wasn't the only graduate getting it that night, and that wasn't the only party. Nobody teased me about it. But it was a gang bang, and I didn't make the slightest move to stop it." She added thoughtfully, "The thing that worries me is that I might do it again. I know I would. So I don't drink at all anymore. I know I can't handle it."

"Why, Winnie, you've had a drink with me, more than once."

"That's not the same thing. Uh, if you wanted me to get drunk with *you*—I would. I'd be safe." (Safe? Little does she know.) (Eunice, we haven't done more than snuggle and you know it.) (She's asking you to step up the pace.) (Well, I won't! Not much, anyhow.)

"Winnie! Winnie dear! Look at the time."

"Uh? Oh, my heavens! Ten minutes after midnight. I—" The little redhead seemed about to cry.

"Are you late? He'll wait. Oh. I'm sure he will—for Winnie."

"Not late yet. He's off duty at midnight and it takes a while to get here. But— Oh, dear, I don't want to leave *you*. Not when we were—I was, anyhow—so happy."

"Me, too, darling," Joan agreed, gently untangling herself from Winifred's arms. "But big sister is always here. Don't keep your man waiting. Check your lipstick and hair and such in my bath if there is any chance that he may already be in your room."

"Well. All right. Miss Joan, you're good to me."

"Don't you dare call me 'Miss' at a time like this or swelp me, I'll make you miss your date. Rush, rush, hon; go get beautiful. Kiss me good-night; I'll be asleep before you are out of the bath. And, Winsome—no exercises tomorrow."

"But—"

"Smile, I didn't break your dolly. I want to sleep late and I want *you* to sleep late so that I won't wake up from knowing you are fidgeting. You'll get all the classic postures you need in bed tonight. Stop blushing. Give him something special from me, only don't tell him. Or do, I don't give a darn. Kiss me quick and let me go to sleep."

Her maid-chum-nurse kissed her not too quickly and left hurriedly. Joan Eunice pretended to be asleep when Winifred walked silently from the bath through the room, on into her own room, and the door sealed behind her.

(Well, twin, you lucked through again, didn't you?) (Eunice, I've told you time and again that I am *not* going to stroll Gay Street while I'm a virgin. Might be habit-forming.) (Could be, with our cuddly little pet who enjoys a

255

gang bang. But I didn't mean *her*. I meant at Safe Harbor.)

(You call that *luck?* I call it the most frustrating thing that ever happened to me. Eunice, I needed the Money Hum as badly as Jake did.) (I call it luck. Boss darling, I may be dead but I can still read a calendar. I was steady on twenty-eight-and-a-half days for more than ten years—and we've still been on it since we amalgamated. We're fertile as a turtle, Myrtle, this minute—and will be, for two or three days. Jake has promised you that the next time won't be frustrating . . . and you'll be as carefree as a cheerleader I told you about. Scan me, Fanny? So run don't walk and get that implant—about ten o'clock tomorrow morning. Unless you plan to get us benched right away. Do you?)

(Eunice, you're talking non— No, you're not. I *will* do something about it. Tomorrow. But 'benched right away' is an exaggeration. I'm new at this while you've been through one pregnancy. But your aunt probably watched you like a hawk—) (She did. Elsie Dinsmore had a livelier time.) (—but I've sat through three, as a husband. 'Benched' is just a short time, at the end. And pregnancy doesn't kill a woman's interest. My angelic first wife, Agnes, would have tried it on the way to the hospital if I hadn't had more sense about it than she had. Just the same, I'll be good. I'll be careful, rather.)

(Joan, I wasn't trying to talk you out of it. I just didn't want us knocked up by accident. Say through a playful romp with Judgie Wudgie. Or Alec. But if you want to, that's fine. Marry Jake and get pregnant at once. Or get pregnant by him and then marry him; he might be more tractable.)

(Eunice, I'm not planning on getting married in any hurry if at all.) (So? I've heard you propose to Jake at least four times.)

(Yes, yes! If Jake agreed, I would; I wouldn't let him down. But he won't, if ever, until these legal finagles are cleared up. Which might take years. Do you remember how long it took to get the courts to okay the Sky Trails stock conversions? That was clear-cut compared with this and did not involve as much money. Eunice, I propose to Jake for his morale; I don't care whether he makes an 'honest woman' of me or not, I just want him to take us to bed. Marriage doesn't figure.)

(Twin, your naïveté surprises me. Didn't you hear Winnie? Marriage isn't planned, it just happens. No girl is more likely to wind up in a hotel room, married to a man she didn't even know at sundown the night before, than a chick who isn't going to get married 'any time soon.' Boss, you marry Jake. Marry him as soon as he will agree to it—for you were talking sense when you pointed out that no other man could both understand you and not be dazzled by your money. In the meantime, it's smart to go contra.)

(All right. What are the girls using today?) (Oh, most of them use implants. Some use pills, both the daily ones and the monthly ones. But if you miss with either sort, you are on a very short fuse. I never liked monkeying with my body's economy; I'm not convinced that anything that changes a woman's femaleness that much is a good idea. Not superstition, Boss, I did some careful reading after the time I got caught. There are hazards to all chemical methods. My body worked fine the way it was; I didn't want to tamper with a successful organization—I'm quoting you, only you were talking about business.) (I see your point, Eunice, even though we're talking about monkey business. A body is far more complex than a corporation, and the one you turned over to me is a jewel; I don't want to tamper with it, either. But what *did* you use? Self-restraint?)

(Never had any in stock, dearie. Oh, there are lots of other loving things you can do without getting pregnant—if you can shake off your early training and be twenty-first century—) (Look, infant, I knew about—and used—every one of those other things in high school. I keep telling you: You kids did *not* invent sex.) (You didn't let me finish, Boss. Those are emergency measures. A girl who depends on them alone is going to add to the population explosion. Joan, I looked into it carefully, when I turned eighteen and was licensed . . . and settled on one of the oldest methods. A diaphragm. They are still available; any physician will fit them. I wore one six days every month, even at the

257

office—because, as the doctor who fitted me pointed out, most diaphragm failures result from leaving them at home while you run out for a pound of sugar, be right back.)

(I suspect he's right, Eunice.) (I'm sure of it, Joan. I never liked them—I never liked *any* contraception; I seemed to have a deep instinct that told me to get pregnant. Boss . . . the thing—the *only* thing—that I really mind about being dead . . . is that I always wanted to have a baby by you. And that's silly, as you were already too old—or maybe almost too old—when I first met you. But I would have tried, if you had offered.)

(Darling, darling!)

(Oh, I'm happy with what I have. Om Mani Padme Hum. I'm not kicking about my karma. I'm not just content, I'm *happy* . . . to be half of Joan Eunice.)

(Eunice, would you still be willing to have a baby by me?)

(What? Boss, don't joke about it. Don't mock me.)

(I'm not joking, beloved.)

(But, Boss, the necessary part of you is *gone*. Pickled in alcohol, or something.)

(They use formalin, I think. Or deep freeze. I'm not talking about that old wreck we discarded. We can go down and get an implant.)

(Huh? I don't understand.)

(Do you remember a tax-deductible called the Johanna Mueller Schmidt Memorial Eugenics Foundation?)

(Of course. I wrote a check for it every quarter.)

(Eunice, despite the purposes set out in its charter, the only *real* purpose does not appear in the fine print. When my son was killed I was already fairly old. But I was still virile—potent—and tests showed that I was fertile. So I got married—I think I told you—to have another son. Didn't work. But I had my bet hedged and never told anyone. Sperm bank deposit. In the cryogenic vault of the Foundation is a little piece of Johann. Hundreds of millions of extremely little pieces, that is. Presumably they are not dead, just asleep. That's what I meant by an implant. With a syringe. Or however they do it.

(Eunice? Are you still there?) (I'm crying, Boss. Can't a girl cry happy? *Yes!*)

(Tomorrow morning, then. You can change your mind up till the last minute.)

(I'll *never* change my mind. I hope you won't.)

(Beloved.)

17

Next morning Joan found that Jake had left the house before she woke; there was a note on her tray:

"Dear Joan Eunice,

"I slept like a baby and feel ready to fight wildcats—thanks to you and Winnie. Please extend my thanks to her and say (to both of you) that I will most gratefully join your prayer meetings any time I am invited—especially if I've had a tiring day.

"I will not be back until late—treasure hunting, locating links of evidence. Alec is off to Washington for one link. If you need me, call my answering service or Judge McCampbell's chambers.

"I've instructed Jefferson Billings to let you draw against your petty expenditures account—about four hundred thousand in it, I believe—on your old signature and new thumbprint. He'll pay drafts and hold them and I'll countersign until you make out a new signature & thumbprint card—he says he knew Eunice Branca by sight, no problem. If you wish, he will call on you with a new sig-print card—we assume that your signature is now somewhat changed."

(Boss, I guess Jake doesn't know that I sign your signature better than you do.) (I don't think anyone knows, dearest. I don't know how that would figure in court—for us, or against us?)

"If you need more pocket money, let me make you a personal loan rather than have it show in my conservator's report. Your 'Brother Mac' is most helpful, but the financial end of this nonsense should appear ultra-conservative until such time as he can, with full justification, relieve me as your conservator. Caesar's wife, you know.

"Speaking of Caesar's wife, I told you a chuckle about two of our friends. This morning I phoned one of them and the other answered and, after the usual query as to sight & security, they seemed unworried about what I saw or heard or might infer. I was flattered. Little imp, if you must misbehave, you can trust them—for they have your welfare at heart. Sorry I was stuffy yesterday."

(I'm glad to learn *that*, Boss.) (Eunice, I can't see that it's our business what Alec and Mac do in their spare time. Jake shouldn't gossip about them, even to us.) (No, no, Boss! Jake is telling you that he was being a cube yesterday—and he's sorry—and now he's granting you absolution in advance. We had best marry Jake—nevertheless I've fretted that Jake might be jealous. Possessive. His age, his background. Could be doom, twin—as you are a tart at heart and we both know it.)

(Oh, nonsense, Eunice! I would never rub Jake's nose in it—and anyhow you're wrong. A smart man—which Jake is—doesn't get excited over a go on the tiles; what worries him is fear of losing a wife he values. If Jake marries us, I will *never* let him worry about losing us.) (I hope you can make that stick, Boss honey.) (With your help I'm sure I can. Let's finish his letter—)

"Don't count on me for dinner, as what I must do today is urgent—more urgent than something that seemed dreadfully urgent yesterday. And was. And will be, I hope.

"This was meant to be a love letter but I've had to mention other matters—and other people, so I must urge you to tear it up and flush it down the W.C. It is no accident that I am thumbprinting the seal and will hand it to Cunningham with a promise to have his head on a platter i

262

it leaves his person before it reaches you. I've learned to like Cunningham; he's and 'honest thief.'

"My love to you, dearest, and the biggest kiss possible—so big that you can break off a piece and deliver it to Winnie when you thank her for me. She's a charming girl, and I'm pleased that she's mothering you so well.

"J."

(Why, the horny old bastard. Joan, Jake has his eye on Winnie's pretty tail while he's patting ours.) (She'll have to stand in line!) (*Jealous*, twin?) (No. But I repeat—I'm going to scalp him first. Darn it, Eunice, I had him all set yesterday—and it's been a long struggle. Not the Whim-Wham-Thankee-Ma'am *you* managed with him. And all it got me was a spanking. I do hope he comes home tonight.) (Three hurdles even if he does, twin.) (*Three?*) (Hubert . . . . . . and Winnie . . . and that 'implant.' Boss darling? You're not going to do me out of having *your* baby by letting Jake get at you first—are you?) (Of course not, little stupid. I was coping with intrigues without getting shot long before your grandmother was born. Mmm—I'll need cash.)

(Jake told you how to get all the cash you want.) (Oh, sure—on my signature and *his* countersignature. Like a cat covering up on linoleum. Eunice my love, I'll bet you never paid a bribe in your life.) (Well . . . not with *money*.) (Don't tell me, let me guess. Hon, what we're sitting on might be worth a million—but today I need used bills in medium denominations from no recorded source. Come along, little snoopy, and I'll show you something that even my secretary—a sweetly deceitful girl named Eunice, remember her?—didn't know about.)

(Do you mean that safe hidden in your bath, Boss?) (*Huh?* How the hell did *you* know about *that?*) (I'm snoopy.) (Do you know the combo?) (I ought to take the Fifth.) (Why bother? You'll know it in two minutes. Or can you pick it out of my mind?) (Boss darling, you know by now that *I* don't know anything in your memory until *you* think about it . . . and *you* don't know anything in mine until *I* think about it. But— Well, if I had to open the safe,

263

I think I would start with the numbers that mean your mother's birthday.)

Joan sighed. (A girl doesn't have any privacy these days. All right, let's see if we've been robbed.)

She went into her bath, sealed the door, bolted it by hand, removed a stack of towels from a lower cabinet, fiddled with the ceiling of the cabinet; the back panel slid aside, disclosing a safe. (You think my mother's birth date will open it?) (I'd switch on the sun lamps over the massage table first, then run the cold water in the hand basin.) (No privacy at all! Honey, did you really pay a bribe with your pretty tail once?) (Not exactly. I just improved the situation. Let's see if we've been robbed.)

Joan opened the safe. Inside was money enough to interest a bank auditor. But the packets had not been packaged in a bank; they were not that neatly jogged and the total for each was hand-printed. (Plenty of moola, dear—and either nobody found this safe, or they never figured out the additional bolts. Either way, it settles one thing. We won't put Jake's sweet note down the hopper.) (Let him think we did, huh?) (If he asks.) (Then cry on him later and admit that we couldn't bear to part with it.) (Eunice, you have a mind like a pretzel.) (That's why it fits so well into yours, twin.) (Could be.)

Joan put the letter inside, took out two packets, put them into a purse in the dressing room end—closed the safe, shut off the sun lamps, shut off the water, spun the dial, slid the panel back, replaced the towels, closed the cabinet. Then she stepped to the bath's intercom, pressed a touchplate. "Chief O'Neil."

"Yes, Miss Smith?"

"I want my car, one driver, and both Shotguns in thirty minutes."

There was a short silence. "Uh, Miss Smith, Mr. Salomon apparently forgot to mention that you would be leaving the house."

"For excellent reason. He did not know it. Did he mention that I am no longer a ward of the Court? If not, have you learned it from some other source?"

"Miss, I haven't learned it from an *official* source."

"I see. Then you are learning it from me. Officially."

"Yes, Miss."

"You don't sound happy, O'Neil. You could check by phoning Judge McCampbell."

"Why, yes, of course."

"Are you going to, O'Neil?"

"Perhaps I misunderstood, Miss. Weren't you telling me to?"

"Are you recording?"

"Certainly, Miss. I always do, with orders."

"I suggest that you play it back and answer your own question. I'll hold. But first—how long have you been with me, O'Neil?"

"Seventeen years, Miss. The last nine as your Chief."

"Seventeen years, two months, and some days. Not enough for maximum retirement but it has been long, faithful, and unquestioning service. You can retire this morning on full pay for life, if you wish, O'Neil; faithful service should be appreciated. Now please play back while I hold." She waited.

"Be switched, Miss—I must need a hearing aid. You didn't *tell* me to call the Judge. You just said I *could*."

"That is correct. I pointed out that you could check on what I told you—officially—by making such a call. You still can."

"Uh, Miss, I don't see what you are driving at."

"I'm sure you can figure it out. Do you wish to retire today? If so, send up Mentone; I want to interview him."

"Miss, I've no wish to retire at all."

"Really? You gave the impression that you were looking for another job. Perhaps with Mr. Salomon. If so, I do not want to stand in your way. Retirement at full pay is available to you, O'Neil."

"Miss, I like it here."

"I'm pleased to hear it. I hope you will stay for many years. O'Neil, have you ever discussed my comings and goings with anyone?"

"Only when you've told me to, Miss. In which case I always have your order on tape."

"Fine. Wipe this tape and I'll hold while you do so."

Shortly he said, "Wiped, Miss Smith."

"Good. Let's start over. Chief O'Neil, this is Miss Johann Sebastian Bach Smith speaking. I want my car, one driver, and both Shotguns in thirty minutes."

"They will be ready, Miss Smith."

"Thank you. I'll be shopping. Is there anything I can pick up for Mrs. O'Neil?"

"That's most kind of you, Miss. I don't think so. Shall I ask her?"

"If you do, it is only necessary to say that my *car* is going out. If she has a list, I'll be happy to have Fred or Shorty take care of it. Off."

(Boss, you scared the pee out of him. Was that nice?) (Running a feudal enclave in the midst of a nominal democracy isn't easy, Eunice. When Johann said 'Frog,' everybody hopped—my security boss especially. O'Neil has got to know—they've *all* got to know—that Johann is still here . . . and that no one, not even darling Jake, reviews or vetoes what I say. Unless he marries us, in which case I'll go female and let him decide everything.) (That'll be the day!) (I might, dear one. Tell me, did you obey Joe?) (Well . . . I never bucked him. I suppose you could say I obeyed him. Except that I fibbed, or sometimes kept my mouth shut.) (I'd do just about the same. I think a perfect arrangement would be to do exactly what a man tells me to do . . . but wangle it so that he tells me to do what I've already decided to do.)

Joan felt, rather than heard, her chuckle. (Boss, that sounds like a recipe for a perfect marriage.)

(I find I like being female. But it's different. Now what shall we wear?)

Joan settled on a bandeau, a knee skirt, an opaque cloak with hood and yashmak, plus low-heeled sandals, all in subdued colors. She was ready in less than thirty minutes.

(How's our face, Eunice?) (Okay for a 'shopping' trip. No need to call Winnie; the little baggage probably hasn't had much sleep.) (Nor do I want to call her; she might want to come along. Let's go, sweet—we're out to break a two-thousand-year record with no help from the Holy Ghost.) (Boss, that's not a nice way to talk!) (Well, I'll be frimped!

266

Eunice, I thought you weren't a Christian? Zen. Or Hinduist. Or some such.)

(I'm not any of those things, Boss. I simply know some useful spiritual disciplines. But it is rude to joke about anything someone else holds holy.) (Even in my *mind*? Are you telling me what I must not *think*? If I could reach you, I'd spank you.) (Oh, you can say anything to *me*, Boss—just don't say such things out loud.) (I didn't and don't and never have. Quit nagging me.) (Sorry, Boss. Love you.) (Love *you*, little nag. Let's go get knocked up.) (*Yes!*)

She took the front lift to the basement; O'Neil met her and saluted. "Car is ready, Miss—and both drivers and both Shotguns."

"Why both drivers?"

"Well, Finchley should be on call. But Dabrowski is bucking my authority a touch. Claims he's senior to Finchley. Do you wish to settle it?"

"Of course not; *you* must. But perhaps I can smooth some feathers."

"Yes, Miss."

He conducted her to her car; both teams were lined up by it, they saluted in unison. She smiled at them. "Good morning, friends. I'm glad to see you all looking so well. It's been a long time."

Dabrowski answered for them, "It has indeed, Miss Smith—and we are glad to see *you* looking so well."

"Thank you." Her eyes traveled across them. "There is one thing no one has told me . . . about the tragedy that started this strange sequence of events. Which team was driving the night Mrs. Branca was killed?"

For a long moment no one spoke. Then O'Neil answered, "Finchley and Shorty had the duty that night, Miss Smith."

"Then I must thank them—for Mrs. Branca and for myself. Although I know that Dabrowski and Fred would have acted as bravely, as promptly." She looked at Finchley, then at Shorty, her face unsmiling but serene. "Which one of you avenged Eunice? Or was it both of you?"

Finchley answered. "Shorty got him, Mrs.—Miss Smith. Bare hands, one chop. Broke his neck."

She turned to Shorty—six feet six of smooth-black soul, two hundred ninety pounds of sudden death—and a preacher in his time off. She looked up at him and said gently, "Shorty, from the bottom of my heart—for Eunice Branca—I thank you." (I *do* thank him, Boss! This is news to me. I was dead before that lift opened.) "If she were here, she would thank you—not just for herself but for other girls that killer will never kill. I'm glad you killed him in the act. If he had gone to trial, he might be out by now. Doing it again."

Shorty had said nothing up to then. "Miss—Finch got 'im, too. Zapped him. Couldn't rightly say which one got him first."

"Nor does it matter. Any of you four would have protected Mrs. Branca with your life. She knew it—and knows it, wherever she is. I know it, and Chief O'Neil knows it." Joan felt tears start, let them flow. "I—all of us!—just wish to Heaven she had waited indoors until you two arrived. I know that each of you would rather see me dead than her. I ask you to do me the honor of believing that I feel the same way. Shorty, will you say a prayer for her tonight? For me? I don't know much about praying." (Damn it, Boss, you've got me crying.) (Then say a Money Hum. For Shorty. He's still blaming himself for the unavoidable.)

"I will, Miss. I have every night. Although—Mrs. Branca—doesn't need it. She went straight to Heaven." (So I did, Boss. Though not the way Shorty thinks.) (And we shan't tell him. Have I said enough?) (I think so.)

Joan said, "Thank you, Shorty. For me, not for Eunice. As you say, Eunice doesn't really need prayers." She turned to O'Neil. "Chief, I want to go to Gimbel's Compound."

"Certainly, Miss. Uh, Finchley, man the car. Both Shotguns." O'Neil helped her in, locked her in; she locked herself in. The armor door lifted and the big car rolled out into the street. (Joan, what in the world are you going to buy at Gimbel's?) (A gag. For you. I'll change that order in a moment. Eunice, where did you buy clothes? You were

268

the most smartly dressed gal in town—even when you were
the nakedest.)

(Pooh, I was never naked; Joe's designs made all the
difference. Joan, where I shopped you should never shop.)
(Can't see why not.) (Johann might but *you* can't; it
wouldn't do. Mmm . . . while I could not afford the stylish
places, I know of them. Come to think of it, two of them
lease space inside Gimbel's Compound.) (So that's where
we'll go—second. I'll tell Finchley the change . . . and tell
him to have Fred escort me; I think Fred feels left out.)
(Wups! Fred can read.) (So? *Oh!* Well, Fred can guard
me later.) She thumbed the order switch.

"Finchley."

"Yes, Miss?"

"I got so preoccupied that I forgot one other stop. Please
drop Shorty and me at the unloading zone where State
passes over Main."

"State and Main, Miss."

"Please have Shorty hang the radio link on his belt;
there's no parking around there. Or was not the last time I
was downtown. How long has that been? Over two years."

"Two years and seven months, Miss. Sure you don't
want both Shotguns with you?"

"No, they can take turns staying with the car. If you
have to get out, I want you covered."

"Oh, I'll be all right, Miss."

"Don't argue with me. You wouldn't have argued when I
was old Johann Smith; I assure you that *Miss* Johann
Smith still has his poison fangs. Pass the word along."

She heard him chuckle. "I'll do that, Miss Smith."

When the car stopped, Joan hooked up her yashmak,
concealing her identity—either or both of them—from the
curious. Shorty unlocked her and handed her out. On the
crowded pedestrian walk of Main Street Joan felt suddenly
vulnerable . . . except for the tower of strength beside her.
"Shorty, the building I'm looking for is in the thirteen
hundred block—thirteen-oh-seven. Can you find it?" The
question was to make him feel useful; she knew where the
Roberts Building was, she owned it.

"Oh, sure, Miss—I read numbers real good. Letters, too—just words bother me."

"Let's go then. Shorty, how do you manage in your real profession? Not being able to read the Bible, I mean."

"No trouble, I use talking books—and as for *the* Book, I got every precious word memorized."

"A remarkable memory. I wish I could say the same."

"Just takes patience. I had the Book down pat while I was still in prison." He added thoughtfully, "Sometimes I think I ought to learn to read . . . but I can't seem to find *time*." (The poor dear probably never had a teacher who could teach, Boss.) (Never tamper with a successful organization, Eunice; he's found his niche.)

"This must be it, Miss. 'One, three, oh, seven.' "

"Thank you, Shorty." She was not asked for her I.D. at the building entrance, nor did she offer it, for she had none, either as Johann Smith or Eunice Branca. The guard noted the "Licensed & Deputized" shield (which matched his own) on Shorty's uniform, released the cage turnstile, and waved them on through. Joan Eunice smiled at him with her eyes—and made note that security at the Roberts Building should be tightened; the guard should have photographed Shorty's I.D. and logged his shield number. (Boss, he *can't* handle so many people that way; he has to use his judgment.) (Look who's talking! If that apartment house you used to live in had had tight security, you would never have been mugged. If we can't stop violence outdoors, we must try to keep it from coming indoors.) (I won't argue, Boss darling—I'm *excited!*) (Me too; this veil is a help.)

On the twelfth floor they went to the suite occupied by the Johanna Mueller Schmidt Memorial Eugenics Foundation, H. S. Olsen, M.D., Sc. D., Director, Please Ring and Wait. The guard let them in, went back to his picture magazine. Joan noted with approval that there was a goodly number of women and couples in the waiting room. She (Johann) had jacked up Olsen about the (public) purpose of the Foundation—to offer superior anonymous donors to licensed and qualified females—in her last letter

270

accompanying a quarterly check; apparently it had had good effect.

"Wait here, Shorty; there's video over there."

She went to the barrier desk separating the waiting room from the outer clerical office, avoided the sign "Applications" and got the reluctant attention of the only male back of the barrier, motioned him to her. "What is it, Ma'am? If it's an application, go to the far end, present your I.D. and fill out the questionnaire, then wait. You'll be called."

"I want to see the Director. Dr. Olsen."

"Dr. Olsen never sees anyone without an appointment. Give me your name and state your business and possibly his secretary will see you."

She leaned closer, spoke softly. "I *must* see him. Tell him that my husband has found out."

The office manager looked startled. "Your name?"

"Don't be silly. Just tell him that."

"Uh . . . wait here." He disappeared through a rear door.

She waited. After a remarkably short time he appeared at a side door of the waiting room, motioned her to him, then conducted her down a passage toward a door marked "Director—Keep Out" and to a door near it marked "Secretary to the Director, Ring & Wait." There he left her with a woman who reminded Joan of Johann's third-grade teacher, both in appearance and authoritarian manner. The woman said frostily, "What is this nonsense? You may start by showing me your I.D." (Three fingers stiff into her solar plexus, Boss, and say she fainted!) (Maybe. We'll try my way first.)

Joan answered in still more frozen tones, "Not likely, Miss Perkins. Why do you think I'm veiled? Will you announce me? Or do I call the police and the news snoops?"

Miss Perkins looked startled, left her stenodesk, and entered the private office behind it. She came out shortly and said angrily, "You may go in."

Olsen did not get up as Joan entered. He said, "Madam, you have chosen an unusual way of getting my attention.

Now what is it? Come to the point."

"Doctor, don't you offer chairs to ladies?"

"Certainly. If they are ladies. A point you have gone to some trouble to render dubious. Speak up, my good woman, or I shall have you removed." (Boss, did you see him glance at the mike? That old bat in the next room is taking down every word.) (So I assumed, Eunice. So we won't talk yet.) Joan stepped close to the Doctor's desk, unhooked her yashmak, let it fall to her left shoulder.

The Doctor's expression changed from annoyance to startled recognition. Joan Eunice leaned across his desk, flipped off the dictation microphone. Then she said quietly, "Anything else still recording? Is this room soundproof? How about that door?"

"Miss—"

" 'Miss' is enough. Are you ready to ask me to sit down? Or shall I leave—and return with my lawyer?"

"Do please sit down—Miss."

"Thank you." Joan waited until he got up and moved a chair to a correct "honored-guest" position near his own. She sat down. "Now answer the rest. Are we truly private? If we are not—and you tell me that we are—I will eventually know it . . . and will take such steps as I deem appropriate."

"Uh, we're private. But just a moment." He got up, went to his secretary's door, bolted it manually. "Now, Miss, please tell me what this is about."

"I shall. First, I've been supplementing my original endowment with quarterly checks. Have you been receiving these during my incapacitation?"

"Eh . . . one check failed to arrive. I waited six weeks, then wrote to Mr. Salomon and explained what your custom had been. It seems he checked the facts, for soon after we received two quarterly payments at once, with a letter saying that he would continue to authorize payments in accordance with your custom. Is there some difficulty?"

"No, Doctor. The Foundation will continue to receive my support. Let me add that the trustees are—on the

272

whole—satisfied with your management."

"That's pleasing to hear. Is that why you came today? To tell me that?"

"No, Doctor. Now we get to the purpose. Are you *quite certain* that our privacy cannot be breached? Let me add that the answer is *far* more important to *you* than it is to me."

"Miss, uh—Miss, I am certain."

"Good. I want you to go into the cold vault, obtain donation 551-20-0052—I will go with you and check the number—and then I want you to impregnate me with it. At once."

The Doctor's face broke in astonishment. Then he regained his professional aplomb and said, "Miss—that is impossible."

"Why? The purpose of our institution, as defined in its charter—which I wrote—is, to supply qualified females with donor sperm—on request, without fee, and without publicity. That's exactly what I want. If you wish to give me a physical examination, I'm ready. If you want to know whether or not this body is licensed for child-bearing, I assure you that it is—although you know that, in *this* case, a fine for unlicensed pregnancy means less than nothing. What's the trouble? Does it take too long to prepare the sperm to do it all in one day?"

"Oh, no, we can have it warmed and viable in thirty minutes."

"Then impregnate me thirty minutes from now."

"But, Miss—do you realize the trouble I could get into?"

"What trouble?"

"Well . . . I do follow the news. Or I would not have recognized you. I understand that there is a question of identity—"

"Oh, that." Joan dismissed it. "Doctor, do you bet on the races?"

"Eh? I've been known to. Why?"

"If we are truly private, you can't possibly get into

trouble. But there comes a time in every man's life when he must bet. You are at such a crisis. You can bet on a certain horse—on the nose, you can't hedge your bet. And win. Or lose. As you know, the other trustees of this corporation are my dummies; *I* am the Foundation. Let me predict what will come to pass. Presently this identity nonsense will be over and the real Johann Sebastian Bach Smith will stand up. At that time the endowment of this institution will be doubled. At that same time the salary of the Director will be doubled. If you bet on the right horse, you will be the Director. If not—you'll be out of a job."

"You're threatening me!"

"No. Prophesying. Old Johann Sebastian Bach Smith was a seventh son of a seventh son, born under a caul; he had the gift of prophecy. No matter which way you bet, the endowment will be doubled. But only you and I will ever know what is done today."

"Mmmm . . . there are procedures to satisfy. I do have authority to permit any adult female to receive a sperm donation if I am satisfied that she qualifies—and let's say that I am. Nevertheless there are routines to go through, records that must be kept."

(He's ready to geek, Boss. So sing him a Money Hum, with a different tune.) (Eunice, a cash bribe is to push him over if he won't fall. Let's see if he'll sell it to himself.)

Joan shook her head. "No records. Just do it to me and I'll hook my veil over my face and leave."

"But, Miss—I don't do these things *myself*. A staff doctor carries out the donation procedure, assisted by a nurse. They would think it strange if no records were kept. Very."

"No nurses. No assistants. You alone, Doctor. You are an M.D. and a specialist in genetics and eugenics. Either you can do this . . . or you don't know enough to head this institution—which the trustees would regretfully notice. Besides that, I go with you and check the number on that donation . . . and stick at your elbow until you place it inside me. Do we understand each other?"

The Doctor sighed. "I once thought a general practice was hard work! We can't be sure that a placed donation will result in impregnation."

"If not, I'll be back in twenty-eight and a half days. Doctor, quit stalling. Or bet on the other horse and I'll leave. No harsh words, now or later. Just that prophecy." She stood up. (Well, Eunice? Will the frog hop?) (Can't guess, dear. He's seen so many female tails he's bored with them. I can't figure him.)

Olsen suddenly stood up. "You'll need a cold suit."

"All right."

"Plus the advantage that a cold suit covers so thoroughly that a man would not recognize his own wife in one. I have a spare here, for V.I.P.s"

"I think you could class me as a V.I.P." Joan said dryly.

Forty minutes later Dr. Olsen said, "Hold still a moment longer. I am placing a Dutch cap, a latex occlusive cervical pessary, over the donation."

"Why, Doctor? I thought those things were for contraception."

"Usually. And it will serve that purpose, too—mean to say, some of our clients wish to be protected at once from any possibility of impregnation from any other souce. But in your case my purpose in installing this temporary barrier is to make certain that the donation *does* impregnate you. To give those wigglers a chance to reach target and to keep them from swimming downstream instead—follow me? Leave it in place until sometime tomorrow—or later, it doesn't matter. Do you know how to remove it?"

"If I can't get it out, I'll call you."

"If you wish. If you fail to skip your next menses, we can try again in four weeks." Dr. Olsen lowered the knee supports, offered his hand. She stepped down and her skirt fell into place. She felt flushed and happy. (Eunice, it's done!) (Yes, Boss! Beloved Boss.)

Dr. Olsen picked up her cloak, held it ready to lay around her shoulders. She said, "Doctor—don't worry about the horse race."

275

He barely smiled. "I have not been worrying about it. May I say why?"

"Please."

"Um. If you recall, I have met Johann Smith—*Mister* Johann Smith—on other occasions."

"Eleven occasions, I believe, sir, including a private interview when Dr. Andrews nominated you to succeed him."

"Yes, Miss Smith. I'll never forget that interview. Miss, there may be some legal point to clear up concerning your identity. But not in *my* mind! I do not think that any young woman of your present physiological age could simulate Mr. Johann Smith's top-sergeant manner—and make it stick."

"Oh, dear!"

"Pardon me?"

"Dr. Olsen, this sex change I've undergone is not easy to handle. It is fortunate—for both of us—that you were able to spot Johann Smith behind the face I now wear. But—darn it, sir!—I've got to acquire manners to match what I am *now*. Will you call on me—oh, say three weeks from now when I hope to have cheerful news—and let me show you that I *can* simulate a lady when I try? Come for tea. We can discuss how the Foundation's work can be expanded under a doubled endowment."

"Miss Smith, I will be honored to call on you whenever you wish. For any reason. Or none." (Wups! Hey, Eunice, I thought you said he was bored with female tails?) (So I did. But we have an unusually pretty one, Joan, even from that angle. Gonna kiss him?) (Eunice, can't you treat just one man impersonally?) (I don't know; I've never tried. Aw, don't be chinchy; he's been a perfect lamb.) (Now you be a lamb, too—let's get out of here.)

Joan let the doctor lay her cloak around her shoulders; it brought his head close to hers. She turned her face toward that side, wet her lips and smiled at him.

She could see him decide to risk it. She did not dodge as his lips met hers—but did not put her arms around him and let herself be slightly clumsy, stiffened a little before giving in to it. (Twin! Don't let him put us back on that

276

able—make him use the couch in his office.) (Neither one, Eunice. Pipe down!)

Joan broke from it, trembling. "Thank you, Doctor. And you see I *can* be a girl if I try. How do I get back to the waiting room without passing your Miss Perkins?" She hooked her yashmak.

18

A few minutes later Shorty handed her into her car, locked her in, and mounted into the forward compartment. "Gimbel's Compound, Miss Smith?"

"Please, Finchley."

Once inside the compound Joan had Fred escort her to Madame Pompadour's. The fact that she had a private bodyguard got her immediate attention from the manager, who was not Madame Pompadour even though he wore his hair in the style made famous by the notorious Marquise and had manners and gestures to match. (Eunice, are you sure we are in the right place?) (Certainly, Boss—wait till you see their prices.) "How may I serve Madame?"

"Do you have a private viewing room?"

"But of course, Madame. Uh, there is a waiting room where—"

"My guard stays with me."

The manager looked hurt. "As Madame wishes. If you will walk this way—" (Eunice, shall we walk *that* way?) (Don't try, twin—just follow him. Or her, as the case may be.)

Shortly Joan was seated facing a low model's walk; Fred stood at parade rest behind her. The room was warm; she unfrogged her cloak and pushed back its hood but left the yashmak over her features. Then she dug into her purse, got out a memorandum. "Do you have a model who comes close to these measurements?"

The manager studied the list—height, weight, shoulders,

bust, waist, leg. "This is Madame?"

"Yes. But here is another specs list even if you can't match me. A friend for whom I wish to buy something pretty and exotic. She's a redhead with pale skin to match and green eyes." Joan had copied Winifred's measurements from the exercise records the two had been keeping.

"I see no problems, Madame, but in your own case permit me to suggest that our great creative artist, Charlot, will be happy to check these measurements or even to design directly on—"

"Never mind. I am buying items already made up. If I buy."

"Madame's pleasure. May I ask one question? Will Madame be wearing her own hair?"

"If I wear a wig, it will be the same color as my hair, so assume that." (Eunice, should I buy a wig?) (Be patient and let it grow out, dear. Wigs are hard to keep clean. And they never *smell* clean.) (Then we'll never wear one.) (Smart Boss. Soap and water is the world's greatest aphrodisiac.) (I've always thought so. Though a girl should smell like a girl.) (You do, dearie, you do—you can't help it.)

"Madame's hair is a beautiful shade. And now, since Madame indicated that her time is short, perhaps it would suit her convenience to let our accounting department record her credit card while I alert the two models?"

(Watch it, Boss!) (I wasn't a-hint the door, dearie.) "I use credit cards with several names. Such as McKinley, Franklin, and Grant. Or Cleveland." Joan reached into her purse, fanned a sheaf of bills. "The poor man's credit card."

The manager repressed a shudder. "Oh, goodness, we don't expect our clients to pay *cash*."

"I'm old-fashioned."

The manager looked pained. "Oh, but it's unnecessary. If Madame prefers not to use her general credit account—her privilege!—she can set up a private account with Pompadour in only moments. If she will permit me to have her I.D.—"

"Just a moment. Can you read fine print?" Joan pointed

at a notice near a portrait of President McKinley. " 'This note is legal tender for all debts, public and private.' I shan't get tangled up in a computer. I pay cash."

"But, Madame—we aren't set up for cash! I'm not certain we could make change."

"Well, I don't want to put you to any inconvenience. Fred."

"Yes, Miss?"

"Take me to La Boutique."

The manager looked horrified. "Please, Madame! I'm sure something can be arranged. One moment while I speak to our accountant." He hurried away without waiting for an answer.

(Why the fuss, Boss honey? I've bought endless things for you, against your personal-expenditures account. Jake said we could use it.) (Eunice, I've despised those moronic machines since the first time I was trapped by a book club. But I'm not just being balky. Today is *not* a day to admit who we are. Later—after we're out of court—we'll set up a "Susan Jones" account for shopping in person. If we ever do again. I can see it's a bloody nuisance.) (Oh, no, it's fun! You'll see, twin. But, remember—I hold a veto until you learn something about clothes) (Sho', sho', little nag.) (Who are you calling a nag, you knocked-up bag?) (Happy about it, beloved?) (Wonderfully happy, Boss. Are *you?*) (Wonderfully. Even if it wasn't romantic.) (Oh, but it was! We're going to have *your* baby!) (Quit sniffling.) (I'm *not* sniffling; you *are*.) (Maybe we both are. Now shut up, here he comes.)

The manager beamed. "Madame! Our accountant says that it is perfectly all right to accept cash!"

"The Supreme Court will be pleased to hear it."

"What? Oh! Madame is jesting. Of course there is a service surcharge of ten percent for—"

"Fred. La Boutique."

"Please, Madame! I pointed out to him how unfair that is . . . and found the most wonderful solution!"

"Really?"

"Truly, Madame. Anything you choose to buy, I'll simply charge against my personal account—and you can pay me cash. No trouble, I'll be happy to. My bank doesn't make the least fuss over accepting cash deposits. Really." (Watch it, Boss; he'll expect a fat tip.) (If he can show us something we want, he may get it. Cost is no huhu, Eunice; we can't get rid of the stuff.) (It's the principle of the thing, Boss.) (Forget it and help me spend money.) (All right. But we don't buy unless we like it.)

For the next two hours Joan spent money—and was dazed to discover how expensive women's clothes could be. But she suppressed her early upbringing and paid attention only to an inner voice: (Not that one, twin—it's smart but a man wouldn't like it.) (How about this one, Eunice?) (Maybe. Have her walk it around again, then have her sit down. Show some leg.)

(Here comes 'Winnie' again. Is that girl a real redhead, Eunice?) (Probably a wig but doesn't matter; she's almost exactly Winnie's size. That would be cute on our Winsome. Twin, see what they have in fancy gee-strings—green, for a redhead. Winnie ought to have at least one outfit intended to be seen by no one but her new boy friend.) (Okay, we'll give 'Bob' a treat. Who do you think he is, beloved?) (Haven't the faintest—and we don't want to guess. Do we? I just hope he's nicer to her than Paul was.)

"Mr. duValle? Do you have something exotic in a minimum-gee for a redhead? Green, I suppose. And matching cups would be interesting, too. Something nice—an intimate present for a bride." (Bride?) (Well, it might help Winnie become a bride, Eunice—and it steers him away from thinking I'm buying it for my sweetheart.) (Who cares what *he* thinks?)

"Jeweled perhaps? Emeralds?"

"I wouldn't want a bride to be mugged over a wedding present. Nor do I wish to buy her something more expensive than her bridegroom can afford. Bad taste, I think."

"Ah, but these are synthetic emeralds. Just as lovely but quite reasonable. Yola dear—come with me."

Several thousand dollars later Joan quit. She was getting hungry and knew, from long experience, that being hungry made her unwilling to spend money. Her subconscious

282

equated "hungry" with "poor" in a canalization it had acquired in the 1930's.

She sent Fred to fetch Shorty to help carry while her purchases were being packaged and while she paid the startling sum. (Eunice, where shall we eat?) (There are restaurants inside this compound, Boss.) (Uh, darn it—no, *damn it!*—I can't eat through a yashmak. You know what will happen. Somebody who watched video yesterday will recognize us. Then the news snoops will be on us before you can say 'medium rare.') (Well . . . how about a picnic?) (Wonderful! Eunice, you win another Brownie point. But—where can we go?—a picnic with grass and trees and ants in the potato salad—but private so I can take off this veil . . . and yet close enough that we won't starve on the way?)

(I don't know, Boss, but I'll bet Finchley does.)

Finchley did know. Shorty was appointed to buy the lunch at The Hungry Man inside the compound—"Get enough for six, Shorty, and don't look at the prices. Be lavish. But there must be potato salad. And a couple of bottles of wine."

"One is enough, Miss. I don't drink, wine is a mocker, and Finchley never drinks when he is on call to drive."

"Oh, think big, Shorty; I may drink a whole bottle myself—you can save my soul tomorrow. Today is special—my first day of freedom!" (Very special, beloved.) (Very, *very* special, Boss!)

Down into the crosstown chute, up onto Express Route South, out to the unlimited zone, then fifty miles at three hundred feet per second—a speed that Finchley did not use until Joan was protected by full harness plus collision net. The fifty miles melted away in fifteen minutes and Finchley eased it down and over, ready to exit. They were not shot at, even where Route South skirts the Crater.

"Finchley? Can I get out of this pesky cocoon now?"

"Yes, Miss. But I'd feel easier if you would wear the Swedish belt. Some of these drivers are cowboys."

"All right. But tell me the instant I can take it off." (Eunice, the engineer if-that's-the-word who designed if-that's-the-word these goddam straps did *not* have women

283

in mind!) (You've got it rigged for a *man*, Boss—of course you're pinching a tit. Move the bottom half closer in and shift the upper anchor point after we stop; that's the way they rigged it for me. Some man has used it since the last time I did.) (Jake, probably, sometime when his own car was laid up. Sweetheart, how many things do I have to learn about being a woman before I can avoid tripping over my feet?) (Thousands. But you're doing all right, Boss—and I'm always here to catch you.) (Beloved. Say, this doesn't look like picnic country. I wonder if Finchley is lost.)

They were passing through solid masses of "bedroom" areas—walled enclaves, apartment houses, a few private homes. The trees looked tired and grass scarce, while the car's air-conditioning system still fought smog.

But not for long—Finchely turned into a secondary freight route and shortly they had farms on each side. Joan noticed that one belonged to her—to a subsidiary of Smith Enterprises, she corrected, and reminded herself that she no longer held control.

Nevertheless she noted that the guard at a corner watch tower seemed alert and the steel fence was stout and tall and capped with barbed wire and an alarm stand, all in good maintenance. But they were past without her seeing what was being cropped—no matter; Johann had never tried to manage that slice of conglom, he had known his limitations. (Eunice, what are we raising back there?) (Joan, I can't see if you don't look—and you never looked.) (Sorry, dearest. Speak up if you don't like the service.) (I will. I think it was a rotation crop. This soil has been farmed so hard and long that it has to be handled carefully.)

(What happens when the soil no longer responds to management?) (We starve, of course. What do you expect? But before that they'll build on it.)

(Eunice, it's *got* to stop, somewhere. When I was a boy I was a city kid but I could *walk* in less than an hour to green fields and uncut woods . . . woods so private I could play Tarzan in my skin. I wasn't 'just lucky'—even in New York City a boy with five cents could ride to farms and

284

woods in less time than it took me to walk it.)

(Doesn't seem possible, Boss.) (I know. It's taken a fast car and a professional driver to do what I used to do on bare feet—yet this isn't real farm country; these are open-air food factories with foremen and time clocks and shop stewards and payroll deductions and house-organ magazines and you name it. A dug well and a tin dipper would cause a strike—and they'd be justified; those open wells and tin dippers spread disease. Just the same, the tin-dipper era was a *good* time in this country . . . and this one isn't. *Where do we go from here?*)

The inner voice failed to answer. Joan waited. (Eunice?)

(Boss, I don't know!)

(Sorry, just sounding off. Eunice, all my life I did the best I knew how with what I had. I didn't waste—shucks, even that white-elephant house keeps a lot of people off Welfare. But every year things got worse. I used to get sour consolation from knowing that I wasn't going to be around when things fell to pieces. Now it looks like I will be. That's why I say: '*Where* do we go from here?" I don't know the answer, either.)

(Boss?)

(Yes, dearest?)

(I could see it, too. Moving from an Iowa farm to a big city made me see it. And I did have plans, sort of. I knew you were going to die, I couldn't help but know, and I figured that Joe would get tired of me someday—no kids and no prospect of any, and me someday no longer with a fine job that took care of everything Joe needed. I underrated Joe; nevertheless I never forgot that he could hand me a pink slip anytime. So I had plans, and saved my money. The Moon.)

(The Moon! Hey, that's a fine idea! Take one of Pan Am's package tours—deluxe with private courier and all the trimmings. Do it before we bulge so big we can't climb through a hatch. What do you say, little imp?)

(If you want to.)

(You don't sound enthusiastic.) (I'm not against it, Boss. But I wasn't saving money for a tourist trip. I meant to put my name on the list and take the selection exams . . . and be able to pay the difference, since I didn't have one of the subsidized skills. Out-migrate. Permanently.)

(I'll be durned! You had this in mind—and never said a word?) (Why talk about if and when? I didn't plan to do it as long as you or Joe needed me. But I did have reason to be serious. I told you I was licensed for three kids.)

(Yes, surely. I've known it since your first security check.) (Well, three is a high quota, Boss—more than half a child over replacement. A woman can be proud of a three-baby license. But I wanted more.)

(So? You can, now. Fines are no problem, even though they've upped them again and made them progressive. Eunice, if you want babies, this one is just a starter.)

(Dear Boss. Let's see how we do with this one first. I knew I could not afford fines . . . but Luna has no restrictions against babies. They *want* babies. I think we're there.)

Finchley turned in at a gate—Agroproducts, Inc., Joan noticed—a competitor. He parked so as not to lock the gate, then got out and went to the guard post. He had parked at such an angle that Joan could not see what was going on, the armor between her and the control compartment cut off her view.

Finchley returned, the car rolled through the gate. "Miss Smith, I was told to hold it under twenty miles per hour, so no safety belts is okay now."

"Thank you, Finchley. How much was the bribe?"

"Oh, nothing to matter, Miss."

"So? I expect to see it on O'Neil's Friday Report. If it is not there, I will have to ask you again."

"It'll be there, Miss," the driver answered promptly. "But I don't know yet what the total will be. Have to stop at their Administration Building and get us cleared through a back gate. To where you picnic."

"To where *we* picnic." Joan stopped to think. It irked her to pay a bribe when her status as a major competitor (retired, conceded) entitled her by protocol to red-carpet treatment. But she had not sent word ahead, a minimum courtesy in visiting a competitor's plant, to allow him time to sweep dirt under the rug or to divert the visitor away

286

from things. Industrial espionage could not with propriety be conducted at top level. "Finchley, did you tell the gate guard whom you were driving?"

"Oh, no, Miss!" Finchley sounded shocked. "But he checked the license even though I tell him it's your car—best to tell; he has a list of all private armoreds in the state, just like I have. What I tell him was, I'm driving guests of Mr. Salomon . . . and let him think it was a couple of Vips from the Coast with a yen to picnic in a safe spot. Didn't tell him anything really, except Mr. Salomon's name. That okay?"

"Just fine, Finchley." (Eunice, I feel like an interloper, being inside without giving my name. Rude.) (Look at it this way, Boss. *You* know who you are. But the public doesn't—not after that silly carnival yesterday. I think it's best to be Jake's guest . . . which is true, in a way.) (I still feel that I should tell Finchley to give my name to the Chief Agronomist. But would the word get out? Or, rather, how *soon*?) (Thirty minutes. Long enough for some clerk to phone in and a news copter to fly out. Then some snoop will try to interview you by loudspeaker because the boys won't let him land.)

(Some picnic!)

(If he does land, Shorty and Fred will be elbowing each other for a crack at him. Eager. Too eager. Boss, maybe you haven't noticed, but, while they call you 'Miss Smith,' they treat you exactly as they treated me. In their heads they know you are *you* . . . but in their guts they feel you are *me*.) (That's not far wrong, Eunice. In my head I am *me* . . . but in my guts—your pretty belly— I am *you*.)

(Boss, I like that. We're the only one-headed Siamese twins in history. But not everything in our belly is me. There's one wiggler swimming faster than the rest—and he is 'Johann,' not Joan, not Eunice—and if he makes it to the finish line, he's more important than both of us put together.)

(My love, you're a sentimentalist.) (I'm a slob, Boss. And so are you.) (Nolo contendere. When I think about Johann and Eunice—both dead, really—getting together in Joan to make a baby, I come unstuck and want to cry.)

287

(Better not, Joan; the car is stopping. Boss? How long does it take a wiggler to get there? I know a spermatozoon has to move several inches to reach the ovum—but how fast does he swim?) (Durned if I know, dear. Let's leave that cork in place at least a couple of days. Give the little bastard every possible chance.) (Good!) (Do you know how to take it out? Or do we have to see Dr. O'Neil? We don't want to let Winnie in on this.) (Boss, I've seated them and taken them out so many times I can do it in my sleep. No fret, Annette. I've worn out more rubber baby bumpers than most girls have shoes.)

(Bragging. Boasting.) (Only a trifle, Boss dearest. I told you I had always been an ever-ready. For years and years, any day I missed was not my idea. I knew my purpose in life clear back when I was a Girl Scout, no breasts, and still a virgin.)

Finchley returned to the car, spoke after he had buttoned in. "Miss?"

"Yes, Finchley."

"Farm boss sends greetings and says guests of Counselor Salomon are honored guests of Agroproducts. No bribe. But he asked if the main gate guard had put the squeeze; I told him No. Correct?"

"Of course, Finchley. We don't rat on other people's employees."

"Don't think he believed me but he didn't push it. He invited you both—assumed there was two and I didn't correct it—to stop for a drink or coffee on the way out. I let him think you might, or might not."

"Thank you, Finchley."

They continued through the farm, came to another high gate; Fred got out and pressed a button, spoke to the security office. The gate rolled back, closed after them. Shortly the car stopped; Finchley unloaded the passenger compartment, offered his hand to Joan Eunice.

She looked around. "Oh, this is lovely! I didn't know there were such places left."

The spot was beautiful in a simple fashion. A little stream, clear and apparently unpolluted, meandered between low banks. On and near its banks were several sorts of trees and bushes, but they were not dense and there was a carpet of grass filling the open spaces. From its lawnlike texture it had apparently been grazed. The sky was blue and scattered fair-weather cumulus and the sunshine was golden warm without being too hot. (Eunice, isn't it grand?) (Uh huh. 'Minds me of Iowa before the summer turns hot.)

Joan Eunice stripped off her sandals, tossed them into the car on top of her cloak. She wiggled her toes. "Oh, delicious! I haven't felt grass under my bare feet for more than twenty years. Finchley, Shorty, Fred—all of you! If you've got the sense God promised a doorknob, you'll take off your shoes and socks and give your feet a treat."

Shotguns looked impassive; Finchley looked thoughtful. Then he grinned. "Miss Smith, you don't have to tell me twice!" He reached down and unclicked his boots. Joan Eunice smiled, turned away, and wandered down toward the stream, judging that Shorty would be less shy about it if she did not stare.

(Eunice, is Iowa this beautiful? Still?) (Parts of it, hon. But it's filling up fast. Take where we lived, between Des Moines and Grinnell. Nothing but farms when I was a baby. But by the time I left home we had more commuter neighbors than farm neighbors. They were beginning to build enclaves, too.) (Dreadful. Eunice, this country is breeding itself to death.) (For a freshly knocked-up broad you have an odd attitude toward reproduction, twin. See that grassy spot where the stream turns?) (Yes. Why?) (It takes me back . . . it looks like a stream bank in Iowa where I surrendered my alleged innocence.) (Well! Nice place for it. Did you struggle?) (Twin, are you pulling my leg? I cooperated.) (Hurt?) (Not enough to slow me down. No reason for it to. Boss darling, I know how it was in your day. But there is no longer any issue over tissue. Girls with smart mothers have it removed surgically when they reach menarche. And some just lose it gradually and never know where it went. But the girl who yells bloody murder and bleeds like a stuck pig is a rare bird today.) (Infant, I must again set you straight. Things haven't changed much. Except that people are more open about it now. Do you

289

suppose that water is warm enough to swim in?)

(Warm enough, Boss. But how do we know it's clean? No telling what's upstream.)

(Eunice, you're a sissy. If you don't bet, you can't win.)

(That was true yesterday . . . but today we're an expectant mother. A babbling brook can be loaded with nineteen sorts of horribles.)

(Uh . . . oh, hell! If it's polluted, it'd be posted.) (Back here where you can't reach it without being passed through two electric gates? Ask Finchley; he may know.)

(And if he says it's polluted?) (Then we go swimming anyhow. Boss, as you pointed out, if you don't bet, you can't win.) (Mmmm . . . if he *knows* it's polluted, I'm chicken. As *you* pointed out, beloved, we now have responsibilities. Let's go eat, I'm hungry.) (*You're* hungry? I was beginning to think you had given up the habit.) (So let's eat while we can. How soon does morning sickness start?) (Who dat, Boss? The other time the only effect it had was to make me hungry morning, noon, and night. Let's eat!)

Joan Eunice trotted back toward the car, stopped dead when she saw that Shorty was laying the car's folding table—with one place setting. "What's that?"

"Your lunch, Miss."

"A picnic? On a table? Do you want to starve the ants? It should be on the ground."

Shorty looked unhappy. "If you say, Miss." (Joan! You're not wearing panties. If you loll on the ground, you'll shock Shorty—and interest the others.) (Spoilsport. Oh, all right.)

"Since it's set up, Shorty, leave it that way. But set three more places."

"Oh, we eat in the car, Miss—we often do."

She stomped her foot. "Shorty, if you make me eat alone, I'll make you walk home. Whose idea was this? Finchley's? *Finchley!* Come here!"

A few moments later all four sat down at the table. It was crowded as Joan had insisted that everything be placed on it at once—"Just reach," she explained. "Or starve. Is there a strong man here who can open that wine bottle?"

The dexterity with which Shorty opened it caused her to suspect that he had not always been a teetotaler. She filled her glass and Fred's, then reached for Finchley's. He said, "Please, Miss Smith—I'm driving," and put his hand over it.

"Give it to me," she answered, "for four drops. For a toast. And four drops for you, Shorty, for the same purpose." She put about a quarter of an inch in each of their glasses. "But first—Shorty, will you say grace?"

The big man looked startled, at once regained his composure. "Miss Smith, I'd be pleased." He bowed his head. (Boss! What's eating you?) (Pipe down! Om Mani Padme Hum.) (Oh! Om Mani Padme Hum.) (Om Mani Padme Hum.) (Om Mani Padme Hum.............)

"Amen."

"Amen!"

(Om Mani Padme Hum. Amen.)

"Amen. Thank you, Shorty. Now for a toast—which is a sort of a prayer, too. We'll all drink it, so it must be to someone who isn't here . . . but should be." (Boss! You must *stop* this—it's morbid.) (Mind your own business!) "Will one of you propose it?"

Finchley and Shorty looked at each other—looked away. Joan caught Fred's eye. "Fred?"

"Uh—Miss, I don't know how!" He seemed upset.

"You stand up"—Joan stood, the others followed —"and say whatever you like about someone who isn't here but would be welcome. Anyone we all like. You name the person to be honored." She raised her glass, realized her tears were starting. (Eunice! Are *you* crying? Or am *I*? I never used to cry!) (Then don't get me started, Boss—I told you I was a sentimental slob.)

Fred said uncertainly, "A toast to . . . someone we all like . . . and who should be here. *And still is!*" He suddenly looked frightened.

"Amen," Shorty said in sonorous baritone. " 'And still is.' Because Heaven is as close as you'll let it be. That's what I tell my people, Fred . . . and in your heart you know I'm right." He poured down, solemnly and carefully, the symbolic teaspoonful of wine in his glass; they all drank.

Joan said quietly, "Thank you, Fred. She heard you. She heard you too, Shorty. She hears me now." (Boss! You've got them upset—and yourself, too. Tell them to sit down. And *eat*. Tell 'em *I* said to! You've ruined a perfectly good picnic.) (No, I haven't.) "Finchley. You knew her well. Probably better than I did . . . for I was a cranky old man and she catered to my illness. What would *she* want us to do now?"

"What would . . . Mrs. Branca? . . . want us to do?"

"Yes. Did you call her 'Mrs. Branca'? Or 'Eunice'?" (They called me 'Eunice,' Boss—and after the first week I kissed them hello and good-bye and thanked them for taking care of me. Even if Jake could see. He just pretended not to notice.) (Busybody. You're a sweet girl, beloved. Anything more than kiss them?) (Heavens, Boss! Even getting them to accept a kiss in place of the tips they wouldn't take took doing.) (I'll bet!—on *you*, that is—sister tart.) (Knocked-up broad.)

"Uh, I called her 'Mrs. Branca' at first. Then she called me 'Tom' and I called her 'Eunice.' "

"All right, Tom, what does Eunice want us to do? Stand here crying? I see tears in your eyes; I'm not the only one crying. Would Eunice have us spoil a picnic?"

"Uh—She'd say, 'Sit down and eat.' "

"That she would!" Shorty agreed. "Eunice would say, 'Don't let hot things get cold and cold things get hot—*eat!*"

"Yes," agreed Joan Eunice, sitting down, "as Eunice was never a spoilsport in all her short and beautiful life and wouldn't let anyone else be. Especially me, when I was cranky. Reach me a drumstick, Fred—no, don't pass it."

Joan took a bite of chicken. (Twin, what Shorty said sounded like a quotation.) (It was, Boss.) (Then you've eaten with him before.) (With all of them. When a team drove me late at night, I always invited them in for a bite. Joe never minded, he liked them all. Shorty he was especially glad to see; he wanted Shorty to model for him. At first Shorty thought Joe was making fun of him—didn't know that Joe rarely joked and never about painting. They never got to it, though, as Shorty is shy—wasn't sure it was all right to pose naked and scared that I might show up

292

while he was posing. Not that I would have.) (Not even once, little imp? Shorty is a beautiful tower of ebony.) (Boss, I keep telling you—) (—that nudity doesn't mean anything to your generation. Depends on the skin, doesn't it? *I* would enjoy seeing our black giant—and that goes for Johann as well as for Joan.) (Well—) (Take your time thinking up a fib; I've got to make conversation.) "Tom, do you have those mustard pickles staked out, or may I have some? Shorty, you sounded as if you had sampled Eunice's cooking. Could she cook?"

Finchley answered, "You bet she could!"

"Real cooking? Anybody can flash a prepack—and that's what kids nowadays seem to think is cooking." (Boss, I'll spit in your soup!) "But what could she have done faced with flour and lard and baking powder and such?"

"Eunice would have done just fine," Shorty said quietly. "True, she mostly never had time for real cooking—but when she did—or whatever she done, anyways—she done just perfect."

(My fan! Boss—give him a raise.) (No.) (Stingy.) (No, Eunice. Shorty killed the vermin who killed you. I want to do something for him. But it can't be money; he would not accept it.)

"She was an artist," agreed Fred.

"You mean 'artist' in the general sense. Her husband was, I recall, an artist in the usual sense. A painter. Is he a good one? I've never seen any of his work. Do any of you know?"

Finchley said, "I guess that's a matter of opinion, Miss Smith. I like Joe Branca's paintings—but I don't know anything about art; I just know what I like. But—" He grinned. "Can I tell on you, Shorty?"

"Aw, Tom!"

"You were flattered, you know you were. Miss Smith, Joe Branca wanted to paint that big ape on your right."

(*Bingo!*) (Trouble, Eunice?) "And did he, Shorty?"

"Well, no. But he *did* ask me. He did." (Don't you *see*, Boss? This is that clincher. A fact you first learned from *me* and nowhere else . . . and then had confirmed to the

293

hilt. Now you know I'm *me*.) (Oh, piffle, darling.) (But Boss—) (I've known you were you all along, beloved. But this isn't proof. Once I knew that Joe and Shorty had met, it was a logical necessity that Joe would want him to model—*any* artist would want to paint him.)

(Boss, you make sick! It's proof. I'm *me*.) (Beloved darling without whom life would not be worth living even in this beautiful body, I *know* you are you. But flatworms don't matter, coincidences don't matter, no mundane proof matters. There is no proof that some cocksure psychiatrist could not explain away as coincidence, or déjà vu, or self-delusion. If we let *them* set the rules, we're lost. But we shan't. What *does* matter is that you have me, and I have you. Now shut up; I want to get them all so easy with me that they'll call me Eunice. You say they used to kiss you?)

(Oh, sure. Friendly kisses. Well, Dabrowski used to put zing in it but you know how Poles are.) (I'm afraid I don't.) (Put it this way, Boss. With a Pole don't advertise unless you mean to deliver—because *his* intentions are as honest as a loaded gun. With Dabrowski I was very careful not to let it go critical.)

(I'll remember. Just as well he isn't here. Because the situation is like that with Jake, only milder. Little baggage, you caused all my mobile guards to fall in love with you. So now I've got to get them to accept that you are dead while feeling that you are still alive, equally. If they call me 'Eunice,' I'm halfway there. If they kiss me—) (*What?* Boss! Don't try it!)

(Now see here, Eunice! If you hadn't played 'My Last Duchess' to half the county, I wouldn't be having to repair the damage.) ('Damage,' huh? You're *complaining?*)

(No, no, my darling! Never. I was the prime beneficiary of your benevolence. But to lose something of value is a damage, and that is the damage I must repair.) (Well . . . I won't argue, dearest. But in this case you can let it be; I never let it warm up that much.) (And *I* say you don't know what you are talking about. Cool you may have meant to keep it. Unsexy—or as unsexy as you could manage which isn't very. But all four of my mobiles were willing to die for you—correct?) (Uh—) (Let's have no silly talk. Do you think the fact that I paid them had anything to do with their willingness? Careful how you answer.)

(Uh . . . I don't *have* to answer! Boss, what's the use of stirring them up over my death?) (Because, my darling, from now on they will be guarding *me*—as I now am, inside your lovely body—just as they guarded you. They've got to *want* to guard me, or they'll never be happy in this weird situation. It's either that, or fire them or retire them—) (Oh, no!) (Of course not. To paraphrase Sherlock Holmes; when you have eliminated what you can't do, what remains is what you *must* do. Besides, dearest and only, this is stern practice for the much harder case we still face.) (Jake? But Jake is—) (Little stupid! Jake has already accepted the impossible. I mean *Joe*.)

(But, Boss! You must *never* see Joe.)

(God knows I wish I could avoid it. Never mind, beloved; we won't see him until you know—as I do—that we must. Now either shut up, or coach me in how to handle these brave men.)

(Well . . . I'll help all I can. But you'll never get them as easy as they were with me—'kissing-friends' easy, I mean. *I* was an employee. *You* are the Boss.)

(If that argument were valid, queens would never get pregnant. Sure it makes it harder. But you've given me a lot to work with. Want to bet?)

(Oh, sure, I'll bet you a billion dollars you can't kiss even one of them. Don't be silly, Boss; we can never make a real bet, there is no way to pay off.) (You don't have much practice being an angel, do you, little imp? You still think in earthy terms. Certainly we can make a bet and pay off to the winner. This baby in us—) (Huh! Now wait a moment—) (*You* wait a moment, Eunice. If I win this bet, I name our baby. If I lose, *you* have the privilege. Fair bet?)

(Oh. All right, it's a bet. But you'll lose.)

(We'll see.)

(Oh, yes, you will, Boss. You'll lose even if you win. Want to know why?) (Planning on cheating?) (Not necessary, Boss darling; you're going to find that you *want* to name the baby whatever name *I* want it to have. Because you're a sucker for a pretty girl, Boss, always have been

295

and still are.) (Now wait a moment. I used to be, but now I *am* that 'pretty girl' and——) (You'll find out. Do you want coaching? I'll help you win if it can be done. It can't.) (Yes, but tuck your advice in edgeways; I've been chewing this bone too long.) "Fred, I'll trade you one of these Danish sandwiches for more wine. Then keep our glasses filled; Shorty doesn't drink and Tom won't and I want company in getting tiddly, this is my freedom celebration."

(Fred might be easiest if you can get him over seeing ghosts when he looks at you.) "I don't mind another glass, Miss, but I mustn't get tiddly, I'm on duty."

"Pish and tush. Tom and Shorty will get us home even if they have to drag us. Right, Shorty?" (Shorty is your impossible case. I managed it only by being 'little girl' to him——which you can't be, Boss.)

"We'll certainly try, Miss Smith."

"Do I have to be 'Miss Smith' on a picnic? You called Mrs. Branca 'Eunice,' did you not? Did she call you 'Shorty?' "

"Miss, she called me by my name. Hugo."

"Do you prefer that to your nickname?"

"It's the name my mother gave me, Miss."

"That answers me, Hugo; I will remember. But it brings to mind a problem. Anybody want to fight me for the last black olive? Come on, put up your dukes. But that's not the problem. I said I didn't want to be called 'Miss Smith' under these circumstances. But I don't want to be called 'Johann' either; that's a man's name. Hugo, you have christened babies?"

"Many times, Miss——uh, Miss——"

Joan cut in fast. "That's right, you don't know what to call me. Hugo, having named so many babies you must have opinions about names. Do you think 'Joan' pronounced as two syllables would be a good name for a girl who used to be a man named 'Johann?' "

"Yes. I do."

"Tom? What do you think?" (Tom would kiss you at the drop of a hint if you weren't his employer. I don't think he ever did give up hoping to catch me alone . . . so I was as careful not to let that chance come up as I was with
296

Dabrowski. All it took with Tom was to say, 'Tom, if you're going to be stuffy about letting me pay for extra service'—it was an after-midnight run, Boss; a rare-blood call—'at least you can kiss me good-night.' So he did, quite well. After which Hugo was too polite not to lean way down and give me a fatherly little peck. But what worked for Eunice can't work for 'Miss Smith.') (So watch me switch decks on them, young'un.)

"It sounds like a good name to me," the driver-guard agreed.

"Fred? Do I look like 'Joan' to you?" She sat up straight and lifted her chest. (You look like you're going to break that bandeau, if you aren't careful.) (Pfui, little hussy; it can't break. I want him to realize that I'm female.) (He realizes it. Winnie ought to be here to take his pulse.)

"I don't see why anybody should get a vote but you. But, sure, I like it."

"Good! I still have to sign papers with my former name—but I'm 'Joan' in my mind. But, friends, this country must have a thousand 'Joan Smiths' in it; I need a middle name. But I *want* one for a much better reason." She looked with solemn seriousness at the giant black. "Hugo, you are a man of God. Would it be presumptuous of me to call myself . . . 'Joan Eunice?' " (Boss, if you make my friend Hugo cry, I'll—I'll—I won't speak to you the rest of the day!) (Oh, quit nagging! Hugo won't cry. He's the only one of the three who believes you're here. He has faith.)

"I think that would be beautiful," the Reverend Hugo White answered solemnly and sniffed back tears.

"Hugo, Eunice would not want you to be sad about it." She looked away from him, her own eyes bright with unshed tears. "That settles it. My new name will be—*is!*—Joan Eunice. I don't want anyone ever to forget Eunice. Most especially I want you, her friends, to know this. Now that I am a woman, Eunice is my model, the ideal I must live up to, every hour, every minute, of my new life. Will you help me? Will you treat me as Eunice? Yes, yes, I'm your employer; somehow I must be both, and it's not easy. But the most difficult part for me is to learn to

297

behave and think and feel as *Eunice* . . . when I've had so many weary years as a cranky, self-centered old man. You are her friends—will you help me?" (Boss, did you ever sell real estate in Florida?) (Damn it, if you can't help, keep *quiet!*) (Sorry, Boss. That was applause. As Hugo would say, 'You done perfect.')

Tom Finchley said quietly, "We'll help. That goes for Dabrowski too. By the way, she called him 'Anton.' First she called him 'Ski' like the rest of us. Then she learned his first name and called him by it."

"Then I will call him 'Anton.' Will you all call me 'Eunice'? Or at least 'Joan Eunice'? To help me? Oh, call me 'Miss Smith' when others are around; I know you won't feel easy otherwise. You probably called her 'Mrs. Branca' if other people were—"

"We did."

"So call me 'Miss Smith' when it would be natural for you to call her 'Mrs. Branca.' But when you called her 'Eunice,' call me 'Joan Eunice' and—dear and trusted friends! —any time you feel that I have earned it, please call me 'Eunice.' It will be the highest compliment you can pay me, so don't use it lightly. Leave off the 'Joan' and call me 'Eunice.' Will you?"

Finchley looked at her, unsmiling. "Yes . . . Eunice."

"Tom, I haven't earned it yet."

Finchley did not answer. Fred said, "Let me get this straight. 'Joan Eunice' is for everyday . . . but 'Eunice' means we think you've done and said just what Mrs. Branca would have."

"That's right, that's what I said."

"Then I know what Tom meant. Uh, this has been a touchy day—worse for you, I'd say, but not easy for any of us. Shorty—Hugo, I mean—said she was an angel. Or meant it, anyhow. I can't argue; Shorty is a preacher and knows more about angels and suchlike than I do. But if she was—is, I mean—still, she had a lot of salt and pepper in her, too. You remember an hour back when you snapped at Shorty and yelled for Tom?"

She sighed. "Yes, I remember. I lost my temper. I've got a long way to go. I know it."

298

"But that's just what I'm *saying* . . . Eunice. She had a lot of spunk. If we had tried to make her eat by herself, she would have kicked the gong. Right, Shorty?—I mean 'Hugo.' "

"Amen! Eunice."

Finchley said, "Fred read my mind close enough . . . Eunice. But I was thinking of other things, too. I never thought of her as an angel, partic'arly. She just treated us like people."

"Tom—"

"Yeah, Shorty? Hugo."

"My name's Shorty to you—and to you, Fred. Don't put on any fancies. Hugo was Mama's name for me. And hers. Yours, Eunice. But I near forgot what I had to say. Tom, that's all anybody wants. To be treated 'like people.' She done it that way—Eunice. And now you do, too. 'Like people.' Mr. Smith didn't quite manage it. But he was old and sick, and we made allowances."

"Oh, dear! I feel like crying again. Hugo—when I was Mr. Smith, I never meant to be anything but people. Truly I didn't."

"Sick people can't help being cranky. My Daddy got so mean before he passed on, I run away from home. Worst mistake I ever made. But I don't fault him for it. We do what we do, then we live with it. Eunice—the first Eunice—is an angel now, my heart tells me and my head knows. But she had her little human ways, same as everybody. The dear Lord don't fault us for that."

"Hugo? If it had been me and not her, would I have made it? To Heaven?" (Om Mani Padme Hum! Watch it, Boss! He'll drag you over to that creek and wash your sins away.) (If he wants to, I'll let him. Shut up!)

"I don't rightly know," the preacher said softly. "I never knew Mr. Smith that well. But the Lord do move in mysterious ways. Looks like He give you a second chance. He always knows what He's doing." (Oh, all right, twin. Try not to get water up our nose.)

"Thank you, Hugo. I think He did, too—and I'm trying to justify it." She sighed. "But it's not easy. I try to do what Eunice would do. At least justify the second chance *she* gave me. I think I know what she would do now. But I'm not certain." (I'd knock off all this talk, that's what *I'd* do.) (Pipe down and give me a chance.) She looked around. "I don't know how well you knew her and I keep learning things about her. I think you three—you four; I include Anton—must have been her closest friends, at least in my household. Certainly you knew her better than I had thought. Tom?"

"Yes, Eunice?"

"Did you ever kiss her?"

Her driver looked startled. "Yes . . . Joan Eunice."

"Meaning Eunice would never ask such a question, she would just do what her heart told her to. I wanted to, Tom—but I was scared. Not yet used to being a girl." She jumped up, stood by his chair, took his hands, pulled.

Slowly he got to his feet. She put her arms around his shoulders, put up her face—waited.

He sighed and almost scowled, then took her in his arms and kissed her. (Twin, he can do lots better.) (He will. The poor dear is scared.) Joan let him go without forcing it beyond his willingness, whispered, "Thank you, Tom," and quickly left his arms.

—went on to Fred, took his hands. Again Fred looked frightened but he got up promptly. (What about Fred, Eunice? Sexy or sisterly?) (Too late, twin!) Fred embraced her with unexpected force, met her mouth so quickly that Joan was caught with her lips open and he at once answered it, savagely.

But briefly. He broke from it and both were trembling. (Eunice! What is this? You didn't warn me.) (So I goofed. Later, dear. Slow march now and say three Money Hums and be darn sure to be an innocent child with Father Hugo.)

Joan went slowly around the table the long way, stopped by Hugo, waited. He got up from his chair, looked down at her. She moved closer, put her hands on his chest, looked up, face solemn, lips closed, eyes open.

Gently he put his arms around her. (My God, Eunice, if he really hugged us, he 'ud break us in two!) (He never will, twin; he's the gentlest man alive.)

Hugo's lips met hers in soft benediction, unhurried but quickly over. She stayed in his arms a moment. "Hugo? When you pray for her tonight, will you add a prayer for me? I may not deserve it. But I need it."

"I will, Eunice." He seated her with gallant grace, then sat down again. (High, low, jack, and game, twin—what are you going to name him?) ('Eunice,' of course!) (Even if he's a boy?) (If he's a boy, he'll be named Jacob E.—for 'Eunice'—Smith.) ('Johann E Smith' is better.) (I won the bet, so shut up. I won't wish 'Johann' on a boy. Now what's this about Fred?) (You won't believe it.) (By now I believe anything. All right, later.) "Fred, is there any wine in that bottle? Hugo, will you open the second bottle? I need it, I'm shaky."

"Certainly, Eunice. Hand me the bottle, Fred."

"I'm going to eat some more, too, and I hope all of you will. Tom, am I still 'Eunice'? Or am I a hussy who doesn't understand how a lady behaves?"

"Yes, Eunice. I mean 'No , Eunice.' I—Oh, hell!"

She patted his hand. "That's the nicest compliment I've had yet, Tom. You would never have said 'Oh, hell' to Miss Smith . . . but you know that Eunice and Joan Eunice—is human." She looked around the table. "Do you know how *good* it is to be touched? Have you ever watched kittens snuggling? For over a quarter of a century no one kissed me. Except for an occasional handshake I don't think anyone ever touched me. Until nurses and doctors started handling me. Friends—dear friends—you have taken me back into the human race, with your lips. I am so very grateful to Eunice—to Eunice Branca—that she kissed you before I did, and won your friendship—your love? I think so. For it meant that you let me in—treated me as 'people'! Uh, tell me this, I must know—even if it makes you, Tom, call me 'Joan Eunice' again. Did Eunice kiss Anton, too?" (Boss, I'm not going to tell you *anything* until we're alone!) (Didn't ask *you*, dear.)

"Won't anyone tell me? Well, I suppose it's an unfair question."

Finchley said suddenly, "Teams shift around. I drive with Fred, and Shorty with Ski, and so forth. Been times
301

when I rode Shotgun for Ski. Eunice, she treated us all alike. But don't never think anything bad about it—"

"I don't!"

"—because there wasn't any such. She was so warm and friendly—and *good*—that she could kiss a man friend just for, uh—"

"For lovingkindness," Shorty supplied.

" 'For lovingkindness.' Kissed us thank-you and good-night as quick with her husband there as any other time. Always did, if we stopped for a late bit o' supper with them." (All right, twin. Fred and Anton. Not Tom and Hugo. Happened only once. Oh, Tom would have, but no chance, so I kept it cool. Hugo—nobody gets past Hugo's guard and I never tried. He has moral character—something you and I don't know anything about.)

"Thank you for telling me, Tom. I'll never let Anton guess. But he'll find me easy to kiss if he wishes to . . . now that I know that she shared lovingkindness with him. Abrupt change of subject: Tom, is that pretty little stream polluted? It looks so clean."

"It's clean. Clean as a creek can be, I mean. I know because I found out about this place through the company lending it to our guild for a picnic. Some of us went swimming after the farm super told us it was okay."

"Oh, wonderful! Because I want to swim. I last went swimming in natural water—old swimming hole style, I mean—let me see . . . goodness! More than three-quarters of a century ago."

"Eunice, I don't think you should."

"Why?"

"Because it can be polluted another way. Dropouts. Not all the dropouts are in the A.A.s; any wild countryside attracts them. Like this. I didn't make a fuss but when you walked down to the bank by yourself, Fred had you flanked one side and me the other."

"Well, heavens, if you can keep me safe on the bank, you can keep me safe in the water."

"It ain't quite the same, truly it ain't. I was a few seconds late once, I won't be again. Some dropouts are real nasty weirdos, not just harmless nuts."

302

"Tom, why argue? I want to get into that water, feel it all over me. I intend to."

"I wish you wouldn't . . . Joan Eunice."

She jerked her head around at the last two words. Then she grinned and pouted her lower lip. "Okay, Tom. Darn it, I've handed you three a leash you can lead me by any time you see fit. And yet I'm supposed to be boss. It's comical."

"It's like the Secret Service," Finchley answered soberly. "The President is the top boss of any . . . but he gives in when his guards tell him not to do something."

"Oh, I wasn't complaining; I was wryly amused. But don't jerk that leash too much, Tom; I don't think Eunice would stand for it and neither will I."

"I'm hoping you won't pull on the leash as much as she did. If she, uh—well, things coulda been different."

Fred said, "Tom, don't cry over spilt milk."

Joan said quickly, "I'm sorry. Boys, I think the picnic is over. Maybe someday we can all have that swim somewhere safe and just as beautiful." (Eunice, can you swim?) (Red Cross lifesaver—you knew that, it was in my snoopsheet. Never went out for the team, though; cheerleader was more fun.) (I could make a comment.) (Look who's talking! No-Pants Smith.) (Who taught me?) (You didn't need teaching; you have the instincts.)

19

A short time later they were again in the car. Finchley said, "Home, Miss Smith?"

"Tom, I can't hear you."

"I asked did you want to go home, Miss?"

"I understood that part but this intercom must be out of order. I heard something that sounded like 'Miss Smith.' "

There was a silence. "Eunice, do you want to go home?"

"Not until dinnertime, Tom; I want all of this lovely day I can have."

"Okay, Eunice. Do I cruise? Or go somewhere?"

"Uh . . . I have one more item on my list, and there's time enough for anything you three may want to pick up, too, so check around."

"Will do. Where do we take you for what you want, Eunice?"

"I don't know. I lost touch with such matters years ago. Tom, I want to buy a present for Mr. Salomon, something nice but unnecessary—presents should be unnecessary, a luxury a person might not buy himself. So it probably would be a men's shop that stocks luxurious unnecessaries. Abercrombie & Fitch used to be that sort—but I'm not certain they are still in business."

"They are. But let me ask Fred and Shorty."

Shortly Finchley reported: "There are a dozen places that would do. But we think The Twenty-First Century Stud has the fastest stock."

"Roz. Let's giddyap and get there."

"That is, if you don't mind their prices. 'Twigs and leaves.' "

"I don't mind; I've met thieves before. Tom—all of you. I came out of this operation with more money than I had last year . . . and it's a nuisance. I've played the money game and I'm bored with it. Any time any of you can think of a good way to help me get rid of some—a *good* way, I said; I won't be played for a sucker—you'd be doing me a favor to tell me. Hugo, are there any poor people in your church?"

His answer was slow. "Lots of them, Eunice. But not *hurtin'* poor, just Welfare poor. I'd like to think about it . . . because it don't do a man no good to plain *give* him what he ought to root for. So the Book says, in different words."

"That's the trouble, Hugo. I've given away money many times, and usually did harm when I meant to do good. But the Book also says something about the eye of the needle. All right, think about it. Now let's go see those thieves. I'll need a man to help me. Which one of you dresses the most far-out when you aren't in uniform?"

She heard Fred laugh. "Eunice, it's no race. You should *see* the getups Tom wears. A Christmas tree. A light show."

Finchley growled, then said, "Don't listen to him, Eunice."

"He's probably jealous, Tom. All right, if there is parking inside or near this shop, you come help me."

As they passed through the second gate Finchley said, "Crash belts, Eunice?"

"I'm wearing the Swedish—and it's comfortable now that Hugo has adjusted it. Could we get along with just it and the collision net if we didn't go so fast? Or does that make me 'Joan Eunice' again?"

"Uh—Will you wear the forehead strap?"

"All right. It's just that I don't like to be tied down all over. It reminds me—well, it reminds me of the way the doctors kept me strapped down after the operation. Necessary, but I hated it." She did not mention that a forehead strap was what she disliked the most.

"We heard about that—musta been horrid. But you

306

need the forehead strap. Say I'm doing only a hundred, a slam stop could break your neck. If you don't wear it."

"So I wear it."

"I don't see the light on the board."

"Because I haven't put it on yet. There. Did the light go on?"

"Yes. Thank you . . . Eunice."

"Thank *you*, Tom. For taking care of me. Let's mush. I wasn't pulling on the leash, truly I wasn't." (Says you. Boss, you're mendacious, untruthful, and a fibber.) (Where did I learn it, dearie? They're sweet boys, Eunice—but we've got to work out a way to live so that we don't have to clear everything with forty other people. Good servants are priceless—but you work for them as much as they work for you. Life should be simpler. Honey, how would you like to go to India and be a guru and sit on a mountain top and never have any plans? Just sit and wait for your grateful chelas to gather around?)

(Might be a long wait. Why not sit at the bottom of the mountain and wait for the boys to gather around?) (One-track mind!) (Yes. Yours, you dirty old man.) (Conceded. But I try to act like a lady.) (Not too hard, you don't). (As hard as you ever did, little trollop. I was called 'Joan Eunice' *once* . . . and the issue had nothing to do with sex.) (You'd be surprised how much sex had to do with it, Joan.) (Well . . . from that point of view, yes. But as long as they call me 'Eunice' I'll go on believing that I've 'done just perfect.' Honestly though, good servants can be smothering. Take Winnie. She's a darling—but she's underfoot every minute. Eunice, how the devil can we manage that 'actively female' life you want—sorry, *we* want—with so much chaperonage?)

(Take a tip from Winnie.)

(How dear?)

(Let her in on your plans. Then she'll keep your secrets and never ask a question, just as you do for her. Try it.)

(I may have to. I'm sure she won't talk . . . and will happily listen to anything I need to spill. But, Eunice, if I go outside the house, it's going to be hard to keep Tom and Hugo, or Anton and Fred, from guessing. You saw the

307

elaborate maneuver I had to use today.)

(You didn't have to, Boss; they won't talk.)

(Perhaps they won't, but I don't want them even to *think*. They're beginning to think I'm an angel—named Eunice—and I'd rather keep it that way.)

(Boss, they know darned well that Eunice is no angel. Even Hugo knows it . . . because Hugo is the smartest of the four, even if he is an illit. Knows people. Understands them from having been there himself. Forgives them their transgressions and loves them anyhow. Boss dear, they loved me the way I was, feet of clay and all—and they'll love you the same way.)

(Maybe, I hope so. I know I love you more, knowing more about you and things I never suspected, than I did before we consolidated. Immoral little wench. What's this about you and Fred and Anton? Did you really?)

(Wondered when you'd get around to that. Those good-night kisses did start out just friendly. Brotherly. Fatherly in Hugo's case. Never got past that with Tom, as we were always either under Hugo's eye, or Jake's, or both—I just knew darn well a *man* was kissing me. But Fred and Anton weren't much chaperonage for each other and they were both charged up over me. So, when a chance turned up, I thought 'Why not?')

(Pure charity, eh?)

(Was that sarcasm, Boss? Anyhow, they took me home late one night. Not a blood donation call, just working late with Jake when we were very rushed getting things arranged for you. The 'warm body' project. I invited them in for a Coke and a snack, as usual. Only it turned out Joe wasn't home.)

(So human nature won—again.)

(You seem to have a low opinion of human nature, Boss darling.)

(I have a *high* opinion of human nature. I think it will prevail in spite of all efforts of wowsers to suppress it. But that's all it took? *Two* men? Cold sober? And a chance that your husband might walk in? Lovely fallen angel, your story not only has holes; it is inconsistent. I do know something about men, having been one. What they'll risk, what they won't. Plenty, that is, for a woman. But two men tend to be wary of each other, and still more so when a husband might show up. Darling, you've left out something—this does not sound like a first time.)

(Boss, cross our heart, it *was* a first time . . . and the only time, for I was killed soon after. All right, I'll fill in the holes. Joe wasn't likely to walk in and they knew it. *Couldn't*, as our door was hand-bolted from the inside whenever either of us was there. Joe was even more careful about it than I was, as he had always been a city boy. But they knew also that Joe was not due home until midnight . . . and they brought me home about twenty-one thirty. No hurry, no worry, no flurry. While Joe can't read, he can tell time—you know those little dummy clocks some one-man shops use? Back at such-and-such a time, and mark the time by setting the hands?

(We had one of those, to tell the other one when he would be back. That night the door opened to my voice, so I looked for the dummy clock and found it set for midnight—and told Anton and Fred that I was sorry but Joe wasn't going to be home soon enough for a visit.)

(Called attention to it, minx. Sounds like a setup.)

(Well, I knew what I was ready for, once I knew we had the place to ourselves. Oh, shucks, Boss, I'm still trying to be your 'nice girl.' I had had my ear cocked for a late arrival with that team for over a month. When Jake asked me to work after dinner, I phoned Joe, just as usual. And set it up under Jake's nose. Short-talked it—almost another language if spoken by a husband and wife. What Jake heard was me telling Joe that I wouldn't be home until twenty-one thirty. What Jake didn't hear, or would not understand, was that I was asking Joe if he minded being elsewhere, in family short-talk code we used if we wanted that favor. It was all right, Boss darling; I made myself scarce for Joe's sake oftener than I asked it of him. The only question was: Was he painting? Turned out he was not, so I was home free.

(Joe asked if I wanted him to be away all night. What he said was: 'Roz. Punch or phone?' Not that Joe *ever* punched me to wake me, but I answered, 'Judy,' meaning

309

that it was up to him but I hoped he would punch me, and added, 'Blackbirds,' and gave him a phone kiss and signed off. All set, no sweat—knew what I would find at home.)

('Blackbirds?')

('Four and twenty blackbirds, baked in a pie'—set midnight on the clock even if you stay out all night, Joe darling. Oh, it could have been 'pumpkin' or 'Christmas Eve' or 'Reach' or 'solid gold.' But what I used was 'Blackbirds.')

(Did you kids ever talk English?)

(Of course we did, Boss. Joe speaks good English when he needs to. But short-talk settled it in a dozen words. Without giving Jake any hint that I was late-dating him. If I had had Betsy at hand, I would have used hush and spoken standard English. But we weren't actually working late, not that late. I was using the phone you used yesterday, with Jake only feet away from me. Had to be short-talked.)

(Let me get this straight. Joe set the dummy clock, saying he would not be home until midnight. Did he come home then?)

(About ten minutes after midnight. Joe wouldn't embarrass a guest by being too prompt. Joe is a natural gentleman, never had to learn; he just *is*. It was the first thing that attracted me to him, and the quality that caused me to ask him to marry me. An illit, certainly—but I'll take an illit gentleman over an Ivy-League squeak any year.)

(I agree, beloved. The more I hear about Mr. José Branca the better I like him. And respect him. And regret his tragic loss—meaning *you*, beloved little strumpet. I was just trying to get the schedule straight for what must have been a busy night. Okay, Joe got home shortly after midnight. But early that evening you phoned him and set things up for this date with Anton and Fred. Then you go back into bed with Jake—)

(Oh, dear! Boss, I've shocked you again.)

(No, my darling. Surprised, not shocked. I find you memoirs fascinating.)

(Shocked. That schedule sounds like a whore on payday. But it wasn't that at all, Boss. It was love—love an
310

respect for Jake, love and affection for Anton and Fred, love and devotion and understanding and mutual trust and respect with Joe. If my husband didn't disapprove, what right have you—or anybody!—to look down your nose at me?)

(Darling, darling! I was *not* shocked, I have *never* been shocked by you. Damn it, it's that Generation Gap. You can't believe that I packed far more offbeat behavior into my long years of lechery than you possibly could have crowded into the fourteen years you claim. You've been a busy body, that's clear—but I had more than five times as many years at it and quite as much enthusiasm. Probably not as frequent opportunities, but beautiful girls get asked oftener than do homely boys. But it was never for lack of trying on my part, nor do I have any complaints, as I received more cooperation than I had any reason to expect.)

(I think you were shocked.)

(No, little innocent. Sheer admiration—plus surprise at your endurance. You must have been half dead the next day.)

(On the contrary I felt grand. Glowing. Happy. You remarked on it. You may even recall it . . . it was the day Joe painted me with tiger stripes and a cat's face makeup.)

(Be darned if I don't! You were bouncy as a kitten—and I said you looked like the cat who ate the canary. Darling girl, I was hurting that day; you cheered me up.)

(I'm glad.)

(How much sleep did you get?)

(Oh, plenty. Six hours. Five at least. Plus a nap stretched out on my tummy while Joe did most of the stripes. Joan, a well-loved woman doesn't need as much sleep as a lonely one—you'll find out. As for it being too much for me—Boss, who told me just last week that nothing encourages sex the way sex does? *You*, that's who.)

(Yes. But I was speaking from a man's viewpoint—)

(Works the same for a woman, twin. You'll see.)

(I hope so. I know that most people—in my day—assumed the opposite. But it's not true. Sex, whatever else it is—much else!—is an athletic skill. The

311

more you practice, the more you can, the more you want to, the more you enjoy it, the less it tires you. I'm glad to hear—very personally glad—that it works that way for a woman, too. But you aren't the first girl to tell me so. Uh . . . first time I heard a girl say that, or roughly that, was when Harding was President. Not a girl, a very sweet young married woman who had more in common with you than you are likely to believe. Almost certainly dead now, God rest her soul; she would be over a hundred years old)

(What was her name?)

(Does it matter? Little busybody, you were telling me about Fred and Anton. I still don't understand how you swung it. The setup, yes—but how did you gentle them to it? Did you split the time and take them into your apartment separately?)

(Oh, heavens, no! That would be rude. And embarrassing for everyone. It would have turned me off utterly. It was a Troy.)

(Well?)

(Boss, can you imagine how excited two men can get while kissing—fondling—the same girl? If she's willing? If they trust each other? Which they did, they were driver and Shotgun together.)

(Yes, that's true but I can't visualize—wups! I just remembered something that happened so many years ago I had almost forgotten it.)

(Tell me.)

(No, no, you go on. Just that history repeats itself—as it always does. Go on.)

(Well, they do, Boss. Excite each other even if they don't touch each other at all. Just her. 'Heterodyning' is the term I learned for it in secretronics; I don't know what the kinseys call it. But I had been kissing them good-night almost every other night for weeks, and kissing them when they picked me up in the mornings. And the kisses got warmer and it's never been my nature to discourage a man if I like him—which I did; I felt affectionate toward both of them; they're nice people.

(Presently we were stopping for a necking session —could no longer call it a good-night kiss—in the base-

ment parking before they would take me up the lift. I
had to slow that down by saying, 'Watch it, boys. You're
not only getting body paint on your uniforms, you're
getting me so mussed up I'll have trouble getting neat
enough that Joe won't notice it.' Which did slow them
down, more on my account than any fret about uniforms;
they liked Joe—everybody likes Joe—and did not want to
cause me worry at home. Didn't tell them that Joe wasn't
fooled; his artist's eye sees much more than most people
see.

(But we settled it that night, Boss. I told them that I was
not a tease and that I was as eager as they were . . . but that
I was *not* going to be spread in a basement. But that I
would find a chance. They are both nice boys—oh, men,
sure; Anton is forty and Fred is as old as I am. Was. So
they waited, and didn't do more than kiss me and grab a
friendly feel. Then twice we almost had it made but Joe
was busy painting, which I would not interrupt to take the
President to bed.

(Then we hit the jackpot. Almost missed at the last
minute; Jake was going to send me home in his car. He told
me to cancel the call I had put in for my car. Yours, I
mean. I surprised Jake by being balky—told him that I
didn't feel safe with Charlie unless he, Jake, was along.
True, as far as it went; Charlie is a bad one, not like our
four.

(So dear old Jake was going to get dressed and ride with
me—I said that was silly, that Finchley and Shorty—I
never referred to them as Tom and Hugo and wouldn't
advise you to—)

(I'm not stupid, dearest. When I'm 'Miss Smith,' they are
'Finchley' and 'Shorty.')

(Sorry, Boss darling, I know you're not stupid. But I
have more experience in being a woman than you have.)

(So you have, and you keep me straight, darling. But
what's this about Tom and Hugo?)

(Misdirection. I knew who was on call that night. So
Fred and Anton picked me up and I was tempted to tell
them—getting excited all the time, myself. Couldn't.
Would have spoiled it some for them, since men enjoy so
313

much spreading a married woman without her husband knowing it—even sweet old Jake relished me more for that naughty reason. I always went along with this quirk because it gave me more control over a situation not easy to control once a man has had you. Gives you a lever. You might remember that, Joan.)

(I will. But I'll need a husband to make use of it.)

(You'll get us a husband, never fear, dear—I still think we ought to marry Jake. He'll come around. But don't hold out on him, Joan; Jake is not a man you can pressure that way.)

(Eunice, I won't hold out on Jake one-half second. I've never had any respect for that female tactic and won't use it now that *I* am female.)

(I have never used it, Boss, I've used almost every other female deception—but not that one. That one is whoring but not honest whoring. 'Minds me. How do you feel about whores, Boss?)

(Me? Why, the way I feel about any professional who performs a personal service. Say a dentist, or a lawyer, or a nurse. If he's honest, I respect him. If he is competent as well, my respect is limited only by his degree of competence. Why?)

(Have you ever patronized whores? Hired their services, I mean, not 'patronize' in the snooty sense.)

(If I give that a simple affirmative will you get on with your story? We're already downtown, damn it.)

(Yes, sir. I mean, 'Yes, twin sister you knocked-up virgin.' Got home, went up the lift with them, was 'surprised' to find Joe not at home, found the dummy clock propped on the sink, hands set at midnight, and told them what it meant. That did it. Finis.)

(*Hey!*)

(What is there to tell? You already know what we did.)

Joan sighed. (That is the skimpiest account of a gang bang I ever heard in my long and evil life.)

(*What?* But it wasn't a gang bang, Boss! Quit dragging your feet and come on into this century. A Troy is *not* a gang bang. Nor is it a frimp session, or needn't be and this was not. A Troy is friendly and loving. They are both

314

married and they treated me as sweetly as they would treat their wives—and I loved the way they treated me and loved both of them, quite a lot and still do, long before the evening was over . . . when up to then it had been just affectionate, sex-charged friendship. Boss, one of the regrets I have about being killed is that I was never able to offer them the second chance at me they had earned—and I had promised. Mmm . . . do you think you might make it up to them?)

(Huh? As you pointed out, I'm their boss; it wouldn't be easy. And besides . . . well, hell, I'm scared. *Two* men?)

(You didn't seem scared of Mac and Alec.)

(Not quite the same thing.)

(Nothing ever is, Boss—especially about sex. But I want to tell you this. A Troy—if it works right, and it can't unless there is trust and respect all the way around—if it works, it is the nicest thing that can happen to a woman. Not just twice as nice because she gets twice as much of what she wants so badly. That's not it; she might even get less than some rutty young stud could manage alone. It's the warm and friendly and loving and trusting aspect that makes it so good. Four times better, at least. Maybe eight. Oh, arithmetic can't measure it. But, Joan darling—listen to me—until you have been in bed between two sweet and loving men, men who love each other almost as much or even more than they love you . . . with your head pillowed on both their arms and surrounded by their love—until that's happened to you, you still have one virginity to go, and an important one. Darling, I was crying most of the time they were with me . . . cried again when I kissed them good-night . . . was still crying happy after they left . . . then jumped out of bed and rushed to unbolt the door when Joe got home a few minutes later—and blubbered all over him and took him straight to bed and told him all about it while he was being especially sweet to me.)

(Did he want to hear about it?)

(Wouldn't *you* want to?)

(Yes, but no two men are alike and some husbands get headaches from horns.)

(Some do. Maybe most of them, Joan. I was always
315

careful of Joe's feelings. Sometimes I strayed and carefully kept it from him—I never told him about Jake.)

(Why not? I would think that Joe would approve of Jake for you if he approved of anyone. Jake respects Joe very highly—you know it, too; you heard him.)

(Yes. But Jake is rich and Joe is dirt poor. Perhaps Joe could have accepted Jake—I now think he could have. But I wasn't sure, so I didn't risk hurting him. But Anton and Fred—well, they are just mobile guards; Joe treated them as friends and equals, and secretly—I think—felt a little superior to them, since he is an artist and they are just stiffs. I knew they wouldn't trouble Joe's mind . . . and I was right; he was delighted for me. Happy that I was happy. Can't explain it, Joan; you get an instinct for it. But a man's pride is a fragile thing and it is all the armor he has; they are far more vulnerable than we are. You have to be oh so careful in handling them. Or they droop.)

(I know, Eunice. Literally droop in some cases. Did I tell you that my second wife made me psychically impotent for almost a year?)

(Oh, you poor darling!)

(Got over it. Not through a shrink. Through the warm and generous help of a lady who didn't assume that it was my fault. And I was never troubled again until I was too feeble for any sort of proper physical functioning.)

(I'm glad you found her; I wish I could thank her. Joan . . . I wasn't born knowing this about men; I found out the hard way. Twin, I made some bad mistakes in high school. Look—males are so much bigger and more muscular than we are, I didn't *dream* that they could be so fragile. Until I hurt one boy's pride so badly he dropped out of school . . . and I've tried never to hurt any boy, or man, since. I was stupid, Boss. But I did learn.)

(Eunice, how long has it been since I last told you I love you?)

(Oh, at least twenty minutes.)

(Too long. I love you.)

Finchley's voice interrupted her reverie. "We're about to park, Miss Eunice."

"What's this 'Miss Eunice' nonsense? We're not in public."

"Seemed like a good compromise."

"It does, huh? Why just dabble your toes? Why not go whole hawg and call me 'Miss Smith?'—and I won't kiss you good-night."

"Very well—Miss."

"Oh, Tom, don't tease me. It's been a perfect day; don't remind me that I must be 'Miss Smith' again. You know I'll kiss you good-night if you'll let me . . . or the real Eunice wouldn't speak to me. Hugo, make him behave!"

"I'll fix his clock, Eunice. Tom, you call her 'Eunice,' real nice."

"I'm sorry, Eunice."

"That makes me feel better, Tom. Are you going to be able to park this wagon close enough that you can come with me?"

"Sure thing, Eunice—but keep quiet right now, please; I've got to work close with the traffic computer to get us in."

20

"Good evening, Chief." Joan rested her hand on O'Neil's forearm, stepped lightly down.

"Good evening, Miss. Message from Mr. Salomon. His respects to you and regrets he will not be back for dinner. Twenty-one o'clock, he hopes."

"I'm sorry to hear it. Then I shan't dine downstairs; please tell Cunningham or Della that I want trays in my lounge for Winnie and me. No service."

"Two trays and no service, Miss—right."

"And tell Dabrowski that I want him to drive me tomorrow."

"He's gone home, Miss. But he knows he has the duty. He'll be ready."

"Perhaps you didn't understand what I said, Chief. I want to tell him, now, that *I* want him to drive me tomorrow. Ten, possibly—not earlier. So after you phone the pantry, call Dabrowski and give him that message from *me*. Leave the call in until you reach him. And phone me at once when Mr. Salomon's car returns, no matter what hour. Don't consult him; do it. Before Rockford unbuttons."

"Yes, Miss. Phone the pantry. Phone Dabrowski immediately thereafter. Phone you instantly when Mr. Salomon's car returns, before he is out of his car. If I may say so, Miss, it feels good to have your firm hand back at the controls."

"You may say so, to me. But not to Mr. Salomon. For

his firm hand has been invaluable. As you and I know."

"As we both know. He's a fine gentleman, Miss; I respect him. Shall I tell Cunningham to send down for your packages?"

"No, Finchley and his guns can handle them—though I did go on quite a shopping spree." Joan gave her security boss Eunice's best happy-little-girl grin. "I was drunk with excitement, bad as a kid on Christmas, and tried to buy out the town. Finchley. Split those packages three ways and you three come up with me. Yes, I know it's not your work, so don't report me to your guild."

Packages, three men, and one woman almost filled the front lift. Joan waited until Finchley had punched for her floor and the lift had started, then she quickly punched the "Stop" touchplate, held them between floors. "Put those packages down."

She went first to Shorty, took his face between her hands. "Thank you, Hugo. Thank you most of all, as your gentle wisdom got us all straightened out." She pulled his face down, kissed him softly and unhurriedly, lips closed. "Good night."

She turned to Fred. "Thank you, Fred. I thank you—and Eunice thanks you." As his arms closed she let her lips come open. (See what I mean, twin? That's a sample.) (I see—I shall be *very* careful not to get him alone unless I expect more than a sample.) "Good night, Fred."

"Tom, it's been the best day of my life. I hope you enjoyed it half as much as I did. Thank you." Joan went straight into the kiss without waiting for Finchley to answer, her face up, eyes closed—and with her back to Shorty in case her driver decided to take advantage of it.

—which he did. (Goodness! Eunice, are you *sure* you never laid him?) (Quite sure, darn it! Are *you* going to?) (I don't know, I don't know!)

Breathless she broke from him, turning her back to all of them to punch again for her floor and trying to regain her composure.

The car stopped and she said, "Put everything in my bedroom, boys. Winnie! Wait till you see!"

The little redhead had been waiting at the lift. "Miss

Joan! You've been gone all day!"

"And why not? Put them anywhere, on the floor, on the bed. Winnie, have you had dinner? That's all, thanks. Good night and thank you all."

"Good night, Miss Smith."

As soon as the door sealed, Joan hugged her maid, lifting her off her feet. "You didn't answer. Did you eat with the staff? Or did you wait?"

"Couldn't eat. Oh, Joan, I've been *so* worried. You ran away and didn't tell anybody where you were going. Bad girl—to worry me so."

"Pooh. I had guards with me; you knew I was safe."

"But guards aren't nurses. I'm supposed to watch you, for Dr. Garcia."

"And pooh all over dear Doctor, too. Winsome, I'm no longer a patient, I'm no longer a ward; I'm a free woman and healthy as a horse and you can't mother me every minute like a broody hen. All right, we've got supper coming up and they'll leave it in the lounge and we'll eat when we feel like it."

"I know, I was backstairs when the order came in—so I hurried up the service lift and thought I had missed you as the indicator was stopped. Then it started again."

"Something wrong with that lift, it stalled. But we kept punching buttons until the Yehudi woke up. Too many gadgets in this house." (Eunice, I thought a stalled elevator was a safe as a grave. Is there no privacy *anywhere?*) ('Fraid not, Boss honey. But I never worried much about such things; I just worried about hurting people.) (I stand corrected. Ever been caught with your legs up, hussy?) (Only once when it was embarrassing—and that's all it was. It's nothing to worry about.)

"Shall I tell maintenance about the lift?"

"No, Finchley will report it. Winsome, maintenance is no part of your duties; you're here to giggle with me and to give me a shoulder to cry on and to cry on mine—and to keep dear Doctor from fussing." Joan started undressing. "Get your clothes off; we're going to model clothes, I've been shopping. Boy oh boy, did I shop! Gave the economy a shot in the arm, I did. Get those duds off—have you had

321

your bath, you dirty girl? Or are you going to bathe with me? Come here and let me smell you."

"Had a bath when I got up."

"You smell all right, I fear me I'm well marinated; it's been a busy day. Okay, we'll dunk together and get stinking good later. Before giving dear Jake another lesson in how to relax. But now we model. Give us a kiss first." (Eunice, will that rubber dingus stay in place in the tub?) (It'll stay seated anywhere—or I would have left a dozen orphans behind me. You can even use the fountain—and you had better.)

"Joan, since you were going shopping, why didn't you take me along? Meanie."

"Complaints, complaints, complaints. I thought you needed sleep, dear. Or didn't Bob show up?"

Winifred blushed clear down her breasts but she answered happily, "Oh, yes, he did! But I would have been up at once if you had called me—love to shop."

"What time did you wake up?"

The blush renewed. "Not till almost thirteen. Long past noon."

"The defense rests. Winsome baby, I didn't take you along because I bought things for *you*, too . . . and if I had had you along, you would have fussed every time I spent a dollar on you. And to set a precedent, too. I'm not a prisoner any longer. I'm free to come and go just as you are. If I don't take you along, you mustn't ask why and I may not tell you where or what."

The younger girl looked crushed. "Yes, Miss Joan. I'll remember." So Joan Eunice again took her in her arms. "There, there, pet; don't quiver your lip. I'll take you with me, mostly. And if I don't, I'll tell you about it, mostly. But I might tell you a fib instead. I might have a date with some horny interns and would not want to shock my Winsome."

"You're teasing me."

"Not mean teasing. I'm at least half serious. Winnie, if you want to see your Bob, no one in this house cares but me and my interest is friendly. But *me?* There are forty-odd people staring down my neck. If I ever have a man in my bed, the whole household will know it, and it's at least
322

fifty-fifty that some member of my ever-loyal staff would sell the fact to a news snoop and it would be on the morning gossip program—phrased so that I can't sue without making it worse. Not?"

"Uh . . . sounds horrible. But I guess it could happen."

"You know it could. Every gossip column, every gossip program, proves it. Hon, if a person is too rich, or too prominent, all the public lets him wear is the Emperor's New Clothes—and what they like best is bad news, good news is too bland. Back when I was running it, Smith Enterprises spend many thousands of dollars every quarter to give me a totally false 'public image'—poisonous phrase!—for business reasons. But that's done with and now I'm fair game. Still more interesting fair game now that I'm miraculously young and female and pretty. No, 'beautiful'—let's be fair to Eunice Branca. You saw what they did yesterday; you watched the babble box. What would they do if they could prove something on me?"

"Uh, something nasty, I guess."

"I *know* they would, I'm not guessing; I've had too many years of trying to avoid the spotlight. The old Romans knew what they were doing when they tossed living victims to the lions; most people are fairly decent—but collectively they love blood. I'm going to do something about getting out of the spotlight but in the meantime, I'm vulnerable. Winnie, what would you do if I woke you some night and asked you to let me slide a man into your bed—so that *you* could be caught, not me. Be certain to be caught, I mean, public as a show window. So caught that Bob would know, too."

The little girl took a deep breath. "I'd do it! Bob would understand."

"Ah, but if I begged you *not* to explain it to Bob? Just take the rap for me?"

"I'd still do it."

Joan kissed her. "I know you would. But you won't have to, sweet Winsome. If—no, *when*—I slip, I won't load it onto my chum. But I may ask you to tell lies for me someday—jigger for me—help me cover up. Would you?"

"Of course I would."

323

"And I knew it and didn't need to ask. It might be soon, I'm feeling more female every day. Now let's play Christmas—I think that round, flubsy box is for Winnie."

Shortly Winifred was parading in front of mirrors with an awed look on her face. "Oh, Joan, you shouldn't have!"

"That's why I made you stay home. It's a maid's uniform, dear—an allowable deduction for me by terms of the Cooks, Domestics, and Hotel Workers approved contract."

" 'Maid's uniform' indeed! It's a Stagnaro Original straight from Rome; I read the label."

"As may be, I'll tell my accountant to list it as a deduction just to annoy the I.R.S. Take it off, dear, and let's see what else we find. Hey, here's one for *me*." Joan quickly got dressed. "What do you think? Of course with this I ought to have my body painted."

"I wouldn't use paint, if I were you. You look yummy and that off-white sets off your skin. It's a delicious design even though kind o' wicked. Joan, how do you know so much about buying women's clothes? I mean, uh—"

"You mean, 'How does an old man who hasn't picked out a dress for a woman in at least half a century manage it?' Genius, dear, sheer genius. You ought to hear my bird imitations." (Hey! Don't *I* get any credit?) (Not unless you want to break your cover, Mata Hari. The men in the white coats are just outside that door.) (Pee on you, twin. Maybe someday we can tell Winnie.) (I hope so, darling—I not only love you, I'm proud of you.) (*Kiss!*)

They worked down to two boxes which Joan had held back. When Winifred saw the synthetic emerald set—gee patch and two half-moon cups shaped for bare nipples—she gasped. "Oh, goodness! Put it on, Joan, and let me find your highest heels!"

"*You* find *your* highest heels, darling—those green rhinestone stilts you were wearing earlier. They didn't have stilts to match this outfit in your size. I've ordered them."

"This is for *me*? Oh, no!"

"Then put it down the trash chute; gee-strings can't be exchanged. Winsome, that dress was designed for a redhead—and the cups are too small for me. Put it on.

That envelope contains a floorlength transparent skirt, silk with a hint of matching green. With the skirt it's just right for formal dinner parties. You could wear one emerald on your forehead. Not any other jewelry. Nor paint."

"But, Joan, I never go to that sort of party—I've never ever been invited to one."

"Perhaps it's time I gave one; the banquet hall hasn't been used in ten years. You would look beautiful—junior hostess at the other end of the long table. But, dear, besides an ultra-formal party, it's intended—without the skirt—for most informal occasions. Would you enjoy wearing it for Bob—and would he enjoy taking it off?"

Winifred caught her breath. "I can't wait."

"Got a date tonight, hon?"

"No, that's why I said 'I can't wait.' Because I can't resist it—want Bob to see me in it . . . want him to take it off me. Joan, I shouldn't accept it, it's much too expensive. But I will, I do. Goodness, you make me feel like a kept woman."

"You are one, dear; I'm keeping you. And enjoying it very much."

The little nurse stopped smiling. Then she faced her mistress, looked up directly into her eyes. "Joan, maybe I shouldn't say this, maybe it'll spoil everything. But I think I must. Uh——" She stopped and took a deep breath. "Two or three times it's seemed to me you almost made a pass at me."

(There's the pitch, twin! Too late for me to help.) "It's been more than three times, Winifred."

"Well . . . yes. But why did you stop?"

Joan sighed. "Because I was scared."

"Of me?"

"Of me. Winsome darling—I've done many hard things in my life. Such as waiting in a landing boat, bobbing around and seasick and stinking with fear . . . then dropping off into four feet of water with machine guns raking us and killing my buddies on both sides. But this is the hardest thing I've ever tried. Being a woman. I have to think about it every instant—do consciously the things you do automatically. Goodness, today I came within a split

325

second of walking into a men's toilet instead of the ladies' powder room. And now *you*. Darling, can you guess what a temptation you are to me? Can you realize that old Johann is looking at your winsome loveliness out of Joan's eyes? Winnie, there hasn't been a moment but what I've wanted to touch you. Hold you in my lap. Kiss you. Make love to you. If I were a man . . . I'd be trying my damnedest to crowd Bob out. Or at least make room for me."

"Joan."

"Yes, dear?"

"There's room for you."

Joan found that she was trembling. "Darling! *Please!* Can't we wait? You have Bob . . . and I have still to learn to be a woman." She started to cry.

And found Winifred's arms around her. "Stop it, dear. Please stop. I didn't mean to upset you. I'll help, of course I'll help. We'll wait. Years if you need that long. Until you're calmed down and sure of yourself—and want me. But Winnie isn't trying to seduce her Joanie. Oh, it can be sweet, truly it can. But you're right and I do have Bob and my nerves aren't frayed the way yours must be. Someday you'll fall in love with a man, and may forget all about me. Wanting to touch me, I mean—and that's all right, as long as I can love you and be your friend."

Joan dashed away a tear, and sniffed. "Thank you, Winnie. I've made a fool of myself again."

"No, you haven't. I just have trouble remembering, sometimes. Do you want a tranquilizer?"

"No. I'm all right now."

"Would you rather I didn't touch you?"

"No. I want you to kiss me, Winnie. Hard. Best you ever have. Then put on the green gee-string dress and let us look at it. Then we'll eat. And then grab some soapsuds and make me smell better for our prayer meeting with Jake—I need those prayers tonight; they're the right tranquilizer. Put it on, dear. But kiss me first."

Winnie kissed her—started to hold back, then flared like a prairie fire and did make it "best she ever had."

(Break, twin, before the house burns down. That's the fanciest tap dancing since Bojangles died.) (What do you

326

know about Bojongles? You *can't* know about him.) (Ever hear of classic films, Boss? Now see to it that Bob marries her; you owe her that, for the hurdles you make her jump.) (How can I when I don't know who he is?) (You can find out. Cheat. O'Neil knows. After you know who he is, find out what he wants; he'll geek. *Men!* Boss, I love you, but sometimes I'm not sure why.)

After Winnie modeled the emerald dress, she fetched in their trays from Joan's upstairs lounge while Joan opened the last package. It contained her present for Jake. "Winnie, tell me what you think of this."

It was a necklace rich and simple—a heavy gold chain with tripled linkage, supporting a large gold ankh, a crux ansata. Winifred took it in her hands. "It's lovely," she said slowly. "But it's not a woman's necklace, you know. Or did you?"

"It's a man's necklace. A present for Jake."

Winifred frowned slightly. "Joan, you do want me to help you learn how to behave as a woman."

"You know I do."

"Yes, I know. When I see that you are about to make a mistake, I must tell you."

"You don't think Jake will like this?"

"I don't know. He may not know what it means. And you may not know. This cross with a loop is called an 'ankh'—and it's what my grandaddy would have called a 'heathen symbol.' It means—well, it means most of the things our meditation prayer means, life and goodness and love and so forth. But specifically it means *sex*, it's an ancient Egyptian symbol for the generative forces, both male and female. It's no accident that the loop looks something like a vulva and that the rest of the design could be interpreted as a male symbol. The way it's used *now*—among people my age, people the age you have become—is . . . well, a wife could give it to her husband, or a husband could give a smaller one to his wife. Or they might not be married—but it *always* means sexual love—flatly and no nonsense about it. If that's not what you mean, Joan, if you just want to give him a nice necklace, take it back and exchange it for another that isn't
327

so specific in its symbolism. Any necklace means love—but perhaps you want one that a daughter could give her father."

Joan shook her head. "No, Winnie. I've known what the ankh means since a course in comparative religion, oh, three-quarters of a century ago. I assume that Jake knows, too; he has solid classical training. I hadn't been sure you kids knew its ancient meaning—I see I was mistaken. Winnie, this present is no accident; I've asked Jake to marry me several times. He won't. Because of age."

"Well . . . I can see why he might feel that way."

"It's ridiculous. Sure, I'm a quarter of century older than he is—but it no longer shows and I'm healthy enough for marriage. Even though dear Doctor thinks I may drop dead."

"But Dr. Garcia doesn't really think you'll drop dead. And I didn't mean *you* were too old, I meant he—oh, dear!"

"Yes, yes, I know. He's being 'noble,' damn him! But he doesn't have to *marry* me, Winnie. I'll accept any crumb I'm offered. This present is intended to say so."

Winifred looked solemn, suddenly kissed the ankh and handed it back. "You and me both, Joan—any crumb we're offered. Well, I wish you luck. With all my heart."

"Good Winnie. Let's sop up some calories; it's getting latish and Jake will be home—I hope—by twenty-one. I want to be clean as a kitten and just as pretty and smelling even prettier when the stubborn darling gets here. Help me?"

"Love to. And look, Joanie, we douse you in 'Harem Breeze,' both the cologne and the perfume—and the powder. And I won't wear any scent. I'll scrub off what I'm wearing."

"No, we'll renew the bait on you, too. Maybe we'll heterodyne."

" 'Heterodyne'?"

"Term that used to be used a lot in radio. In this case it means that if one girl isn't enough, two might do the trick. Last night Jake was polite about not staring . . . except that

328

he was noticing my Winsome with both eyes all the time he was pretending not to. I'm not trying to crowd you into a Troy—but I have no scruples about staking you out as bait."

They were out of the tub and working on the finishing touches when the house phone sounded. "Miss Smith. Mr. Salomon's car just rolled in."

"Thank you, O'Neil."

A few minutes later Joan phoned the Green Suite. "Jake dear? This is your resident guru. If you wish to share a prayer meeting, guru and chela will call on you whenever you say."

"That's welcome news; I'm tired—and last night was the best sleep I've had in years, Guru."

"I'm glad. Have you had dinner?"

"At the Gib, hours ago. Ready for bed now. If you'll let me have, oh, twenty minutes, for a tub."

"Shall we be there in exactly twenty minutes? I don't want to run into Hubert."

"I sent him to bed. Nobody here but just us chickens."

"Twenty minutes, dear. Off."

Again two girls went barefoot down the hallway. Joan was wearing, under a negligee, the ankh necklace. The door opened for them and Jake came toward them. He was wearing a bathrobe and had a book in hand with a finger marking his place. "Hello, my dears. You both look charming. Joan, I took the liberty of stopping in your downstairs library and borrowing this book."

"It's not a liberty and you know it. What is it, Jake?"

He handed it to her. "Vishnudevananda's Yoga text. Thought there might be some of the simpler postures I could try. But I'm afraid I must stick to meditation."

Joan looked puzzled. "This was downstairs?" She glanced at the endpaper, saw her bookplate: "Ex Libris— J S B Smith." "I had forgotten I owned it."

"You're a pack rat, dear. This house must have ten thousand books in it."

"More, I think. There were that many the last time I had them catalogued. Well, after you're done with it Win-

nie and I will look through it. We might find exercises we
haven't tried." She handed it back; he put it aside. "Ready
for autohypnosis?"

"Ready for prayers and I'm sorry I sounded disparaging
last night."

"I can't see what difference a name makes, Jake. But
first—" Joan opened her robe, lifted the necklace from her
neck. "A present for you, Jake. Bend your head down."

He did so. She placed it around his neck with the
ceremonial kiss. He lifted the ankh, looked at it. "Thank
you, Eunice. It's a beautiful present. Am I to wear it now?"

"As you wish. Or wear it in your mind—I know you've
never been one for much jewelry. Ready, Winnie?" Joan
Eunice dropped her robe, melted into Lotus; Winnie
followed her. Jake got out of his bathrobe, leaving the
necklace on, joined them.

"Jake, will you lead us tonight? No need to say 'hold' or
'breathe,' we'll stay in step. Just like last night, a prayer for
each of the four parts. Keep the tempo slow."

"I'll try. Om Mani Padme Hum!"

(Om Mani Padme Hum.)

Jake Salomon appeared to fall asleep instantly once they
put him to bed. The girls quietly left the darkened room.
Joan stopped a few feet down the hall. "Winnie, will you
do something for me?"

"Anything, dear."

"What time do people start stirring in the morning?"

"I don't know what time Cook gets up. About six,
maybe. Mostly seven or near it, for the others; staff
breakfast is at seven-thirty."

"Della doesn't matter, she never comes upstairs. I mean
this floor."

"Well, cleaning starts at nine. But no one cleans near
your room until you phone down for your tray. Have
you been disturbed?"

"No. And I don't mean to be. I guess Hubert is the only
one who worries me. I'm going back and sleep with Jake."

"Oh!"

"I'm not going this instant, I want to be sure he's sound
330

asleep. If he sleeps all night, I shan't wake him; the poor dear needs his rest. But sleep with him I will! I don't want Hubert barging in. Can you think of a way to divert him?"

"Oh, I see. I'm pretty sure Hubert never goes to Mr. Salomon's room until Mr. Salomon sends for breakfast and Hubert takes it up. Some mornings I've eaten downstairs and seen Hubert sit and drink coffee and watch the news, oh, quite a long time. Waiting for Mr. Salomon to phone."

"That's a relief. It's not likely that anyone but you will know it, then. Not that I mind for myself, but I would hate to be the cause of Jake being dragged into a gossip item. All right, will you do three things for me? Read or sleep in my bed a while, muss it up. Stay all night if you like but muss yours, too. And will you set your alarm for eight and if I'm not in my own bed by then, phone the Green Suite? I'm sure Jake would rather know that you knew than have us caught by someone else. Then one other thing. Would you fetch me lounging pajamas and slippers? Then, if anything slips, I'll put a bold face on it—I'll be dressed and to hell with snoops. While you get them I'm going to put my robe down here and say a few more Money Hums. My mind is made up but I'm a touch nervy. Afraid Jake will scold me, I guess. (Afraid Jake *won't* scold you, *I* guess.) (Don't you want us to, Eunice?) (*Yes!* Quit yattering and get on with it.)

"Right away, Joan. Oh, I'm excited myself! Uh, I think I'll sleep in your bed. If you don't mind."

"You know I don't. But I may come back and wake you, most any time."

"Don't mind. If you need a shoulder to cry on, I want to be there. Or maybe just for snuggle."

"Or I might have something to tell you. You don't fool me a bit, Winsome. Never mind, I *would* like to find you there when I return, no matter when or why."

A few minutes later Joan slipped silently into the bedroom of the Green Suite, dropped her clothing without lighting a light, found her way to the bed by Jake's soft snores. Cautiously she got into bed, felt the radiant warmth of his body close to hers, sighed happily, and went to sleep.

Some indefinite time later Joan felt a hand on her in the

dark, came instantly awake. (What?) (General Quarters, twin! It's *now*.) (I'm scared!) (I've taken over, dearest—the body remembers. Say a Money Hum.)

Without a word Jake firmly took possession of her.

(Oh, God, Eunice! Why didn't you *tell* me?) (Tell you what?) (That for a woman it's so much *better!*) (Is it?) (Ten times, a *hundred* times—I don't know; I'm fainting.) (How could *I* guess that it's better? Kiss him as you faint.)

21

The occupation of the Oklahoma State House by the People's Agrarian Emergency Government continued. The Martian Manned Field Laboratory reported finding artifacts (age 1.4×10^6 plus/minus 14% years) indicating extinct human-equivalent intelligence. A second report signed by the Chinese members of the expedition denied that the exhibits were artifacts but were simply automatic and instinctive by-products (analogous to coral rings, or to honeycombs) of sub-intelligent life closely related to the anaerobic life now present on Mars. The International Flat Earth Society in annual convention in Surrey, England, passed its usual sanctions on any national government wasting taxpayers' money on alleged "space travel."

The suicide rate was up for the nineteenth successive year, as were also rates for death by accident and by violence. World population appreciation passed 300,000 persons per day and continued up, with six babies born every second vs. 2.5 persons dying each second, for a net gain of seven people every two seconds.

A hen in Izard County, Arkansas, laid an egg with the Sign of the Cross on it. A spokesman for the Treasury Department, speaking off the record, announced that the Administration would not push the Administration bill for total abolition of paper currency in favor of universal credit cards and computer accounting. "We must face the fact," he told the Washington Press Club, "that black market transactions, bribes, and other quasi-legal exchanges are as much part of our economy as is interest on the National Debt, and that to create conditions which would make these voluntary exchanges impractical would bring on a depression the country could not stand. To put it poetically, gentlemen, the small amount of physical currency still in circulation—only a few billions—is our lubricant for the gears of progress. You have my assurance that the President recognizes this truth."

The First Satanist Church, Inc., (forty-four branches in California, five in other states) brought suit in Federal Court for relief from "discriminatory taxation." The First Disciple stated: "If other churches aren't badgered and taxed and investigated concerning their sacred objects, a Glory Hand should enjoy the same protection—that's American as apple pie!" Reno again repealed its ordinance for licensed prostitution. The City Manager stated that the fees weren't sufficient to pay the inspectors . . . and besides, there wasn't all that much commercial prostitution anyhow since the closing of the Federal Youth Training Center.

The Rally for Human Beings gained speed in its drive to fold, spindle, and mutilate computer cards and drop them into the nearest mail box—despite arrests by Postal Inspectors there was almost no cooperation by local police and no jury had brought in a verdict of guilty no matter how compelling the evidence. The Post Office's Chief Inspector stated that the mutilated cards were almost always bills and that, so far, no mutilated checks or money orders had been reported—and that the government had no great interest in the matter but he was getting damn sick and tired of the country's mailboxes being used as trash baskets.

The chairman of the Rally for Human Beings answered that the country's mailboxes had been trash baskets for years and both the Postmaster General and Congress knew why. The traffic computer for downtown Houston went into spastic breakdown during the evening rush hour, leaving thousands of people stranded on the streets overnight; the estimated deaths exceeded seven thousand, including heart stoppage, smog poisoning, and mugging, but excluding suicide. The Southern States Automobile

Assurance Companies Trade Association repudiated all claims based on the incident on the theory that deaths or injuries in stationary vehicles were not covered by the (fine print).

The Lunar Colonies dedicated two more superlarge "balanced-aquarium" Food Caves, the *George Washington Carver* and the *Gregor Mendel*, and the Commission again announced an increase in subsidized out-migration quota but again with no relaxation in standards (the injunction against the Commission issued by Mr. Justice Handy of the United States Supreme Court was quietly ignored on the grounds of no jurisdiction). The common stock of Las-Vegas-in-the-Sky continued to move up against the downward trend of the Market: most investment advice peddlers remained bullish basing their expectations on past correlations between weather, the Market, and women's styles. The Interstellar Advisory Subcommittee to the Lunar Commission settled on Tau Ceti rather than Alpha Centauri for the first attempt. Jodrell Bank lost touch with the Manned Pluto Probe. The (official) casualties in Ukraina dropped below the (official) casualties in Matto Grosso—and in both places the dead did not argue

"—whereas 'id' is *not* a scientific concept; it is merely the first syllable of '*idiot!*' . . . as my esteemed colleague should know best" "—will be order in the courtroom." "—let me cite the incontestable conclusions of that *great* scientist—" "garbage in, garbage out! Any graduate assistant can draw pretty graphs and make half-bright conclusions from irrelevant data." "May I ask my esteemed colleague to repeat that slur outside the courtroom?" "—Bailiff is directed to keep order during—" ("Jake, with any luck we'll get this so fouled up that *nobody* can play left field.")

"—with those bright lights. Don't shine them in *my* eyes, or KPOX will lack your services a few days." "—inquire of the Court whether esteemed Counsel has any serious purpose in subjecting the Court and these spectators to the offensive sight of this grisly carcass?" ("—can't stand it myself, Jake; did I *really* look that bad? I still think we

335

should take a dive on this." "Hush, dear, Mac knows what he is doing and so do I.") "—respectfully suggest that the witness himself should be conclusively identified before his testimony can be used to identify another person." "—State and County. This set of prints I am now projecting on the screen you have just seen me take from the cadaver marked exhibit MM. I will now compare them with prints supplied by Veterans Administration Archives and previously marked as exhibit JJ, using jump-stereo superposition—" "—personally take those photographs which you now hold and which have been tentatively marked as exhibit SS, numbers one through one hundred twenty-seven?"

"—will *not* be cleared. This will be a public hearing. But the Court will take time to sentence for contempt as needed, and Evelyn, you can start by putting that spectator, *that* one, the woman with the glasses and the fright wig, on ice for ten days. Get her name, give it to the Clerk, take her away. Any more morons who can't keep quiet? You back there, eating a candy bar; stuff it into your pocket, this is not a lunchroom."

"Is Counsel for the challenged party suggesting that this is *not* José Branca?" "Goodness, no, I'll help identify him if you need me. I'm simply urging that you lay a proper foundation." ("Jake, Joe looks ghastly. I *must* go see him as soon as this nonsense is over." "Do you think that is wise?" "I don't know, Jake. But I know that I *must*.")

"Look around you, Mr. Branca. Tell the Court—tell the Judge, that is—whether or not your wife is in this room?" "Not here." "Mr. Branca, look where I am pointing." "Not here, I told you!" "Your Honor, we are faced with a reluctant witness. It becomes necessary to lead him." "Very well. But Counsel is reminded that he cannot impeach his own witness." "Thank you, Your Honor. Mr. Branca, I am pointing at this young woman, look at her closely. I have my hand on her shoulder—" "Keep your hands to yourself! Judge, if he puts a hand on me again, I'll bite it!" "Order. Counsel, it is not necessary to touch the challenged party, and you will not do so again. Your witness—knows which young woman you mean." "Very well, Your Honor—and if I have given offense to this young lady, I am sorry. Mr. Branca, I put it to you that this is your wife, Eunice Branca née Evans."

"Not Eunice. She dead. Judge, do I gotta take this kark? That lyin' fixer knows t' score, he talk to me two, three hours. Sure, that's Eunice' *body*. But she's *dead*. Everybody knows what happen."

"Sorry, Your Honor. Mr. Branca, please confine yourself to answering my questions. You say your wife is dead . . . but did you ever *see* your wife Eunice Branca dead?"

"Huh? No. This operation—"

"Just answer the question. You never at any time saw her dead. I put it to you that you were paid one million dollars to testify that this woman is not your wife Eunice Branca." ("Jake, can they do this to Joe? Look at him." "I'm sorry, darling. I didn't call him.")

"Judge, this karky bastard's *lyin'!* They got this club, see? Rare Blood. I got this funny blood, see? Eunice, too. Save lives. Sure, they offer money, thousand, million, I I don' know, don' care. You think I'm a pimp, maybe? For *Eunice*? I tell 'em shove it. I—"

"Your Honor, I pray your help in bringing this witness to order."

"I think he's making a responsive answer to your question. Go on, Mr. Branca. They offered you money. For what?"

"Oh. Eunice got a boss, see? Mr. Smith. Johann Smith. So rich he karks in gold pot. But poor old muck is dying, see? Only the medicares don' let him die. Pitiful. But he's got this same funny blood, see? Like me, like Eunice. I tell 'em, sure, he can have Eunice' body, she don' need it no more—but *not* for money. So we rig a swindle—me and his fixer over there, Mr. Jake Salomon. He knows how I feel, he helps. 'Eunice Evans Branca Memorial Fund for *Free* Rare Blood'—all paid to t' Rare Blood Club. Ask Mr. Jake Salomon, he knows. I . . . don' . . . touch . . . one . . . God damn' frimpin' *dime!*" ("Jake—he won't even look at me."

337

"Put your veil up, dear, and cry under it.")

"Does Counsel for Petitioners have any more questions to ask this witness?"

"No, Your Honor. Counsel may inquire."

"No cross-examination, Your Honor."

"Does either counsel wish to question this witness at a later time? This is not a trial, and the Court intends to allow the widest latitude for inquiry even at the cost of permitting irrelevancies to creep into the record. Counsel?"

"Petitioners have no further use for this witness."

"No questions now or later, Your Honor."

"Very well. Court will reconvene at ten tomorrow morning. Bailiff is directed to provide this witness with transportation home or wherever he wishes to go, and to protect him from annoyance in so doing. Off the top, Evelyn, he's been harried enough."

"Judge? Can I say sump'n?"

"If you wish, Mr. Branca."

"That. karky fixer—not Mr. Salomon, other one. Gets dark every night. Some night he winds up in Bird's Nest turf."

"Order. Mr. Branca, you must not make threats in court."

"Wasn't no threat, Judge. Was *prophesying. I* wouldn't hurt anybody. But Eunice had lots and lots and *lots* of friends."

"Very well. You're excused, Mr. Branca; you won't have to come back. Clerk will take charge of exhibits. Bailiff will provide heel-and-toe guards. Recessed."

"All rise!" "—greatest possible respect for the scholarly qualifications of my distinguished colleague, nevertheless the opinions he has expressed are the most arrant nonsense, as proved by that *great* scientist in his paper of 1976 from which I now quote: 'The very concept of "personality" is but a shadow of a figment of a fantasy of a pre-scientific speculation. *All* life phenomena are fully explained by the laws of biochemistry as exemplified—' "

"—even an existential phenomenology requires a teleological foundation and I so concede, but a close study of dialectical materialism proves to any but the hopelessly biased that—" "Who's in charge here?" "An unborn child is not person; it is merely an inchoate protoplasmic structure with a potentiality to become *from its environment*—" "—mathematical laws of genetic inheritance account for every possible event misnamed—" "—in words familiar to the Court and to everyone: 'Father, forgive them, for they know not what they do.' "

"—*shocked* to discover that the learned judge presiding over this trial is in fact a fraternity brother of Johann S. B. Smith. This clandestine relationship may be verified in records open to the public and I ask that this Court today, and any later courts seeing this record, take judicial notice, and I demand that opposing Counsel stipulate the fact."

"Stipulated." ("Jake, how did they find out?" "We leaked it. Through Alec, last night. Time to get it into the record, rather than in an appeal.")

"Aha! This damning fact having been stipulated, Petitioners are now forced to demand that the Judge presiding disqualify himself and declare this a mistrial." ("Jake, seems to me they've got us on the hip. Much as I like Mac and Alec, I have to admit that this has the flavor of finding a strawberry mark on a missing heir." "No, my dear. In the course of a long life a prominent man acquires direct linkage to every other prominent man. If it hadn't turned out that you and Mac were in the same fraternity, it would have been some other link as close or closer. How many members of the Supreme Court do you know?" "Uh . . . I think it's five." "There's your answer. At the top of the pyramid everybody knows everybody else.") (And sleeps with them.) (Shut up, Eunice!)

"Counsel, I find this interesting. First let me set you straight on a point of law. Twice you have used the word 'trial' and now you speak of a 'mistrial.' This is, as you know, not a trial, it is not even an adversary situation; it is merely an inquiry for the purpose of determining the identity of the young woman there who calls herself 'Miss Smith.' She is charged with no crime, no civil suit against her is before this court; it is simply that her claimed identity has been challenged by petitioners who assert an

339

interest. So this court is assisting in a friendly investigation—helping like a good neighbor in attempting to straighten out a mixup. *Not* a trial."

"I stand corrected, Your Honor."

"Please be careful in your use of technical language. If there is no trial, there can be no mistrial. Do you agree?"

"Perhaps I should use other language, Your Honor. Petitioners feel that, under these disclosed circumstances, you are not the judge who should preside over this, uh, friendly investigation."

"That is possible. But the matter *has* reached me in the course of due process and it will continue to remain before me unless compelling reasons are shown why I should step aside. Again on the matter of language, you used the word 'clandestine.' The Court will not *at this moment* consider whether or not Counsel's choice of this word implies contempt—"

"Your Honor, I assure you—"

"Order. I am speaking. Nor will *you* discuss that aspect at this time. We will now consider only the meaning of this word. 'Clandestine' means 'hidden, secret, concealed' with a flavor or connotation of surreptitious, or underhanded, or illicit. Tell me—this alleged relationship: Could it be verified in 'Who's Who'?"

"Oh, certainly, Your Honor! That's where I found it."

"I know that my own fraternity is noted there; I assume that if appropriate it would be listed in the case of Johann Sebastian Bach Smith. Since you tell me that you have checked it, the Court takes judicial notice for whatever it is worth and requires no further substantiation . . . other than to comment that we could hardly have been members of the same chapter at the same time since we differ by almost half a century in age. Did your investigations show that Johann Smith and I were jointly members of other organizations? For example Johann Smith was a founding member of the Gibraltar Club—and I am a member, and Miss Smith's counsel, Mr. Salomon, is a member . . . and *you* are a member. In what other organizations do I share membership with Johann Smith? Now or in the past."

"Uh . . . Petitioners have not investigated."

"Oh, come now, I feel sure that you could turn up others. The Red Cross, for example. Probably the Chamber of Commerce at some time. I seem to recall that when I was a Scout Commissioner Johann Smith was one also. Possibly we're both in other fraternal bodies. Almost certainly we have served as trustees, or such, for the same charitable or service groups, either simultaneously or successively. I note that you are a Shriner, so am I. Care to comment on the fact?"

"No comment, Your Honor."

"But you and I almost certainly share several fraternal bonds. The Court takes notice of the wry fact that, since lawyers are not permitted to advertise, as a class they tend to join more organizations—fraternal, social, service, and religious—then do laymen as a class. Since you choose not to comment on the ones that you and I share in common, the Court will on its own motion investigate and place the results in the record. Now as to my alleged obligation to disqualify myself, do you wish to clarify your reasoning? Think it over while we take a recess, as your answer will go into the record. Ten minutes."

"Order. Counsel for the Petitioners? You have had time to think."

"Petitioners move that all remarks concerning fraternal associations and like matters be struck from the record."

"Motion denied. *Nothing* will be struck from this record. Come now, Counselor, you must have had *some* theory. State it."

"Your Honor, at the time I raised the point it seemed important. I now no longer think so."

"But you must have had a theory or you would not have raised it. Please speak freely, I want to know."

"Well . . . if Your Honor will indulge me, the disclosed fact seemed to admit of the possibility of prejudice on the part of the Court. No contempt is intended."

"And the Court will assume that none exists. But your answer is less than complete. Prejudice in favor of whom? The Petitioners? Because of my fraternal relationship with their grandparent?"

341

"What? Oh, no, Your Honor—prejudice in favor of, uh, of Miss—the challenged party."

"You are stipulating that she is *indeed* Johann Sebastian Bach Smith?" ("My God, Jake, Mac's got him biting his own tail." "Yes. *Who* has got *whom* on *whose* hip?")

"No, no Your Honor, we are not stipulating *that*. That is the very matter we are challenging."

"But Counsel cannot have it both ways. If this young woman is *not* Johann Sebastian Bach Smith—as Petitioners allege—then she is *not* of my college fraternity. Conversely, under your own theory, she *is* Johann Sebastian Bach Smith. Which way will you have it?"

"I'm afraid I have been guilty of faulty reasoning. I pray the court's indulgence."

"We all reason faultily at times. Are you quite finished? Shall we go on with examination of witnesses?"

"Quite finished, Your Honor."

"But, Dr. Boyle, do you *know* that you removed the brain from this body—this cadaver, and transplanted it into the body of that woman?"

"Don't be an ass, old chap. You heard my answer."

"Your Honor, Petitioners feel that this is proper cross-examination and ask for the Court's assistance."

"The Court orders the witness to answer the questions as stated."

"Judge, you don't scare me, y' know. I am here as a voluntary witness—and I am not and never was a citizen of your quaint country. I am now a citizen of China. Your State Department promised our Foreign Affairs Minister that I would have full immunity during my entire stay if only I would appear. So don't bother to throw your weight around; it won't go. Care to see my passport? Diplomatic immunity."

"Dr. Boyle, this court is aware of your immunity. However, you have been induced to come here—at considerable expense I would assume and clearly at some inconvenience to you—to give evidence that only you can give. The Court *requests* you to answer all questions put to

342

you, as fully, explicitly, and clearly as possible, in terms a layman can comprehend, even if it means repeating yourself. We want to find out exactly what you did and what you know of your own knowledge, which might directly or indirectly assist this court in determining the identity of this woman."

"Oh, certainly, my dear fellow—put that way. Well, let's go back and run it through again, from A to Zed. A year ago, more or less, I was approached by that old bugger over there—sorry, I mean 'barrister'—Mr. Jacob Salomon—to do what the Sunday sheets call a 'brain transplant.' I accepted the commission. After this and that—you can get the trivia from him—I did it. Moved a brain and some ancillary parts from one human skull to another. That brain was alive in its new digs when I left.

"Now as to *whom*. The brain donor was a very elderly male, the body donor was a young mature female. And that is about the size of it—they are covered, y' know, sterile sheeting and such, before the surgeon in charge comes in. Prepped. I can add only these hints: The male was in bad shape, kept alive by major supportive means. The female was in worse shape, she was dead—massive trauma to skull and cortex about *here*—head bashed in, I mean to say, and the yolk spattered. Dead as Queen Anne save that her body had been kept alive by extreme support measures.

"Now that unsightly hunk of pickled meat over there has had its brain et cetera removed in a fashion consistent with my own—unique—surgical techniques; I doubt if there is another surgeon alive who can do it my way. I have examined that cadaver carefully; I conclude that it is my work—and, by elimination, I conclude that it *must* be the body Salomon hired me to carve on; there is no conflicting evidence and the cadaver is not from any other case of mine.

"Identifying the young female is another matter. If her head were shaved I might look for scar tissue. If her skull were X-rayed I might look for prosthesis; teflon vitae does not throw the same shadow on a plate as does natural bone. But such tests would be only indicative; scar tissue is easily come by, and other trephining could produce similar X-ray shadow without disturbing the central nervous system."

"Dr. Boyle, let us stipulate momentarily that you removed a living brain from exhibit JJ, the cadaver—"

" 'Stipulate?' I *did* do so, you heard me say so."

"I am not contradicting you, I am simply using appropriate language. Very well, you have so testified and you have also testified that you transplanted that brain into a young female body. Look about and see if you can identify that female body."

"Oh, you're being an ass again. I am neither a witch doctor nor a beauty contest judge; I am a surgeon. No, thank you. If that young woman—that composite human, female body, male brain—survived and is alive today—a point on which I have no opinion of my *own* knowledge and I assure you that I have had strong reason to acquaint myself both with relevant forensic medicine and medical jurisprudence; you are not about to trip me into being the ass you are—I would not today be able to single her out with certainty from ten thousand other young women of approximately the same size, weight, build, skin shade, and such. Counsel, have you ever seen a human body hooked up for extreme life support and prepared for such surgery? I'm sure you have not or you would not ask such silly questions. But I assure you that you would not recognize your own wife under such circumstances. If you want me to perjure myself, you've come to the wrong shop."

"Your Honor, Petitioners seem unable to get a responsive answer on this key point."

"The Court finds it responsive. Witness states that he can and does identify the male body but is unable to identify the female body. Doctor, I confess that I am puzzled on one point—perhaps through not being a medical man myself; nevertheless I am puzzled. Are we to understand that you would perform such an operation without being certain of the identity of the bodies?"

"Judge, I've never been one to fret about trivia. Mr. Salomon assured me, in legalistic language, that 'the fix was on' if I have your American idiom correct. His

344

assurances meant to me that the paper work was done, the legal requirements met, et cetera, and that I was free to operate. I believed him and did so. Was I mistaken? Should I expect an attempt to extradite me after I return home? I think it would be difficult; I have at last found a country where my work is respected."

"I am not aware that anyone has any intention of trying to extradite you. I was curious, that's all. What Counsel was getting at is this: There is present in this room a woman who claims to be that composite from your surgery. You can't point her out?"

"Oh, certainly I can. Though not as a sworn witness. It's that young lady seated by Jake Salomon. How are you, my dear? Felling chipper?"

"Very much so, Doctor."

"Sorry if I've disappointed you. Oh, I *could* make positive identification . . . by sawing off the top of your skull, then digging out your brain and looking for certain indications. But—heh heh!—you would not be much use to yourself afterwards. I prefer seeing you alive, a monument to my skill."

"I prefer it, too, Doctor—and truly, I'm not disappointed. I'm eternally grateful to you."

"Your Honor, this is hardly proper!"

"Counsel, I will be the judge of that. Under these most unusual circumstances I will permit a few human amenities in court."

"Miss Smith, I'd like to examine you before I go home. For my journal, you know."

"Certainly, Doctor! Anything—short of sawing off my skull."

"Oh, just chest-thumping and such. The usual rituals. Shall we say tomorrow morning, ten o'clockish?"

"My car will be waiting for you at nine thirty, Doctor. Or earlier, if you will do me the honor of having breakfast with me."

"The Court finds it necessary to interrupt. I'm sorry to say that both of you will be *here* at ten o'clock. The hour of recessing is almost on us and—"

"No, Judge."

"What, Dr. Boyle?"

"I said, 'No.' I will not be here tomorrow morning. I speak this evening at twenty o'clock at a dinner of one of your chop-'em-up societies. The American College of Surgeons. Until shortly before that time I am at your disposal. I suppose you can require the presence of Miss Smith tomorrow morning, but not mine. I'm off to merry old China as quickly as possible. No shortage of opportunities for research there—you would be amazed what condemned prisoners will agree to. So I shan't waste another day on silly-ass questions. But I am willing to tolerate them now."

"Mmm—I'm afraid that the Court must concede that this is a case of Mahomet and the Mountain. Very well, we will *not* recess at the usual hour."

"Witness will stand down. Do Petitioners offer more witnesses?"

"No, Your Honor."

"Counsel?"

"Miss Johann Smith offers no further evidence."

"Mr. Salomon, is it your intention to present an argument or summary?"

"No, Your Honor. The facts speak for themselves."

"Petitioners?"

"Your Honor, is it your intention to bring this to a terminus *today*?"

"That's what I am trying to find out. We've been at this for many weary days and I find myself in sympathy with Dr. Boyle's attitude: Let's sweep up the mess and go home. Both sides agree that there are no more witnesses, no more questions, no more exhibits. Counsel for Miss Smith states that he will not offer an argument. If Petitioners' counsel wishes to argue, he may do so—in which case Miss Smith, in person or through counsel or both, is privileged to rebut. What I had in mind, Counsel, was a recess . . . then, if you have your thoughts in order, you can say what you wish. If you can't, we can let it go over till tomorrow morning. You may at that time argue for a postponement—but I warn you that a lengthy postponement will not be tolerated; the

346

Court has become impatient with delaying tactics and red herrings, not to mention language and attitudes flavored with contempt. What is your wish?"

"May it please the Court, if we continue this evening, how long a recess does the Court contemplate?"

"—and rebuttal having been concluded, we are ready to rule. But first a statement by the Court. Inasmuch as a novel point in Constitutional Law is involved in this matter, if an appeal is made, the Court will, under the Declaratory Relief Act of 1984, on its own motion send the matter directly to Federal Appellate Court with recommendation that it be referred at once to the Supreme Court. We cannot say that this will happen but there are aspects which lead us to believe that it could happen; this matter is not trivial.

"We have heard the petition, we have heard witnesses and seen exhibits. It is possible to rule in one of four ways:

"That both Johann Sebastian Bach Smith and Eunice Evans Branca are alive;

"That Eunice is alive and Johann is dead;

"That Eunice is dead and Johann is alive;

"That both Eunice and Johann are dead.

"The Court rules—please stand up, Miss Smith—that this person before us is a physiological composite of the body of Eunice Evans Branca and the brain of Johann Sebastian Bach Smith and that in accordance with the equitable principle set forth in 'Estate of Henry M. Parsons v. Rhode Island' this female person is Johann Sebastian Bach Smith."

"—take it that you are offering me your lovely body. Sorry, m'dear. I have no interest in women. Nor in men. Nor in rubber garments or high heels or other toys. I'm a sadist, Miss Smith. A *genius* sadist who realized quite young that he must become a surgeon to stay out of the clutches of Jack Ketch. Sublimation, y'know. Thanks just the same. A pity, you do have a magnificent body." (Well, Boss, you got turned down. It's a lesson every woman must learn. So you bresh your hair and start all over again.)

(Eunice, I'm relieved. But he was entitled to the lagniappe if he wanted it.) "I'm your Galatea, Dr. Boyle; I owe you anything you care to name—short of sawing off my skull. The debt remains on the books. All I was offering was symbolic down-payment. But you don't respond like a typical Australian—nor sound like one, either."

"Oh, that. I'm a fake, dear. From the Sydney slums into a sadists' finishing school—a stylish British boarding school, a 'public' school right out of the second drawer. Then on to the University of London and the best surgeons in the world. Put your pretty robe on and I'll be going. I say, would you mind having that extr'ordinary slow-motion somersault filmed in stereocinema for my archives?"

"Where shall I send it, Doctor?"

"Jake Salomon knows. Keep your pecker up, m'dear, and try to live a long time; you're my masterpiece."

"I'll certainly try." ˙

"Do. Ta ta!"

An unidentified flying object roughly disc-shaped was reported to have landed in Pernambuco and its humanoid crew to have visited with local yokels; the report was denied officially almost faster than it reached the news services. The number of licensed private police in the United States reached triple the number of public peace officers. Miss Joan née Johann Smith received over two thousand proposals of marriage, more than that number of less formal proposals, one hundred eighty-seven death threats, an undisclosed number of extortion notes, and four bombs—not any of which she received in person as they were diverted to Mercury Private Courier Service under procedures set up years earlier. The waldoes of one package-opening bunker had to be replaced; the other bombs were disarmed.

The Postmaster General died from an overdose of barbiturates; the career Assistant Postmaster General declined an interim appointment and put in for retirement. A woman in Albany gave birth to a "faun" which was baptized, dead, and cremated in eighty-seven minutes. No flowers. No photographs. No interviews—but the priest wrote a letter to his seminary roommate. The F.B.I. reported that recidivism was up to 71%, while the same rate figured only on major felonies—armed robbery, rape, assault with a deadly weapon, murder, and attempted murder—had climbed to 84%. The paralysis at Harvard University continued.

"Jake, the last time you refused to marry me, you *did* promise me a night on the town if we won."

Mr. Salomon put down his cup. "A delightful lunch, my dear. As I recall, you told me at the time that a nightclub check was no substitute for a marriage license."

"Nor is it. But I haven't nagged you about marrying me since you accorded me the honor of first concubine. Uh . . . erase 'first.' I have no idea what you do with your time when you're not here. Well, I don't have to be 'first.' " (Twin, never crowd a man about sex. He'll lie.) (Pussy cat, I'm *not* crowding Jake about *sex*; I'm confusing the issue. He's going to take us nightclubbing and we're going to wear that lush blue-and-gold job—it's meant to be seen, not just modeled for Winnie and put away.)

"Eunice, surely you don't think I have anyone else?"

"It would be presumptuous of me to have an opinion, sir. Jake, I've stayed close to home all during this hearing—a little shopping, mostly with Winnie along. But now we've won and I see no reason to be a prisoner. Look, dear, we can make it a party of four—a girl for you and a boy for me—and you can come home early and not lose any sleep you don't want to."

"You surely don't think that I would go home and leave you at a nightclub?"

"I surely think I can stay up all night and celebrate if I want to. I'm free, over twenty-one—my *God*, am I over twenty-one!—and can afford a licensed escort. But there is no reason to keep you up all night. We'll call Gold Seal Bonded Escorts and fill out our party. Winnie's been teaching me what the kids call dancing—and I've been teaching her real dancing. Say, maybe you'd rather escort Winnie than some dollikin picked out of a catalog? Winnie thinks you're wonderful."

"Eunice, are you seriously proposing to hire a gigolo?"

"Jake, I'm not going to marry him, I'm not even going to sleep with him. I expect him to dance with me, smile, and make polite conversation—at about what a plumber charges. This is doom?"

"I won't have it."

"If you won't—and Heaven knows I would rather be on your arm than that of a paid escort—will you take a nap? I'll get a nap, too. Do you need help to get to sleep? Money Hums, I mean, not horizontal calisthenics. Although we have that in stock, too."

"I don't recall saying that we were going out. Nor is there anything to celebrate, Eunice. We haven't won until the Supreme Court rules on it."

"We have plenty to celebrate. I'm legally *me*—thanks to you, darling—and you no longer have to report as my conservator; my granddaughters have lost on all points. If we hold off celebrating until the Supreme Court maunders over it, we might both be dead."

"Oh, nonsense! You know I'm about to leave for Washington; I expect to be able to arrange for an early spot on the calendar. Be patient."

" 'Patient' is what I'm *not*, dear. Surely, you'll arrange it; you always do arrange things—and the Administration owes me that and will expect more from me. But, Jake, your jet might crash—"

"That doesn't sway me, it's my death-of-choice. Since my genetic background doesn't permit me to hope for heart failure, I've been counting on cancer. But a crash is still better. Anything but a long, slow, helpless dying."

"You're rubbing my nose in the mistake I made, sir. Will you let me finish? You once pointed out that you had only ten or twelve years, based on the actuarials—whereas I had at least half a century. Not true, Jake. *My* life expectancy is null."

"Eunice, what the devil are you talking about?"

"The truth. Truth you have conveniently forgotten—but which I am aware of every golden second. I'm a transplant, Jake. A *unique* transplant. No statistics apply to me. Nobody knows, no one can guess. So I live each wonderful day as all eternity. Jake my beloved master, I'm not being morbid—I'm being happy. When I was a little boy there was a prayer Mama taught me. It goes—

"Now I lay me down to sleep;

"I pray the Lord my soul to keep.

"If I should die before I wake,

"I pray the Lord my soul to take.

"It's like that, Jake. I had not used that prayer in almost ninety years. But now I use it . . . and go happily to sleep, unworried about tomorrow." (Twin! You lying little bitch! All you ever say is a Money Hum.) (It's the same thing, Puss. A prayer means what you want it to mean.)

"Joan Eunice, you once told me that you had no religion. So why do you say this child's prayer?"

"As I recall, what I told you was that I had been a 'relaxed agnostic'—until I was dead for a while. I'm still an agnostic—meaning that I don't have any answers—but I am now a *happy* agnostic, one who feels sure deep in her

352

heart that the world has meaning, is somehow good, and that my being here has purpose, even if I don't know what it is. As for that prayer, a prayer means whatever you make it mean; it's an inner ritual. What this one means to me is a good intention—to live every moment as Eunice would live it, *did* live—serenely, happily, and unworried by any later moment including death. Jake, you said you were still worried about Parkinson."

"Somewhat. As a lawyer, I don't see how he can get his hands on it again. But as a shyster at heart—don't quote me!—who has taken part in many a back-room deal, I know that even the Supreme Court is made up of men, not angels met in judgment. Eunice, there are five honest men on that court . . . and four from whom I would never buy a used car. But of the honest ones, one is senile. We'll see what we shall see."

"So we will, Jake. But don't give Parky a thought. The worst he can do is to strip me of money. Which I wouldn't mind; I've discovered that more money than is needed for current bills is a burden. Jake, I've got enough tucked away that even you don't know about that I'll never miss any meals. Parky can't touch it. As for Parky himself, I've erased him from my universe and suggest that you do likewise. He's damned by his own I.Q.—leave him to nature."

Salomon grinned. "Okay, I'll try."

"And now you go do whatever it is you have to do and forget that I tried to inveigle you into a pub crawl." (Twin, you're giving up too easily.) (Who is giving up?)

"Eunice, if you really want to—"

"No, no, Jake! Your heart's not in it. While you are in Washington I may sample the fleshpots of this decadent village but I promise you that I will be closely guarded. Shorty, probably; he frightens people just with his size. Nor will I go alone; Alec told me that he and Mac didn't have much trouble slipping the leash, and Winnie can make a fourth."

"Eunice."

"Yes, dear?"

"I am like hell going to step aside for those two wolves."

353

"Why, Jake, you sound jealous!"

"No. God save me from falling prey to *that* masochistic vice. But if you want to see the seamy side of this anthill, I'll find out where the action is and take you there. Dress for it, girl—I'm going to shake the moths off my drinkin' clothes. Formal, I mean."

"Bare breasts?" (Could you have done better, Pussy Cat?) (Pick up the pup, twin. I concede.)

" 'Much too good for the common people.' Unless you intend to paint heavily, plus a lot of that sparkly glitter stuff."

"I'll try to do you proud, dear. But you *will* take a nap? Please."

"A long nap at once and a dinner tray in my room. H-hour is twenty-two hundred. Be ready or we jump off without you."

"I'm scared. Want help to get to sleep? Me? Or Winnie? Or both?"

"No, I've learned how to do it by myself. Perfectly. Though I admit it's more fun with two pretty little girls chanting with me. *You* get a nap. I may keep you up all night."

"Yes, sir."

"And now, if I may be excused." Mr. Salomon stood up, bent over her hand and kissed it. "Adios."

"Come back here and kiss me right!"

He glanced over his shoulder. "Later, my dear. I don't believe in letting women be notional." He left.

(Who won that round, Boss?) (He thinks he did, Eunice—and you tell me that's how it ought to be.) (You're learning, twin, you're learning.)

They had been lunching in her lounge. She went into her boudoir, sat down at her stenodesk to phone—picking it rather than the viewphone because its phone was *not* a viewphone. She used it with hush, and with ear plugs.

Shortly she was answered: "Dr. Garcia's office."

"This is Mrs. McIntyre's secretary. Is the Doctor in and, if so, can he spare a moment to speak to Mrs. McIntyre?"

"Please hold. I will inquire."

Joan passed the time reciting her meditation prayer, was

calm when he ânswered, "Dr. Garcia speaking."

"Mrs. McIntyre's secretary, Doctor—hush and secure?"

"Of course, Eunice."

"Roberto dear, do you have news for me?"

" 'The Greeks have captured Athens.' "

"*Oh!* You're certain?"

"No possible doubt, Eunice. But *don't* panic. You can have a D. and C. at once with no chance of your privacy being breached. I'll get Dr. Kystra, the best possible man and utterly trustworthy. I'll assist, there won't even be a nurse present."

"Oh, Roberto, no, no, no! You don't understand, dear—I'm going to have this baby if it's the last thing I ever do. You've made me terribly happy." (Now we've *really* got something to celebrate, Boss darling. But don't tell Jake, huh?) (Nobody, just yet. How soon does our belly bulge?) (Not for weeks, if you don't eat like a pig.) (I want pickles and ice cream this instant.) (So don't.)

The Doctor answered slowly, "I misunderstood the situation. But you seemed quite nervous when I took the specimen."

"Certainly I was, dear; I was scared silly that I might *not* have caught."

"Uh . . . Eunice, I can't help feeling personally responsible. I know you're wealthy—but a marriage contract can exclude any 'fortune hunter' possibility and—well, I'm available."

"Roberto, I think that's the sweetest—and bluntest —proposal a knocked-up broad ever got. Thank you, dear; I do appreciate it. But, as you pointed out, I am wealthy— and I do not care what the neighbors think."

"Eunice, I am not simply accepting my responsibility . . . I want you to know that I do not regard marrying you as a chore."

"Roberto darling, it is *not* your responsibility. For all you know I've been sweetheart to the regiment." (We've tried, haven't we, twin!) (Don't joggle my elbow, dear; he wants to be noble.) "It's *my* baby. Who helped me is my business."

"Sorry."

"I meant that you mustn't feel *any* responsibility. If you *did* help me, I'm grateful. I'm grateful even if you didn't. Roberto? Instead of trying to make an honest woman out of me—difficult—why don't you remove that implant from Winnie's pretty thigh, then place another sort of implant where it will do the most good . . . then make an honest woman out of *her*. Much easier, she leans that way."

"It's a thought. Truthfully it's a thought I've considered quite a lot lately. But she doesn't want to leave you."

"She need not. Oh, she could stop pretending to be my maid, but this is a big old barn, several spare suites. If you get her pregnant, she and I could chum and giggle about it and have our babies almost together. I'll shut up and stop trying to run your life. Two questions—I had planned to go out on the town tonight, to celebrate the good news I expected to hear from you. Must I stick to soft drinks now?"

"Not at all. Shortly we'll put you on a diet and limit your drinking. But tonight you could get stinking drunk and the only effect would be a hangover. You don't lose a baby that easily . . . as millions of women have learned."

"May not get stinking but I may soak up several glasses of bubbly. Last question— If you're able to sign off, would it suit you to lose a night's sleep helping me celebrate? Officially it's to celebrate our court victory. That 'the Greeks have captured Athens' will stay secret a while longer."

"Uh—"

"You sound fretted, dear."

"Well, to tell the truth I have a date with Winnie."

"Oh! I expressed myself badly. *I* have a date with Jake; I hope that you and Winnie can make it a four. I wasn't asking you to spend a night with me in that sense—although I certainly would not be averse if it could be managed some other time without hurting our Winsome. The moments you and I have been able to steal have been too short, dear. I think you are a man it would be sweet to be leisurely with."

"I *know* that you are such a woman, Eunice."

"Go along with you, you tell that to all your female

356

patients. Doctor, you are a delightful wolf. Will you wait ten minutes before phoning Winnie? I have a favor I want to ask of her."

"Ten minutes."

"Thank you, Roberto. Off."

Joan switched to the house intercom. "Winnie? Are you busy, dear?"

"Just reading. Be right in."

Joan met her at their connecting door. "Nothing much, hon. I want you to call O'Neil and tell him that I wish to speak to Finchley. In my lounge. Sure, I could phone O'Neil myself, sweet, but I want it to look more formal."

"Sure, Joanie. Do I stay and chaperon?"

"Winsome, you know darn well that all I ever want is fake chaperonage—and sometimes a jigger. This time I don't need a jigger—but I do want to ask Finchley something privately and he will speak more freely if you aren't around. So let him into my lounge, come tell me he has arrived, and don't come back in. Go on into your own room and close the door. Then stay there—you are going to receive a phone call in about eight minutes."

"I am?"

"Yes, and a nice one. You and I and Jake and Dr. Garcia are going nightclubbing tonight."

"*Oh!*"

"And when we get home just keep him here the rest of the night and I'll see to it that Jake doesn't twig. Or does he know who 'Bob' is?"

"Uh . . . yes, he does. I told him."

"It may still suit dear Doctor to cover up; men are shy. Now skedaddle, dear, and phone O'Neil."

Four minutes later Winnie announced Finchley, and left the lounge. He said, "You sent for me, Miss?"

"Tom Cat, these doors are soundproof; you can stop being formal."

He relaxed a little. "Okay, Pussy Cat."

"So give us a kiss and sit down. That hall door locks itself. Winnie is the only one who could walk in and she won't."

"Pussy Cat, sometimes you make me nervous."

"Oh, piffle." She moved into his arms. "I do have a question to ask you—advice that I want. You can discuss it with O'Neil and get his advice, and any of the guards. But it is *your* advice I want; the rest is cover-up."

"Woman, quit talking and shove me some mouth."

Joan did so, a long thorough kiss. Presently he said hoarsely, "You don't have much on under this."

"I don't have *anything* on under it. But don't get me distracted, Thomas Cattus; let me get my question in. I'm going nightclubbing tonight—Jake and me, Winnie and Dr. Garcia. They're going to want to take us to cubes. *I* want to see *rough* places. I figure you know where they are."

"Mmm . . . Eunice, the up-high places are all in bad turf."

"Well, are they safe once we're inside? And can one get inside safely?"

"Uh . . . there's one, has its own inside parking and as good armor as the doors you have. Look, I'll bring up a list, addresses and so forth, and everybody's suggestions. But I'll star my own."

"Good. Thank you, Tom Cat."

"God, but you feel good. Do we have time? Can I lock that other door?"

"If I'm not worried about Winnie, why should you be? Grab a pillow and put me on the floor."

The party made rendezvous in Joan's lounge. Jake Salomon had elected to dress with ultra old-fashioned formality: maroon tuxedo jacket and trousers, with white turtleneck. The silky knit made a splendid background for his gold ankh necklace. Dr. Garcia was just as formal in modern mode: scarlet tights boldly padded, stretch-fit white mess jacket with jabot of pearls and black lace. Little Winifred wore her new emerald dress with floor-length skirt—no body paint as Joan had advised but blushes caused her skin to change again and again from extremely fair to rosy glow. On her forehead in caste-mark position was a single emerald.

Jake looked at her. "Little one, what holds that solitaire in place? Insurance?"

She blushed again but answered saucily, "It's on a corkscrew, sir. Shall I unscrew it and show you?"

"No, I'm afraid you might be telling the truth."

"Never in mixed company, sir. Actually it's the adhesive we use on bandages. Won't come loose even with soap and water but alcohol takes it right off."

"Then be careful not to spill your drinks that high."

"Oh, I don't drink, Counselor; I learned my lesson long ago. I'll be drinking Cuba Libre without the 'libre' and screwdrivers with no drive to them."

"Doctor, let's leave her at home; she's just a chaperon."

"Would you make me stay home, Counselor? Just for not drinking?"

"Just for calling me 'Counselor' if you do it again. And for calling me 'sir'. Winifred, men my age do not care to be reminded of it by pretty little girls. After sundown my name is Jake."

"Yes, Counselor," Winifred answered meekly.

Jake sighed. "Doctor, someday I hope to win an argument with a woman."

"If you do, tell Dr. Rosenthal. Rosy is writing a book on the difference in mental processes between male and female."

"A dreamer. Eunice, does that thing cover you any better when you stand up? And what is it?"

"It's a hula skirt, Jake. And it does." Joan Eunice was wearing a floor-length skirt, with her torso covered with a myriad glittering stars. They faded out gradually at neck and shoulders. The skirt was thousands of gold nylon threads overlying more thousands of deep blue threads.

As she was seated, the mass of threads fell away from her graceful legs. Now she stood up; the threads fell back into a solid curtain. "See, Jake? A plain gold skirt. But when I move"—she walked—"the blue underneath keeps flashing through."

"Yes, and you, too. Panties?"

"A rude question. The Polynesians never heard of pants until the missionaries corrupted them."

"That's not a responsive answer—"

"Wasn't meant to be."

"—but as long as you are standing, let's get rolling."

"Yes, dear." Joan Eunice put on a matching opaque yashmak, let Jake lay an evening cloak around her shoulders. Jake hooked on a maroon domino which covered his distinctive aquiline nose—he had been too often on video lately and felt that there was no point on concealing Miss J. S. B. Smith's face if his own face broke her cover. The Doctor donned a small white domino—having been asked to help keep the party in character—and Winifred wore a filmy green harem veil that was only a symbol, being of the same material as her skirt.

As they entered the lift Joan Eunice said, "Where are we going, Jake?"

"Woman, you aren't supposed to ask. The Gaslight Club, as a starter."

"It sounds like fun," Joan agreed. "A piano player with sleeve garters and such?"

"And derby hat and fake cigar—he can sing and play anything written a hundred years back. Or fake it."

"I want to hear him. But, Jake, since this is to celebrate my uhuru, would you indulge me a little?"

"Probably. Show your openers."

"There's a club I've heard about . . . and while you were napping, I reserved a table for four for twenty-two thirty. I'd like to try it."

"Winnie, you haven't been coaching her enough. Eunice, you're not supposed to be capable of making such a decision—less than the dust beneath my chariot wheels and all that. All right, where is this dive? What's its name? We'll try the Gaslight later—there is a waitress there alleged to have the most pinchable bottom in the state."

"Probably foam rubber; Winnie has that distinction. It's the Pompeii-Now, Jake—I have the address in my purse."

Mr. Salomon's eyebrows appeared over his domino. "We won't need it, Eunice. That box is in an Abandoned Area."

"Does that matter? They have inside parking and

360

assured me that they are armored against anything short of a nuke bomb."

"We would still have to get there and back."

"Oh, I have confidence in Finchley and Shorty. Don't you?" (Twin, that's a crotch chop. Not nice.) (Big sister, do you want to go to the Gaslight and listen to bad piano and watch Jake pinch bottoms? If so, say so.) (I just said it wasn't nice.) (So you phrase the next answer. Jake's a tough case.)

"Joan Eunice, when I take a lady out for the evening, we go in *my* car. Not hers."

"Whatever you say, Jake; I was trying to be helpful. I asked Finchley and he said there was a route in that the—what do they call it?—the Organization—keeps open. No doubt Finchley can tell Rockford."

"*I* call it the Mafia. If there is an acceptably safe route, Rockford knows it; he's the most expert driver in town—more experienced than your boys, he drives more."

"Jake, you don't want to go there. So let's go to the Gaslight. I want to try sticking a pin in that rubber fanny."

They went to the Pompeii-Now.

There was no trouble getting inside and the club had a card lounge for its patrons' mobile guards. The maître d'hôtel led them to a ringside table across from the orchestra, swept a "Reserved" sign from it. "Will this be suitable, Mr. 'Jones'?"

"Yes, thank you," agreed Salomon. Two silver-bucket stands with champagne appeared as they sat down; the maître d'hôtel took a magnum from the sommelier and displayed it to Salomon, who said, "That's a poor year for Pol Roger. No Dom Pérignon ninety-five?"

"At once, sir." The sommelier hurried away. The maître d'hôtel asked, "Is there anything else not to your liking, sir?"

Joan Eunice leaned toward Jake. "Please tell him that I don't like this chair. It was designed by Torquemada."

The floor manager looked upset. "I'm sorry Madame feels that way about our chairs. They were supplied by the number-one hotel and restaurant supply company."

"As may be," Joan answered, "but if you think I'm going to spend an evening perched on a shooting stick and pretend that it's fun, you are mistaken. Jake, we should have gone to the Gaslight."

"Perhaps, but we're here now. Just a moment, dear. Maître d'hôtel—"

"Yes, sir."

"You have an office here, no doubt."

"Why, yes, sir."

"With a desk and a chair. Probably a padded swivel chair with arms and an adjustable back. A man who is on his feet as much as you are wants a comfortable chair when he does sit down."

"I do have such a chair, sir, and—while it's hardly suitable for a dining room—Madame is welcome to it if it pleases her. I'll send for it."

"One moment. In a club with so many activities—you have a gaming room, do you not, and other things?—I feel sure that it is possible to round up four such chairs."

"Uh, I'll try, sir. Although our other patrons might find it odd if we supply one table with special chairs."

Mr. Salomon looked around. The place was less than half filled. "Oh, I imagine that if you explained to anyone who asked just how expensive such special service is, he might not want it. Or you might find it possible to accommodate him, too, if he is willing to pay. I think those guards pretending to be waiters standing around the edge of the room can handle anyone who is unreasonable."

"All our staff are guards, sir—in a crunch. Very well, sir, if you will be patient a few moments your party will all have desk chairs." Quickly he distributed wine cards and drug lists, and left.

Roberto and Winifred were already dancing. Joan leaned toward Jake again and said, "Jake, will you buy this place for me?"

"Does it attract you that much?"

"No, I want to make a bonfire out of these chairs. I had forgotten what indignities nightclubs expect their customers to put up with."

"You're spoiled."

"I intend to be. Jake, much of what is wrong with this world would be righted if the customer screamed every time he feels cheated. But I'm not out to reform the world tonight; I simply want a comfortable chair. The cover charge—I checked it when I made reservations for 'Mr. Jones'—is high enough to *buy* a decent chair. What are these 'other activities'? A whorehouse upstairs, maybe?"

"Eunice, see those three tables of beautiful people over in the corner? Attractive men and women, all young, all smiles, no frowns, and each with a champagne glass that may hold ginger ale? It's high odds that, if the Greeks had a word for it, they have a price for it."

"Why, one of those girls doesn't look more than twelve."

"She may not be that old. Who's going to check on her age, in an Abandoned Area? I thought you weren't going to reform the world tonight, my dear?"

"I'm not. If the government can't police these areas, I certainly cannot. But I hate to see children exploited." (Twin, that pretty child may have an I.Q. of eighty and no other possible profession—she may think she's lucky. Proud of her job. And seeing where she is, she's either got an implant or cut tubes—not like that cheerleader I told you about.) (Eunice, doesn't it bother you?) (Some, chum, but only some. People usually are what they are because it suits them—I learned that from Joe. The girl's mother may be one of the other pretties there—two gets you seven. Want to rescue them both?) (Oh, shut up, darling; let's have fun.) (I'm willing.)

A waitress came past, refilled their glasses. She was pretty and was dressed in sandals, cosmetics, and careful depilation. She smiled and moved on. "Jake, is she one?"

"Couldn't say, I don't know the house rules. Shocked, Eunice? I told you not to come here."

"Shocked at *skin*? Jake dear, you forget that *my* generation thinks nothing of nudity."

"*Hrrmph!* One more remark like that and I'll call you 'Johann' the rest of the evening."

"I'll be good. Mostly. Darling, our waitress suddenly reminded me of the Chesterfield Club. Kansas City in the palmiest days of the Pendergast machine. Nineteen-thirty-four."

"In nineteen-thirty-four I was barely out of diapers, Eunice. It was something like this?"

"Not as much fake swank and lower prices even allowing for inflation. But otherwise much the same. It specialized in complete nudity even at high noon at the 'Businessman's Lunch.' Just up the street from the Federal Reserve Bank. Jake, she's headed back. Find out for me."

"How? I don't even have a hat to tip."

"Simply ask her, dear, ask her if she's available. Slip her ten dollars as you do; she won't be insulted."

The waitress came back, smiled, and said, "Have you looked over our drug list? All illegal drugs at the controlled international prices plus twenty-five percent. Guaranteed pure, we obtain them from government sources."

"Not for me, thank you, dear. Eunice? Want a trip?"

"Me? I don't even take aspirin. But I want a steady supply of champagne. And I could use a sandwich, or something. Chiquita, is there a kitchen?"

"There is always a gourmet chef on duty, Ma'am; it says so at the bottom of your wine card. Anything from snacks to Maine lobster. Would you like to see a menu?"

"No, thank you. Maybe a big platter of little sandwiches for all of us, Jake. And don't forget that other matter."

Joan Eunice saw Jake get out a ten-dollar bill. It disappeared and Joan decided that the girl must have folded it with one hand and palmed it. Jake spoke to her in a voice lower than the music.

She smiled and answered clearly. "No, sir, I'm not even allowed to dance with customers—and I'm not in that branch of the business; I'm married. But I can arrange it." The waitress glanced toward the 'beautiful people' and looked back. "For you sir? Or for both of you?"

"No," Jake answered. "It was just curiosity."

"*My* curiosity," Joan put in. "I'm sorry, dear; I shouldn't have made him ask you."

"Ma'am, a high roller can be as inquisitive as he wishes. Baby needs shoes." She smiled. "Twins. Boys. Two years old. I was licensed for two and now I'm arguing with the

Board as to whether twins use up my license. Since twins are okay under a one-baby license. I'd like to have a little girl, too."

"Jake, be a high roller again; I want to ask" —Joan leaned forward, read the girl's name written or tattooed above her left breast—"Marie another question."

"He's paid for more than one question, really, Ma'am." But a second note disappeared as quickly as the first.

"Marie, do you live inside the turf? With kids?"

"Oh, goodness, no! My husband would never permit that. An armed bus picks me up after supper and delivers me home around breakfast time. Most of us use it. Except—" She indicated the exception by inclining her head toward the corner. "My husband is on night shift at Timken—we match up pretty well."

"Who takes care of your twins at night? Nursery?"

"Oh, no, Mama lives with us. No huhu. Actually, Ma'am, this is a good job. I've been a waitress where I had to wear uniforms—and the work was hard and the tips were small. Here the work is easy and the tips are usually high. Oh, sometimes a customer gets drunk and gropy, but I don't bruise all that easily—and drunks are often the highest tippers. Never any trouble; the guards watch everything." She smiled at Joan. "You could get a job here in two seconds, Ma'am. All it takes is a friendly manner and a good figure—and you've got both."

"Thank you, Marie."

"I'd better go, the maître d' is bringing a party to another of my tables. 'Scuse, please—sandwiches will be right in."

The girl left. Joan said, "Jake, would you say that she has found her niche?"

"Seems so. As long as she keeps her figure and saves her money. She doesn't pile up Social Security points here; this doesn't count as a job under the rules, it's off the map."

"She doesn't pay income tax?"

"Oh, certainly! The fact that her income doesn't exist, legally, means nothing to revenooers. Though she may hold out a good portion—I would. My dear, do you want to try this music?"

"Jake, I thought you didn't dance?"

365

"I don't dance this modern stuff. But I can try, if you want to. I wonder if that combo can play Rock? This new stuff has so little beat I don't see why they call it dance music."

Joan chuckled. "I'm so much older that I despised Rock instead of liking it. Swing was my era, Jake, and on back clear to the Bunny Hug—though I didn't learn to dance until the fox-trot crowded out the rest."

"I can fox-trot, I'm not all that young. But I doubt if that bunch of disappointed harpists can play one. Eunice, can you tango?"

"Try me, just try me! Learned it when Irene Castle was alive—and with this new body I'm eight times as good as I was then. Been teaching it to Winnie. Do you have a firm lead?"

"Firm enough for you, wench. I'm going to flag the maître-d'—it's possible that they can play one. It's the only tempo that has stayed evergreen through all the passing fads."

"Of course, Jake. Because the tango, danced correctly, is so sexy that you ought to get married afterwards. See if they can play one."

But they were interrupted by busboys arriving with four swivel chairs and Joan decided that it would be polite to sit in hers a while, since she had made a fuss over chairs. Then sandwiches arrived and more champagne and she found she wanted both—bubbly to make her tiddly and sandwiches to soak it up so that she wouldn't get tiddly too fast. Roberto and Winifred returned to the table; Winnie said, "Oh, food! Good-bye, waistline! Bob, will you love me when I'm fat?"

"Who knows? Let's operate and find out," he answered, reaching for a sandwich with one hand and champagne with the other.

"Winsome, pour that Coke into the wine bucket and have champagne."

"Joanie, you know I mustn't. My Nemesis."

"But this time there's food to go with it . . . and not the other hazards."

Winifred blushed. "I'll get drunk. I'll get silly."

"Roberto, will you promise this poor child that, if she passes out, you'll get her home safely?" (What's safe about *home*, twin? You ought to hang out a red light.) (Nonsense, Eunice! Our man won't marry us—so what do you want me to *do*? I don't give myself to men I don't respect—and I've got *years* to make up for. I'm nearly ninety-five years old—and knocked up—and healthy—and *can't* hurt anyone physically and *won't* hurt anyone socially . . . a man's pride or anything else. Why shouldn't I be 'No-Pants Smith'?) ('Methinks the lady doth protest too much.' Boss, your Bible-Belt background is chafing you again. Certainly sex is no sin—but *you* don't really believe it.) (I do so! Always have. I've been almost enough of a busybody to keep *you* happy. Why do you needle me?) (Beloved Boss. You've shown amazing talent for juggling eggs and I've enjoyed every second of it and I hope you have, too.) (You *know* I have. So much I'm scared of losing my judgment. My caution, rather, Eunice, I never *dreamed* how much *more* it is, to be a woman. It's our *whole* body.)

The cabaret was crowded now; the lights changed and the floor show began—two comics. Joan listened, tried to look amused, and tried to amuse herself by trying to remember how long ago she had heard each "new" gag. She could see only one improvement in the routines: The "dirty" story of her (his) youth had disappeared. Being based on shock of breaking taboo, the dirty story had bled to death when there were no more taboos. There was sex humor—the comics used plenty of it; sex remained forever the most comical thing on a weary globe. But it was harder to work out real comedy than it once had been simply to shock.

But she applauded the comics as they left. There was a black-out and the dance floor changed instantly into a farmyard scene—she found herself more intrigued by trying to guess the mechanics of that "magic" than she had been by the comics.

The farmyard set was used for one of the oldest (possibly the oldest, she decided) of all sex stories, and it was done in stylized, very old symbols in both costume and props: the Farmer, the Farmer's Daughter, and the City Slicker with his Hundred-Dollar Bills. It was pantomime, with theme music from the orchestra.

She whispered to Jake, "If she's a farm girl, I'm Adolf Hitler."

"What do you know about farms, my dear?"

"Plenty, for a city boy. On one nearly every summer when I was a kid. Followed the harvest in high school and college—good money, plus occasionally a farm girl. Always was a peasant at heart—wanted the biggest manure pile in the valley . . . and got it, save that it was cash. Jake? Couldn't we buy an abandoned farm? A simple little place, with drawbridge and moat, and our own plant and water supply? Get out of this dying city?"

"If you say to, dear. Getting bored with this? Want to move on?"

"Not during their act, dear." (I'm curious to see how he fakes it.) (Me, too!)

To her surprise the entertainers did not fake it. Money caused the "farm girl" to go from offended, to coy, to consent, to active cooperation, with a haystack as locale of consummation—and actor and actress made certain that the audience could see that it was in no way faked. Winifred blushed to her waist and never took her eyes off it.

The ending had a variation that Joan-Johann conceded was new to her-him. As motions grew vigorous and the orchestra kept time to loud squeals and grunts, the "Farmer" showed up (as expected) with pitchfork. But the hay caught fire, apparently from the action, and the "Farmer" dropped his pitchfork and grabbed a seltzer bottle conveniently at hand on an empty table and doused his "Daughter" and the "City Slicker" in putting out the fire—aiming first at the apparent source of the fire.

Joan decided that it rated applause. Winifred hesitantly joined in, then clapped hard when Roberto did. Jake joined in but was interrupted. "What is it, Rockford?"

Joan turned her head, surprised. Jake's driver-guard was looking very upset. "Mr. Salomon—I've *got* to speak with you."

"You are. Speak up."

368

"Uh—" Rockford tried to make it just to his employer but Joan watched his lips. "That crazy fool Charlie has gone got hisself killed."

"Oh, for God's sake! Where? How?"

"Just now. In the guards' lounge. Not drunk. This is a tight joint, they won't let a guard drink. We were playing stud and Charlie kept needling this Polack. No excuse and I told him to knock it off. But he didn't. Polack got sore, but tried to avoid a showdown. Charlie kept crowding him and—oh, what's the use; the Polack broke his neck. Before I could get around to that side of the table." Rockford said, "Boss? Seeing where we are, I could dump him. Best, maybe?"

"Of course not. I have to report it, the body has to go to the morgue. Damn it, Rocky, I'm his parole officer."

"Yeah, but maybe you don't know about it? He skipped. Dropped out."

"Shut up." Salomon turned to Joan. "My dear, I'm terribly sorry."

"Jake, I should never have asked you to take me into an A.A."

"That has nothing to do with it. Charlie was a congenital killer. Rockford, get the maître-d'. No, take me to the manager. Friends—Bob, Winnie—stay here please, I've got to take care of something."

Garcia said, "I caught most of it. Take me with you, Jake. I can certify death—and it's smart to get that done at once."

"Uh . . . who's going to stay with the girls?"

Joan put her hand on Jake's arm. "Jake, Winnie and I are safe—lots of guards. I think we'll go to the powder room. I need to, Winnie probably does, too. Coming, Winnie?"

The party was over but it was two hours before they were home; too many details—tedious ones rather than legal complications, as Dr. Garcia certified death, and he, the manager, Mr. Salomon, and Rockford endorsed the certificate that death had occurred in an Abandoned Area at the hands of a party or parties unknown—in fact unknown, as the cardroom was empty save for the body.

There was no point in inquiries; it had happened in an Abandoned Area and was not a crime de facto nor in any practical sense de jure. Nor did anyone weep; even Rockford did not like his driving partner, he simply respected him as a fast gun in a crunch. To Garcia Jake groused that he should have known better than to try to rehabilitate a congenital—and got no sympathy, as Garcia believed that such creatures should be exterminated as soon as identified.

Both tried to keep the grisly aspects from the ladies.

Winifred and Joan Eunice spent an hour alone at the table, fiddling with champagne and trying to look amused, while the men tidied up the mess. But Joan helped on one point : The body had to be sent to the morgue and Jake was unwilling to leave it to the management, he was certain they would dump it. Nor was he willing to send Rockford without someone to ride shotgun. So a phone was brought to Joan and she called O'Neil—was answered instantly and she wondered if her Chief ever slept.

Finchley and Shorty were on duty; O'Neil said they would be rolling at once. But Joan ordered him to have them first pick up Fred, to ride shotgun for Rockford. As an afterthought she told O'Neil to have the night pantryman place a cold supper and a case of chilled champagne in her lounge—the "night on the town" had turned out a dismal flop; she was darned if she would let it stay that way. Charlie was better dead and his death did not rate one crocodile tear. Ten thousand human beings had died around the globe in the hour since his death—why weep over a worthless one? (Eunice, what happens to a kark like Charlie after he's dead?) (I'm no authority, Boss. Maybe the bad ones die dead—like a potter destroying damaged work. Ask the Front Office.)

(I don't know its wavelength, sweetheart. Maybe you can tell me this—How can I get this party rolling again? Look at Winnie—drinking champagne but not smiling.) (Boss darling, I recommend more champagne and Money Hums, mixed fifty-fifty.) (Eunice, I thought you didn't approve of liquor?) (Never said that, Boss. I didn't drink because I didn't need it. But nothing is good or bad in

370

itself, just in its effects. Try it. Can't hurt, might help.)

So when at last the four reached the big, ugly fortress, Eunice insisted that they go to her lounge for a nightcap and a snack. "Who knows? We might feel like dancing yet. Roberto, has Winnie introduced you to our relaxing routine? The Money Hum?"

"I've tried to teach it to him, Joanie. But Bob is a dreadful cynic."

"Jake, let's uncynic Robert. I've thought of a new way to recite it. Sit in a circle and pass around a loving cup. Three recite while one drinks, and pass the cup to the next one."

"I vote Yea," Jake answered. "Doctor, if you want to be cynical, go do so by yourself—you can have the guest bed in my suite. We'll form a triangle instead."

"I had better stay to keep the party orderly."

"Very well, sir. But one unseemly word while we are at our devotions and you will be severely punished."

"How?"

Joan Eunice answered, "By having to down the loving cup unassisted, of course, and then start it again."

Joan Eunice woke up feeling rested but very thirsty. She glanced at the ceiling, saw that it was after ten and thought idly of turning on floor lights as a gentle preliminary to stronger light.

Then she realized that she was not alone. Should she wake Jake—gently—for a pleasant good morning? Or slide out softly and sneak back to her room and hope not to be seen? Or did it matter? Was she already a topic of gossip in her own house?

Better not wake Jake in any case; the poor darling planned to go to Washington tonight. She started to slide out of bed.

The man by her reached out and pulled her to him. She at once gave in, went soft and boneless. "Didn't know you were awake, dear. I meant to—*Roberto!*"

"You were expecting Santa Claus?"

"How did you get here?"

"You invited me."

"I did? Well, yes, I did. I mean I told you that you were

371

welcome in my bed, quite a while back. But where's Jake? Did he go to sleep on us? And what about Winnie?" She thumbed on the floor lights, saw that she was, as she was beginning to suspect, in her own bed.

"Winnie's next door. In her bed. With Jake."

"Good God, Roberto—I've finally spent a night with you. And don't remember it." (*I do! Whee!*) (Well, *I* don't, Eunice, Not in detail. Confused.) (You're a drunken little bitch, Boss. But we had fun.) (I'm sure we did. I wish I remembered it.)

Dr. Garcia sighed. "Ah, well. I should not complain."

"It's coming back to me," she lied. "Just disoriented as I woke up. You were especially sweet to me."

"You didn't think so when I wouldn't let you go to bed with your makeup on."

Joan allowed enough general illumination to come on to let her see herself, noted that the star sequins were gone as well as body paint they had adhered to. She had not scrubbed it off herself; ergo, someone else had. Not Winnie—Winnie had been potted as a palm. "That's part of what I meant by 'especially sweet', Roberto. Not many men would take such good care of a drunken wench. Was I hard to handle?"

"Not really. But you were pretty tight."

"Too tight?"

"Not too tight. Just pleasantly so."

"I'm not sure I understand that and don't think I want to. Roberto darling, even if I did fuss over it, thank you for washing me. Only a slut leaves paint on when she goes to bed. I'm a tart but I don't want to be a slut." (*Hi*, slut!) "And thank you most of all for a wonderfully sweet night. I hope I wasn't too drunk to make it sweet for you, too."

"Eunice, you would be more woman passed out cold than most can manage at their best."

"I'm glad you said 'would be' rather than 'are.' But, Roberto, I'm uneasy. Not about you and me, dear, but about Winnie. Does this affect that thought you've been considering? About Winnie, I mean."

"On the contrary, Eunice, it was Winnie's idea—her notion of how to celebrate our engagement—"

372

"Wait a moment! Am I engaged to *you*?"

"Eh? No, no—I'm engaged to Winnie."

"Oh. Roberto, I would happily marry you, you would make a numero-uno esposo. But I don't need one, and Winnie does. Did I know this last night? About you two?"

"You seemed to. You said that was why you wouldn't wait to scrub off your sparklers—you were right-now about it."

"Roz. I remember being terribly eager but I seem to have drawn a blank as to why. Roberto? Did I spill the news about the 'Greeks capturing Athens'?"

"I don't think so, Eunice. Not when I was around. I'm fairly sure Winnie doesn't know it."

"I'll tell Winnie; it's Jake I want to keep in the dark."

"Eunice? Did Jake do it? Capture Athens and the Parthenon as well."

"Watch that Hippocratic Oath, dear. Parthenogenesis might be the answer. Let me keep this up in the air a while longer. You say this was *Winnie's* idea? After you told her you would marry her?"

"Yes."

"How did she ever get up her courage to propose? I've been urging her to—but she's so damn' shy. Dutch courage?"

"Yes. But my own. Sure, she's shy—but under her blushes Winnie is as rugged as a nurse has to be. She said All right—if I would let her tie it down tight that she is no angel. I told her I had no use for angels, in bed or out. She said she hoped I meant that, because she was about to ask Jake to sleep with her."

"Roberto, I missed a lot of this. How much champagne did I drink?"

"Who counts? Jake kept opening bottles and we kept passing the loving cup around. While reciting that amphigory. You got your share. We all did."

"Uh . . . am I engaged to Jake?"

"Not that I know of."

"That's good. Because when Jake finds out I'm knocked up, he's going to be noble. Just as you were, dear, but Jake will be much more difficult. And I've discovered that I

373

don't need a husband; I just want loving friends. You. Jake. Winnie. Some others. People who'll love me as I am, clay feet and all—not because of a contract. Did Jake make any fuss over the sleeping arrangements?"

"Uh, truthfully I don't think anyone was displeased with Winnie's suggestion. Jake picked Winnie up under one arm and announced that he was reenacting the Rape of the Sabines."

"The faithless old darling."

"So I picked you up and carried you in and scrubbed you . . . and you squealed and protested and told me that was a hell of a way to run a rape."

"Mmm, I think I was right. 'In vino veritas.' "

"So now I'm going to put a pillow over your face so that you can't squeal and protest."

"You won't need a pillow; just put your hand over my mouth if I'm noisy. But all these doors are soundproof."

"You think I don't know it? When I lived here for most of a year? Miss Johann Smith, I know more about your house than you do."

"Oh, you bastard! Call me 'Eunice.' Or put a pillow over my face so I can't hear you, Roberto—I'm so *happy* that you're going to marry our Winsome."

"So am I, Eunice. Now shut up."

"Yes, sir." (*Unh!* Eunice, nobody ever tells me anything.) (Shut up, twin, and pay attention to what you're doing!)

Joan Eunice reached for the intercom by her bed, tapped it for Cunningham, then reached for Roberto's hand.

"Yes, Miss?"

"Cunningham, I want breakfast for four, served in my lounge."

"Yes, Miss."

"Placed in my lounge, rather, with warmers and coolers. No service. I have no idea when Mr. Salomon and Dr. Garcia will wake up, but I want to be hostessish and ready to serve them myself when they do. But Winnie and I want to eat." She winked at the doctor, squeezed his hand.

"Certainly, Miss."

374

"They need their sleep. Tell me, Cunningham—you've known me a long time. Have you ever pinned one on?"

"Pardon me, Miss?"

"Go on a luau, get so fried you can't find the floor with both feet. Drunk and disorderly."

"I have sometimes—in the past—come down with that ailment."

"Then you know what a delicate condition we are in—Winnie and myself at least and I have reason to believe that the gentlemen will not be in much better shape. But there was excellent excuse."

"I heard about the trouble, Miss. Too bad."

"Cunningham, I did *not* mean Charlie. This may be callous of me . . . but he was a bully who picked a fight, and lost."

"Oh. If I may say so, Miss, he was not liked belowstairs. Uh, we really did not like having him in the house."

"I know. I would have put a stop to it long ago except that he worked for Mr. Salomon, not me—and I owe Mr. Salomon a great deal. No, the 'excellent excuse' was something else. We were celebrating an engagement."

Cunningham said cautiously, "Should I offer congratulations, Miss?"

"Yes, but not to me. Dr. Garcia is marrying Winifred."

"*Oh!* That's fine, Miss. But we'll miss her."

"I am hoping that we will not have to miss her. This is a big house, Cunningham, much too large for one person. Or for two whenever Mr. Salomon can be persuaded to honor us. Not often enough, that is to say—but the Counselor is afraid that he will cause gossip about me."

"Uh, may I speak plainly, Miss?"

"Any time you don't, Cunningham, I shall be offended."

"Mr. Salomon is a fine gentleman. But if he worries about that—well, it's silly, that's all I can say. The staff do *not* gossip about his presence. They respect him."

"Perhaps you can tell him, he won't listen to me. But today I'm simply concerned that he sleep as late as possible. He must go to Washington tonight, you know. When you bring up breakfast, don't go past his door; go around the other way. You can't disturb me or Winnie; we

375

are awake. And be certain that Hubert doesn't come fussing around until Mr. Salomon sends for him."

"He won't, Miss; he never does."

"He used to, sometimes, when he was tending me—be a touch noisy when he thought I should be up. So keep him off this floor. Keep everyone off this floor until I call you—that includes all cleaning, everything. Except, of course, that I want you to bring up breakfast—with whatever help you need—promptly."

"Yes, Miss. Perhaps coffee and juice at once?"

"No, we don't want to be disturbed twice; my ears might fall off. You'll find evidence of the debacle in my lounge—a case lot of empty magnums. Remove them—quietly—for Heaven's sake don't bang one against another; I can hear an ant stomp this morning. Pencil ready? We need a simple, nourishing breakfast. At least four cups of coffee each, double orders of orange juice, half grapefruits, either pinks or the big Arizonas, scrambled eggs, poached eggs, some link sausages and breakfast steaks. Better include cold cuts and sliced cheeses. Oh, toast and muffins and jam and such. Flatbread. And a big pitcher of ice-cold milk for cereal, I think this is a cereal morning. Some decent, quiet, well-brought-up cereal that doesn't snap, crackle, or pop. That's all. Unless you know a remedy for a hangover."

"Well, Miss, when I was tending Mr. Armbrust before I went to work for you, I used to mix something that he thought well of."

"Yes?"

"Silver fizz, Miss, using vodka rather than gin."

"Cunningham, you're a genius. One each, plus largish dividends, in thermos glasses. How soon will breakfast be ready?"

"Can't be sooner than twenty minutes, Miss, even though Della has started the sausages. But I could still fetch up coffee and juice."

"One trip only. Then steal quietly away on stocking feet. This is a hospital zone, Cunningham. Winnie and I need at least twenty minutes to put our eyeballs back in, they're bleeding. I'll expect you not sooner than twenty minutes,

376

not later than twenty-five. Off."

She put down the bedside intercom, said, "Doctor, did I handle that?"

"Eunice, sometimes I think you're not truthful."

"And sometime I'm going to be a hermit and not have to dodge servants. Where are your clothes, Roberto? In the lounge?"

"Yes. I had better get into them."

"Better think again. We've got twenty minutes of privacy, we'll use it."

"Oh, Eunice!"

"Courage, comrade; I'm not a black widow spider. We'll use it to gather up *all* clothes in the lounge, toss feminine items in here, fast—then take your clothes and Jake's down to his suite—where I'll grab a robe and pajamas and slippers for Jake, and a second set of his for you. If you're a sissy, you'll stay there and put them on. If you're not, you'll stay in skin and come back here with me, and dress when you feel like it. Then I'll switch on a light that tells Winnie I'm awake—better than phoning the love bugs, they might be love-bugging, and even a bug hates to be disturbed at such times. Come on, you bony, hairy, wonderful man. Sixteen minutes—we can do it in twelve, I'll bet."

"Pussy Cat, sometimes you make me nervous."

"Oh, piffle, I own this house. Although I may sell it and buy a nudist resort in California—then run it just for me and my friends. Roberto, I *like* skin—when it's the wonderful skin I have now. It's meant to be seen and *touched*—not hidden away in clothes. Did you like our waitress last night?"

"A healthy young woman, apparently."

"Oh, piffle twice. I'll bet you were thinking about her when you took me to bed last night. I know men, darling—I *was* one, much longer than you've been alive. Fifteen minutes. Let's move."

23

Dabrowski handed her out and Fred locked the car. They escorted her to and into the lift. Joan Eunice looked around. "This must be where it happened."

Her driver said, "Eunice, I wish you would change your mind."

"Anton, Tom and Hugo should have driven me today, but I was afraid the poor dears would get upset when they saw the inside of this lift. I thought you and Fred could stand it. Fred, are you nervous?"

"You know damn well I am, Eunice."

"Over what? *She* entered this lift *alone*. I've got the two with me."

"Well . . . you're a stubborn one. I don't know what Ski is going to do but *I* am going to wait outside the door until you come out." (Eunice, what do you do with stubborn men?) (It's hard, twin, especially when they love you. You had best use female jujitsu—let them have their own way until it turns out it's your way.) (I'll try.)

"Fred, Eunice lived here for years. Utterly safe . . . except for one mistake. I have the radio link and I promise you both, solemnly, that I won't stir outside Joe's door until I *know* you're waiting for me."

"We'll be waiting, all right—all the time. Right, Ski?"

"Right! Eunice, you don't even know Joe Branca still lives here."

"But I do. It's just that he didn't pay his phone bill, so

they cut him off. Joe's still there, or was at sixteen o'clock yesterday. Look, how does this sound? First, you know that Joe wouldn't hurt me, don't you? Anton?"

"Oh, sure. Joe might not want to see you—but Joe Branca would put a fly outdoors before he would swat it."

"Then I'm safe as long as I'm inside with Joe. But you're right, he may not want to see me. He may not let me in. Or I may be inside only minutes. So wait an hour, then go home. I'll call you when I want you to take me home."

"Two hours?" suggested Fred.

"All right, two hours. But if I don't come home tonight, you are *not* to come back and buzz Joe's door. You can come back tomorrow at noon and wait an hour, or even two, if that will make you feel better. And again the next day. But I'll stay in Joe Branca's studio a full week if it takes that to make his mind easy. Or a month, damn it! Or anything. Boys, I've *got* to do this; don't make it harder."

Anton said glumly, "All right. We'll do it your way."

"Am I 'Eunice' now? Or 'Joan Eunice'?"

He grudged a smile. "You're Eunice. *She* would do it."

"That's why *I* must. Look, darlings"—she put an arm around each of them—"last night was wonderful . . . and I'll find a way to manage it again. Perhaps next time Mr. Salomon is away—you know he fusses over me like a mother hen. But you two do also—and you must *not* . . . except when you're guarding me. Right now I *must* try to find a way to soothe Joe's soul. But I'll be your playmate another day. Be darlings and kiss me; the lift is about to stop."

They did so; she hooked up her veil. They left the lift and headed toward the Branca studio—Joan found she knew the way, as long as she didn't stop to think.

She stopped at the door. "She always kissed you good-bye? Here, with Joe watching?"

"Yes."

"If he lets me in, kiss *me* good-bye the same way. Just don't stretch it out; he might close the door. Oh, I'm shaky!" (Steady down, Boss. Om Mani Padme Hum. Don't use the button; try our voice on the lock. 'Open up!' Like that.)

"Open up!" Joan said. She unhooked her veil, faced the door.

The lock started clicking but the door remained closed. A transparency flashed on the wall: PLEASE WAIT. Joan stood in front of the door peep, wondered if Joe was scanning her. (Eunice, will he let us in?) (I don't know, Boss. You shouldn't have come. But you wouldn't listen to Jake . . . nor to *me*.) (But I *am* here. Don't scold me—*help* me.) (I'll try, Boss. But I don't know.)

Through the door, not as soundproof as her own doors, Joan heard a high voice: "Joe! *Joe!*" (Who's *that!*) (Could be anybody, Joe has lots of friends.)

The door opened, she saw Joe Branca standing in it. He was dressed in much-worn shorts which had been used repeatedly for wiping paint brushes. His face showed nothing. A girl, a wrapper pulled sketchily around her, looked out from behind him. "See? It's *her!*"

"Gigi—get back. Hello, Ski. Hi, Fred."

"Hi, Joe."

Joan tried to keep her voice steady. "Joe, may I come in?"

He finally looked at her. "You want to, sure. Come in, Ski. Fred." Joe stood aside.

Dabrowski answered for them. "Uh, not this time, Joe. Thanks."

"Roz. Other time, any. Welcome. Too, Fred."

"Thanks, Joe. See you." The guards turned to leave as Joan started to enter—she checked herself, remembering that she must do something. "Boys!"

Fred kissed her quickly, nervously. Dabrowski did not kiss her; instead he held his mouth to hers and said almost soundlessly, "Eunice, you be good to him. Or, damn, I'll spank you."

"Yes, Anton. Let me go." Quickly she turned, went inside past Joe, waited. Slowly he refastened the hand bolts, taking an unnecessarily long time.

He turned and glanced at her, glanced away. "Sit?"

"Thank you, Joe." She looked around at the studio clutter, saw two straight chairs at a small table. They seemed to be the only chairs; she went to one of them,

381

waited for him to remove her cloak—realized that he was not going to do so, then took it off and dropped it, sat down.

He frowned at her, seemed uncertain, then said, "Coffee? Gigi! Java f' Miss Smith."

The girl had been watching from the far end of the room. She tightened her wrapper and went silently to a kitchen unit beyond the table, poured a cup of coffee, and prepared to flash it. Joe Branca went back to an easel near the middle of the room, started making tiny strokes on it; Joan saw that it was an almost finished painting of the young woman addressed as "Gigi." (That's a cheat pic, Boss.) (A what?) (Project a photo onto sensitized canvas, then paint over it. Joe does them if someone wants cheesecake, or a cheap portrait, or a pet's picture—but claims they aren't art.)

(Can't see why, Eunice; it's still an original oil painting.) (I can't, either—but it matters to an artist. Boss, this place is filthy, I'm ashamed of it. That bitch Gigi.) (She lives here, you think?) (I don't know, Boss. Could be Joe's sloppy housekeeping. He likes things clean—but won't stop to do it. Only two things interest Joe. Painting . . . and tail.) (Well, he has both, looks like. I see he's kept your Gadabout.) (I'll bet it won't run by now. Joe can't drive.)

Gigi fetched coffee, placed it on the table. "Sugar? Isn't any cream." She leaned closer, added in a fierce whisper, "You don't belong here!"

Joan answered quietly, "Black is fine. Thank you, Gigi."

"Gigi!"

"Yes, Joe?"

"Throne."

The girl turned and faced him. "In front of *her?*"

"Now. Need you."

Slowly Gigi obeyed, untying her wrapper as she moved, dropped it as she stepped up onto the throne, fell into pose. Joan did not look, understanding her reluctance—not modesty but unwillingness to be naked to an enemy. (But I'm *not* her enemy, Eunice.) (Told you this would be rhino, Boss.)

Joan tried the coffee, found it too hot—and too bitter, after the delicately fragrant—and expensive—high-altitude

382

brew Della prepared. But she resolved to drink it, once it had cooled.

She wondered if Joe recognized what she was wearing. La Boutique had reconstructed, at great expense, a costume Eunice Branca had once worn, one in last year's "Half & Half" style, scarlet and jet, with a tiny ruffle skirt joining a left-leg tight to a right-side half sweater. Joan had hired the most expensive body-paint artist in the city and had rigidly controlled him in reconstructing the design Eunice Branca had worn with it, as nearly as memory and her inner voice could manage.

(Eunice, was Joe too upset to notice how we dressed?) (Boss, Joe sees *everything*.) (Then he's gone back to painting *not* to notice us.) (Maybe. But Joe wouldn't stop painting for an H-bomb. That he let us in at all is a blue moon—in the middle of a painting.)

(How long will he paint? All night?) (Not likely. He does that only for a real inspiration. This one's easy.) It did not look easy to Joan. She could see that the artist was working from an exact cartoon, one that looked like a dim photograph of Gigi as she was posed—but he was working also from his model, yet he was not following either model or photograph. He was enhancing, exaggerating, simplifying, making flesh tones warmer, turning flat canvas almost into stereo, realistic as life, warmer than life, sensuous and appealing.

Perhaps it was not "art"—but it was more than a photograph. It reminded Joan of a long-dead artist Johann had liked. What was his name?—used to paint Tahitian girls on black velvet. Leeteg? (Eunice, what do we do now? Walk out? Joe doesn't seem to care either way.) (Boss, Joe cares *dreadfully*. See that tic on his neck?) (Then what do I *do?*)

(Boss, all I can tell you is what I would do.) (Wasn't that what I said?) (Not quite. Any time I came home and found Joe working from another model, I kept quiet and let him work. First I would get out of my working clothes, then shower and get off every speck of paint and makeup. Then tidy things—just tidy, heavy cleaning had to wait for weekends. Then I would get things ready to feed them, because Joe and his model were going to be hungry once they stopped. They always did stop; Joe won't overwork a model. Oh, he sometimes painted me all night but he knew I would ask to stop if I got shaky.)

(Are you telling me to strip down? Won't that upset him still more?) (Boss, I'm not telling you to do *anything*. This visit wasn't *my* idea. But he's seen our body thousands of times—and you ought to know by now that nakedness isn't upsetting, it's relaxing. I felt that it was rude to stay dressed when a model was nude—unless I was certain she was easy with me. But I'm *not* telling you to do this. You can go look out the peep and see if Anton and Fred are still there—they will be—and unbolt the door and leave. Admit you can't put Humpty-Dumpty together again.)

(I suppose I should.) Joan sighed, stood up—kicked her sandals off, peeled the half-sweater down, shoved the ruffle skirt down, and got out of the tight. Joe could not see her, but Gigi could—Joan saw surprise in her eyes but she did not break her pose.

Joan looked at her and put a finger to her lips, then picked up dress and cloak and sandals, headed for the bath unit while avoiding (she thought) Joe's angle of vision—hung her clothes on a rack outside the bath and went in.

It took only minutes of soap and shower to rid her body of jet and scarlet. (Face makeup off, too?) (Forget it, you don't wear as much as I used to. Towels in the cabinet under the sink. Or should be.)

Joan found one clean bath towel, three face towels, decided that it wasn't fair to grab the last bath towel, and managed to get dry with a face towel, looked at herself in the mirror, decided that she was passable—and felt refreshed and relaxed by the shower. (Where do I start?) (Here of course. Then make the bed but see it if needs changing. Sheets in the box with bed lamp on it.)

The tiny bath took little time as scouring powder and plastic sponge were where they almost had to be. The toilet bowl she was forced to give up on—she got it clean but stains left by flushing water did not respond to scrubbing.

Joan wondered why a civilization that could build mighty spaceships could not cope with plumbing?

Or was it a civilization?

She washed her hands and went out. The bed seemed to have been slept in no more than a couple of nights; she decided it would be presumptuous to change sheets. As she was straightening the bed she noticed lipstick on one pillow—turned it over, (Gigi?) (Might be, Boss, it's her shade. Proves nothing.)

(Now what?) (Work around the edges—don't *ever* touch Joe's stuff. You can pick up a tube of paint and dust under it . . . but *only* if you put it down exactly where you found it.)

The edges kept her busy for a time. It seemed likely that Joe must have noticed her—but he gave no sign. The painting seemed finished but he was still working on it.

The sink was loaded; she found soap powder and got busy.

Once she had dishes washed, dried, and put away, and the sink was sparkling as the dishes, she looked over the larder. (Eunice, did you keep house with so few staples?) (Boss, I didn't keep many perishables on hand—but this is skimpier than *I* ever kept it. Joe doesn't *think* about such things. I never let him shop—because he would come back with some new hungry friend, having forgotten the bread and bacon and milk I had sent him for. Try the freezer compartment.)

Joan found some Reddypax in freeze—dinners, a carton of vanilla ice cream almost full, spaghetti, pizza of several sorts. There were more of the last, so she decided she could not go wrong offering them pizza. What else? No fresh vegetables—- Fruit? Yes, a small can of fruit salad, hardly enough but she could put it over scoops of ice cream, plus wafers if she could find any. Yes, lemon snaps. Not much of a meal but she didn't have much to work with. She started getting things ready.

Set the table for three? Well, she was either going to be accepted—or sent home; she set it for three. (Eunice, there are only two chairs.) (The kitchen stool adjusts in height, Boss.) (I'm stupid.) (Wouldn't have bet you could find your
385

way around a kitchen at all.) (Maybe I wouldn't have learned if Mama had had a daughter. I'll bet I've cooked more meals than you have, sweetheart—not that this is cooking.)

Just as Joan had everything laid out she heard Joe say, "Rest, Gigi."

She turned around. "Joe, will you two have supper now? It's ready to flash."

Joe Branca turned at her voice, looked at her—started to speak, and with pitiful suddenness went to pieces.

His features broke, he started to sob, his body slowly collapsed. Joan hurried toward him—and stopped abruptly. (*Boss!* Don't touch him!) (Oh, God, Eunice!) (Don't make it worse. Gigi has him. Down on the floor, fast! Om Mani Padme Hum.)

Joan dropped into Lotus seat. "Om Mani Padme Hum." Gigi had given him a shoulder, eased him down. He sat on the floor with his head against his knees, sobbing, while Gigi knelt by him, her face showing the ages-old concern of a mother for a hurt child. "Om Mani Padme Hum." (Om Mani Padme Hum.) (Can't I help her, Eunice?) "Om Mani Padme Hum." (No, Boss. Ask Gigi to help *you*.) (How?) "Om Mani Padme Hum." (Ask for a Circle. Om Mani Padme Hum.)

"Gigi! Help me form a Circle. *Please!*"

The girl looked up, looked very startled as if seeing Joan for the first time.

"Om Mani Padme Hum. Help me, Gigi—help us both."

Gigi slid into Lotus seat by her, knee to knee, reached for Joan's left hand, took Joe's right hand. "Joe! Joe, you must listen! Close the Circle with us. *Now!*" She started chanting with Joan.

Joe Branca stopped sobbing, looked up, seemed not to believe what he saw. Then slowly he straightened his legs, moved until he filled the third side of the triangle and tried to assume the Padmasana. His paint-smeared shorts were too confining; they got in the way. He looked down, seemed puzzled, then started unfastening them. Gigi let go his hand and Joan's, helped him get them off. Then he settled easily into Lotus, reached for their hands. "Om Mani Padme Hum!"

As the Circle closed Joan felt a shock through her body, somewhat like electricity. She had felt it before, with three, with four, but never so strongly. Then it eased off to a sweet feeling of warmth. "Om Mani Padme Hum."

The prayer rolled around the Circle, rolled back, and was chanted in unison. They were still softly whispering when Joan stopped feeling or hearing anything—other than utter peace.

"Wake. Wake up. Come back."

Joan fluttered her eyelids, felt her eyeballs roll down. "Yes, Winnie? I'm awake."

"You said you had supper ready to flash. Want to do it? Or shall I?"

"Oh." She became aware that the Circle was still closed. "I'll do it. If I may."

Joe looked inquiringly into her face, his own face serene. "You okay? Good vibes?"

"She's okay," Gigi answered. "Go take a pee and we'll get supper on. Wash your hands; I left turpentine in the medicine cabinet."

"Okay." He got up, gave a hand to each of the girls, pulled them to their feet together, turned to do as he was told.

Joan followed Gigi to the kitchen unit, noticed the clock of the flash oven. "Gigi, is that clock right?"

"Near enough. Do you have to leave? I hope not."

"Oh, no, I can stay. But how long did we hold the Circle?"

"An hour, hour and half, maybe longer. Long enough. Does it matter?"

"No." Joan put her arms around the other girl. "Thank you, Gigi."

Gigi put her arms over Joan's, hugged her. "Thank *you*. This is the first time I've seen Joe truly at one with the All, accepting his karma, at peace with it, since, uh, since—"

"Since Eunice was killed?"

387

"Yes. He's kept coming back to the crazy notion that, if he hadn't gone to Philly to see his Maw, it wouldn't have happened. He knows that's not so—but now he knows it in his belly, I can tell." (Boss? Say hello to Gigi for me.) (Break cover?) (Oh, hell, we'd better not. I don't *think* she'd tell Joe—but we can't risk it. And things are okay the way they are.)

"Gigi, I think Eunice would want to thank you. If she could. Things look okay the way they are, now."

"Looks like. Say, what do I call you? I can't say, 'Hey, you!' But 'Johann Sebastian Bach Smith' seems like a hell of a name for a girl."

"My name is Joan, now. Uh, my full name is 'Joan Eunice Smith.' But my middle name is, well, sort of a memorial. Rozzer?"

"Roz. That's nice, I think that's perfect—Joan Eunice." (I think *you're* perfect, Boss. You *did it!* You know why I didn't want to come here? I was scared for Joe . . . but twice as scared for *me*.) (I knew, sweetheart. We both were scared. And so was Joe.)

"Gigi, better not use my middle name. Joe might be upset. Bad vibes."

Gigi shook her head. "I don't think so. If I'm wrong, if he needs to soak in the Circle some longer, tonight we've got the right Circle. Might not have, if he found out later."

"All right, Gigi, I'll tell him."

"Yes, but wait until after we eat. A Circle is fine and I can stay in one all day, if needed. But I'm starved. Sandwich about five hours back and I don't eat much breakfast." Gigi pulled her closer, kissed her. "So let's eat."

"Somebody say 'eat'?"

"In a minute, Joe; we got to talking. And we need a crack at the plumbing, too. First dime is yours, hon; I'll flash the packs."

"Go ahead, Gigi."

"Oh, come along. Joe, you flash the packs."

"—like your 'Eunice Evans Branca Memorial,' Joe. Because I don't want anyone *ever* to forget Eunice. Especially me."

Joe Branca nodded soberly. "Is good. Eunice 'd like."

388

Suddenly he smiled. "You okay, Joan Eunice." He put down his cup, started stacking dishes, and added, "Getup you had on, same like one Eunice had."

"It was one I had seen her in, Joe, so I had one made like it."

"Good job. Dress, not skin paint. Sign painter, maybe?"

"Joe, I didn't have anyone of your skill to do that; I had to use whom I could find. Uh, is it possible that you might paint me—body paint, I mean—sometimes? Professional job, professional fees, no obligations."

He smiled and shook his head. "Not cosmetics man, Joan Eunice. Sure, paint body for Eunice, she liked. Gigi, too, when she wants. Paint *you*, sure. But no fee."

"Joe, I won't take up professional time of an artist without paying. But I see your point. Cosmetic painting for your wife is one thing—but it isn't your real work."

"But fun," he answered. "Maybe do jet-and-scarlet job right before you go home, huh?"

"That would be sweet of you, Joe, but don't bother; I wouldn't be showing it, I'll go straight home. But let me ask one question, please, about body paint. Do you remember that you once painted Eunice as a mermaid, and she wore it to work?"

"Sure."

"Well—Gigi, this was when I was Johann Smith and very old and very ill. I hurt *all* the time but couldn't stand heavy dosage of painkillers. Had to tough it. But here was Eunice, lovely as a flower and cute as a kitten, painted to look like a mermaid, and—Joe, this is the silly part. I don't think I noticed any pain all day long, I was so busy trying to figure something out. And never could. Was that a *real* brassière Eunice had on? Or paint?"

Joe looked smugly pleased. "Paint. Fool-the-eye." (Boss, I *told* you that.) (Yes, little imp—and sometimes you fib, too.)

"You certainly fooled *my* eye. I could see those big sea shells, I could almost feel their rough texture. Then Eunice would turn in profile—and I wouldn't be sure. I spent that whole day staring while trying to seem not to. Joe, you're a great artist. It's a shame you prefer canvas to skin."

"Not quite right. Like to paint *skin* on *canvas*. Fool-the-eye forever. Not just one day."

"I stand corrected. Like that one." Joan nodded at the easel. "Gigi, let me do the dishes, please. I want to."

"Pile in sink," Joe ordered. "Inspiration. Two-figure compo."

"Okay, Joe," Gigi answered. "Joan Eunice, do you feel up to posing late? Joe said 'Two-figure' so he means you, too. But I warn you, when Joe says 'Inspiration,' you don't get much sleep."

"No," Joe denied. "Can short it. Cheat some. Get pose right, shoot eight, nine, ten shots. Then——" He suddenly looked distressed, turned to Joan. "Maybe not here tomorrow? Or could be, not want to pose. Damn, I forget! Think you sleep here. Crazy. Damn!"

Joan said, "I don't have to be anywhere at any time, Joe, and I would be greatly honored to pose for you. But——" She turned to Gigi. "May I stay tonight? Is it all right?"

"Oh, sure!"

"I wonder. Since you showed me your wedding ring I've been wondering how much I am butting in."

Gigi giggled. "Hon, if you think that's a ring in Joe's nose—well, *I'd* better never think so. Joan, I left Sam a good month before I let Joe give me that ring and marry me. Cubical and comical, couldn't believe he meant it. I can't think of another couple we know who are *married*. It's nice—but I still get the giggles. Sure you stay if you want to. We got a cot to set up—not much but we'll put Joe on it."

(Watch it, Boss! This is dynamite—ten to one *Joe* won't be on that cot.) (Of course not. *I* will be. Think I'm a fool?) (Sadly, I do, Boss. You're lovable—but you just barely have sense enough to stay out of lifts. Not out of beds.) (Joe wants me to pose, I pose! If he wants anything else, he can have that, too! *Anything*.)

(That's what I thought.) (Eunice, Joe doesn't want *me*. Gigi is his woman now.) (Okay, twin. But when did I last hear you say that marriage isn't a form of death?)

Joe Branca appeared to regard the matter as settled; housekeeping details seemed of no interest to him. He said,

390

"You oil after shower?" and reached out and fingered Joan's left ribs. "No. Gigi."

"Chop chop, Joe." Gigi ducked into the bath, returned with a bottle of olive oil. She said to Joan, "Lanolin is as good, but I'd rather smell like a salad than a sheep. Joe, get her ribs; I'll do her leg. Then we give you a quick oiling all over, hon, and wipe you down. Get all off that your skin doesn't absorb. Mmm, some red paint back here where you can't see, but olive oil cuts it. Joan, I've had twice as good a complexion since Joe has been making me take care of my skin."

"You have a perfect skin, Gigi."

"Joe's a tyrant about it. Now for a wipe down."

"Not too much wipe," Joe warned. "Need highlights in cheat shots."

"Easy on the wipe down. Some oil on me, Joe?"

"Da."

"Okay, Maestro. Joan, we'll polish each other bone dry before we go to bed. If we're not too tired to care—no importa, disposable sheets. Joe, are you going to tell your slaves what this pic is?"

"Sure, need acting. *Gut* acting. Lez pic."

"*Hunh?* Joe, you can't put Joan in such a pic. You *can't.*"

"Wait, Mate. I don' draw comic books. You know. Pic so square can hang in church. But symbols so gut-loaded old butch pays top money. But—Joan Eunice, can change face if you say?" He looked anxious.

"Joe, paint the way you want to. If somebody recognizes me in one of your paintings, I'll be proud."

"Okay." Rapidly Joe Branca built a low platform of boards on boxes, heaped floor cushions on top, covered it all with a ragged heavy cloth. "Throne, Gigi first. Gigi butch, Joan Eunice sweetheart." He moved them like lay figures, shoving them into position like a butcher handling meat, so that Gigi was supported by cushions while she held Joan in her arms and looked into Joan's eyes. Joan's position figleafed Gigi; Joe raised Joan's left knee so that she figleafed herself. Then he placed Gigi's right hand under

Joan's left breast, not cupping it but touching—stepped back and scowled.

—stepped forward, changed the composition slightly, moving them so little that Joan could not guess what difference it made. Apparently satisfied, he shoved cushions in more tightly so that each could hold the pose without strain.

He placed a platter just below them, slanted with careful casualness. "Is Greek lyre," he said. "Title, 'Bilitis Sings.' Song just pau, action not yet. Golden moment between." He looked at them carefully, still scowling. "Joan Eunice, you knocked up?"

Joan was very startled. "Does it show? I haven't gained an ounce." (Erase and correct—nineteen ounces.) (Yes, but not enough to *show*. Aside from pizza just now, I've stuck to Roberto's diet. You know I have.)

Joe shook his head. "Figure not show. You *happy*, Joan Eunice?"

"Joe, I'm dreadfully happy about it. But I haven't told anyone yet."

"Be easy, Louisie; Gigi don' yatter." He smiled in benison and Joan saw for the first time how beautiful he could be. "What counts, you happy. Happy mama, happy baby. Knocked-up broads look different. Better. Skin glows, muscles firm, folds under eyes fill out. Whole body better tone. Eye can *see* but most can't see what they see. Lucky I got you for model right now. But solves problem been eatin' me."

"What, Joe? How?" (Eunice, is this all right?) (Sure, twin. Joe approves of babies as long as he doesn't have to bother with them. He's pleased that you are happy—and doesn't think about how it happened or what you'll do about it. But not callous. If you were broke, he would take you in and try to support your baby and still not ask where you got it. He doesn't find the world complex, dear—so it isn't . . . to him.)

"Puzzle problem. You *look* like Eunice, how else? But look *better*. Impossible. Know why now. Any broad looks best doin' her thing."

"Joe, do you think pregnant women are beautiful later?
392

Say eight, or nearly nine months gone?"

"Sure!" Joe seemed surprised that she would ask. "*More* beautiful. Healthy, happy woman ready to drop—how not? Top symbol of The All. Shut up now. Work."

"Please, Joe, one more question. Will you paint me when I'm big as a house? Between eight and nine months? Could be a cheat job. Might have to be, I might not be able to pose very long when I'm heaviest."

He smiled in delight. "You bet, Annette! Artist don' get that chance much. Most broads silly about it. But now shut up. Must look gutsy, so *think* gutsy. Don' act—*be*. Sweaty, eager. Joan Eunice, Gigi's got you set up, eager. But scared. Virgin. Gigi, you just eager. Maybe gloating, but *think*, don't *do*. Not even face. Just *think*."

He stopped to reposition lights, scowled at his models, changed his lights a little, brushed an oily rag on Gigi's right shoulder and breast. "Is right! Nipples up? Joan Eunice, can't you get 'em tight? Try thinking about men, not Gigi."

"I'll fix it," Gigi assured him. "Listen, darling." She started whispering, telling Joan in blunt detail what this ancient Grecian Lesbian was about to do to the virgin helpless in her arms.

Joan found that her breasts tightened so hard that they hurt. She wet her lips and looked back at Gigi, hardly noticed that they were being photographed.

"Break," announced Joe. "Off throne, pau tonight. Got good shots."

Joan straightened up, peered across the room at the clock. "My goodness! Blackbirds already?"

"So bed," he agreed. "Pose tomorrow."

Gigi said, "I'm still going to do those dishes, Joe. You set up the cot."

"I'll do them, Gigi."

"I'll wash, you can wipe."

By the time they finished, Joe was in the cot and apparently asleep. Gigi said, "Which side do you like, hon?"

"Either one."

"Crawl in."

24

Joan woke with her head on Gigi's shoulder. Gigi was looking at her, which helped Joan to remember where she was. She yawned and said, "Good morning, darling. Is it morning? Where's Joe?"

"Joe's getting breakfast. Had enough sleep, dear?"

"Guess so. What time is it?"

"I don't know. The question is, are you rested? If not, go back to sleep."

"I'm rested, I feel grand. Let's get up."

"All right. But I charge one kiss to get past me."

"Outrageous," Joan said happily, and paid toll.

But Joe was not at the kitchen unit; he was projecting the photographs he had taken the night before. Gigi said, "Look at that, Joan. Forgotten all about offering to get breakfast."

"It's no matter," Joan said softly.

"Don't bother to keep your voice down, Joe can't hear when he's working. Unless you shout. Well, let's scrounge, then we'll try to get him to eat. Hmmm . . . not much to offer a guest."

"I don't need a big breakfast. Juice and toast. Coffee."

"No juice." Gigi poked around futilely. "I could give you a Reddypak. Spaghetti or something. I've got a grocery-shop. Send Joe out for groceries and he comes home with a new picture book and some paint, happy as a kid. No use scolding him."

Joan Eunice caught an undertone in Gigi's voice, said softly, "Gigi, are you broke?"

Gigi did not answer. She kept her face turned away, got out half a loaf of bread, prepared to make toast. Joan persisted, still speaking quietly, "Gigi, I'm rich, I suppose you know. But Joe won't take a dime from me. You don't have to be that stubborn."

Gigi measured out powder for six cups of coffee. Then she said almost as softly, "Joan, I was a whore when Big Sam and I were together. Somebody had to pay the rent and half his pupils never paid what they promised, and the rest paid so little it hardly made up for the coffee and doughnuts they ate. Hell, some of them came to class just to eat. So somebody had to work. I never hustled men much—Sam didn't like it if I made it with another man—unless it was a swing scene that he had set up. But an old butch is often generous. When we had to have money I would go sit in one of the Lez coffee shops and bring some money home—Sam didn't mind that.

"I finally got wise that I was being used, not just supporting him. Those swing scenes—a guru needs a young chela for openers or it won't get off the ground. Joan, a woman will do anything for a man—but she hates to think it's a one-way street. Now take Joe. Doesn't sell many paintings and we usually have to split fifty-fifty to get them hung. But Joe doesn't *use* a woman no matter how thin things are." She looked around at Joan.

"When I first posed for Joe he paid me guild rates, none of this kark about a fin now and another fin when he sells the picture. He had some money from Eunice. Insurance, I suppose. But Joe is a soft slob and everybody borrowed it and everybody spent it and nobody paid it back and it was gone before I shacked in with him and started minding his money. Somebody's paying the rent and utilities on this studio. You, maybe?"

"No."

"You know about it?"

"Yes. A man who greatly admired Eunice took care of it. Joe can live here the rest of his life if it suits him. And I can drop a hint and the phone will be turned back on. The phone was an oversight when the rent and power and water and such were arranged for."

"We don't need a phone. I think half the people on this level used Joe's phone as a free public phone—some still try and get sore when I tell 'em there's no phone here, please go away; Joe is working. Uh, that man who admired Eunice—named 'Johann' maybe?"

"No, not 'Johann' and his name isn't 'Joan' now. Gigi, I can't tell you without his permission and I don't have it. Has Joe ever said anything about the rent?"

"Truthfully I don't think he's thought about it. He's a child, some ways, Joan. Art and sex—doesn't notice other things until he bangs his nose into them."

"Then maybe he wouldn't notice this. I've got my car radio link in my purse, I can call for it. If you tell Joe you've got to grocery-shop, he'll let you go, won't he?"

"Oh, sure. Won't even fuss—even though he has his heart set on painting us all day today."

"So you tell him you must and I offer to take you in my car. We can pick up a *big* load, with a car and two guards to carry for us. Maybe Joe won't suspect that I've paid for it. Or maybe you can tell him that a picture sold."

Gigi looked thoughtful. Then she sighed. "You tempt me, you cuddlesome little broad. But I had better hold off and eat pizza till we sell another painting. And we will. Best not to monkey with a setup that works, I think."

(She's right, Boss. Leave it alone.) (But, Eunice, there's not a thing for breakfast but coffee and dry toast. That's no matter but there are only four Reddypax in there and three pizzas—we ate three last night. A few other items, not much. I *can't* leave it alone.) (You've *got* to leave it alone. You trying to cut off his balls? Or split him up with Gigi? Gigi's good for him, she'll find a way. Do I, or do I not, know more about Joe than you do?) (You do, Eunice—but people have to eat.) (Yes, Boss, but it doesn't hurt to miss a couple of meals.) (Damn it, girl, what do *you* know about being hungry? *I* went through the thirties.) (Okay, Boss, louse it up. I'll keep quiet.) (Eunice—*please!* You said I did fine last night.) (So I did, and you certainly did. Now keep up the good work by leaving them alone or by finding some

397

way to let Gigi come by groceries honestly . . . but don't *give* them anything.) (All right, sweetheart, I'll try.)

"Gigi, here in the fridge—bacon grease in this can?"

"Yes, I save it. Can be useful."

"Can indeed! And I see two eggs."

"Well, yes. But two eggs split three ways is sort of feeble. But I'll fry one for you and one for Joe."

"Go soak your head, cuddle baby; I'm going to teach you Depression cooking I learned in the nineteen-thirties."

Gigi Branca suddenly looked upset. "Joan, you gave me goose bumps. I can't realize how old you are—but you're not, really—are you?"

"Depends on which rubber ruler you use, dear. I remember the Great Depression of the thirties; I was about as old as you are now. By that scale I'm ninety-five. Looked at another way, I'm only weeks old and not able to crawl without help. Always making mistakes. But by still a third way to measure it I'm the age of this body—Eunice's body—and that's how I like to be treated. Don't let me be a ghost, dear—hug me and tell me I'm not." (What you got against ghosts, Boss?) (Nothing at all, some of my best friends are ghosts—but I wouldn't want my sister to marry one.) (*Very* funny, Boss—who writes your gags? We *did* marry a ghost—in Dr. Olsen's examining room.) (Ouch! Sorry about it, Eunice?) (No, Boss darling, you're just the old goat—old ghost, pardon me!—I want for our little bastard.) (Love you, too, Busybody.)

Gigi hugged her.

"First we melt the bacon grease and make sure it's not rancid—or not too rancid. Then we soak the bread in it and fry it. We scramble the eggs and since we don't have cream to stretch them, we use what we find. I'll settle for powdered milk, or flour, or cornstarch. Even dry gelatin We don't salt the eggs, the grease may be salty enough—salt to taste, afterwards. But if you have Worcestershire sauce, or A-l, or anything like that, we add a little before we scramble. Then we spoon this goop onto six slices of fried bread, two to a customer, and garnish with paprika, or dried parsley, or chopped most anything, to make it look fancy.

This is creative cookery à la W.P.A. We set the table the best we can manage—fancy cloth and real napkins, if you have them. A flower, even an artificial one. Or a candle. Anything to swank it up. Now—do I fry the bread while you stretch the eggs? Or vice versa?"

Joe reluctantly came to the table, absentmindedly took a bite—looked surprised. "Who cooked?"

"We both did," Joan answered.

"So? Tasty."

"Joan showed me how and we'll have it again sometime, Joe," Gigi amended.

"Soon."

"All right. Joan, you can read, can't you?"

"Why, yes."

"Thought you could. There's a letter from Joe's mother, been here three days. I've been meaning to find somebody to read it, but Joe's kept me busy posing and Joe is particular who reads his mother's letters."

"Gigi, Joan's company. Not polite."

"Joe, am I company? If I am, I won't finish breakfast and I won't pose—I'll call Anton and Fred and go home!" ('That's telling him, Fat Lady!') (That's a vulgar joke, Eunice.) (I'm vulgar, Boss. Come to think about it, you're about as vulgar as they come yourself, though I wasn't sure of it till I woke up inside your head.) (I give up. But Joe can't make us 'company.') (Of course not. Quiver your chin and make him kiss you—he's never kissed you with the lights on.)

Joe said soberly, "Sorry, Joan Eunice."

Joan pouted her lip. "You ought to be. You ought to kiss me and tell me I'm family. *Not* 'company.' "

"She's right," agreed Gigi. "You've got to kiss and make up."

"Oh, hell." Joe stood up, came around to Joan Eunice's chair, took her face, tilted it up and kissed her. "Family. Not company. Now eat!"

"Yes, Joe. Thank you." (He can do better.) (So we both know.) "But, Joe, I won't read your letter unless you want me to. Gigi, you startled me when you indicated you could not read. I thought I could tell by the way a person talks. Is it your eyesight?"

"Eyes are okay. Oh, I'm a real Talking Woman. Had some coaching, done some little theater. Probably should have learned to read—though I can't say I've missed it. Computer fouled up my pre-school test records and I was in sixth grade before anybody caught it. Then it was sort o' late to change tracks and I stayed on the 'practical'. There was talk of putting me through a remedial but the principal put his foot down. Said there wasn't enough budget to handle the ones that could benefit from it." She shrugged. "Maybe the fact that he was a third had something to do with it. Anyhow I don't miss it. Joe, shall I find the letter?"

"Sure. Joan Eunice is family."

Joan found Mother Branca's handwriting difficult, so she read the letter to herself to be sure she could read it aloud—and ran into trouble. (Eunice! How do I handle this.) (Twin, never tell a man anything he doesn't need to know. I censored as necessary. Even some of *your* mail, when you were sickest.) (Know you did, baggage, as I reread some you had read aloud.) (Boss, some went straight into the shredder. And this one should have gone there—so censor it.) (You were married to him, sweetheart, but I'm not. I have no *right* to censor his mail.) (Twin, between being 'right' and being kind, I know which way *I* vote.) (Oh, shut up, I won't consider Joe's mail!)

"Takes a while to get used to strange handwriting," Joan Eunice said apologetically. "All right, here it is:

" '*Darling Baby Boy,*

" '*Mama don't feel so—*' "

"Don't read all," Joe interrupted. "Just tell."

"That's right" agreed Gigi. "Joe's mother puts in a lot of kark about noisy neighbors and their pets and people Joe never heard of. All he wants is news. If any."

(You see, twin?) (Eunice, I'm still not going to censor. Oh, I can leave out trivial gossip. Uh, maybe edit the wording.) (You damn well better, Boss, and you know it.)

"All right. Your mother says her stomach is troubling her—"

("Mama dont feel so good and cant seem to get no relief nohow. The medicare man says it's not stomach cancer but what does he know? Sign says he's an internist and everybody knows an internist is a student, not a real doctor. What do we pay taxes for when just a student can half kill me like I was a dog or a cat or something they're always cutting up behind locked doors like they say on teevee?")

"Joe, she says that her stomach has been bothering her but she's been getting tests from an internal medicine man—that's a doctor who specializes in such ailments, they are very learned—and he has assured her that it isn't cancer or anything of that sort."

("The new priest aint no help. He's a young snot that thinks he knows it all. Wont listen. Claims I get just as good treatment as anybody when he knows it aint true. You got to be a nigger to get anything around here. We white people that built this country and paid for it are just so much dirt. When I go to medicare clinic, they make your Mama wait while Mexican women go in first. How about that?")

"She says that there is a new priest in your parish, a younger one than the last, and that he has investigated and has reassured her that she is getting the proper treatment. But she says that she sometimes has to wait a long time at the clinic."

"Why not?" said Joe. "Got nothin' but kill time. Don' work."

("Annamaria is going to have a baby. That snot priest says she ought to go to a Home. You know what terrible places those Homes are and its Unamerican to bust up families. They don't do that in the Old Country and that's what I told the Visitor. Youd think the way they throw away money on people that dont deserve it they could spend a little on a decent family that just wants to be left alone and not bothered. The other Johnson twin—not the one that dropped out, the one I told you was out on parole again—got busted again and about time! There's a family the Visitor could look into—but oh No, he just told me to mind my own business.")

"Someone named Annamaria is pregnant."

Gigi said, "Which one is that, Joe?"

"Baby sister. Twelve. Maybe thirteen." Joe shrugged.

"Well, your parish priest thinks she ought to go into a home for expectant mothers but your mother feels that she would be better off at home. There is something about a neighbor family named Johnson."

"Skip."

(*"Baby Boy, Mama dont hardly never get a letter from you since Eunice died. Aint there no letterwriter in your block? You dont know how a mother worries when she dont hear from her little boy. I watch the mailbox every day, be sure nobody swipes it fore I get it. But no letter from my little Josie—just ads and once a month the Check."*)

"She says she hasn't heard from you in a long time, Joe. I'd be glad to write one for you before I go, anything you dictate—and send it by Mercury to be sure she gets it."

"Maybe. Thanks." Joe did not seem enthusiastic. "See later. Paint first. Any more? Just tell."

(Eunice, here comes the tough part.) (So skip it!) (I can't!)

(*"I seen you in the teevee and almost dropped dead when you said you gave away a thousand million dollars you had every right to. Dont your own mother mean nothing to you? I didnt raise you and love you and take care of you when you busted your collarbone to be treated like that. You go straight to that Miss Yohan Bassing Bock Smith and tell her she can just wipe that nasty sneer off her face because I want my rightful share of whats coming to me and I'm going to get it. I already been to a lawyer and he said hed take my side for fifty-fifty as soon as I paid him a thousand dollars for expenses. I told him he was a thief. But you just tell that stuckup Miss Smith to pay up or my lawyer will put her in jail!!!!*

"Sometimes I think the best thing is just pack up everybody and go visit you till she pays up. Maybe just stay. Would be hard to leave all our old friends here in Philly but you need somebody to keep house now that you havent got no wife to do for you. It wont be the first time Ive made sacrifices for my darling boy.

"Your Loving Mother.")

"Joe, apparently your mother watched my identity hearing on video and heard your testimony. She seems disappointed to learn that you gave money to establish a memorial to Eunice, when you could have kept it."

Joe made no comment.

Joan went on: "She says she may pack up all the family and pay you a visit but the way it's phrased I don't think she will. That's all except she sends you her love. Joe, I can see how your mother could be disappointed in what you did about—"

"My business. Not hers."

"May I finish, Joe? From this letter I think she must be poor and I have been poor myself and know how it feels. Joe, I think that your memorial to Eunice was a wonderful thing, the most gallant tribute of a husband to the memory of his wife I've ever heard of. I heartily approve and I think Eunice must feel honored by it." (I do, Boss. But maybe he overdid it, huh? Jake could have set up a little annuity for Joe—eating money, I mean—with part of it. But Joe never did know how to do anything part way—whole hawg, or nothing; that's Joe.) (Maybe we can fix it, dear.)

"Joe, if I paid your mother an allowance—you *know* I can afford it!—it wouldn't be *you* accepting money from Eunice's death."

"No."

"But I would *like* to! She's your mother, it would be sort of an additional memorial to Eunice. Say enough to—"

"No," he repeated flatly.

Joan Eunice sighed. "I should have kept quiet and arranged it through Jake Salomon." She memorized the return address, intending to do it anyhow. "Joe, you are a lovable man and I can see why Eunice was devoted to you—I've fallen in love with you myself and I think you both know it—without any intention of crowding you out, Gigi; I love you just as much. But, Joe, sweet and gallant as you are . . . you are a bit stiff-necked, too." (Sure he is, Boss darling, but it's no use trying to change people. So drop it. You didn't need to sneak that address; I could have told you.)

"Joan."

403

"Yes, Gigi?"

"Hate to say this, hon—but Joe's right and you're wrong."

"But—"

"Tell you later, we'll talk while we pose. Grab the bathroom if you need to while I put dishes to soak; Joe wants to start."

Joan was surprised to learn that she could visit with Gigi while they posed. But Joe assured her that he had the expressions he wanted from the photographs; he simply wanted them to hold still. He took even more pains to get them arranged than he had for the camera. Talk did not bother him as long as it was not to him. Nevertheless Joan tended to whisper while Gigi used the normal tones of a face-to-face conversation.

"Now I'll tell you why you must not send money to Joe's mother. But wait a sec—he's done it again. Joe! *Joe!* Put on your shorts and quit wiping pigment on your skin." Joe did not answer but did so. "Joan, if you've got money to throw away, flush it down the pot but don't send it to Joe's mother. She's a wino."

"Oh."

"Yeah. Joe knows it, her Welfare Visitor knows it; they don't let her have her family allowance in cash—she gets one of the pink checks, not a green one. Just the same she'll take groceries around the corner and trade 'em for muscatel. That stomach trouble—forget it. Unless you want to help her drink herself to death. No loss if you did. The kids might be better off."

Joan sighed. "I never will learn. Gigi, all my life I've given money away. Can't say I did any good with it and I know I've done lots of harm. Me and my big mouth!"

"Your big heart, dear. This is one time not to give it away. I know, I've had a lot of her letters read to me. You trimmed that one, didn't you?"

"Did it show?"

"To me it did—because I know what they sound like. I learned from the first one never again to have somebody just read them aloud to Joe; he gets upset. So I listen—I'm a quick study, used to learn my sides and cues just from two readings aloud when I was finding out I wasn't an actress—and then I trim it to what Joe needs to hear. Figured you were smart enough to do it without being told and I was right—except that you could have trimmed it still more and Joe would have been satisfied."

"Gigi, how did such a nice person as Joe—and so talented—come from such a family?"

"How does any of us happen to be what we are? It just happens. But—look, it's never polite to play the dozens, is it?"

"I shouldn't have asked."

"I meant it isn't polite for *me* to. But I'm going to. I've often wondered if Joe was any relation to his mother. He doesn't *look* like her; Joe has a picture taken when she was about the age he is now. No resemblance."

"Maybe he takes after his father."

"Well, maybe. But Paw Branca I'm not sure about; he left her years back. If Paw Branca is his Pop. If she has any idea who his father is."

"I guess that's often the case. Look at me—pregnant and not married; I can't criticize."

"You don't know who did it, dear?"

"Well . . . yes, I do. But I'm never, never, *never* going to tell. It suits me to keep it to myself and I can afford to do it that way."

"Well—none of my business and you seem happy. But about Joe—*I* think he's an orphan. Somebody's little bastard who wound up with this bitch though I can't guess how. Joe doesn't say so. Although he never talks much—unless he has to explain things to a model. But his mother has had one good influence on him. Guess."

"I can't."

"Joe won't drink. Oh, we keep beer for friends, when we can, but Joe never drinks it. He won't touch pot. He won't join a Circle if it calls for a high. You know how it is with drugs—all of them against the law but as easy to buy as chewing gum. I could show you three connections in this one complex where you can buy you-name-it. But Joe won't touch any of it." Gigi looked sheepish. "I thought he was

405

some kind of a freak. Oh, I was never hooked but I couldn't see any harm in an occasional trip with friends.

"Then I shacked with him and he was broke and I was, too, and groceries were our only luxury and—well, I haven't touched anything since he married me. And don't *want* to; I feel grand. New woman."

"You certainly look happy and healthy. Uh, this 'Big Sam,' did he have a habit?"

"Not a habit. But Sam would eat, drink, or smoke anything somebody else paid for. Oh, he didn't mainline—doesn't fit the image for a guru and needle marks show—and he was proud of his body."

"What did you do before you were his chela?"

"His meal ticket, you mean. Same thing—model and whore. What else is there to do? Babysat. Served drinks in my skin for a while but they let me go when they found a girl who could write—discrimination and I could have fought it as I never got my orders mixed up; my memory is better than people who have to write things down. But, hell, no use trying to hang on when they don't want you. Joan, you said you'd been giving money away all your life."

"I exaggerated, Gigi. Never had much until after World War Two. I just meant I wasn't stingy even as a kid, when every nickel came the hard way."

" 'Nickel'?"

"A five-cent piece. They used to be minted from a nickel alloy and were called that. Dimes and even dollars used to be silver. We actually had gold money when I was a kid. Then during the Great Depression I was flat broke for about six months—and other people helped me—and then later I helped some, sometimes the same people. But giving money away on a large scale I didn't start until I had more money than I could spend or wanted to invest, and the tax laws at that time fixed it so that you could do more giving it away than by keeping it."

"Seems a funny way to run things. But of course I've never paid taxes."

"You just think you haven't. You started the day you were born. We may eliminate death someday but I doubt if we'll ever eliminate taxes."

"Well . . . I won't argue it, Joan, you must know more about it than I do. How much money have you given away?"

"Oh, it didn't amount to more than a few thousand until after War Two and most of that was loans I knew I would never collect. Kept records for years—then one day I burned the record book and felt easier. Since then—I'd have to consult my accountant. Several millions."

"Several *millions*! Dollars?"

"Look, cuddly, don't be impressed. After a certain point money isn't money, it's just bookkeeping figures or magnetized dots in a computer."

"I wasn't exactly impressed. Confused. Joan, I don't have any feeling of any sort for that much money. A hundred dollars I understand. Even a thousand. But that much is like the National Debt; it doesn't mean *anything* to me."

"Nor does it to me, Gigi; it's like a chess game—a game played just for itself, and one I'm tired of. Look, you wouldn't let me buy groceries even though I am helping to eat them. Would you accept a million dollars from me?"

"Uh . . . no! It would scare me."

"That's an even wiser decision than the one you made before breakfast. But page Diogenes!"

"Who's he?"

"Greek philosopher who went around searching for an honest man. Never found him."

Gigi looked thoughtful. "I'm not very honest, Joan. But I think I've found an honest man. Joe."

"I think so, too. But, Gigi, may I say why I think you were smart to say No? Oh, it was a gag, sort of, but if you had said Yes, I would not have welched. But I would hate to do it to you. May I tell you why?—what's wrong with being rich?"

"I thought being rich was supposed to be fun."

"It's fun, some ways. When you're really wealthy—and I am—money is power. I'm not saying that power isn't worth having. Take me, if I hadn't had that much raw power, I wouldn't be here chatting with you; I'd be dead. And I *like* it here, with your arms around me and Joe painting a picture of us because he thinks we're beautiful—and we *are*. But power works both ways; the man—or woman—who has it can't escape it. Gigi, when you're rich, you don't have friends; you just have endless acquaintances."

"Ten minutes," said Joe.

"Rest time," said Gigi.

"Huh? But we've *been* resting."

"So get up and stretch, it'll be a long day. If Joe says we've posed fifty minutes, we have; he uses a timer. And have a cup of coffee; I'm going to have one. Coffee, Joe?"

"Yes."

"Can we look?"

"No. Lunch break, maybe."

"Must be going well, Joan, or Joe wouldn't even make a guess. Joe, Joan tells me that a rich person can't have friends."

"Hey, wait, I didn't finish. Gigi, a rich person *can* have friends. But it has to be someone who isn't interested in his money. Like you. Like Joe. Even that doesn't mean he's a friend. First you have to find him. Then you have to *know* this about him, which may be—*is!*—hard to find out. There aren't many such people; even other rich people aren't likely to qualify. Then you have to win his friendship . . . and that's harder for a rich man than it is for other people. A rich man gets suspicious and puts on a false face to strangers—and that's no way to win friends. So in general, it's true—if you're rich, you don't have friends. Just acquaintances, kept at arm's length because you've been hurt before."

Gigi suddenly turned around from the kitchen unit. "Joan. We're your friends."

"I hope so." Joan looked soberly from Gigi to her husband. "I felt your love in our Circle. But it won't be easy, Gigi. Joe looks at me and can't help remembering Eunice—and you look at me and can't help wondering what effect it has on Joe."

"We don't! Tell her, Joe."

"Gigi's right," Joe said gently. "Eunice dead. She wanted you to have what you got. Me—over my gut ache, all done in t' Circle." (Boss, do you mind if I get out for a moment

408

and trot around in my bones? A girl likes to be missed a *little*.) (Eunice, we must not hurt him. It was all we could manage to heal him.) (I know. But the next time he kisses us I'm going to be tempted to speak up and tell him I'm here.) (Om Mani Padme Hum.) (Om Mani Padme Hum—and kark on you and Diogenes both. Let's go home and phone Roberto.) (Sweetheart, we'll stay here until we've cracked the bone and eaten the marrow.) (Okay, okay. That Gigi is as cuddly as Winsome, isn't she?)

"Joe, I want us three to be friends and never break our Circle in our hearts. But I'm not going to put too much strain on it. Not fair to you, not fair to Gigi—not even fair to me. Gigi, I wasn't saying I didn't have *any* friends. I do have. You two. A doctor who took care of me and honestly doesn't give a damn about money. The nurse he is about to marry who is the nearest thing to a sister I've ever had. My four driving guards—I've tried very hard with those four, Joe, because I knew they were your friends and Eunice's. But that's an odd situation; I'm more their baby they take care of than I am either employer or friend. And one, just *one*, friend left over from the days when I was Johann Smith—rich and powerful and mostly hated."

Joe Branca said softly, "Eunice loved you."

"I know she did, Joe. God knows why. Except that Eunice had so much love in her that it spilled over onto anyone around her. If I had been a stray kitten, Eunice would have picked me up and loved me." (More than that, Boss.) (Sweetheart.) "And Joe, you know, or at least have met, my one friend who carried over. Jake Salomon."

Joe nodded. "Jake okay!"

"You got to know Jake?"

"Close. Good aura."

Gigi said, "Joe, is he the one you told me about? The fixer?"

"Same." Joe looked back at Joan Eunice. "Ask Jake. Throne now."

"Come on, Joan. He bites if you don't pose the instant rest period is over."

Joe fussed over getting them back into position, then

409

moved both of Joan's legs and one of Gigi's into positions
somewhat different from the original pose—stepped back
and scowled at the change . . . turned to his easel and
started scraping part of the canvas with a palette knife. Gigi
said quietly, "Now we won't get to look at lunch break."

"Why not?"

"God only knows. I'm not sure Joe knows why he makes
a change. But something was wrong and now he's
abandoned the cartoon and is working directly from us. So
it won't be far enough along that he'll be willing to let us
look at it that soon. So freeze, darling. Don't sneeze, don't
get an itch, don't even breathe deeply."

"Not talk?"

"Talk all we like as long as we don't move."

"I won't move. Gigi, I was *so* pleased to learn that Joe
and Jake got to know each other well. Did you know Jake,
too?"

"I've met him. Just in passing. Me leaving and Mr.
Salomon arriving, it was while I was a hired model before I
moved out on Big Sam." (Twin, she's being vague about
this—and Jake has never mentioned laying eyes on Joe
after clearing up business matters a long time ago.) (Eunice,
what are you getting at? It was probably while Jake was
straightening out your bank account, and the lease, and
things.) ('—and things,' you are so right. Look, Boss, don't
be naïve. They were crying over the same girl—me—and
Joe is ambi as an oyster when it suits him.) (Eunice, you
have a dirty mind! (*Coo!* This from 'No-Pants Smith.' I
know whereof I speak, twin; I lived with Joe for years.
Don't be so darned twentieth century.) (Eunice, of course
you know Joe better than I do and I would never criticize
Joe no matter what. I meant Jake.) (What makes you think
you know Jake better than I do? And take a look at
Joe—purty, ain't he? Jake has eyes. Boss, what are we
fussing about? Find out what Gigi knows.)

"I suppose," Joan said carefully, "that Jake had to come
here on business. Eunice died without a will and I know
Jake arranged it so that Joe could draw against her bank
account. There may have been insurance to clear up, too;
I'm not sure."

410

"Joan, I don't know. Why don't you ask Jake, as Joe suggested?" (Because Jake will lie about it, Boss. Forget it, men lie about such things, far more than women do. Who cares where a man has lunch as long as he gets home in time for dinner? Not *me*. You give my 'dirty mind' quite enough to keep it busy. But, Boss, you're a devious little slut—you can't be truthful even to yourself.) (Wench, if I could get my hands on you, I'd spank you!) (And if you could, I'd let you. Kind o' fun to be spanked, isn't it, dear? Gets the action moving like a rocket.) (Oh, stuff it!) (Where, twin? What? And how big is it?)

"I have no need to ask Jake, Gigi. I know they met through business matters, I know that Jake admires Joe's integrity. I simply hadn't realized that Jake thought of Joe as a close friend. If he does."

Gigi Branca looked thoughtful. "I couldn't say. I was working Guild hours then, as Joe was paying me. Mr. Salomon—Jake, you call him—showed up one evening as we were quitting, and Joe introduced him to me as his former wife's fixer—lawyer, he said; Joe doesn't use jive when he doesn't want to. Saw him a couple more times, I think, about the same way. But he hasn't been here since we got married." (Double talk, Boss. All it means is that she won't spill other people's secrets. Well, that's nice to know—considering.)

"No importa. Gigi, how did Joe get his art education? Or is it native genius with no instruction?"

"Both, Joan. Let me tell it bang as it would take you forever to get it out of Joe. Joe says that all an artist can teach is technique. He says creativity can't be taught and that each artist has his own sort. If he has any—Joe thinks that most people who call themselves 'artists' haven't any. He calls 'em 'sign painters' and adds that he would rather be a *good* sign painter than a fraud who calls himself an artist.

"You've seen what Joe has. That one of me he did yesterday and others around the studio. You'd see lots more if you prowled the coffee shops and bookstores and art shops at this end of town. Nudes that look better than life—you wouldn't need to look for his pinxit. Most of them kind o' square except that they grab. Oh, Joe can do sex pix,

I've seen him prove it, then scrape off the paint—because I asked him *why* he didn't do sex pix since they sell so well. He shrugged and said those weren't his symbols.

"Joe knows he's not Goya or Picasso or Rembrandt or any of the masters—and doesn't want to be; he just wants to paint *his* symbols, *his* way, and sell enough for us to eat. Oh, sometimes I get so *mad*, knowing that if he would paint just *one* frimp scene as grabby as he so easily can, it would keep us eating for months. But I've given up suggesting it because Joe just shrugs and says, 'Don' paint comic books, you know that, Gigi.' Joe is Joe and doesn't give a damn what any other artist does or whether his own work makes him famous or a lot of money or anything. He cares so little—well, many of our friends are artists or call themselves artists but Joe isn't interested in what they paint and won't talk shop. If they're good people, warm people, good vibes, Joe likes to go see them or have them here . . . but Joe wouldn't waste a floor cushion on Rembrandt if Joe didn't like the way he behaved. Joe just wants to paint—his way. And not have to sleep alone."

Joan said thoughtfully, "I don't suppose Joe has had to sleep alone very often."

"Probably not. But Joe wouldn't sleep with Helen of Troy if he didn't like her attitude. You mentioned your Brink's boys—the two who brought you here, and there are two more, aren't there? One a big soul? Hugo?"

"You know Hugo?" Joan asked in delight.

"Never met him. He sounds like an African myth. I know just two things about him. Joe wants to paint him . . . and Joe loves him.

"Spiritual love, I mean—although I'm sure Joe would sack in with Hugo if Hugo wanted to." (He'll have to stand in line! I saw Hugo first.) (Shut up, you bang-tail.) "Can never happen, I gather—and Joe never makes a pass. Never made one at me, I never made one at him; we just sacked in our first time without a word and combined as naturally as ham and eggs." (Hmm! Some girls have all the luck. *I* had to trip him.) (You're the eager type, sweetheart; Gigi isn't.) (You'll pay for that crack, Boss.)

"I'm sure Joe never crowded Hugo about posing; he

412

would rather have Hugo's friendship than have him as a model—though Joe told me he has two pix in mind. One would show Hugo on an auction block. Historical background and honkie ladies in the crowd—close shot, full figure, Hugo looking patient and weary, and just heads and shoulders of the honks . . . and the honk females just barely not slobbering.

"But Joe says he *can't* paint that one; it would stir up old trouble. The second he really aches to paint—just Hugo, big as a mountain and no sex symbols at all—except that a big stud can't help being sexy, *I* think—just Hugo, strong and wise and solemn dignity—and loving. Joe's words, pieced together by me. Joe wants to paint it and call it 'Jehovah.' "

"Gigi! Maybe I can help."

"Huh? You can't just tell Hugo to pose for Joe; Joe wouldn't like that. Wouldn't hold still for it."

"Dear, I'm not foolish. But maybe I can make Hugo see that it's all right to pose for Joe. Can't hurt to try." (Boss, let Hugo know that you have been posing naked for Joe. Then let it soak.) (Of course, Eunice, but that's just the gambit.) (Twin! You're not thinking of trying to *seduce* Hugo, are you? Damn it, I won't stand for it! You leave Father Hugo alone.) (Eunice, I'm not *that* much of a fool. Hugo can have anything I've got; he killed the creep who killed you. But I would never offer what he won't accept. If I did, I think he'd quit—and then pray for me. I vote with Joe; I'll take Hugo as he is, never try to twist his arm.) (You couldn't. His arms are bigger than our thighs.) (I meant 'psychologically,' twin, and you know it.)

"Just one thing, Gigi— Joe would have to give up that title for the pic."

"You don't know Joe, Joan. He won't change the title."

"Then he'll have to carry it just in his mind. Hugo is as firm in *his* rules as Joe is in his. He won't let a picture of himself be titled 'Jehovah.' It would be sacrilege in his eyes. But if Joe is willing to keep the title a secret, I think I can deliver the body. You talk to Joe. But you never did tell me where Joe got his training."

"Oh. Joe could always draw; I'm sure he could have learned to read, he remembers what he sees. When he was

413

about fourteen, he was being held overnight with some other boys in the precinct lockup and the desk sergeant got a look at some sketches Joe had done while he was killing time, waiting to be taken up in front of the judge and warned. One was of the desk sergeant—and Joe had seen him only a few minutes.

"That was Joe's break. The desk sergeant turned him over to the priest and got him off the blotter and both of them took him to a local artist, and showed him the kid's sketches.

"This artist was a mixture, fine art and commercial—I mean he made money. He was another sort of mixture, too. An oyster. He may not have been impressed by Joe's sketches but he made a deal with him. Modeling. Joe could hang around his studio and use his materials and sketch from his models—if Joe would pose when he needed him. They both won on the deal; you know how Joe looks now; at fourteen I'd bet he was more beautiful than any girl—and no doubt that oyster thought so.

"So Joe did and soon he was eating and sleeping there and got away from his mother entirely, best thing that ever happened to him. Joan, it was a one-bed studio like this one."

"You mean Joe was his sweetheart? Gigi, I decline to be shocked. Even though I'm ninety-five, I try to think modern."

"Joan, I never can believe that's your age; it isn't real, like that million dollars. I said 'oyster' not 'homo.' The artist was married, or shacked, with his number-one model. Possible she got Joe's cherry. Either way, she taught him plenty and mothered him and was good to him, and it was a happy Troy.

"But the artist—Mr. Tony, as Joe speaks of him—while he gave Joe the use of his studio and table and bed and wife—was nevertheless a strict master. He wouldn't let Joe paint with a palette knife or a wide broom or do distortions or abstracts or psychedelics—he made him learn to draw. Anatomy. Composition. Brush techniques. Color values. The whole endless drill of academic art, and wash brushes and sweep out the studio. Joe says that if it hadn't been for

414

Mr. Tony, he would still be sketching sausage skins. Joe found out what he could do, what he wanted to do, and learned to do it. But, so he told me, not what his master did—but in both cases founded on old-fashioned academic training. The hard way. Oh, Joe's learned short cuts. But he can paint directly on canvas—he's been doing it since our last break—and make it as close to a photograph as he cares to. Or as different."

"—never said that poor is better than rich, Gigi; it is *not*. But both 'rich' and 'poor' have shortcomings—somewhere between is probably best, if you could get off the treadmill at that point. But— Look, does Joe guard you when you go grocery-shopping?"

"Huh? Of course not. Oh, sometimes he comes along and helps carry—but not to guard. Well, he does ride down the lift with me if it's a time of day when it might be empty—I mean, he's no fool and neither am I and I don't go *looking* for a mugging. Same coming back up and if I'm later than I said I would be, he's always there waiting. But I move around by myself, always have; I'm just not foolish about where and when."

"Gigi, I'm sure you're not foolish, I doubt if you ever go into a park—"

"Not even at high noon! I've been raped once and didn't like it. I'm not looking for a gang bang where they take turns holding you down. They ought to bulldoze every park in the city."

"Bulldozing the whole city might be better. But, Gigi, you move around rather freely. I *can't*. I don't dare appear even with guards around me without being veiled, I can't risk being recognized. I have to be wary all the time. Sure, you bolt your door—but *my* house has to be strong enough to take a bomb tossed against it—that's happened several times since I built it. I have to watch for everything from kidnappers and assassins to mere nuisances who want to touch me.

"I'm talking both about the way I am now and the man 'Johann' I used to be—too much money attracts crackpots and criminals and there is *nothing* I can do about it but keep

415

guards around me day and night, and live in a house that's a fort, and try to avoid being recognized at *any* time, and never, never try to live what is called a 'normal life.' Besides that—Gigi, can you imagine what a treat it is to me to be allowed to wash dishes?"

Gigi looked startled. "Huh? Joan, you've lost me. Oh, I know how complicated it is to be rich; I've watched video. But washing dishes isn't a treat; it's a horrid bore. Too often I've left them in the sink, then had to face them before breakfast. By the time breakfast is ready, I don't want any."

"Let me give you a tip, Gigi. I did know something about Joe's mother; Eunice was my secretary for years." (I never mentioned her, Boss!) (Will you let me tell this lie my own way?) "She was—and is—a pig and lives like one. This place isn't big; if you'll keep it spotless, Joe won't care when you get wrinkles—and we all do, someday. But a dirty toilet bowl or dishes in the sink reminds him of his mother."

Gigi said, "Joan, I *try*. But I can't clean house and pose at the same time."

"Do your best, hon. If necessary, lose sleep. Joe is a man worth making extra effort to keep. But I was talking about doing dishes—it's a nuisance to you but a luxury to me. Washing dishes means 'freedom' to me. Look, here we are, three of us, no servants—and presently I'll be gone and you'll be alone with your husband and the world shut out. I *can't* shut it out. Uh . . . let me think— Four mobile guards, a security chief, twelve in-house watchmen under him, three always on duty and the others on call, which means the married ones—which is most of them—have their families under my roof—a personal maid, a valet who used to tend me and now takes care of guests—couldn't fire him; I *never* fire anyone without cause—a butler, a head chef, three—oh, I don't remember; there were about sixty adults in my house the last time I asked."

"My God, Joan!"

"Yes, 'My God!' To take care of *one* person. Yet not one could I let go without replacing him. I planned that house and kept tabs on the design, intending to keep staff down to a minimum. So it's loaded with gadgets. Things like robofootmen, and a trick bed that was designed to let me

416

get along without a nurse a few more years as I got older. Do you know what that means? I *lost*. I have to have a building superintendent and maintenance mechanics—or the gadgets don't work. All this complication—and never any real privacy—just to take care of one person who doesn't want it that way."

"Joan, why don't you get rid of it? Move—and start over."

"Move *where*, dear? Oh, I've thought about it, believe me. But it's not actually to take care of one person—it's to take care of too much money, money that is fastened to me . . . so that I can't risk kidnappers or anything else. I can't even cash it and flush it down the pot; that's not the way big money works. And even if I could and did—nobody would believe I had. I would just have taken off my armor and probably would not stay alive two days. Besides— Do you like cats?"

"Love 'em! Got a kitten promised now."

"Good. Now tell me—how do you get rid of a cat you've raised?"

"Huh? Why, you don't. Not if you're decent."

"I agree, Gigi. I've lived with many cats. You keep them. If you are forced to it, you have a cat humanely destroyed—or if you have the guts, you kill it yourself so that it won't be bungled. But you *don't* give away a grown cat; it is almost impossible. But, Gigi, you can't kill *people*."

"I don't understand, Joan."

"What would I do with *Hugo*? He's been with me many years; he's doing the only thing he knows how to do—except preach, which doesn't really pay. Gigi, loyal servants are 'Chinese obligations' just like a cat. Sure, they can get other jobs. But what would you do if Joe told you, 'Get lost. We're finished.' "

"I'd cry."

"I don't think my servants would cry—but I would."

"But I'd get along!"

Joan sighed. "And that platoon I have around me would get along, I think; they're able or I wouldn't have them—and I've got money enough to make sure that ones
417

like Hugo are taken care of; that's one of the *good* things about being rich—if money is all it takes to remedy something, you can. Gigi, there is some solution to this silly fix I'm in and I'm going to find it—I was just trying to show you that it isn't as simple as it looks on video. The solution may be something as easy as changing my name again and changing my face with plastic surgery and going somewhere else."

"Oh, no, you mustn't change your face."

"No, you're right; I must not change this face. It's Eunice's; I'm only its custodian. If I changed it, Joe would not like it—nor several other people. (Starting with *me*, Boss.) (I won't change your lovely face, sweetheart. I'll cherish it.) "I'll keep it as it is—but I have to keep it veiled. It's been on video too much, photographed and printed too many million times. But there's *some* way to tackle it."

Joan Eunice looked at the nearly finished painting almost with awe. She knew what a beautiful body she had inherited; she knew that Gigi was a beauty of another sort; she could see that these "Grecian damsels" were herself and Gigi and she could not see any detail in which the painting was not a perfect likeness of each.

Yet Joe Branca's "realism" was fantasy. These two nymphs in a glade were voluptuous, sensuous, enticing in a way that she *knew* that she and Gigi had not been—sprawled on a platform of boards and gossiping about everything from an alcoholic to dirty dishes.

"What do you think?" Gigi asked. "Say what you like; Joe doesn't give a hoot about any opinion but his own."

Joan took a deep breath, sighed. "How does he do it? Here I am with my nipples tight just from looking at it—and yet it's you and me, and we lay there talking for *hours* and never got in a sweat about it. Discussed everything *but* Topic 'A'—wasn't even a cuddle because we had to hold still. Yet this paint-and-canvas reaches out and grabs you by the gonads and *squeezes*. I'm certain it would have just as much effect on a man."

From behind them Joe said, "Fool-the-eye."

Joan answered, "Fool-the-eye, hell, Joe. My eyes are not
418

fooled, I'm enchanted. I want to buy it!"

"No."

"Huh? Oh, kark. You planned to sell it to some old butch. God knows ninety-five is old—and I feel butch enough to qualify when I look at the painting."

"Yours."

"Huh? Joe, you can't do this to me. You intended to sell it, you said so. Gigi, back me up."

Gigi chose not to answer. Joe said stubbornly, "Yours, Joan. You want it, you take it."

"Joe, you are the most stubborn man I've ever met and I don't see how Gigi puts up with you. If you *give* me that painting, I'm going to destroy it at once—"

Gigi gasped. "Oh, no!"

Joe shrugged. "Your ache. Not mine."

"—but if you'll *sell* it to me at your going rates, I'll take it with me and give it to Jake Salomon to hang at the end of his bed so he'll wake up happy each morning." (You bombed him, twin! Now swing back and strafe the survivors.) "That's the choice, Joe. *Give* it to me and I'll chop it into shreds. But *sell* it to me—and Jake Salomon gets it. Oh, you could welch, then hang it for sale—and put me to the trouble of hiring detectives to follow it to where you hang it so that I can buy it through an agent. What I do with it then, I won't tell. Or you could even keep it for your own jollies; it's quite a job."

Gigi said, "Quit being stubborn, Joe; you know you'd like Jake to have it."

"Gigi, what does Joe charge for a painting like that?"

"Oh, I set the prices. Mostly I sell them by the yard. By size."

"So? How much is this size?"

"Well, I try to get two hundred and fifty for that size."

"Ridiculous!"

"Really, Joan, considering that it took both my time and Joe's all yesterday evening and today—not to mention your time, but you're buying it, so I didn't add on for the second figure in it—considering all that and the commission we pay, it's not very much—"

"Darling, I meant 'ridiculously' *low*. I haven't bought

419

much art the last twenty years but I do know that is not less than a thousand-dollar picture—then up like a kite to whatever the traffic will bear. I can tell you this: When Jake dies and that painting is auctioned off, it won't go for as little as a thousand . . . and it might be much higher because I'm certain to be at that auction and in no mood to let it get out of the family. But I'm not raising the price now; I never do that. You named a price of two-fifty; I accept. It's a sale."

"Joan, you never did let *me* finish."

"Oh. Sorry, hon."

"I try to get two hundred and fifty for that size when I hang it in a shop. But half of that goes to the owner of the shop; that's the only way I can get space. So the price to you is a hundred and twenty-five."

"No."

"Why not?"

"Just 'No' the way Joe said it to me. As good business practice you should *never* undercut your retailer. I think he's robbing you; the commission should be twenty-five percent, no more. But don't undercut the price you want *him* to ask—that's no way to stay in business. I don't know much about art . . . but I know one hell of a lot about business. Cash, or check?"

"Cash is fine. If you have that much with you. Or pay when you feel like it."

"I want to pay now and get a receipt so that it will be legally mine—before your stubborn husband can thwart me again. Shall I write the receipt for you, Gigi girl?"

"Oh, I've got Woolworth's printed forms for that, and I can write numbers and sign my chop. No huhu."

"Good. But I want something else."

"What, Joan?"

"I want to be kissed. I've been a good girl and posed all day and haven't even been kissed for it. So I want Joe to kiss me for being so stinky difficult—and I want to kiss you for helping me with him. Joe, will you kiss me?"

"Yes."

"That's better. Joe, will you escort two nice girls—me and Gigi, I mean, and no smart cracks—down to the

420

supermarket? If Gigi will buy us a steak to celebrate, I want to prove I can broil it. Will you buy us a steak, Gigi?"

"Sure! Beef, or horse?"

"Uh ... hon, I'm forced to admit that I haven't shopped for groceries in years. What do you think?"

"Well ... it had better be horse."

"Whatever you say. As long as they don't sell us the harness."

25

In the United Nations the Burmese delegation charged that the so-called Lunar Colonies were a cover-up for a conspiracy by China and the United States to build military bases on the Moon. The Secretary of Conservation and Pollution Control denied a report that deer in Yosemite National Park were "dying in hordes from polluted water and emphysema." He stated that a healthy ecological rebalancing was taking place—no need for alarm—and the new herd would be stronger than ever.

The Reverend Dr. Montgomery Chang, D.D., Most Humble Supreme Leader of The Way, Inc., testified before the Subcommittee on Unwritten Law of the Senate Judiciary Committee in support of the pending bill to require Federal licensing of teachers of Zen Buddhism and related disciplines as "therapists de facto et de jure:" "These bootleg gurus are giving rational mysticism a bad name. A man should no more be allowed to teach meditation, asanas, or transcendental philosophy without strict control by a licensing board than he should be allowed to ski, or to surf, or to frame a picture without passing an examination. The idea that this bill would abridge the sacred guarantees of the First Amendment is the sheerest nonsense; it protects and frees them." Under questioning he stated that he would be humbly willing to serve as chairman of such a board if such sacrifice were asked of him. Survivors of Hurricane Hilda were still being rescued and the known death toll now stood at 1908.

The Department of Internal Defense placed a temporary exception on interstate transmittal of intelligence concerning public disorders involving more than three persons, then placed a second exception with strict penalties on the publicizing of the first censorship order. The Secretary reported to the President that news services and video nets were cooperating voluntarily in the interests of the general welfare. In re the matter of identity of Conglom Tycoon Johann S. B. Smith the Supreme Court, in a declaratory relief opinion made notable only by Mr. Justice Handy waking up in the middle of its reading, slapping the desk and roaring, "Divorce granted!" then going back to sleep, ruled seven to two to sustain a lower court in expanding and clarifying the principle originally set forth in *Estate of Henry M. Parsons v. Rhode Island*. Four of the majority and one dissenting justice ruled also that a legal sex change was involved in the matter; two justices thought otherwise; one justice (Mr. Handy) used twenty pages to prove that such a composite of sexes was contrary to public interest and to the laws of God and that both Johann Smith and Eunice Branca were legally dead and that the resultant monster had no legal existence of any sort; the ninth justice, in a one-sentence separate assent, opined that sex was irrelevant in the entire matter; one of the majority, in another separate assenting opinion, stated that the donor body should have been sterilized surgically in the public interest and that the Congress would do well to make such sterilization mandatory in any future similar situation. No mention was made by any justice of thirteen *amici-curiae* briefs and one petition filed with the Court. In an opinion issued the same day (*Illinois v. Sam J. Roberts*) conviction was set aside on the grounds that the householder (deceased) had not advised Roberts of his rights before attempting to place him under citizen's arrest.

On the basis of evidence submitted by the Chinese delegation the U.N.A.E.C. eased the tolerance levels for strontium-90 for whole milk. The Reverend Thomas Barker of Long Beach, California, in an Equal-Time-for-God videosermonette declared that the World had ended at midnight December 31st 1999 PCT, and that all since that time was "illusion of the Devil, without form, substance, or reality."

Miss Smith greeted O'Neil and asked him to have Dabrowski and Fred fetch upstairs with her two big flat packages, one so large that it had to be tilted to get it through the door of the lift. When packages, mobile guards, and she herself were fitted inside, she locked the door and pressed the "Hold" touchplate without signaling a floor, then dropped her cape. "Let me kiss you thank-you-good-bye, boys, but for Heaven's sake don't get paint on you or muss it. Better just hold my face in your hands—but no need to hurry."

Shortly thereafter she looked at herself in the lift's mirror, decided that makeup and hairdo had suffered only minor wear and tear, let Dabrowski lay her cape around her, then punched for her floor and fastened all the cape's frogs so that she was again fully covered. When the lift stopped she hooked up her veil.

"These go in your boudoir, Miss? Or your lounge?"

"First let's see if Mr. Salomon is receiving." They followed her down the long hall to the Green Suite. Joan noted that the please-don't-disturb ruby light was not burning over the door of Jake's lounge, so she touched the door signal.

The speaker above it bellowed, "Come in!" The door

opened; she went in. "Put them inside and that will be all."

"Very good, Miss."

As they left and the door closed Jake came out of his bedroom, looking tousled. He stopped abruptly. "Well! Where the hell have you been?"

"Out."

"Hrrrmph! Five days. Five *whole* days!"

"So? Chickens fed? Hogs slopped? Cows milked?"

"That's not the point. I—"

"That *is* the point, Jake. Nothing has been neglected through my being away. You won't marry me, so I am not answerable to you when I come and go. Though as a courtesy I *did* leave a note with Cunningham telling you where I had gone. Did you receive it?

"Yes, but—"

"Then you knew I was safe—and in emergency could have sent me a message. Or joined me; you would have been welcome. You *know* Joe would have made you welcome—and Gigi is friendly as a puppy."

" 'Gigi'?"

"You know her. You've met her, I mean. Mrs. Joe Branca."

"*What?*"

"Why the surprise, Jake? People do remarry—especially if an earlier marriage was happy. Joe's was, and now he has, and I'm happy for him—and certain that Eunice is happy for him, too." (Sure I am, Boss. But let's not be too 'noble.' Being 'noble' is a male prerogative. So *they* think.)

"I can't believe it."

"What's odd about a widower remarrying?"

"I can't imagine anyone who had been married to Eunice ever marrying some other woman." (My fan! Twin, we're going to be especially nice to Jake tonight.) (If he doesn't start being nice to *me*, he's going to sleep alone tonight! But *I* shan't. I wonder if Anton and Fred have left the house?) (Calm down, Boss. And get Jake calmed down.) (Not yet, I won't! He's wrong and I'm right.) (Twin honey, how long is it going to take you to learn that being 'right' has nothing to do with getting along with a man? Men aren't logical, their minds don't work that way. But it's 'the only game in town,'

426

so when a man is wrong and you are right, it's time to apologize. Tell him you're sorry—and *mean* it. Om Mani Padme Hum.)

(Om Mani Padme Hum—sometimes I find being a woman just too frimping difficult. If it weren't so darned much fun. Okay, sweetheart, watch me take him.) "Jake dearest, I'm sorry it upsets you that Joe has remarried—but why not wait before deciding that he has made a mistake? Joe *needs* a wife—even if she's not Eunice. And I'm terribly sorry that I worried you by not being here when you got home . . . and sorry on my own account; I expected to welcome you—with open arms and a happy smile. But I didn't expect you to be away less than a week and I had an impression that you expected it to take longer—possibly much longer."

"Well, yes, I did think I might have to sit it out quite a while. But I got in to see the Chief Justice the second day and he assured me that he would put it at the top of the calendar . . . and that he had seen—unofficially—an advance transcript of the record. And that was that."

"Hm! Campaign contributions are sometimes worthwhile."

"Joan Eunice, don't *ever* talk that way. Especially in reference to the Chief Justice of the United States. Yes, this is your house. Nevertheless it might be bugged."

"I'm sorry, Jake. It was a thoughtless remark. My appreciation really goes where it belongs. To *you*."

"To Mac more than to me, my dear; that boy has been on the ball. How he got an advance copy to, uh, the right man so quickly is something I don't want to inquire into."

"I appreciate Mac's efforts, I appreciate Alec's efforts—but mostly I appreciate my darling, always dependable, utterly wonderful Jake." (Is that too thick, Eunice?) (Boss, I keep telling you: it's *impossible* for a woman to lay it on too thick with a man. If you tell a man he's eight feet tall and say it often enough, with your eyes wide and a throb in your voice, he'll start stooping to go through seven-foot doors.)

Jake looked pleased, so Joan went on: "I suppose it will all be settled soon, then?"

"Little one, don't you ever listen to the news?"

"Not if I can avoid it."

"Well, you should. It *is* over. You've won, finally and completely."

"Really? I never doubted that we would win, Jake, the wonderful way you've handled everything. My surprise is solely that it has happened so fast. Yes, I suppose I should follow the news. But I haven't been able to, these last few days. Had this difficult job to do—Joe, I mean—and while you were away seemed the best time . . . so I gritted my teeth and tackled it."

"Joan Eunice, I told you never to go near Joe. I *told* you. If this new marriage of his ever stood a chance—yes, intellectually I know that a man should remarry—if it ever *did* stand a chance, you must have put a horrible strain on it. Too much strain, probably. Uh . . . how did he take it? Badly?"

"Jake, I stayed five days. If it had gone badly, would I have been there even *one* day? I accomplished the mission; everything is all right."

Jake looked surprised, then thoughtful. "Hmmm! That's a one-room studio . . . and if I follow your meaning, you stayed right there the whole five days. My dear, just *how* did you 'accomplish your mission'? Or have I no right to ask?"

She looked up at him and spoke seriously. "Jake, I owe you so much that you will always have the right to ask me anything. Including my comings and goings and I should not have given you a snippy answer." (Didn't quite tell him he had a right to a *truthful* answer, did you, Boss honey? Devious little bitch.) (Eunice, I don't lie to Jake—) (Oh, what a *whopper*!) (—more than is necessary to his happiness.)

"Jake, I accomplished my mission—I set Joe's mind at rest about Eunice—through a 'prayer meeting.' With Gigi's utterly necessary help, which is only part of why I feel sure that she's good for him. But if you mean I offered him a zombie—his dead wife's reanimated body—I knew that was not the way to do it. Joe hasn't touched me. Oh, he does touch me now, easily and without strain, the way he might touch his sister." (Any incest in Joe's family, twin?

428

I've never been sure.) (Oh, shut up!) "He even kisses me the same way. But, Jake—"

"Eh? What, dear?"

"If Joe *wanted* this body I'm wearing, of *course* he could have it; I owe him anything I can give him. You see that, don't you? You agree? Or am I wrong?"

"Uh . . . yes, I agree. But I think it's well that Joe does not want to. It could be disaster for him . . . and a terrible strain for you."

"I know it would be a strain for me. But I would do my best to smile and never let him guess. As it is, I am honored—and relieved—and deeply grateful that Joe has given me his loving friendship instead." (Okay, Eunice?) (Okay. Now get him off that subject.)

"I'm glad, Eunice."

"Jake, do we have to stand here, me still in street clothes? I have presents for you—welcome-home presents." She smiled her best happy-little-girl smile. "Want to see them?"

"Of course I want to see them! And where are my manners, letting you stand? Here, let me seat you and take your cloak. Sherry?"

"Later. Or champagne, to welcome you home. To welcome us both home." She turned and let him take her cape. He turned to lay it aside and turned back just as she did so, too.

"Holy *Cow!*"

"Didn't know you were a Hindu, Jake." She posed, in graceful and calculated display.

"You wore *that* all the way across the city? Just paint?"

"Why not, dear? It's your first present—from Joe to you, sent with his love. I had my cape over it before I left Joe and Gigi's studio, and then kept it on when I got home—until you unwrapped your 'present.' Didn't want my mobiles to see it, of course." (Oh, of *course*, twin—except that Joe let them watch every brush stroke, once Gigi was sure you didn't mind. Say, Joan, Gigi would go for a Texas Star with Anton and Fred, I feel certain. And Joe would go along; he likes them. What do you think? Easy way to keep your promise to them, huh?)

(Eunice, we've got *this* man on our hands now.) (Oh,

poor you. Best way in the world to work up steam with *one* man is to let your mind rove about *other* men. You've still got some Puritan in you, girl.) (Which Puritan? When? And why didn't I notice? You can't mean Jake; he's Jewish. Speaking of Jake, has he noticed that slight omission in this getup? And why haven't we been raped?) (I doubt it, his eyeballs are spinning. As for the latter, I have hopes.)

"Joan Eunice, do you realize that that is a reproduction—exact, I think—of a body-paint design Eunice once wore?"

"Of course I realize it; she wore it *here* . . . and I wasn't so near dead that I didn't stare. Could never make up my mind whether these were sea shells or paint. Now I know. Joe wanted to be sure that you had seen it that first time, when Eunice wore it. I told him that I was almost certain that you had been here that day."

"Well, yes, I was. Briefly. That's why I recognized it."

"So? It had seemed to me that I recalled that as one of the days you took Eunice home. Hmmm?"

"Joan, are you trying to be snoopy?"

"Yes."

"Woman, I will not satisfy your prurient curiosity."

"How do you feel about satisfying prurience itself? Mine, I mean."

"That's another matter."

"I was wondering. So far you haven't even kissed me. Shall I take a shower first? Or let me put it this way: Did Eunice take time to get the paint off first?"

"Let *me* put it *this* way: Shut up and keep quiet and pipe down and not another damn word out of you until I give permission."

"Yes, sir."

She obeyed in essence for a reasonable time.

"May I talk now?"

"Yes, as long as you limit yourself to polite words of endearment. Some of your spontaneous remarks were quite unladylike."

"That's because I'm quite unladylike, Jake my only darling. I'm a failure as a lady. But I'll go on doing my best to simulate one in public—be a credit to Eunice."

"Joan Eunice——"

"Sir?"

"That's the way Eunice herself did it. A perfect lady in public . . . utterly uninhibited in private. It was a major part of her great charm. Some of *her* spontaneous expressions at such times were far more 'unladylike' than any I've heard you use."

"Really, Jake? Did she know any that I don't? And do you like them?"

"Hmm, I don't think she knew any that you don't know; she was just easier about it once she trusted me. Yes, I do like them. Used spontaneously."

"Jake, I trust you without limit—and I'll try not to inhibit any future spontaneity. Haven't meant to. Still learning."

"Darling girl, you do just fine when you get your rest. I mean 'my rest.' Now that I've got you helpless—and seeing that you trust me 'without limit'—what *did* happen at Joe's."

"Sir, the fact that I trust you—and I do!—does not mean that I'm going to satisfy your prurient curiosity."

"Hmm— Neither did Eunice, ever."

"Instead, you tell me what happened to *you*—at Joe's."

"We seem to have reached a stalemate. Let's wash off this paint. I wish I had taken a photograph of our mermaid before I smeared it."

"No huhu, Jake my beloved; Joe took several and I have them in my purse. For you. And I have two of Eunice in the same getup—one for you, and one for *me*. And besides that Joe gave me a four-by-five Kodachrome of a most incredible trompe-l'oeil painting he did of Eunice as a mermaid diving . . . plus a smaller transparency which shows how he did it. Same getup minus sea shells."

"Would it surprise you to learn that I've seen them both? Just didn't have the crust to promote Joe for them."

"No, not surprised, I guess. But I did *not* pressure him, Jake; he said he had a present for me—and these photos turned out to be the present. I should refuse? God forbid. But I'm going to put snoops to work and trace down who bought that painting. I intend to own it. Price no object."

431

"Your money won't help you, Miss Smith. Would it surprise you to know that *I* own that original Branca? It's at the Gib."

"I'll be—dipped! Jake, you're a dirty old holdout. I take back ten percent of any compliments I've handed you."

"That's okay; I didn't believe more than ninety percent. But if you're a good girl I'll *give* you that painting."

"I accept! But—well, it's hardly worthwhile opening those packages. They'll be disappointments."

"Would you like a spanking?"

"Yes."

"I'm too tired. Let's open packages."

"Well . . . we might open the smaller one. Let you see what Gigi looks like, if you don't remember. She's worth looking at."

"We'll open both of them."

"Scrub first?"

"I suppose we should."

"Well . . . let's give it a lick and promise, not turn it into a social event."

Joan Eunice insisted on opening 'Bilitis Sings' first. "Well, Jake?"

He gave a respectful wolf whistle. "The boy's a genius."

"Yes. I hadn't suspected. But you already knew it."

"Well, yes. His decision to use strong sunlight on your two contrasting skin colors was inspired."

"Especially as he had no sunlight—just smog-filtered north light, soft as old linen. Those highlights come from photographing us under floods the night before. Then he painted from us the next day. Changed the pose, though—and I don't know how he corrected the highlights. But I'm no genius."

"What's in the big package?"

"Open it."

It was 'The Three Graces'—and all three were Joan Eunice. "Joe calls this a 'cheat pic,' Jake—he photographed me three times—erase and correct—more nearly thirty-three times, against a neutral background, then combined three photos for his cartoon. Had Gigi pose with me each time to get arms-around-waist and so forth, then she would slither out like a snake without disturbing my pose. If he hadn't used 'cheat' the painting would have taken far longer. Aren't those dimples in my behind cute?"

"Woman, you are conceited enough."

"I'm not conceited, Jake; I wasn't handsome even when I was young. I know whose beautiful bottom that is. Well dear? I had intended 'Bilitis' for me and the 'Graces' for you—but you can have your choice."

"What a choice to have to make!"

"The one you let me keep will be no farther away than down the hall. If you had married me when you so obviously should have, you lecherous old rapist, you wouldn't have to make a choice; both would be yours. Jake, what does it cost to buy a job lot of art critics?"

"Well, the present crop ought not to fetch more than ten cents a dozen but everything is higher these days. I take it you have Joe Branca in mind?"

"Of course. He's selling his paintings at ridiculously low prices and paying an outrageous commission—and sells so few that the kids hardly get enough to eat. While freaks and frauds and sign painters are all the rage. I thought—"

"You can stop thinking; I see the swindle. We'll get him a good agent, we'll buy up what he has on the market, using dummies—and keep them ourselves; they're a surefire investment . . . and we'll buy art critics here, then elsewhere as he becomes better known. The question is: How much of a success must he be? Do I have to get him into the Metropolitan?"

"Jake, I don't think Joe *wants* to be famous. And *I* don't want it to be so conspicuous that he might smell a rat. Or that Gigi might; she's a little more sophisticated. Not very, that is. I just want his pictures to sell regularly enough that Gigi can buy groceries without worrying and can have enough disposable sheets that she can change them every day if it suits her. The kid is trying to keep house on scraped icebox and boiled dishrag soup. I tried that in the Depression and it's not funny—and I see no reason why Gigi should have to do it when she's married to an honest-to-God artist who can *paint*—and works at it. One who doesn't spend his time sopping up sauce or blowing weed,

433

and talking about the painting he's going to do. Joe paints. He's a craftsman as well as an artist. Well, maybe I don't know what an artist is but I know what a craftsman is and I respect craftsmen. Too few of them in this decadent world."

"No argument. We'll do it. Even if we have to go as high as fifteen cents a dozen."

"Even two-bits. Let's finish getting paint off—I must send down for olive oil—and you could be a darling and get Winnie to fetch me a heavy robe or get it yourself, pretty please, if she isn't home—no, I can get back to my room in my street cape, no problem, and—"

"Hrrmph."

"Did I goof again?"

"My dear, I have an announcement. Dr. and Mrs. Roberto Carlos Garcia y Ibañez are on their honeymoon."

"*What?* Why, the dirty little rat! Didn't wait for big sister to hold her hand. Good for them! Jake, that's *wonderful*—I think I'll cry."

"Go ahead, you cry while I shower."

"Hell, no, I'll cry when Winnie is back. I'll take that shower with you and you can scrub me. My back, where I can't see the paint; not my front, I'm tired, too. When was it and do you know when they will be home? And, goodness, I must pick out a suite for them; Roberto won't want to be next to mine with a connecting door. And I need to think of a wedding present—I may give them the painting you don't pick; Roberto won't let me give them anything expensive, he's a stubborn man." (Boss, is there another sort?)

"I can't see why Bob wouldn't want to have a connecting door into your bedroom."

"I think that was meant to be an insult. Perhaps he would like it, dear—*I* would like it. But it would not look right to the servants." (Frimp the servants!) (*All* of them, Eunice? I'm kept busy as it is.)

"Eunice, I took the liberty of telling Cunningham to have the Gold Suite set up for the Garcias—"

"Perfect! I'll have a door cut from my lounge into theirs . . . and there already is a lock-off that we can unlock between its foyer and the upstairs library we joined to your

434

suite—and then we can quit this unseemly ducking back and forth through the hall."

"The newlyweds *might* prefer to be left alone."

"Hadn't thought of that. Oh, well, 'I have some friends of my own,' as the old gal said."

"In any case they'll be back too soon for carpentry. I have it from a usually dependable source that a reliably dishonest member of your staff agreed to phone Mrs. Garcia the instant you returned. I assume that the call was made. I assume that they will be back by, oh, nightfall."

"I wonder whom I should fire? That's a hell of a way to run a honeymoon."

"I understand the good Doctor was in on it—the idea being to keep you safe from harm, since between them they constitute your medical staff."

"What nonsense. I'm the Pioneer-Mother type. Rugged. If I had crossed with the prairie schooners, they would have yoked me in with the oxen. But I'm glad they're coming home. I want to kiss them and cry on them."

"Johann, sometimes I can't make up my mind whether you are a silly young girl—or senile."

"The last time you called me 'Johann' you acquired some scar tissue. Dear, has it occurred to you that I might be both? A senile silly young girl?"

"Interesting. A possible working hypothesis."

"If so, I'm a well-adjusted one—Jake, I'm as happy as a cat left alone with the Christmas turkey. With Joe squared away and the Supreme Court being sensible for a change my last fret is gone. Life is one long giddy delight. I'm not even morning sick."

"Can't see why you should be—*huh?*" (Boss, I thought you weren't going to tell him?) (Eunice, he was bound to know soon . . . and I couldn't just let him find out, can't do that to *Jake*. This is the perfect time—he's officially 'first to know.')

"I said I wasn't bothered by morning sickness, Jake. I'm healthy as a horse and the only change I've noticed is that I'm hungry as a horse, too."

"You wish me to believe that you are pregnant?"

435

"Don't give me that stern-father look, Jake. I'm knocked up and happier than Happy Hooligan. I could have kept it to myself a while longer but I wanted to tell you before anyone else could notice. But be a dear and treat it as privileged—because the instant Winnie finds out she'll start mothering me and worrying. Which is not what a bride should be doing. With luck I can keep it from Winnie until she's pregnant, too." (Boss, what makes you think Winnie intends to get pregnant?) (Use your head, Eunice—five to one she's got a Band-aid over the spot where that implant used to be this very minute.) (I don't have a head, Boss—just yours and it doesn't work too well.) (Complaints, huh? Talk that way and I won't marry *you*, either.) (We *are* married, Boss.) (I know it, beloved. Now be quiet; I've got to juggle eggs.)

"Eunice—are you sure?"

"Yes. Test positive."

"Did Bob make the test? Or some quack?"

"A patient's relations with a doctor are confo. But it was not a quack. Don't pursue this line of inquiry, Counselor."

"We'll get married at once."

"The hell we will!"

"Eunice, let's have no nonsense!"

"Sir, I asked you to marry me quite some time back. You emphatically refused. I asked you at a later time. Again I was turned down. I decided not to renew my request, and I do not do so now. I will *not* marry you. But I will be honored and delighted to continue as your mistress until I am benched by biology—and more than pleased to be allowed again to be your concubine when I am back in commission. I love you, sir. But I will not marry you."

"I ought to spank you."

"I don't think it would do me any damage, darling. But I don't think you could bring yourself to strike a pregnant woman." (Now kick him in the *other* shin, Boss. You little hellcat.) (Eunice, stay out of this row. I'm not only a woman scorned; I'm also old Johann Smith who never could be pushed too far. Jake can have us any time, sure. But I'm damned if I'll let him be 'noble' about it when I'm knocked up.) (Boss, aren't we *ever* going to marry him?

This is a mistake, dear; he needs us.) (And we need him, Eunice. Sure, we'll marry him—after we've whelped. *After*.) (Boss, you're making a big mistake.) (If so, I'm making it. I never make little mistakes—just big ones.)

"I didn't say I was going to spank you, Eunice—I said I 'ought' to. What happened? I distinctly remember you telling me that you had taken care of contraception."

"Your memory is good, sir. The exact phrasing, as I phrased it most carefully. I have 'taken care' of such matters in whatever fashion I wished. Every time. With you. With others. Each time I have taken such care as suited me—at that time and with that man."

"Hmmm! That's as unresponsive an answer as I've ever heard. Let me put it more plainly. Eunice, did I get you pregnant?"

"I won't answer. You know that at least one other man has slept with me—and I may have been the bride of the regiment. Jake, you would not marry me when I was a virgin; you still would not marry me when you made me your mistress. So where I got this child in me is not your business and you have no right to quiz me and—much as I love you!—I will *not* tolerate one more question along this line. Not now nor in the future! Whom I chose to father my child is *my* business. But you may be certain that I selected him with care, eyes open and wits about me. You've been acting as if you were a father dealing with a wayward daughter, or a Welfare Visitor trying to establish responsibility for an unlicensed pregnancy. You *know* that is not the situation. I am ninety-five years old—much older than you are—able to afford a dozen bastards if it suits me—and it may—and wealthy enough to tell the world to go pee up a rope. Jake, I was sharing happy news with you. You elect to treat it as bad news and take me to task about it. I won't accept that, sir. I made a mistake in telling you. Will you please treat the matter as privileged—and never mention it again?"

"Eunice."

"Yes, Jake?"

"I love you."

"I love you, Jake."

"Had I been twenty years younger—even ten years!—I would have married you long before now. Since you won't tell me—and since I have no right to quiz you; you are correct—will you forgive an old man's pride if I choose to believe that *I* am the man you picked? I promise that I will not discuss that belief with anyone."

"Jacob, if you choose to believe that, I am honored. But I ask no promises. If you chose to proclaim such a belief, I would never shame my oldest and closest and most beloved friend by denying it. I would smile proudly and let my manner confirm it. But, Jacob my beloved, to *you* I neither affirm nor deny it—and never will. I did this on my own. I *alone* am parent to this child." (Watch your words, Boss! You almost spelled it out.) (He'll take it as rhetoric. Or if he does suspect, investigation will prove that he's wrong. Hank Olsen knows which side of his bed is buttered. Mine, that is.) (And the dates are going to check out so that Jake will be certain it's his. Hmm—) (Still think I'm a fool, Eunice?) (No, Boss—just reckless. You scare the hell out of me at times.)

"Well, Eunice, from the restrictions you *have* put on me that seems to be all we can say about it."

"That was my intention, Jake."

"I understood. What would you like to do the rest of today—at least until our newlyweds return? Play cribbage?"

"If you wish, Jake, certainly."

"I have a better idea. If you want to join me in it. Could be fun, I think."

"*Will* be fun, Jake. Anything is always fun shared with you. Even if it's just cribbage."

"This is a better two-handed game if it's played right. Let's phone Mac, ask him to have his clerk start the ball rolling—and get married. With luck we can be legal by twenty-one or -two—and still get in a couple of boards of cribbage before bedtime."

"Oh, Jake! '*Cribbage*'!"

"Answer me, woman. A simple 'Yes' or 'No'. I won't argue it . . . and I won't ask you again. And blow your nose and wipe your eyes—you're a mess."

438

"Damn you, Jake! *Yes!* Let me go and I'll blow my nose. I think you've cracked my ribs, you big brute. That's a hell of a way to treat an expectant mother."

"I'll do worse than crack your ribs if I have any more nonsense out of you. Now to call Mac—I'll have to think up a plausible lie so that he'll be justified in authorizing the County Clerk to issue a special license."

"Why does it have to be fancy, Jacob? I thought you were going to tell Mac that you had knocked me up?"

"Eunice, is that what you want me to say?"

"Jacob, I'm going to marry you as quickly as possible, I don't care how. I hope Winnie and Roberto show up in time but I'm not going to wait; you might come to your senses. I thought you preferred to claim that you had done me in and I know I agreed to confirm it. So tell Mac so. Tell anybody."

"Doesn't fret you?"

"Jake dearest, maybe that's the best way to handle it . . . because, presently, God and everybody is going to know about the Silent Witness. Jake? Do you recall my first day of freedom? The day after Mac conditionally confirmed my identity and discharged me as a ward of the court?"

"My dear, I am not likely to forget *that* day."

"Nor I. Count two hundred sixty-seven days. That is when the Silent Witness should show up."

"You're telling me that I *am* the father of your child."

"Not at all, sir. I was in heat and had slipped the leash and you may assume if you wish that I spent the day bouncing in and out of beds, going from one man to another." She smiled beatifically. (Boss, that's awfully close to the truth—but it sounds like a whopper.) (It *is* the truth, Eunice; I worded it most carefully. That is the second best way to tell a lie—tell the truth so that it sounds like a whopper.) (And I thought *I* knew how to lie.) (I've had years more practice, Beloved—and as a kid had more reason to lie than you ever had. Lying is a fine art; it is learned only through long practice.)

"Knock off the nonsense, Eunice, or I'll start married life by giving you a fat lip. Okay, we'll tell Mac that; the truth is often the simplest solution. But we have to have health certificates; Mac can get us out of the waiting time but not out of that requirement. My doctor will phony one for me without stopping to take a blood sample and make tests, but how about that quack you mentioned? Will he cooperate?"

"Jake, I don't recall mentioning a quack. If Roberto gets here in time, I think he would take a chance. Or Rosy would, I think. I don't think I'm harboring even a cold bug unless I picked up something from Joe and Gigi. Most unlikely. But how about *you*, darling? Washington, D.C., has the highest V.D. rate in the country. Did you fetch anything home?"

"Oh, nothing but big and little casino."

"A nice girl like me can't be expected to understand such terms."

"You impudent little baggage, I slept *alone* in Washington. Can you make the same claim? For the past five days?"

"Of course not, dear; I've never been interested in sleeping alone—and Gigi is *very* snuggly. I commend her to your attention—take a look at that painting."

"I'm sure she is. Just Gigi, eh? Not Joe?"

"Is Joe snuggly, Jake? Tell me *more!*"

"Woman, you may get that fat lip *before* I marry you."

"The groom's present to the bride? Sir, if you want to give me a fat lip, I'll hold still, smile happily, and take it. Oh, Jake darling, it's going to be such *fun* to be married to you!"

"I think so, too, you dizzy bitch. Mmm, my doctor will phony a certificate for you, too, if I explain the circumstances. But he'll need your blood type."

"Jake, the whole country knows that my blood type is AB-negative. Had you forgotten it?"

"Momentarily, yes. That's all I need. Except— Wedding here? Or in Mac's chambers?"

"Here, if possible. I want our servants for 'family' if Winnie and Roberto don't show up. Jacob, do I dare send a car with a message and ask Joe and Gigi to allow themselves to be fetched here for this purpose? I *do* want them present. Gigi is no problem; she will do as Joe wishes—but I think you know Joe better than I do. I don't even know that he has clothes he would be willing to wear here—all I saw him wear were denim shorts so caked with paint they could stand alone."

"Mmm, I agree that Eunice's former husband is entitled to be invited to Joan Eunice's wedding, though there has never been a protocol established, that's certain. Dear, the clothes Joe wore in court would be okay for a home wedding. How about yourself, Eunice? Going to be married in white?"

"I think I've been insulted again. Wear white so that somebody can sneak a picture and sell it? 'Ninety-Five-Year-Old Sex-Change Bride Wears White.' Dear, if I wear white, let's ask *Life* to send a photographer and cut out the middleman. Jake, I'll wear white if you tell me to. If you don't, I'll pick something but it won't be white. Something."

" 'Something old, something new, something borrowed, something blue.' "

"Erase and correct, Jake. Here is the twenty-first century version:

"The bride is old,
"The license new,
"The body borrowed,
"The groom is blue."

"I am like hell blue, I simply need a shave. Get out now and let me be. Beat it. Go take a bath. Try to smell like a bride."

"Instead of payday at Tillie's? I can take a hint. But *you* take a bath, too."

"Who notices the groom?"

Cunningham had a busy six hours. But so did everyone in the ugly old mansion. To the old-tradition strains of Mendelssohn's "Processional" the bride walked slowly in hesitation-step through the rotunda. (Twin, 'Here Comes the Bride' always sounds to me like a cat sneaking up on a bird. Pum . . . pum . . . tee-pum! Appropriate, hnnn?) (Eunice, behave!) (Oh, I'll behave. But I prefer 'John Jacob Jingleheimer Smith—his name is my name, too!') (You can't know *that* one. It's eighty years old and long forgotten.) (Why wouldn't I know it when you were singing it in your head every second they were dressing us?)

She walked steadily down the center of a long white velvet carpet, through the arch and into the banquet hall, now transformed with flowers and candles and organ into a chapel. (Boss, there's Curt! I'm so glad he made it! That must be Mrs. Hedrick with him. Don't look at them, twin; I'll giggle.) (I'm *not* looking at them and you stop trying to—I must look straight ahead.) (You do that, Boss darling, and I'll count the house. There's Mrs. Mac—Norma—and Alec's Ruth, with Roberto. Where's Rosy? —oh, there he is beyond Mrs. Mac. My, isn't Della dressed fit to kill?—makes us look shabby.)

The bride wore a severely simple dress of powder blue, opaque, with high neck, matching veil, long sleeves, matching gloves, skirt hem brushing the velvet runner and long train sweeping behind. She carried a bouquet of white cattleya dyed blue to match. (Twin? Why that last-minute decision for panties? They make a line that shows.) (Not through this gown; it's not skin-tight. The 'bride's knot,' Beloved—for symbolic defloration.) (Coo! Don't make me laugh, Boss.) (Eunice, if you louse up this wedding, I'll—I'll—I won't speak to you for three days!) (Joan twin, I won't spoil it—Jake wants symbols, he shall have them.) (And *I* want symbols, too!) (And so do I, twin, so do I. It's just that I have never been able to see life as anything but a vast complicated practical joke, and it's better to laugh than cry.)

(Yes, darling—but let's not do either right now. I'm having trouble with tears.) (I thought they were my tears. Doesn't Thomas Cattus look handsome? I heard you order the 'Lohengrin recessional'; that one is even funnier than the Mendelssohn—to an Iowa farm girl it sounds *exactly* like the triumphant cackle of a hen after she lays an egg. I'll laugh then, I know I will.)

(All right to laugh and cry both then, Eunice—and to hang on tight to Jacob's arm. Look, dearest, this is an old-fashioned wedding with all the clichés because Jake and I are old fossils and that's the way it *should* be.)

(Oh, I approve. Cunningham looks worried—can't see why; he's done a beautiful job. Boss, those panties struck me so darn funny because you ordered the 'Bilitis' and the 'Graces' to be placed on easels in the drawing room where everyone at the reception can stare at them. Riddle me that.) (Eunice, there is no inconsistency. A bride is supposed to be covered; those paintings are meant to be looked at. With Joe and Gigi here I darn well *want* them to be looked at!) (They'll be looked at. Stared at. Some wives may look at them with intense interest. Maybe.) (Maybe. Eunice, you know I've never asked a husband *not* to tell his wife anything; it's not right to ask one member of a married couple to keep secrets from the other. Besides, he will or he won't, no matter what you ask—and he should; he knows her better than we do. But those pix are as harmless as the fruit punch we have for those who turn down the champagne. It's irrelevant that I posed for them, I simply want Joe's genius to be appreciated. Enjoyed.)

Joe Branca had used no small part of his genius in making up the bride. Starting with a bare, clean canvas—fresh out of her tub—he had worked long and hard to make up Joan Eunice from head to toe with such restraint that even close inspection could not detect any trace of his efforts. As in "The Three Graces" it was simply Eunice's own beauty, invisibly enhanced—strongly enhanced, better than life, more natural than nature. He turned down the use of a hair fall and simply fluffed her own hair (still far shorter than Eunice's hair had been) and sprayed it slightly to keep it unmussed under her veil.

The bride's matron of honor was made up with much less restraint. Having seen the miracle wrought on Joan Eunice, Winnie had timidly asked Joan if she thought it would be all right to ask Mr. Branca to improve her a little? Since she was part of the wedding party?—and Joan and Gigi had enthusiastically pushed the idea. Joe had studied Mrs. Garcia, then said, "Forty minutes, Joan Eunice—is time? Okay, Winnie, wash face." The result exploited Winifred's red hair, made visible her transparent eyebrows and lashes, livened her too-white skin—yet looked more natural than the stylized face Winnie usually wore.

The matron of honor wore pastel-green tabard and tights and carried a smaller bouquet of green and brown cymbidia. She kept in step to the hesitation march thirty paces ahead of the bride, preceded her into the banquet hall toward the improvised altar.

Chief of Security O'Neil was the last one in, then posted himself in the archway at parade-rest and managed to watch events at the far end of the room while giving his attention to his rear. His features were serene but he was uneasy, alert. The big house was empty save for seventy-five to eighty people in this one room; all armor was up, every door, every real window was locked, hand-bolted, and dogged, and the night net of alarms switched on, and O'Neil had personally made sure of all this before releasing his guards to attend the wedding. But he trusted no gadgets and few people; he did not release himself from duty.

The bride approached the far end. Jake Salomon waited there, with Alec Train at his side. Facing down the aisle were the Reverend Hugo White and Judge McCampbell, matching in dignity. Shorty was wearing a black frock coat, white shirt, string tie, and carried his Book; the Judge was in judicial robes.

(Boss, doesn't Jake look beautiful? But what is that getup?) (It's a cutaway, dearest.) (It's a museum piece.) (I suppose so. Jake probably hasn't worn it in thirty, forty years—or perhaps rented it from a theatrical costumer. I feel certain Alec had to rent his. Doesn't Father Hugo look grand!) (Must be his preachin' clothes, Boss. Joe ought to paint him in *this*, even if he never gets the pix he wants.) (Good idea, Eunice; we'll plant it with Gigi—and one thing may lead to another. I have hopes that seeing 'The Three Graces' will gentle him, too. As Hugo *wants* to pose ... if he can convince himself that it's not sinful. Eunice, my knees are shaking. I'm not sure I can do it!) (Om Mani Padme Hum, baby sister. We had one hell of time getting him off the dime; don't go chicken now.) (Om Mani Padme Hum, Eunice—hold my hand, darling—don't let me faint.)

Joan Eunice stopped in front of judge and preacher. Winifred took her bouquet from her, stepped back to one side. Alec Train moved Jake into place beside Joan Eunice, placed himself to balance Winifred. The music stopped.

444

Hugo lifted his eyes and said, "Let us pray." (Om Mani Padme Hum. You okay, twin?) (I'm all right now. Om Mani Padme Hum.)

When Hugo said, "Amen," Joe Branca slid in from the side, shot his first picture. Thereafter he moved around like a Chinese stagehand, disturbing no one and never moving at a crucial moment—but getting his shots.

Hugo opened his Book, did not look at it. "We read today from the Book of Psalms. It says here:

" 'The Lord is my shepherd; I shall not want.

" 'He maketh me to lie down in green pastures; He leadeth me beside the still waters.

" 'He restoreth my soul; He leadeth me in the paths of righteousness for His name's sake.

" 'Yea, though I walk through the valley of the shadow of death, I will fear no evil ....' "

He closed his Book. "Brothers and Sisters, the Lord saw that Adam was lonely in the Garden of Eden and He said it is not good for man to live alone. So He created Eve to live with Adam. And He said to Adam, My son, you take care of this woman, you hear Me? You treat her right all the time, just like I was watching you every minute. Because I *am* watching you, every minute and every second. You cherish her and protect her like I tell you and you'll be too busy to get into anything wrongful, and she'll be a comfort to you all the days of your life."

He turned to Salomon. "Jacob Moshe, are you going to do that?"

"I will!"

The Reverend looked at the bride. "And the Lord said to Eve, My daughter, you got to cook for this man and wash his clothes and bring up his babies and not go running around when you should be home, and love him even when he's tired and bad-tempered and not fit to speak to, because men are like that and you must take the bad with the good—you hear Me, Eve?

"Joan Eunice, are you going to do that?"

"Yes, Father Hugo."

445

"Judge—"

"Jacob Moshe, does there exist any impediment under our laws and customs to you marrying this woman?"

"None."

"Joan Eunice, is there any reason in law or in your heart why you cannot marry this man?"

"There is none, Your Honor."

McCampbell spoke more loudly. "If any witness knows of any cause which would forbid me to bind these two in marriage, I command him to speak." (Eunice, if anyone even clears his throat, I'll—I'll—) (You'll keep quiet, Boss darling; that's what you'll do. Nobody here but our loving friends. Om Mani Padme Hum.) (Om Mani Padme Hum.........)

"Jacob Moshe, will you love, honor, and cherish her?"

"I will."

"Joan Eunice, will you love, honor, and cherish him?"

"I will love, honor and *obey* him." (Huh? Boss you demon, you haven't the slightest intention of obeying!)

Salomon said, "Wait a moment! Judge, she switched the words! I don't expect that and I won't let her promise—"

"Order. You keep quiet, Jake; I'm not addressing *you*. Joan Eunice, is that what you wish to promise?"

"Yes, Your Honor." (Eunice, stay out of this. I know what I'm doing.)

"I must advise you that such a promise is not legally binding under the civil marriage contract of this State but I must warn you, too, that it is not a promise which should be lightly made in these circumstances."

"I know it, Your Honor." (Boss, you're out of your mind!) (Quite possibly. But it's all *right*, sweetheart. Jake is going to give us exactly the orders we will be humbly pleased to obey. Haven't I been right so far?) (Yes, but you keep scaring me. Suppose he tells us to keep our legs crossed? I've never been any good at *that*.) (He never will. Instead he'll be magnanimously pleased to humor our little follies—since we've promised to obey him. Relax, sweetheart—this is precisely the way my darling Agnes handled *me* . . . when I was not anything like as wise and tolerant as Jake is.)

446

"Let me hear you state your intention again."

"I, Joan Eunice, do solemnly promise to love, honor, and obey Jacob Moshe—and I will, Your Honor, even if he backs out and won't marry me. He doesn't have to marry me. I'd be perfectly happy just to—"

"Quiet, Joan Eunice. That's enough. Reverend, this is getting out of hand; I'm going to wrap it up with the bare legalities and you can plaster them with anything else they need in your closing prayer. All right?"

"Yes, Judge. They don't need much prayer; they're ready."

"I hope you're right. Jake, you heard this stubborn little, uh, lady. Are you willing to marry her anyhow?"

"Yes."

"Jacob Moshe, do you take Joan Eunice to be your lawfully wedded wife?"

"I do!"

"Joan Eunice, do you take Jacob Moshe to be your lawfully wedded husband?"

"I do."

"Uh, where's the ring? Alec. Jake, take her left hand in your left. Now."

" 'With this ring I thee wed.' "

"Under authority vested in me I pronounce you man and wife. Kiss her, Jake. Take it, Reverend." (And *you* told *me* not to louse it up!) (I got us there, didn't I? He's ours. I mean, we're his. Same thing.)

"Let us pray!"

26

On Luna, Kennedy Tunnel B, parelleling Kennedy Tunnel
A between Luna City and the Apollo Industrial Complex,
was completed and both tunnels were then made one-way,
thereby quadrupling the potential traffic. The five- and ten-
year projections caused the Commission to decide to go
ahead at once with tunnels C and D. On the Hong Kong and
New York Stock Exchanges Vacuum Industries, Ltd.,
Selenterprises, Pan Am, and Diana Transport all took
sudden jumps against a generally sagging market. Mercury
Newsletter (subsid of MercServ) sent destructaped messages
by special couriers to their 7-star clients. Nine percent of
these couriers failed to report back, which caused the
managing director of MercServ to decide that a vacation
at Las-Vegas-in-the-Sky would be good for his health even
though there was no proof that Internal Defense agents had
detained the couriers or solved the "destruct" combo. A
source close to the President denied that there was anything
more than seasonal unrest in any city in the country and
denounced "irresponsible rumormongers." CBS's "Today's
Day with Dave Daly" was replaced by a motion picture
with an explanation of technical difficulties. "Today's Day"
resumed the next day without Daly, who was—it was
announced—on sick leave to recover from extreme fatigue.
Miss Molly Maguire, the hottest sensie star of the private
film industry, claimed the title of first woman in history to
give birth to a child during a sky dive. The babe was safely
landed exactly as planned by the midwife team diving with
her, the event was filmed in stereosound and -color from
several angles, and the only casualty was a sprained ankle

for Miss Maguire—she was able to hold a press conference thirty minutes after she landed.

Since plane flight had originated in, and sky dive had started over, Mexican soil, whereas the entire party except the plane had landed in Arizona, it was not clear what laws had been violated or whose, or what nationality the child was—as Miss Maguire's citizenship was Pakistani, with legal permanent residence in the States. The party surrendered voluntarily to the nearest U.S. immigration officer and Miss Maguire apologized most prettily on videocast for having reentered the country of her choice so informally through an inadvertent error in navigation by her pilot, plus a sudden gust of wind. They were released with a warning but the films were impounded—uselessly, as they seemed to show that the child was born, about fifty-fifty, in *both* countries, but factors of angle and parallax and identification of ground markings—in those film sequences in which the ground showed at all—make it impossible to be certain. Grove Press bought an option on the films, then entered suit to have them released, in the interest of justice.

A notorious sex-change case married her attorney but the newsworthy couple managed to leave for their honeymoon before issuance of their license was noted—a famous scoopsnoop chased them to Canada, only to find that the couple he had traced down were a Dr. & Mrs. Garcia, members of the wedding but themselves of no news value. Mrs. Garcia smiled and let herself be photographed (she was quite photogenic) and was interviewed about the wedding; then the Garcias returned home.

Senator James "Jumping Joe" Jones of Arkansas charged that the drive to repeal the XXXIst Amendment permitting prayer in public schools was a plot by the Devil-inspired Pope of Rome and his servile followers. The rebuilding of the Oklahoma State House was halted by labor trouble drummed up (it was alleged) by the underground "Equal Rights for Whites" Action Committee. The contractor's construction foreman said, "Any honk thinks he's discriminated, he can take it to the hiring board and get a fair hearing. Trouble is these people they don't *want* to work."

"Mr. and Mrs. MacKenzie" (Liberian passports) had the penthouse floor to themselves—three baths, four bedrooms, kitchen, dining room, bar-lounge, drawing room, lanai, garden, swimming pool, waterfall, fountain, garden bar-pantry, foyer, private lift, magnificent view of the yacht harbor, beaches, estuary, town, and mountains beyond.

But they were eccentric. Their rent included full hotel service but none of the hotel's staff had been on that level since their arrival. They were not seen at the casinos, nor on the beaches, nor were they known to make use of other attractions of the resort. They sometimes had room-service meals, but the table cart went only as far as the lift; their servants took it up.

It was rumored among the hotel staff that Mrs. MacKenzie liked to do her own cooking, but no one really knew—no one had seen her (save possibly from a copter) and few knew him by sight. Their servants had three suites on a lower floor . . . but were willing to discuss anything but their employers.

She came from the garden into the lounge. He looked up

from his book. "Yes, dear? Too much sun? Or did that copter come back?"

"Neither. Copters don't worry me; I just turn over on my tummy so that they can't photograph my face. Jake darling, I want you to see something pretty."

"Drag it in here, I'm lazy."

"I can't dearest; it's down on the water. A boat of some odd sort, with the gayest, most colorful sails. You were in the Navy; you know about such things."

"I was in the Navy one hitch fifty years back, so I'm an expert already."

"Jacob, you always know everything. And it *is* pretty, and quite odd. Please, sir?"

"Your slightest wish, Madame." He got up and offered her his arm.

They stopped at the seaward rail. "Now which one? All those boats have colored sails. I haven't seen a suit of white sails since we got here—you'd think there was a law against it."

"*That* one. Oh, dear, they're putting down its sails. And it was so pretty a minute ago."

" 'Dowsing her sails,' Eunice. If I'm going to be your resident expert, let me expert. When you lower sails suddenly, you 'dowse' them. Which this laddie is doing because he's standing in to anchor about—yes! There goes the hook. And a vessel is *always* 'she,' never 'it.' Boats and ships are female because they are beautiful, lovable, expensive—and unpredictable."

"Jake, you've always been able to predict what I'm going to do even before I know myself." (Twin, why tell a whopper like that? He knows better.) (He won't argue it, hon.) "But what is it?"

"Oh. It's a trimaran, a yacht with a triple hull. Can't say that I agree that she's pretty. A sloop with a triangular mains'l is my notion of beauty."

"Does look sort of squarish now. But swooping in with all its—sorry!— 'her' sails up, she was lovely." (Twin, ask Jake if he thinks there is any way we could go on it?) (On 'her,' Eunice—not 'it.' Are you a sailor, hon?) (Never been on a boat in my life, Boss. But I'm getting an idea, maybe.)

452

(Maybe I have the same idea. Are you thinking about that talk with Jake when he pointed out a farm would mean even more staff and less safety than our house?) (I don't care who thought of it first, Boss—just make sure that *Jake* thinks of it first.) (I shall, dear—do you think I have to be told that a ship is 'she'? Or can't recognize a trimaran? The real question is: Do *you* get seasick? I used to—and it's miserable. But the fact that we haven't had the tiniest bit of morning sickness makes me think you might be immune to motion sickness.) (So 'let's operate and find out,' as Roberto says.)

"Oh, trimarans have their points, Eunice. You get a lot of boat for your money. Roomy. And they are almost impossible to turn over—safer than most small vessels. I just wouldn't award one a beauty prize."

"Jake, do you think you could get us invited aboard that one? She looks interesting."

"Oh, there's some way to swing it. I might start by talking with the manager. But, Eunice, you can't go aboard a private vessel with your features veiled; it would be rude. Your granddaughters did you no favor when they made you as recognizable as a video star."

"Jacob, a veil doesn't enter into it because I *never* want to meet *anyone* as 'Mrs. MacKenzie.' I'm Mrs. Jacob Moshe Salomon and proud of it—and that's the way I must *always* be introduced. Jake, I doubt if our marriage is news any longer; it can't matter much if I'm spotted."

"I suppose not. The copters might swarm a mite closer for a while and some would have pixsnoops aboard with telescopic lenses. But I doubt if even your granddaughters are anxious to take a shot at you. If the snoops fret you, wear pants to sunbathe, and in the pool."

"The hell I will, it's our pool, Jacob. Anyhow, briefies can't conceal the fact that I'm pregnant, and the sooner that's in the news the less it will interest anyone later. Let them sneak a pic, then you have Doctor Bob confirm it—and it stops being news. No huhu, dear; I learned years ago that you can't 'get away from it all'—you just have to cope. Is it possible, on a boat of that sort, to have a swimming pool?"

"Not one that size. But I've seen trimarans much bigger than that one. Could be done, I suppose, since a trimaran can have so much deck space for its tonnage—I'd have to ask a naval architect. Why the interest, Lively Legs? Do you want me to buy you a yacht?"

"I don't know. But boats look like fun. Jake, I never had much fun in my life—my other life. I'm not sure how one goes about having fun—except that every day is a joy to me now. All that I'm sure of is that I want to do something utterly different this time. Not be a Hetty Green. And not the gay, mad whirl of 'society'—*kark!* I'd rather turn whore. Would *you* like a yacht, Jake? Take me around the world and show me all those places you've seen and I never had time for?"

"You mean you didn't take time."

"Maybe it's the same thing. I do know that, if a man acquires too much money, presently it owns him instead of his owning it. Jake, I've been to Europe at least fifty times—yet I've never been inside the Louvre, never seen them change the Guard at Buckingham Palace. All I saw were hotels and boardrooms—and those are the same all over the globe. Would you care to repair my education, dearest? Show me Rio?—you say it's the most beautiful city in the world. The Parthenon by moonlight? The Taj at dawn?"

Jake said thoughtfully. "The trimaran is the favorite craft of the dropout."

"Excuse me? I missed something. 'Dropout'?"

"I don't mean the barefooted bums in the Abandoned Areas, Eunice, nor the ones skulking around the hills. It takes money to drop out by water. But people do. Millions have. Nobody knows how many because it has been subject to an 'exception' for years—the government does not want attention called to it. But take those yachts below us: I'll bet that at least one out of ten has registration papers for some 'flag of convenience' and the owner's passport is as phony as that of 'Mr. and Mrs. MacKenzie.' He has to be registered somewhere and carry some sort of passport, or the Coast Guard wherever he goes will give him a bad time, even impound his craft. But if he takes care of
454

that minimum, he can dodge almost everything else—no income tax, no local taxes except when he buys something, nobody tries to force his kids into public schools, no real estate taxes, no politics—no violence in the streets. That last is the best part, with the cycle of riots swinging up again."

"Then it *is* possible to 'get away from it all.' "

"Mmm, not quite. No matter how much fish he eats, he has to touch land occasionally. He can't play Vanderdecken; only a ghost ship can stay at sea forever, real ones have to be put up on the ways at intervals." Jake Salomon looked thoughtful. "But it's closer to that antithetical combination of 'peace' and 'freedom' than is possible on land. If it suits one. But, Eunice, I know what I would do—if I were young."

"What, Jake?"

"Look up there."

"Where, dear? I don't see anything."

"*There*."

"The Moon?"

"Right! Eunice, that's the only place with plenty of room and not too many people. Our last frontier—but an endless one. Anyone under the cut-off age should at least *try* to out-migrate."

"Are you serious, Jacob? Certainly space travel is scientifically interesting but I've never seen much use in it. Oh, some 'fallout.' Videosatellites and so forth. New materials. But the Moon itself?—why, it doesn't even pay its own way."

"Eunice, what use is that baby in your belly?"

"I trust that you are joking, sir. I hope you are."

"Simmer down, Bulgy. Darling, a newborn baby is as useless a thing as one can imagine. It isn't even pretty—except to its doting parents. It does *not* pay its own way and it's unreasonably expensive. It takes twenty to thirty years for the investment to begin to pay off and in many—no, *most*—cases it never does pay off. Because it is much easier to support a child than it is to bring one up to amount to anything."

"*Our* baby will amount to something!"

"I feel sure that it will. But look around you; my generalization stands. But, Eunice, despite these shortcomings, a baby has a unique virtue. It is always the hope of our race. Its *only* hope."

She smiled. "Jacob, you're an exasperating man."

"I try to be, dear; it's good for your metabolism. Now look back up at the sky. *That's* a newborn baby, too. The best hope of our race. If *that* baby lives, the human race lives. If we let it die—and it is vulnerable for a few more years—the race dies, too. Oh, I don't mean H-bombs. We're faced with far greater dangers than H-bombs. We've reached an impasse; we can't go on the way we're headed—and we can't go back—and we're dying in our own poisons. That's why that little Lunar colony has *got* to survive. Because *we* can't. It isn't the threat of war, or crime in the streets, or corruption in high places, or pesticides, or smog, or 'education' that doesn't teach; those things are just symptoms of the underlying cancer. It's too many people. Not too many souls, or honks, or thirds—just . . . *too many.* Seven billion people, sitting in each other's laps, trying to take in each other's washing, pick each other's pockets. Too many. Nothing wrong with the individual in most cases—but collectively we're the Kilkenny Cats, unable to do anything but starve and fight and eat each other. Too many. So anyone who can ought to go to the Moon as fast as he can manage it."

"Jacob, in all the years I've known you I've never heard you talk this way."

"Why talk about a dream that has passed one by? Eunice—Eunice-Johann, I mean—I was born twenty-five years later than you were. I grew up believing in space travel. Perhaps you did not?"

"No, I didn't, Jake. When it came along, it struck me as interesting—but slightly presposterous."

"Whereas I was born enough later that it seemed as natural to me as automobiles. The big rockets were no surprise to my generation; we cut our teeth on Buck Rogers. Nevertheless I was born too soon. When Armstrong and Aldrin landed on Luna, I was pushing forty. When outmigration started, with a cut-off age of forty, I was too old;

when they eased it to forty-five, again I was too old—and when they raised it to fifty, I was *much* too old. I'm not kicking, dear; on a frontier every man-jack must pull his weight, and there is little use for an elderly lawyer."

He smiled down at her, and went on: "But, darling, if *you* wanted to out-migrate, I wouldn't try to dissuade you; I'd cheer you on."

"Jake!" (He can't get away from us that easily!) (You're darn tootin' he can't! I'll fix him.) "Jake my own and only, you can't get away from me that easily."

"Eunice, I am serious. I could die happy if I knew our baby was to be born on the Moon."

She sighed. "Jacob, I promised to obey you and I happily do so. But I *can't* go to the Moon—as an out-migrant. Because I'm even farther past the cut-off age than you are—the Supreme Court says so."

"That could be fixed."

"And raise an issue over my identity again? Jacob darling, I don't *want* to leave you. But"—she patted her belly and smiled—"if *he* wants to go to the Moon, we'll help, at the earliest age they'll take him. All right?"

He smiled and gently patted her slight bulge. "More than all right. Because I don't want his beautiful mother to go away for any reason. But a father should never stand in the way of his son."

"You don't. You aren't. You won't. You never would. Jacob Junior goes to the Moon when he's ready, but not *this* week. Let's talk about trimarans and *this* week. Jake, you know I want to close up our house—I'd sell it but nobody would buy it other than as land; it's a white elephant. But two things have bothered me. It has to be left garrisoned, or the Free People will break in despite all armor, and squat—then someday some judge grants them title on adverse possession."

Jake said, "Certainly. Historically, that's where all land titles come from. Somebody standing on it, defending it, and saying, 'This is mine!' And lately the courts have been cutting down the period of adverse possession. Especially in city cores close to Abandoned Areas—and your house is both."

457

"I know, dear—but I don't want to surrender it to squatters. Darn it, that house cost me more than nine million, not counting taxes and upkeep. The other worry is what to do about our in-house staff. I'm sick of being a feudal lord—erase and correct; lady, now." (Erase and correct—'tart' now.) (Certainly, Eunice, but I haven't been too tartish since we got married.) (Not much opportunity, twin—but you're getting restless. Huh?) (*Who* is getting restless? Never mind, twin sister, the day will come. But we won't rub darling Jake's nose in it.) "I can't just let them go; some have been with me twenty-odd years. But if we buy a yacht—and live in it—I think I have a solution to both problems."

"So?"

"I think so. It's an idea I got during our wedding, thinking about that farm."

"Well! Wench, you were supposed to be thinking about *me*."

"I was, dear. But I seem to be able to think about several things at once, since my rejuvenation. Better blood supply, possibly." (My help, you mean, Boss.) (Yes, dear. Same thing.) "Our banquet hall, dressed as a chapel, looked more like a church than it has ever looked like a place to eat. So here's my notion. Give our house to Shorty. Give it to his church in a trust setup, with Alec, maybe, as a trustee, and also Judge Mac if he'll do it. Arrange the trust for perpetual maintenance, with ample funds and a good salary for Hugo as pastor. Is this practical?"

"No difficulty, Eunice, if you really want to unload the house—"

"I do. If you consent."

"It's your house, dear, and I decided a long time ago that being a householder in a big city was more headache than pleasure. We could still keep my little house in Safe Harbor—no fear of squatters—if you want a pied-à-terre. We won't do it quite as you described it but you can give your house to Shorty if you wish to. I'll get Alec to work out a plan. But I wonder if Shorty can cope with it? Squatters might still move in on him—or rioters break in and wreck the place."

"Oh. That fits in with the other half of my idea: What to do about our too-faithful retainers. Offer any with twenty years or close to it retirement at full pay. Encourage the in-house guards and maintenance men to work for the trust, same pay—because you're right; if we hand an illit a place like that, with no one to keep him straight, he'll soon have a shell, not a church. Father Hugo is the best bodyguard I've ever seen . . . but he's a child of God and unsophisticated about management. He needs a practical, cynical man as his in-house steward. Cunningham. Or O'Neil. Or Mentone. Alec can work it out. Jake, I want to hand over to Shorty a complete plant, subsidized and maintained, so that he can put his mind solely on preaching and praying and soul-saving. I think you know why." (I think *I* know why, Boss—but any of the four would have killed that mugger.) (We've managed to thank the other three, beloved—and will go on thanking them. Father Hugo is a special case.)

"Eunice, do you really think Hugo saves souls?"

"I haven't the slightest idea, Jacob; I don't know Who is in charge of this world. Even if what Hugo does has no more real meaning than our 'prayer meetings,' it's still worthwhile. Darling, this is a screwed-up world. Back in the days of the Model-T Ford the United States was a fine country, brimming with hope. But today the best thing most young people can do is stay home, sit still, not get involved, and chant Om Mani Padme Hum—and it *is* the best thing most of them are capable of doing, the world being what it is now; it's far better than dropping out or turning on with drugs. When meditation and a meaningless prayer are better than most action open to them, then what Hugo has to offer is good in the same way. Even if his theology is a hundred percent wrong. But I don't think Father Hugo is any more mistaken than the most learned theologian and he might be closer to the truth. Jacob, I don't think *anyone* knows Who's in charge."

"Just wondered, my dear. Sometimes pregnant women get taken with fancies."

"I'm pregnant down *here*, dearest; up *here* is still old Johann. Protects me somewhat, I think." (Oh, you think so, huh? Boss, if you didn't have me to keep you straight, you'd
459

be as filled with vapors as a cat trying to have kittens in a wastebasket! Remember, I've been through this before.) (I know you have, darling, and that's why I'm not afraid—otherwise I'd be scared silly.) (No worse than having a tooth drilled, Boss; we're built for this. Roomy.) "Jake, did I ever tell you about the time I went into politics?"

"Didn't know you ever had and can't imagine it, Eunice."

"Imagine it for 'Johann,' not for 'Eunice.' Forty years back I let them persuade me that it was my 'duty.' I was easy to persuade—but I realize now that my attraction to the Party was that I could pay for my campaign in a district they were going to lose anyhow. But I learned things, Jake. Learned that being a businessman has nothing to do with being a politician and even less to do with being a statesman. They *clobbered* me, Jake!—and I've never been tempted to save the world since. Maybe someone can save this addled planet but *I* don't know how and now I *know* that I don't know. That's something even if it isn't much. Jake, I could worry about Smith Enterprises when I was running it. I can worry now about sixty-odd people and make sure they're each all right insofar as money can insure it. But no one can solve things for seven billion people; they won't let you. You go nutty with frustration if you try. Nor can you do much for three hundred million, not when the real problem—as you pointed out—is the very fact that there *are* three hundred million of them. I can't see *any* solution short of compulsory sterilization—and the solution strikes me as worse than the disease. Licensing without sterilization hasn't solved it."

Her husband shook his head. "And won't, Eunice. Licensing is a joke; it has more loopholes than the tax laws. Compulsory methods inevitably involve political tests—no, thanks, I prefer the Four Horsemen. And the only effect that voluntary contraception has ever had has been to change the ratio, unfavorably, between the productive and the parasites; the population climbs anyhow. If we were as hard-boiled about weeding the culls as China is, it might not work that way. But we aren't, we never have been—and I'm not sure I'd like it if we were."

"Then there isn't any solution."

"Oh, there is, I mentioned it. The Four Horsemen. They never sleep, they're never off duty. And *there*." He pointed at the Moon. "Eunice, I suspect that our race's tragedy has been played endless times. It may be that an intelligent race has to expand right up to its disaster point to achieve what is needed to break out of its planet and reach for the stars. It may always—or almost always—be a photo finish, with the outcome uncertain to the last moment. Just as it is with us. It may take endless wars and unbearable population pressure to force-feed a technology to the point where it can cope with space. In the universe, space travel may be the normal birth pangs of an otherwise dying race. A test. Some races pass, some fail."

She shivered. "Gruesome."

"Yes. And no way to talk to a gal in what used to be called a 'delicate condition.' Sorry, darling."

"A gruesome thought at any time, Jake. I'm *not* in a 'delicate condition.' I'm doing what this body is designed for. Building a baby. Feels *good*. I'm enjoying it."

"So it appears and that makes me happy. But, Eunice, before you shut down your house and move into a yacht, I must mention one thing. I think you must put it off until you've had this baby."

"Why, Jake? No morning sickness. I doubt if seasickness will be a problem."

"Because you *are* in a delicate condition, no matter how good it feels. I'd feel happier if you were never more than five minutes from medical attention. You'd be okay at home; Bob and Winnie are there. You're okay here—a hotel resident physician and a good one—believe me, I checked on him—and a modern hospital over there, in sight. But at *sea*? Suppose you had a seven-month preemie? We'd lose the baby and probably you, too. No, Eunice."

"Oh." (Eunice, any point in telling him that you carried your first one full term and no trouble?) (No, twin. How are you going to prove it? If you mention me *now*, you're just a female with pregnancy delusions. Boss, this is one argument you're going to lose. So concede it at once. Fall back and find another route.) "Jacob, I can't argue. I lost my first

461

wife with her first baby; I know it can happen. But what would you think of this? Could you persuade Roberto and Winnie to come with us? Then not go very far to sea. If we were anchored where that trimaran is, that hospital could be just as close . . . and Roberto would be aboard. This hotel physician must be all right as you have checked on him but I would rather have Roberto. He knows me inside and out. And never mind wisecracks; I mean as my physician. Or does the fact that you know that Roberto has slept with me make him unacceptable to you as my O.B. man?" (Whew! Twin, that was a foul blow.) (Oh, pooh, Eunice, I'm just confusing the issue.)

Jake Salomon cocked one eyebrow and grinned down at her. "Little one, you can't embarrass me that easily. If Bob is the baby-cotcher you want, I'll do my best to persuade him . . . as long as *you* don't mind Bob's wife being around."

"Pooh to you, sir. If you and Winnie want to stroll down memory's lane, I'll tuck you in and kiss you good-night. She's certain to console you while I'm benched—and you'll need it."

"Thereby giving you carte blanche later. A woman almost always falls in love with the doctor who delivers her first baby."

"Pooh again. I've loved Roberto a long time and you know it. Are you jealous, Jacob?"

"No. Just curious. I suppose that injunction you laid on me on our wedding day still applies? It occurs to me that, with respect to the day you mentioned, Bob had opportunity before, during, and after."

"Is that all it takes, dear? Just opportunity?" (Just about, twin!) She grinned at him and wrinkled her nose. "Sweetheart, all I will admit is the possibility that Roberto's name might be in the hat. But it could have been Finchley. Or Hubert. Or dear Judge Mac. You and Alec were awfully busy that day—but I think you'll find that Mac adjourned court at his usual hour . . . and I wasn't home until much later."

"Is that a confession?"

"Well, there might be a confession in there *somewhere*."

"Quit pulling my leg, my love. There are only two sorts of wives. Those who cheat, and those who have their husbands' friendly cooperation, in which case—"

"Isn't there a third sort?"

"Eh? Oh, you mean *faithful* wives. Oh, certainly. So I've heard. But in my twenty years of general practice, much of it divorce cases, I encountered so few of *that* sort—none I felt certain about—that I cannot venture an opinion. Wives technically faithful form so small a part of the sample that I can't evaluate them. People being what they are, a rational man should be satisfied if his meals are on time and his dignity not affronted. What I was trying to say is, that if you ever want my friendly cooperation, don't assault my credibility with a wet firecracker such as Hubert. Judge Mac I could believe. Tom Finchley is a very masculine person too, and one who bathes regularly—even though he sometimes abuses the sacred English tongue in a manner which causes me to flinch. Bob Garcia shows your good taste. But, *please*, darling, don't expect me to believe that Hubert's name could be in the hat." (Twin, Jake knows us too well. Better not try to fool him too much.) (Ever hear of a 'red herring,' love?)

"Very well, sir; I'll take Hubert's name out of the hat. That still leaves endless possibilities, does it not? And I will try always to respect your dignity. But, speaking of meals on time, I had better get busy or your dinner will be late."

"Why not just cold cuts and such when we feel like it and heat a tin of soup? I was thinking of a nap."

"Shall I join you, sir?"

"I said 'nap,' sweetheart. Sleep. A nap with you is not restful. Old Señor Jacob needs a siesta."

"Yes, sir. May I finish quickly what I was saying? We can take care of anyone who wants to retire, or wants another job, or wishes to stay on with Hugo. But I am hoping that some of them might come with us as crew in our trimaran or whatever. Especially if they've been to sea before and know something about it."

"Finchley does. He was sent up for smuggling or some such."

"I was hoping that all of my mobiles except Hugo—and

463

Rockford, if you want him—might decide to sail with us. They are all strong and able, and not much family problem. Fred's wife split some months back, Dabrowski has no children at home, and Olga might be willing to be a chambermaid—stewardess, I should say—if she likes to sail; she's insisted on doing most of the cleaning and such here even though she doesn't have to. As for the Finchleys, Tom is just what we need—it wasn't smuggling drugs; they were running arms into Central America as I recall, and he was first mate—and Hester Finchley is a good cook. Eve is no problem, she already knows how to read and write and do arithmetic—and if they tell her about this, she'll be teasing her parents to take the job; all kids want to travel. Dear? If you are going in, would you see who's on guard at the lift, and ask him to dig out Finchley? He may know something about trimarans."

"I think he has the watch now. Shall I chuck you a robe?"

"Am I getting too much sun? Doesn't feel so; I've been using the lotion. *Oh!* You mean for Thomas the Tom Cat? But, dear, we've been swimming with him and his family every day. As well as with Fred and the Dabrowskis."

"I don't give a hoot, dear, but I thought you were anxious to preserve appearances."

"Seems silly when I swim and sunbathe with all of them. As for appearances, didn't I see you patting Hester's bottom in the pool yesterday? Or was it Wednesday?"

"It was Tuesday and it wasn't Hester, it was her daughter Eve. Just practicing to be a sex maniac, Beautiful—nothing serious. So don't be jealous."

"Beloved, the day I'm jealous of a little girl I want you to beat me. Not spank me. Beat some sense into me, woodshed style. But it was Hester, not her daughter. My gallant, wonderful Jacob would never bother a little girl."

"Perhaps not but that little girl bothers the hell out of *me*. Furthermore she does it on purpose."

"Poor Jake. Even thirteen-year-olds won't leave him alone. I'm not surprised; I didn't leave him alone, either."

"In this case, she's thirteen-going-on-twenty-one. I'll make you a deal, dearest. I'll carefully avoid chaperoning you with her father if you will be *very* careful *always* to chaperon me with his daughter."

"Yes, sir. To hear is to obey, my lord—though I am chagrined that you think I might need chaperoning—or not chaperoning, as the case may be—with one of our servants. But how about Hester? Must I always be sure to be in sight when she's around?"

"Mind your own business, wench. Uh, no need to be fanatical about it. I want them all to feel easy when they come up here to swim as I don't want *any* of our household ever to swim in that sewage down there. You know the coliform count in that beautiful surf. That was the deal we offered—stay off the beaches entirely and they could swim in our pool at any time. So we sacrifice a little privacy but don't have one of them picking up amebiasis or such and spreading it through our whole family. It evens out—and they are all nice people . . . even our precocious Eve who's doing her best to see if she can upset me."

"I haven't minded, Jacob; it is not good to be too much alone. But we were speaking of Hester's bottom. Shapely, huh?"

"Hon, you're as bad as Eve. I'm going to go and say ten Money Hums and catch that siesta. I'll send out Tom. Don't let me sleep more than an hour. Kiss."

She turned her face up. As he left she dived in, swam a couple of lengths and climbed out, was waiting, staring down at the yacht harbor when Finchley arrived. "You sent for me, Ma'am?"

She smiled. "Thomas Cattus, that's not my name when we're alone."

He glanced over his shoulder, said almost soundlessly, "Pussy Cat, the Boss is awake."

"So he is. But he's gone to his room and closed the door. Siesta. He'll be asleep in almost no time. But I don't mean to scare you, Thomas Cattus dear. Come here to the rail, want to show you something. Have you done any sailing? Or has it all been power?"

"Sailing? Oh, sure, I grew up on Chesapeake Bay. Cat boats and such."

"Ever sail a trimaran?"

"Never skippered one. Crewed in one when I was sixteen."

"What do you think of them?"

"Depends on what for. Okay if you want something more like a houseboat than a racer. But I wouldn't have one without an auxiliary engine. In tight waters they can be as awkward as two people in a bathtub."

"Ever try it in a bathtub, Thomas Cattus?"

"Sure, who hasn't? Okay for a giggle with a few drinks aboard. But a bed is better. Or a floor."

"How about a sunbathing mat?"

"Pussy Cat, you *enjoy* scaring me. You gonna get us caught, yet."

"Rhetorical question, dear; I wasn't twisting your arm. Tell me, do you think Hester and Jake have ever made it?"

"Practically certain they never." He grinned at her. "But I can tell you something."

"Then do. Pretty please. Pretty Tom Cat with the muscles."

"Not Hester's fault they haven't. I know. She told me bang, one night, while we were at it. Said the Boss could have it any time he reached for it. Hester thinks the Boss is God's right hand."

"Well, so do I. But it doesn't keep me from appreciating my Thomas Cat. How would you feel about it? Jake and Hester."

"Me?" He looked astonished. "Look, Pussy Cat, you know if anybody does I don't see no sense in putting a fence around a broad. Just makes her want to jump it. I'd ruther hold open the gate for her, she wants to."

"I said, 'How would *you* feel about it, dear?' "

"Oh." Her driver-guard looked thoughtful. "Wouldn't get my nose out of joint. The Boss is numero uno, da kine. Rozzer?"

"Roz."

"He knocked up a broad, he'd pay. No huhu. But no huhu anyhow; we were only licensed for one and Hester had herself fixed, right after she had Eve. Good broad I married—didn't split when I dropped one, took me back when I was paroled. Oh, she shacked, sure—but just with

466

her boss, she worked. Didn't peddle it. Or kept it to herself, didn't tell me. Hester and the Boss? Sure, if they want to. Told her so, bang. Have fun, I told her."

"Mmm . . . Thomas Cattus, let's give them a chance. Or six chances. Might be insurance for us, later."

He nodded thoughtfully. "Smart thinking, Pussy Cat. But how? And would he? The Boss?"

"I feel sure he would if he knew it was safe. Private, I mean; Jake has courage under fire, just as you have, dear. Main problem is to get Eve out from underfoot. Mmm . . . you could take me shopping or such and I could ask Hester to get Mr. Salomon's lunch . . . then as an afterthought I could invite Eve to come with me. Hmm?"

"With either Fred or Ski up here? No good, Pussy Cat."

"All it needs is a time when you have the guard. Jake won't send for your relief; at most he'll lock open the lift door. He doesn't worry about *him*, he worries about guarding *me*."

"Mmm . . . roz. Could work if he wants it. You're filling out, Pussy Cat. Tits prettier than ever."

"Joe says a woman gets prettier as she bigs out. But I don't think many men think so."

"Hester looked awful cute, clear up to the last minute. And on you it looks good, too. Uh . . . you're sure the Boss is asleep?"

"Certain enough that I'm willing to risk it. But I *don't* mean to scare you, dear. Want to wait and see how our plans for Jake and Hester work out?"

"Uh . . . oh, hell, we might all be dead by then."

"Right here?"

"Uh, copter might cruise by."

"Let's go into the lanai."

27

Harvard University Corporation voted to withhold all funds until the Student Government selected a new university president. Both of the rival student governments and the faculty senate sought court relief from this "reckless and irresponsible action." CONS BEST COPS SEZ FUZZ PREZ—the General Secretary of the Private Police, Guards, and Security Drivers (AFL) at its annual banquet congratulated Milwaukee on joining the growing list of municipalities that had abolished the "clean record" rule in hiring peace officers. "The outstanding success of parolees and probationers as licensed private security officers is finally teaching the politicians to 'hunt ducks where the ducks are.' The Bible says 'To catch a thief you set a thief,' don't it? Who knows more about hoods than a hood? Give a man incentives to keep his nose clean and put him on work he understands and you can count on him in the crunch. My Mom kept telling me that when I was just a punk knockin' over candy stores. Besides, like the Sec'etary of the Treasury told us earlier tonight, '*Look* what it's done for the economy!' In this *great* republic—"

"Today's Day" newscast interviewed a midwife who claimed to have delivered Miss Molly Maguire of child ten days *before* her sensational two-nation sky dive. The sensie star promptly sued newscaster, station, and videonet.

The Lunar Commission made permanent its trial policy of screening out-migration solely on physical and mental examination with no percentage points either plus or minus from past record. The Director said: "In a new world a man must start with a clean slate. No other policy is practical." Under sharp questioning he admitted that contributions for unsubsidized vocations remained unchanged but insisted that this was a fiscal matter controlled by the condominium governments and in no way affected the basic principle. HOT WORDS IN CAP-PUN DEBATE: " '—does not deter!' So he tells us. Is the Senator from the great State of Puerto Rico aware that our major problem is recidivism? Can the Senator cite *one case* in which a killer committed still another murder *after* he was executed?"

"*Whee!* Joe, see how she runs before the wind!"

"Swell."

"Gets me clear down in my gizzard," Joan Eunice said happily. "Let's go aft. Winnie's got the wheel and be sure to be impressed; she's proud as can be that Tom has let her go on the watch list. She's a natural sailor, salt water in her veins. Gigi, what's the matter, dear? You aren't smiling. Feeling queasy?"

"Uh, a little, maybe."

"I must admit that the 'Pussy Cat' does have a rocking-horse motion when she's running free. Love it myself but some don't. Never mind, dear; Doctor Roberto has a surefire pill for tipsy tummy. I'll fetch you one and in five minutes the motion won't bother you and you'll be hungry as a horse."

"I don't take pills, Joan. I'm all right."

"You aren't all right and when we go below you won't want lunch and Hester told me she was fixing something special in your honor. Look, darling, Roberto feeds these pills to *Winnie*—one before breakfast every day and he had her on them for morning sickness before they came aboard. He's a careful doctor, hon; he wouldn't give them to his own wife if they could hurt. Nobody ever gets a pill of any sort in the 'Pussy Cat' unless our ship's surgeon dispenses it. Pretty please? Huh?"

"Gigi."

"Yes, Joe."

"Take pill."

"Yes, Joe. Thanks, Joan, I do feel fluttery. I guess you think I'm silly but I've seen so many kids hooked on pills I'm scared of 'em."

"I don't like pills but I take 'em when Doctor Roberto says to. He's got me on supplements right now for this little monster inside me. You stay up here in the breeze, dear, while I find Roberto."

" 'Sailing, sailing, over the bounding main!' " Mr. Jacob Salomon bellowed, as he swung up into the control console. "Morning, Ski."

"Good morning, Captain. On port tack with basic course one five—"

"I see what it is. Beat it down below and get your breakfast." Salomon slid into the saddle and glanced at the compass as he took the wheel. "We didn't leave you anything but you can scrounge ship's biscuit out of the lifeboat."

"Hester won't let me starve, sir."

"Nor Olga. Now beat it." Jake eyed his sails, decided he could point a touch higher, reached out with his right hand to the running rigging controls, kept tapping a switch to shorten his main sheet, his eye on her mainsail, while he handled the wheel by touch till he had her settled down on a tighter tack. Then he adjusted his jibs and relaxed.

"Good morning, Captain."

"Tom, save that for witnesses. It's all very well for Mrs.

471

Salomon to want me dubbed with an honorary title but we all know who's the sailing master by our ship's papers. You're skipper and have the responsibility; I'm just the owner and unlicensed first mate. Eunice ought not to do it—but we have to cater to the little darlings. Speaking of little darlings, how are your two this fine morning? Didn't see Eve at breakfast."

"She ate before you got up, sir. Seen her and told her she's goin' to have to wear pants from now on, except in the pool or near it."

"Don't see why she should, the other gals don't unless it happens to suit them. I just don't want her swarming into my lap, naked as an eel and twice as lively. Gives me delusions of youth."

"I'll clamp down on her, sir."

"Tom, I *don't* want the child 'clamped down on.' I want everybody to enjoy this cruise—one big happy family. Ask Hester to tell her quietly that old Uncle Jake loves her but doesn't like to be pawed. A lie, that last, but an official lie. Speaking of the pool, how's the filter?"

"Filter's okay, was just a clog in makeup feed line. Kelp. No huhu."

"Has the surgeon tested the water?"

"Safe."

"That's good. Tom, when I was a kid, striking for quartermaster third, we used to swim off the boat booms and thought nothing of it. But today even the Pacific Ocean can't soak up all the crud they dump into it. You can put swimming call on the bull horn and take the Skull-and-Crossbones sign off the pool."

"Aye, aye, sir."

"Half a second while I make eight bells." Jake reached out with his left hand, picked the last touchplate of a row of eight; the quadruple double *Bong!* marking the beginning of the forenoon watch rang through the vessel. He then picked still another touchplate and sounded swimming call himself. "Tom, if a man didn't have to eat or sleep, he could sail this wagon around the world by himself. Three men could do it easily. Even two."

"Maybe."

"You sound doubtful, Tom."

"Even one man could, sir—if nothin' never went wrong. Something always does."

"I stand corrected. And with two pregnant women aboard—three if you don't keep a close eye on Eve—"

"Oh, Dr. Garcia got her on the junior pill. I don't take no chances, sir."

"So? Tom, my respect for you—high—has just increased. She's safe from her Uncle Jacob . . . but I make no promises about any other male in this bucket. There is something in salt air that hikes up the metabolism. And there is much truth in the old saw about 'when they're big enough, they're old enough and nothing can be done about it.' Better to roll with the punch."

"She is and she has and we did—I had this here talk with the Doc. Hester and me don't expect no more from Eve different than we did ourselves. Anybody knows when a broad starts getting broad she's goin' to land on her back."

"Yes, everybody knows it—yet most parents don't believe it when it comes to their own kids. I know, I had a family law practice for years. Tom, you're such an all-around sensible man I'm surprised that you ever got in trouble."

His sailing master shrugged. "Comes o' believing what I was told, sir. 'M chief officer of this rust bucket and Captain says keep my lip tight and see nothin' and we make ten times as much on one voyage. All fixed. Only he got smart and hung onto the bribe money hisself. Thought he could run it in the dark. You'da thought he'd never heard of radar. *Wham!* Coast Guard." Finchley shrugged again. "No complaints, sir, I was a fool. But two years and four months and I get this much better job driving for Mr. Smith-as-was. Smellin' like a rose. Not so trusting now, is all. Don't trust too much, you don't get your ass burned."

"Yet you don't seem cynical. Tom, I think the major problem in growing up is to become sophisticated without becoming cynical."

"That's over my head, Counselor. I just think people are okay, mostly—even that silly skipper—if you don't strain 'em more than they're built for. Like that piece of standing

473

rigging there. Rated three tons. Pro'ly take five and no trouble. *Don't* put six tons on it."

"We've said the same thing, I think, but your illustration is vivid. Beat it, Tom. If there's no work to be done, grab sack time. Or pool time."

"Yes, sir. I want to inspect the starboard hull; it's making extra water. Pump can handle it but I want to know *why*." He touched his cap and swung down off the platform.

Jake cocked his own cap against the sun, relaxed and started to sing:

" 'A sailor's wife a sailor's star shall be!

" 'Yo ho, we go, across the sea!

" 'A sailor's wife a sailor's star shall be,

" 'A sailor's wife his star . . . shall *be*!"

His wife climbed up behind him and kissed the back of his neck. "Is that for me, dear? Or for 'Nancy Lee'?"

"Always for you, my darling. Besides, I can't remember the part with 'Nancy Lee' in it."

"I wonder if you ever remember a girl's name. You call all of us 'darling.' "

"Merely because it's true. But *you* are the only one I call *'my darling.'* And I do remember your name—it's 'Salomon.' "

"Jacob, you must have been a prime menace when you were a bluejacket. With that Hebrew blarney you could talk your way into anything. Then out of it, with no trouble."

"No, Ma'am, I was a sweet, innocent lad. I simply followed the ancient code of the sea: 'When the hook's up, all bills are paid.' "

"Leaving little Jewish bastards behind in every port . . . and thereby improving the breed. How about Gigi? Going to improve the breed there?" She dug her thumb into a spot over his hip where his slight pot bulged out from sitting "Some dish, eh, keed?"

"Madam," he said haughtily, "I do not know what you are talking about."

" 'Tell that to the Marines, the old sailors won't believe you.' Jacob my love, I feel certain that you know the second Mrs. Branca almost as well as you knew the first. But I have no wish to prove it; I simply offer my congratulations. Gigi

474

is a darling, I love her to pieces. I was not throwing asparagus." (Tell him she squeals, twin.) (I will not!)

"Woman, you get your exercise jumping at conclusions."

(Then tell him it happened where Troy Avenue crosses Gay Street, near the Square—a neighborhood *you* know well, twin.) (Eunice, I want Jacob to feel easy about such things—I am *not* trying to harpoon him.) (You aren't equipped to, Joan; Jake is the original Captain Ahab.) (Eunice, you have a dirty mind.) (*Whose* mind? I don't have one. Don't need one.)

Mrs. Salomon dropped the subject, opened her sextant case, took it out.

"Will you give me a time tick, darling?"

"Are you going to shoot the defenseless Sun?"

"I'm going to do better than a Sun sight, dearest. The Sun, the upper limb of the Moon, and—if I'm lucky and can spot it again—Venus, for a three-star fix. Want to bet on how small a triangle I get?"

"Even money on fifty miles for the short side."

"Beast. Brute. Cad. And me an expectant mother. I was more than ten times that close yesterday evening; I'm getting the hang of it. I *could* cheat—I could get a point fix by querying Point Loma, then fudge it on the chart."

"Eunice, why this passion to emulate Bowditch? One would think that radio and satellites and the like had never been invented."

"It's fun, darling. I'm going to hit that nav exam for a flat four-oh and get my limited license. After I've unloaded this pup in the hopper and we no longer have to stick to coastal waters, I'm going to do a 'Day's Work' every day all the way to Hawaii. Betcha I make landfall at Hilo under three miles. Oh, it's not necessary, dear—but what if it turned out to be? Suppose war broke out and everything went silent? Might help to have a celestial navigator aboard. Tom admits that he's hardly taken a sight since he got his mate's ticket."

"If he ever took one. Yes, it could be useful, my darling . . . because if war broke out in earnest and we were at sea, we would not go on to Hilo. We would make a sharp left turn and go south and get lost. The Marquesas. Or farther south, the farther the better. That way our kid might live through it. Easter Island if you think you can hit it."

"Jacob, by then I'll split it right down the middle. Or any island you pick. Sweetheart, I wasn't playing games when I asked for the whole old-fashioned works—all the charts, all the pilots, three key-wind chronometers and a hack, this lovely sextant and a twin like it in case I drop this one . . . and please note that I *always* put the lanyard around my neck. All the H.O.s and the Almanac. I'm no use as a deckhand now—so I decided to become a *real* navigator. Just in case, just in case."

"Mmm. My darling, I hope we never have to run for it . . . but have *you* noticed that I keep this vessel fully stocked at all times even though we anchor almost every night and can shop for supplies any time we wish?"

"I've noticed, sir."

"Nor is it an accident that I gave Doctor Bob an unlimited budget and saw to it that he equipped for any conceivable obstetrical problem."

"I did not notice that, quite."

"You weren't meant to, nor was Winnie—no need to give you gals something to worry about. But since you have been doing the same sort of planning ahead, I decided to tell you. Bob used the time the 'Pussy Cat' was being refitted in taking a refresher in O.B. And he spent twenty times more money on our sick bay than one would expect for a seagoing yacht."

"I'm pleased to hear it, sir. With such foresight, money can do almost anything. Except turn back the clock."

"It even did *that* in your case, beloved."

"No, Jacob. It gave me added years . . . and this wonderful body . . . and *you*. But it did *not* turn back the clock. I'm still almost a century old. I can never *feel* young the way I once did—because I'm *not*. Not the way Winnie is young. Or Gigi. Jacob, I have learned that I don't *want* to be young."

"Eh? Are you unhappy, dear?"

"Not at all! I have the best of two worlds. A youthful, vital body that makes every breath a sensuous joy . . . and a century of rich experience, with the wisdom—if that is the right word—that age brings. The calmness. The long perspective. Winnie and Gigi still suffer the storms of youth . . . which I don't have and don't want. I've forgotten the last time I had a tranquilizer but I think it was the day they unstrapped me. Jacob, I'm a better wife for you than either of those two lovely girls could be; I'm older than you are, I've been where you are now and understand it. I'm not boasting, dear; it's simply true. Nor would *I* be happy married to a young man—I'd have to spend my time trying desperately not to upset his delicate, youthful, unstable balance. We're good for each other, Jacob."

"I know that you are good for me, my darling."

"I know I am. But sometimes you have trouble remembering that I am *not* truly 'Eunice,' but 'Johann.' " (Hey! What is this, Boss? We're *both*.) (Yes, beloved, always—but Jake needs to be reminded of Johann—because all he ever *sees* is Eunice.) "For example, Jacob, a while ago you thought I was twitting you about Gigi."

" 'Thought,' hell—you *were*."

"No, dear. Close your eyes and forget that I have Eunice's voice. Think back at least ten years when I was still in passable health. If your older friend Johann had twigged that you had kicked the feet out from under some young and pretty woman, would he have twitted you?"

"Huh? Hell, yes. Johann would have slipped me the needle and broken it off."

"Would I have, Jacob? Did I *ever*?"

"You never caught me."

"So? I might have congratulated you, Jacob, just as I did today—had I felt that I could do so without offending you. But I would *not* have twitted you. Do you recall a young woman whose first name was—or is—Marian? Last name had the initial 'H'—your pet name for her, 'Maid Marian.' "

"How in the *hell*?"

"Steady, darling—you let your helm fall off. That was sixteen years ago, just before I asked you to spend all your time on my affairs. So I ordered a fresh snoopsheet on you before I put the deal up to you. May I say that the fact that you had dealt so carefully with *her* reputation was a strong factor in my deciding that *I* could trust you with anything,

477

too?—including my power of attorney, which you have held ever since and never abused. May I add, too, that I *wanted* to congratulate you on both your good taste and your success as a Lothario?—for of course I then had to have *her* snooped, too, and her husband as well, before I could entrust *my* grisly secrets to you. But—also of course—I could not say a word."

"I didn't think any part of that ever showed."

"Please, Jacob. Do you recall that you once told Eunice that you could hire a man to photograph her in her own bath—and she would never know it? As we've noted, money can do almost anything that is physically possible. Part of that snoop report was a photograph of you and Marian in what you lawyers call a 'compromising position.' "

"Good God! What did you do with it?"

"Burned it. Hated to; it was a good picture and Marian looked awfully pretty—and you looked all right yourself, you lovable old goat. Then I sent for the head of the snoop firm and told him I wanted the negative and *all* prints *now* and no nonsense—and if it ever turned out that even one print had escaped me, I would break him. Get his license, bankrupt him, put him in jail. Were you or Marian ever embarrassed by such a picture? Blackmail, or anything?"

"No. Not me—and I'm morally certain she wasn't, either."

"I guess he believed me. Jacob, do you still think I was twitting you about Gigi? Or was I congratulating you?"

"Uh . . . maybe neither. Maybe trying to wring a confession out of me. It's no go, wench."

"Please, Jacob. Stipulating that I was mistaken but sincere—which was it? Now that you know how I behaved about Marian."

"Eunice—*Johann!* You should have been a lawyer. Subject to that stipulation, I concede that it must have been a sincere congratulation. But one I can't accept, I haven't earned it. Now, damn it, tell me how you came by this delusion."

"Yes, dear. But not this minute; there comes Gigi herself." Joan put her sextant back into its box. "Sights will have to wait anyhow; this reach has taken us in so close I've lost my horizon for the Sun. Hi, Gigi, you pretty, pretty thing! Give us a kiss. Just me, Jake is on watch."

"I'm not all that busy. Eunice, hold the wheel." He accepted a kiss while still seated, then took the helm back from his wife.

Joan said, "Been swimming, dear?"

"Uh, yes. Joan Eunice, could I see you a minute? Mr. Salomon, would you excuse us?"

"Not by that moniker I won't; you'll have to call me 'Jake.' "

"Stuff it, dear," his wife said cheerfully. "She wants a hen conference. Come along, dear. Captain, try to keep us afloat."

They found a spot in the lee of the lifeboat. "Got troubles, dear?" (Eunice, are we about to have a beef over Jake? Surely not!) (Can't be, twin. That affair started over two weeks ago . . . and both Gigi and Joe were relaxed about it from scratch. Which means just what we thought: It actually is a return engagement—and Jake lied to protect a lady's reputation. Predictable.)

"Well, sort of," admitted Mrs. Branca. "Uh, might as well say it bang. Next time you anchor and send a boat in . . . Joe and I want off."

"Oh, dear! What's wrong, Gigi? I did so hope you would stay at least the month we talked about—then as much longer as you wished."

"Well . . . we did expect to. But I got this seasickness problem and Joe—well, he *has* done some painting but . . . the light's not right; it's too bright and . . ." She trailed off. (Twin, those are excuses.) (Jake?) (Can't be, I tell you. You've got to make her come clean.)

"Gigi."

"Yes, Joan?"

"Look at me. You haven't missed a meal since Roberto put you on the seasick pill. If Joe prefers floodlights to sunlight, we'll clear out the dining saloon and it can be his studio. Put your arms around me and tell me what's *really* wrong."

"Uh—Joan, the ocean's just too darn *big!*" Gigi blinked tears and said, "I guess you think I'm a baby."

"No. It's big. Biggest ocean in the world. Some people don't like oceans. I do. That doesn't mean *you* have to."

"Well, I *thought* I would like it. I mean, you hear about it. What a wonderful thing it is to make an ocean trip. But it *scares* me. Uh, it scares Joe, too; he just doesn't say so. Joan Eunice, you've been awful good to us—but this isn't our scene. Joe and I, we aren't fish—we're alley cats. Always lived in cities. It's too *quiet* here. Especially at night. At night the quiet is so loud it wakes me up."

Joan kissed her. "All right, darling. I knew you weren't having quite the happy time I wanted you to have. Didn't know why. I'll have to visit you at your place—where it's nice for all of us. *I* don't like the city, it scares *me*. But I like it, loads, in your studio—as long as I don't have to go outside. But is that *all* that's wrong? Has anyone upset you? Or Joe?"

"Oh, no! Everybody's been swell."

"You called Jake 'Mr. Salomon.' "

"That was because I was upset—knowing I had to tell you."

"Then you both feel easy with Jake? I know he's impressive, he even impresses *me*. Nothing uptight there?"

"Oh, not a bit! Uh, knowing we were walking out on Jake upset us as much as knowing we were walking out on you."

"Then may Jake and I *both* come visit you? Stay a few days?" (Will she duck this, Eunice?) (Why ask me, Boss? You just asked *her*.)

Mrs. Branca dropped her eyes, then looked up and said bluntly, "You mean a Quartet? All the way?"

"All the way."

"Well, *we* would, I guess you know that. But how about Jake?"

"Well? How about Jake, Gigi? *You* tell *me*."

"Uh, Jake is relaxed with *us*. But he's a little uptight

when you're around, seems like. Joan Eunice, you caught on. Didn't you? Or you wouldn't have braced me for a Quartet."

"I caught on, dear. It's all *right*. No huhu."

"I *told* Jake I thought you had. He said, Oh, no, impossible, you slept like a log."

"I do except that I've reached the point in pregnancy where I sometimes get up to pee. But that wasn't it—Jake could be most anywhere if he's not in bed and I never check on him. What I spotted wasn't proof. Just that a man has a way of looking at a woman he's sure of. And vice versa. Nothing anybody could object to. Just 'not uptight' describes it as well as any. I'm not even mildly jealous of Jake, it simply pleased me. Knowing how sweet you can be for a man—remember, I used to *be* a man—"

"I know. But I don't really believe it."

"I have to believe it and can't ever forget it. Knowing you, I felt smugly pleased for my husband. Tell me, have you made a Three Circle with Jake? Money Hum?"

"Oh, yes, always!"

"Next time—at your studio—it will be a Four Circle. Then our Quartet will harmonize perfectly and no one will ever be uptight again."

"Yes. *Yes!*"

"In the meantime you're not going to have to put up with this great big scary ocean even one more night. We won't anchor, I'll have Tom call for a copter—say for right after lunch. It'll put you down at La Jolla International and you'll jet straight home—copter pilot will see to things for you and Tom will have your reservations—and you'll be home and flashing a pack in your own studio before you can say 'Time Zone.' Feel better?"

"Uh, I feel like a heel but—yes, I do. Oh, golly, Joan, I'm so *homesick!*"

"You'll be home today. I'm going to find Tom and have him get things rolling. Then I'll go tell Jake—and tell him why, he'll understand—and relieve him at the wheel, and tell him he can find you in your stateroom. If you have the nerve of a mouse, little alley cat from the big city, you'll bolt the door and tell him good-bye properly. Uh—Troy? Or twosome?"

"Oh. Troy. Of course."

"Then find Joe and tell him. Ten minutes, maybe fifteen. But Gigi—that painting of Eve. I must buy it."

"No, we'll give it to you."

"We settled that long ago. Joe can give me anything else, but not paintings. I must pay for it because I want it to be a present from me to my husband. Now kiss me and run, dear."

The *Pussy Cat* with her sails dowsed rocked gently on a light sea. Fifty feet above her tallest stick a copter hovered while again lowering a passenger-freight basket. Tom Finchley stood far aft and coached the copter pilot with hand signals. Mr. and Mrs. Branca had already disappeared into the copter cabin, having gone up on the first trip, but their baggage was on the weather deck, waiting to be loaded.

There was quite a pile. Joan had urged them to fetch along "everything you could possibly need for a month or longer—for painting especially, as there will be lots of bodies around—and any of them will model . . . or I'll have them lashed to a grating and flogged, then make them walk the plank. Joe darling, you can do *big* romantic pix if you wish—pirate scenes with lush victims and leering scoundrels. Fun?"

She had sent the invitation by MercServ with tickets and an air-freight order and instructions to MercServ to supply a reader for the message. Joe had taken her literally; he seemed to have cleared out his studio—flood lamps, spots, easels, a heavy roll of canvas, stretchers, cameras, photo equipment and supplies, assorted impedimenta—and one bag each for clothes and personal articles. Seeing what Joe had fetched, Joan was glad that she had ordered a Brink's to get them to the jetport and was careful today to have one meet them at the far end.

The basket took up a load of baggage, came back for the last. Fred and Della's sixteen-year-old, Hank, an eager but

482

untrained deck hand, were loading, taking turns keeping the basket from spinning while the other placed items in it.

Soon they had it all in but one large case, when a gust of wind disturbed the uneasy balance between copter and surface craft. The basket swung wildly; Fred let go and danced aside while Hank went flat to the deck to keep from being hit by it.

Fred recovered and again braced the basket, now ten feet farther forward. Joan Eunice grabbed the handle of the last case, then used both hands. "Whew! I think Joe packed the anchor in this one."

Jake yelled, "*Eunice!* Don't lift that! You want to miscarry?" He grabbed it from her, started for the basket.

Hank was on his feet again. "Here, Captain, I'll get that!"

"Out of my way, son." Jake trudged to the basket, found it too high, got the case into his arms, then up onto one shoulder, placed it carefully inside—and collapsed. Joan rushed to him.

Back aft, Tom Finchley noted when the last item went in, looked up at the copter's pilot and signaled "Hoist away!" and added the hand signal for "That's all—on your way!"

Then he looked down—and started to run.

Joan sat down on the deck, took Jake's head and shoulders to her.

"Jake, Jake darling!" (Eunice! Help me!)

Fred said, "I'll get the Doc!" and rushed for a companionway. The boy stood helplessly by. Salomon gave a long bubbling sigh and all his sphincters relaxed. (Eunice! Where is he?) (Boss, I can't find him!) (You've *got* to find him! He can't be far.) (What in hell?) (Here he is, here he is! *Jake!*) (Eunice, what happened? Somebody slammed me in the side of the head with a brick.) (Does it hurt, darling?) (Of course it doesn't hurt, Boss, not now. It *can't.* Welcome aboard, Melancholy Jacques you lovin' old bastard! Oh, boy, am I glad to see you!) (Yes, welcome home, darling. My darling. Our darling.) (Eunice?) (No, *I'm* Eunice, Jock. Old cocky Jock. That's Joan. Or Johann. Or Boss. No, Joan is 'Boss' only to me; you'd better call her 'Joan.' Look, shipmates, let's get this Troy straight before we get tangled up in our feet. Joan, you call our husband 'Jake' same as always—while I'll call him 'Jock' as I used to. Jock, you call Boss either 'Joan' or 'Johann' as suits you and she's either 'Joan' or 'Boss' to me. And I'm always 'Eunice' to either of you. Got it straight?)

(I'm confused.) (No huhu, Jock beloved, never any huhu again. You'll get used to it, I did. Joan has to drive while we'll sit back and neck and give advice. Tell him, Joan.) (Yes, Jake. You have us both now. Forever.) (Om Mani Padme Hum.) (Om Mani Padme Hum. Join us, Jake. A Thanksgiving.) (Om Mani Padme Hum!) "Om Mani Padme Hum."

"Joan. Let me have him, dear." Dr. Garcia was bending over her.

She shook her head. "I'll hold him, Roberto." (Boss! Knock off the female kark and let dear Doctor work.) (Yes, Eunice. Hang on tight to Jake.) (Never fear, dear; I shall. Jock, can you see now? Out of Joan's eyes. We're going to move.) (Of course I can see. Who's that ugly old wreck? *Me!*) (Of course not; that's just something we don't need any longer. Look away, Joan; you're upsetting Jock.)

"Fred, take her below. Hank, help him. Tom, I need Winnie. Get her."

Dr. Garcia found Joan in the saloon. She was lying down, a wet cloth over her forehead, with Olga Dabrowski seated by her. Tom Finchley followed the doctor in, his face solemn. The Doctor said nothing, took Joan's wrist, glanced at his watch.

Then he said, "It's bad news, Joan."

"I know, Roberto. He was gone before I came down here. (He's *not* gone, Boss. Don't put it that way. Jock is *dead*, as dead as I am. But not *gone*. Right, Jock?) (I think you're splitting hairs, Lively Legs—) ('Lively Legs!' You haven't called me that in a *long* time.) (How about last night?) (You called *Joan* that; you didn't call *me* that, not last night.) (Will you two keep quiet? Or at least whisper? I've got to cope.)

484

(Sorry, Boss. Jock darling, whisper to me *very* quietly. Is Joan better at it than I am?) (Eunice, I can still hear you—and you have your tenses mixed.) (Boss darling, there are no tenses in the eternal Now. I asked Jock a question—and he's too chicken to answer.) (I certainly am!) (Oh, well. With my equipment and my coaching, Joan is probably adequate by now. Plus a good start—you won't believe this, Jock, but Boss has the *dirtiest* mind. That lady-lady act is just an act.) (Twin, quit trying to get my goat. I'm busy, Roberto is worried about us.) (Sorry, twin. I'll be good.)

"Eunice, I want to make one thing clear. It would not have made any difference if it had happened ashore with all possible life-support at hand. Even with Dr. Hedrick at hand. Oh, we could have kept him alive—as a vegetable. Nothing else."

"Jake never wanted that, Robert; I've heard him say so, emphatically. He never approved of the way *I* was kept alive."

"The two cases are a hundred and eighty degrees apart, Joan. Your body was worn out but your brain was in good shape. In Jake's case—well, I gave him that physical before we put to sea; his body was in fine shape, for his age. But I know what the autopsy will show: a massive rupture of a large blood vessel in his brain; he died at once. A cerebral 'accident' we call it, because it's unpredictable. If it's any consolation, he didn't suffer."

('Didn't suffer,' eh? Try it, Bob—it felt like a kick in the head by a mule. But you're right, it was just one blow. Not even a headache, afterward.) (About the same for me, Jock darling, when I got it. Boss had a much rougher time, for *years*.) (What if I had? It's over now. Darlings, *please* keep quiet—we'll talk when they let us alone.)

"Doctor, there will be no autopsy."

"Joan, there should be an autopsy for your peace of mind."

"It won't bring Jake back and he wouldn't like it. As for my 'peace of mind,' I have just one question. Was it . . . too much honeymoon?"

"Oh. No, just too many years. Joan, it wasn't even from lifting that heavy load. Let me explain this sort of 'accident.' It's like a weak spot in an old-fashioned pneumatic tire, worn almost through and ready to blow out—then *anything* can trigger it. Jake could simply have stood up, and keeled over—today, tomorrow, last week. Oh, it *can* happen during intercourse, you often hear men say they want to die 'while tearing off one last load.' But it's a horrible experience for the woman involved—and probably isn't a last orgasm anyhow, more likely he's chopped down just before it.

"Far better the way Jake got it, still virile—I assume—" (You know darn well Jock was 'still virile.' Ask your wife. Ask Gigi. Hell, ask *anybody*.) (Eunice, was my behavior *that* blatant?) (Not blatant at all, Jock you lovin' old goat. But news gets around.) "—or I should say 'I know' as I was his physician. Jake was happy and strong and virile—and then he was through, like snipping a film. Don't worry about 'too much honeymoon.' Getting married may have saved Jake years of hopeless senility. Or it may have chopped two weeks off his life as a small price for much happiness. But more likely it *extended* his life; a happy man functions better. Forget it, dear. When my time comes I hope I get it the way Jake got it—quickly, and happy to the end."

"Then there is no point in an autopsy, Roberto. Will you sign a death certificate?"

"Well . . . when death takes place not in a hospital and not under medical care, it is customary to notify the authorities and—"

"Roberto!"

"Yes, Joan?"

"You're *not* going to do that to Jake. Notify *whom*? Somebody in Washington? We're in Federal waters, and the coroner of San Diego County has no proper interest in this death. But he'd be likely to try to milk it for publicity, once he finds out who Jake is, who *I* am—and I *shan't* let that be done with Jake's death. Jake *was* under medical care—*yours!* You're our ship's surgeon. It might be that

486

you saw him die. Think about it." (Joan, don't ask Bob to lie. It doesn't matter if some coroner has his M.E. chop me up.) (I shan't permit it! Besides, Jake, I'm pregnant. Do you want me to have to go through *that*? Crowds and questions and pulling and hauling and sleepless nights?) (Mmm. . . tell him to make it an airtight lie, dear.) (Boss is a stubborn bitch, Jock—but she's usually right.))

"Hmm—" Dr. Garcia took off his stethoscope, put it aside. "Now that you mention it, there was still some heart action after I reached him. Lacking means to determine the instant of brain failure, I am forced to take cessation of heart action as the moment of death." (That boy would make a good witness, girls—come to think about it, he *did* make a good witness at the identity hearings.)

"In that case, Doctor, it seems to me that the circumstances are not open to question—and you may be sure that I will spend any amount of money to keep anyone from turning Jake's death into a circus at any later time. I would like you to certify death and the circumstances and mail a copy to whatever *Federal* authority should be notified—when next we touch shore. No copy elsewhere, we have no permanent residence other than this vessel. Oh, mail a copy to Alec Train; he has Jake's will, he'll need one for probate. And be sure to supply Captain Finchley with a duplicate original for the log."

"All right, Joan, since that's the way you want it. And I agree: Here we have a natural death and there is no point in letting bureaucrats poke around in it. But—right now I want to give you something to make you sleep. Nothing much, just a heavy dose of tranquilizer."

"Roberto, what was my pulse?"

"That's none of a patient's business, Joan."

"It was seventy-two, dead on normal—I counted my heart beats during that thirty seconds from your first glance at your watch until you let go my wrist. I need no tranquilizers."

"Joan, your heart action should be higher than normal—under the circumstances."

"Then possibly I need a stimulant, not a tranquilizer.

Roberto, you sometimes forget—even though you have been through the whole thing with me—that I am *not* a normal patient. Not a young bride subject to hysteria. Underneath I am a very old man, almost three times your age, dear . . . and I've seen everything and no shock can truly be a shock to me. Death is an old friend; I know him well. I lived with him, ate with him, slept with him; to meet him again does not frighten me—death is as necessary as birth, as happy in its own way."

She smiled. "My pulse is normal because I'm happy—happy that my beloved Jake met death so easily and happily. Oh, I'll go to my cabin and lie down; I usually nap during the heat of the afternoon. But how about Eve?"

"Eh?"

"Have you done anything about *her?* She's young, she's probably never seen death before. She almost certainly needs a tranquilizer—not I."

"Uh . . . Joan, I've been busy. But— Olga. Will you find Winnie and tell her I said that Eve was to have a minimum dose of 'Tranquille'?"

"Yes, Doctor." Mrs. Dabrowski left.

"Now, young lady, I'll take you to the cabin."

"Just a moment, Doctor. Captain, will you get way on with both sails and auxiliary, and make course for the nearest point of the seventy-five-mile limit? I want us to be in international waters before sundown."

"Aye aye, Ma'am. That would be about west by south, maybe basic course two-six-oh. I'll plot it."

"Good. Then pass the word, quietly, that burial services will be at sundown."

"Joan!"

"Roberto, do you think I would turn *Jake* over to an *undertaker?* Taxidermists! He wanted to die like his ancestors; I shall bury him like his ancestors—his dear body untouched and returned home before the sun sets."

" 'To every thing there is a season, and a time to every purpose under the heaven: A time to be born, and a time to die—' "

Joan paused in her reading. The Sun was an orange-red
488

circle almost touching the horizon. On a grating at the rail, steadied by Fred and the Doctor, Jake's body waited, sewed into canvas, with ballast weights at the feet. (A primitive rite, Johann.) (Jake, if you don't like it, I'll stop.) (Jock, you should be respectful; this is a funeral.) (It's *my* funeral, isn't it? Do I have to pull a long face for my own funeral? Johann, I *do* like it. I respect symbols, primitive symbols especially. Thank you for doing this—and thank you most of all for not letting my carcass fall into the hands of licensed ghouls.) (Just wanted to be sure, Jake. I'd better go on; I've marked several more passages.)

(Go on, Johann. Just don't try to pray me into Heaven.) (I shan't, Jake beloved. We three will face whatever comes, together.) (Right, Boss. Jock knows it.)

" 'All go unto one place; all are of the dust, and all turn to dust again. Who knoweth the spirit of man. . . ?'

" 'Two are better than one. . . . For if they fall, the one will lift up his fellow: but woe to him that is alone when he falleth; for he hath not another to help him up. Again, if two lie together, then they have heat: but how can one be warm alone?' " (Boss, that reminds me. Do we have to sleep alone tonight?) (Damn it, Eunice, don't you *ever* think of anything else?) (Come off it, Boss. What else is worth thinking about? Stocks, bonds, and other securities? I've been telling Jock about your discovery—that sex is more intense for a woman than for a man. He doesn't believe it. But he's eager to find out.)

(Jake, are you *that* eager? I intended to show respect for your memory.) (I appreciate the thought, Johann. But you needn't carry it to extremes. I can't see why you should mourn me when I'm still here. Uh, tell me—is it *really* better?) (Let him judge for himself, Boss—whether it's better to spread Eunice . . . or to *be* Eunice. A more scientific comparison than you have been able to make.) (Quit talking like a kinsey, Eunice. All right, partners; I'll think over the changes. But I'll be damned if I'll make a disgraceful spectacle out of us tonight. Not *this* night. It's got to be discreet—or no game.) " 'And if one prevail against him, two shall withstand him; and a three-fold cord is not quickly broken.' "

489

(Boss, I like that. This makes up for the funeral I never had. Not even a memorial service.) (But you did have a memorial service, Lively Legs.) (I *did*? Who was there?) (Just me, dear. I hired a little chapel and an organist. I read a couple of poems you used to like. Some flowers. Nothing much.) (Jock, I'm dreadfully touched. Boss! He really *does* love me. Doesn't he?) (He does, darling—we both do.) (I wish I'd been there, Jock.) (I didn't know where you *were*, dearest. Maybe just as well, you're not very well behaved at funerals.) (Oh, pooh all over you, you dirty old ghost—nobody can hear me.) (Careful whom you call a 'ghost', Lively Legs; it might slop over onto you. Let Joan get through with this and splash it.)

" 'Whatsoever thy hand findeth to do, do it with all thy might—' '—for thy days are few and they are numbered—' '—man goeth to his long home.' 'The silver cord is loosed, the golden bowl is broken.' From the deep we came, let the body of our brother Jacob now be returned to the deep."

Joan closed the Book; Fred and Dr. Garcia lifted the end of the grating; the body fell into the water, disappeared.

She turned away, handed the Book to Mrs. Dabrowski. "Here, Olga. Thank you."

"Joan, that was beautiful. I don't see how you did it."

"Wipe your eyes, Olga; farewells must never be sad—and Jake was ready to go. I knew my husband well, Olga; I knew what he wanted, it was not hard."

She pressed Olga's hand and turned away. "Winnie! Stop that. Stop it at once. Jake does not want you to cry." (What makes you think so, Johann? I feel flattered by having a lovely little creature like Winifred weep over me.) (Oh, pipe down, Jake. You were the star of the show, now stop taking bows. Talk to Eunice.) Joan took the smaller woman in her arms. "You mustn't, Winnie. Really you mustn't. Think of your baby."

Winnie bawled against her shoulder. "Joan, don't you miss him at all?"

"But, darling, how can I miss Jake when he has never left me? The Jewel is *still* in the Lotus, and always will be. Eternal Now."

"I guess so—but I just can't *stand* it!"

490

(Dear Doctor, maybe? He'll be giving Winnie a sleeping pill, surest thing.) (Not Roberto, Eunice. Under his aggressive atheism he's got a touch of what he was brought up on, he'd be shocked. Some other night.) "Roberto, you had better take care of Winnie."

"I will—but are *you* all right?"

"You know I am. I have a prescription for you, however."

"All right. It won't hurt you to take a real knocker-outer tonight. Say phenobarb."

"Let's *not* say 'phenobarb.' My prescription is for Winnie. Get her to eat something. Then sit with her and recite the Money Hum for at least a half hour. Then take her to bed and hold her in your arms and let her sleep. And *you* sleep, sir; you've had a rough day, too."

"All right. Do you want to join us in saying them? We could come to the cabin—then you could go straight to bed. I've learned that it's better than barbiturates."

"Doctor, if you wish, you may come to my cabin at nine o'clock tomorrow morning—and kick me out of bed if I'm not up. But I will be. Don't go there any sooner than that. Tonight I shall recite that hypnotic prayer. With Jake. He'll be able to hear me . . . whether you think so or not."

"Joan, I have no wish to attack anyone's faith."

"You haven't, dear. I appreciate your solicitude. When I need it, I will draw on it—freely. But now you take care of Winnie." (Boss, how about Fred? No one to dodge. Jock, you'll be right in the middle. Lucky Adolf. But Fred won't know it.) (Eunice, you're out of your pointy little head. We almost scared Fred to death once before, just by being *us*. Before we got him gentled. Look at him, he's worse off than Winnie. With nobody to console him. But *we* can't console him, not this night.)

"Captain."

"Yes, Ma'am?"

"Let's bust up this wake. People should not stand around moping. Meal hours have become disorganized; can Hester throw together some cold supper quickly? Perhaps with volunteer help? I'd volunteer but I have something to do." (Oho! The Tom Cat. Jock, this is going to be fun.) (Lively

Legs, is there a man in this vessel you gals haven't spread for?) (Oh, sure, Jock honey. Hank. He's got his eye on Eve and thinks we're an old hag. And now that her Uncle Jock has left her, Eve might trip him.) (Now that I'm dead, I regret having resisted that delicious little jailbait. Wouldn't have cost me more than a million to buy my way out of trouble—and I had a rich wife.) (If you two lechers will shut up a moment, I'll set you straight about something. *Not* Thomas Cattus. Certainly not before the midwatch and could be later with this wind against us. Captain Tom Finchley is going to be busy skippering.) "Captain, I want you to get way on and set basic course for San Clemente Island anchorage."

"Yes, Ma'am." He trailed after her, and added softly, "I better start calling *you* 'Captain' now. Set an example."

She stopped. They were sufficiently alone that she could speak privately by lowering her voice. "Tom Cat."

"Yes?"

"Don't call me 'Captain'—*you* are Captain until I've passed my tests. Then we'll see. And don't call me 'Ma'am.' I'm either 'Mrs. Salomon' or 'Joan,' depending on the company, just as before. But in private I'm still your 'Pussy Cat'. I hope I am."

"Well . . . okay."

"Let's hear you say it."

"Pussy Cat. Brave little Pussy Cat. Puss, you surprise me more, longer I know you."

"That's better. Tom Cat, Jake knew all along about your tomcatting with me." (Oh, what a lie! Eunice, she *never* told me—and I suspected only once and decided I was mistaken.) (I know, Jock. Boss is a deceitful one and not at all truthful and besides she tells fibs even to *me*.)

"He *did*?"

"Yes, Thomas Cattus. But Jake Salomon was a true gentleman and saw only what he was expected to see. He never teased me about my little follies. Simply indulged me. But he didn't tell on himself, either. Do you know if he ever made it with Hester?" (Now see here, Johann—) (Pipe down, Jock; I've wondered, too.)

492

"Uh . . . hell, Pussy, all men are alike, all after the same thing."

"And all women are alike, we've all got it. Well?"

"Hester spread for him first chance we gave 'em. But she didn't *tell* me. Ashamed. Had to catch 'em at it, then twist her arm."

"Surely you didn't hurt her?"

"No, no, Puss, I don't rough a broad, never. Didn't catch 'em, not to hurt, neither. Backed out fast—then *asked* later. Told her I knew for certain, so how about coming clean, was all. She did. She hadn't told me—because of *you*."

"Oh. I trust you then told her about me?"

Her sailing master looked horrified. "Pussy, you think I'm out o' my frimpin' *head*? Look, I like what you got, just fine. But I ain't foolish. I don't rat on broads. If I did, you'd be last on the list. Believe."

"Tell Hester if you wish, dear; it can't matter now. Then at some later time, she would not be surprised if she found me doing what widows so often do." ('They don't tell, they don't yell, they rarely swell—and they're grateful as hell.') (Jock, you're a dirty old ghost.) "Well, let's set our course. What ETA, Tom Cat? If it's later than midnight, I'll relieve you for the midwatch."

"You will like hell, Ma'am—Pussy Cat. You sack in a full night, you need it. I'll put Fred on the wheel now and Hank on lookout—and I'll drag a corking mat back near the helm and catch some sack drill till we get close in. Pussy Cat, you've got to *promise* me you'll stay in your cabin. Not go wandering around, I'll think you're meaning to jump overboard."

"Is that an order, Captain?"

"Uh—yes, damn it, that's an order!"

"Aye aye, sir. It won't be necessary to check on me; I'll be in my cabin, door locked, and I will be asleep. I promise not to jump overboard earlier than *tomorrow* night."

"Pussy Cat, you wouldn't jump? Would you?"

"With Jake's baby inside me? Captain, I do have a concept of duty. Until I have this baby, my life is not my own. I not only must *not* suicide—I would not in any

493

case—but I must also keep calm and happy and healthy and not risk so much as a dirty drinking glass. So don't worry about me. Good night, Tom." She headed for the cabin.

(Nothing doing at that shop tonight, partners—we're faced with nobility. I think Anton is our best bet.) (The Passionate Pole! Jock darling, I'm not sure your heart can stand it.) (Fortunately, my dears, my old pump no longer has to stand anything—and the one you turned over to Joan, Eunice, is a Swiss watch among tickers. Doesn't race even when *she* is racing. But you know that.) (Quit chattering, you two. Either of you have any idea how to get Olga out of the way?)

(Push her overboard?) (Eunice!) (Can't I joke, Boss? I like Olga, she's a nice girl.) (Too nice, that's the problem. Not a tart like you, or me—or Hester.) (Hrrrmph!) (Jake, you're not in court, dear. The subject is tail. Mine. Ours, I mean.) (Johann, I simply wanted to say that, if you took our problem directly to Mrs. Dabrowski, you might find her sympathetic. *I* always found her so.)

(Jake! Are you implying that you've had *Olga*? I don't believe it.) (I don't either, Jock. If you had said 'Eve' I would have boggled—but would have believed you. But *Olga*? Hell, she wears a panty even in the pool.) (Which comes off very easily—in private.)

(Eunice, I think he means it. Well, I'll be *damned*! You and I are pikers. 'Me' at's off 'to the Duke.' All right, Jake—tell us how to go about it.) (About what? Getting her out of the way? Just ask her, she's very sympathetic—and felt my death more than you wenches have.) (Jock, that's not fair. We felt it . . . but we're overjoyed that you decided to stay anyhow.)

(Thank you, my dears. Conversely, if you would like to invite her in—) (Do you mean a Troy?) (I understand that such is the current argot, Eunice; in my youth we called it something else. But wouldn't it be more of a Pentagon? Five?)

(The word is 'Star' today, Jock. But let me give you the first rule of happy ghosting. You must never, never, *never* admit that you are here, nor tease Joan to admit it. Because she might get groused and do so. Whereupon Joan would

494

wind up in a shrink factory—with us along—and there go our happy games. Look, you've been married to Joan quite a while now and jumping her even longer—did you *ever* suspect that *I* was present, too?) (Not once.) (You see? Don't admit it and they leave us alone.)

(Eunice, Jake would never let on. But now about Olga—Jake, did you ever teach her Om Mani?) (No.) (Boss, I begin to see. We've taught it to Anton, Jock. Is Olga limber enough to sit in Lotus?) (Lively Legs, Mrs. Dabrowski is limber enough for *anything*.) (That does it, Joan. Olga will join in, even if she thinks it's heathen—tonight she will. For you. And there is no easier way to get a party peeled down and rolling than by forming a Circle. You've done it again and again.) (As I recall, dears, Joan even used it on *me*. When it was hardly necessary. Okay, let's find the Dabrowskis.)

28

APPOINTMENTS OPEN—FEDERAL GS-19 Assistant Welfare Field Operative (Learner-Visitor) Literacy requirement C. Brown Belt or higher gives 10% preference. Veteran's preference, parolee's preference, relevant-experience preference all semi-cumulative. See local Civil Service or Welfare office for pre-examinations and salary formulas. Latter based on standard scale plus field cost-of-living factor and hazardous area rating, cumulative.

In a compromise vote today the Society for Rational Astrology accepted a "grandfather clause" in the licensing bill before the Nebraska Legislature. The Committee on Agriculture & Mechanical Arts then voted the amended bill "Do Pass" by 7 to 2—tantamount to passage in the state's unicameral legislature. The Protective Association of Intuitive Astrologers called it "the greatest setback for science since Galileo." The Lunar Commission announced that the Colonies are now 102% self-sufficient in foodstuffs but added that the ten-year plan would continue in order to increase out-migration potential. MAY-DECEMBER ROMANCE LOSES . . . at sea in their honeymoon yacht. The young widow remained in seclusion. . . .

"—door for processing. Pleasure meeting you, Mrs. Garcia; good luck, Doctor. Next applicant! Step lively, sit down over there—your husband not with you? Or is it 'Miss'?"

"I am a widow, Mr. Barnes."

"So? We don't get many widows, nor does the Commission encourage them. Out-migration is not an escape for emotional problems. Such as bereavement. Nor do we accept applicants so advanced in pregnancy unless there are overriding advantages to the Commission, not the applicant. Take the couple who went through just before you. She's pregnant—but he is a medical doctor, one of the top categories for subsidized out-migration. So I passed her. Might have passed her on her own; she's a nurse. But unless you have such a special qualification—"

"I know, sir. Dr. Garcia is my personal physician."

"Eh? Even if I accept you, that is no guarantee that he would still be *your* physician on the Moon. Unlikely, in fact. Unless, by coincidence—"

"Mr. Barnes, you have my out-migration proposal in front of you. It has been prepared with great care by my attorney. It might save time to glance through it."

"All in good time. You would be surprised at how many people come in here without having the slightest idea of what they are up against. They seem to assume that the Commission is *anxious* to have them. Nothing could be farther from the truth. Nineteen out of twenty who sit down in that chair I do not permit to go on through the processing door. I make it a practice to get rid of the more obvious time-wasters quickly. Uh, Salómon, Eunice.' Mrs. Salomon, I want to know first—Mrs. '*Salomon*'?"

" 'Mrs. Jacob Moshe Salomon,' maiden name 'Joan Eunice Smith.' "

"Your face *did* look somewhat familiar but your features, uh—"

"—are chubby now. Yes. I've gained twenty-six pounds—which Dr. Garcia finds satisfactory for my height, build, and date of impregnation."

"That brings up other problems. A woman is often mistaken as to the date—and first babies are notoriously in

498

a hurry to arrive. Our Lunar transports aren't planned for new infants, nor for childbirth. I want you to realize the hazards."

"I know them. Need we go into this?"

"*I* must be the judge of that."

"Mr. Barnes, my doctor is satisfied that I know the exact date of impregnation and— Is all of this confo?"

"Mmm. I'll put it this way. None of it is privileged. I am a lawyer but not *your* lawyer. I hear more intimate details from applicants than you can imagine but I haven't time to waste on gossip."

"I am glad to hear that, Mr. Barnes . . . as I would be *much* displeased if what I am about to tell you were to become a matter of gossip."

"Hmmph. I think I felt a chill breeze. Are you trying to impress me with your importance? Don't bother; applicants are all the same size once they come in here. Your money doesn't mean a thing."

"Was my manner unfriendly? I'm sorry."

"Well— Let's stick to the business at hand. A lawyer in the Lunar Commission's Civil Service—a job with no squeeze, believe me—doesn't often find himself dealing with rich people. But it makes no difference; if you don't want to be frank with the Commission, that's your problem. But I won't approve an applicant's proposal until *I* am satisfied about it. *All* about it. Now you implied that you had something pertinent to tell me which you class as 'confo.' I don't accept your restriction. Now . . . do you talk? Or shall we terminate this interview?"

"You leave me no option, sir. This is not a first baby I am carrying, so no 'first baby' hazard exits. If the 'Goddard' lifts on schedule, I have every reason to expect to have my baby on the Moon. Dr. Garcia is not worried about the timing and neither am I."

"So? This brings up other problems. This earlier child—does he, or she, affect your estate?"

"No. That is why this *must* be treated as confo. I did not have that earlier baby."

"Eh? You lost me. Better clarify that."

"Please, Mr. Barnes. I am a sex-change and a brain
499

transplant. Surely you know it—good heavens, the whole world knows it. The first baby this body gave birth to was before that time. It is the reputation of my *donor* I wish to protect, not mine. The child was illegitimate. Common as that is these days—no longer a legal concept in most states and the very word almost obsolete—so great is my gratitude to the sweet and gracious lady who formerly lived in this body, I would be most unhappy were I to be the cause of any tarnish on her memory."

(Boss, you know I don't give a kark.) (Let her handle it, Eunice; this petty bureaucrat can gum up the works if Joan does not divert him just so. Are we kibitzing Joan?—or are we going to the Moon?) (Hell, yes, we're going to the Moon! My 'Yes' vote, plus your 'Yes' vote, plus half of Joan's vote—a natural fence-straddler she is, legs always open—which works out to a five-to-one majority for out-migrating. A landslide!) (So let her alone while she handles him.) (If she didn't have that big belly, she could handle him a lot better. And faster.)

(Hrrmph. Eunice, you claim you were there . . . so why don't you tell poor old melancholy Jacques the straight on that? It was me, wasn't it? It was I?) (Jock old ghost, I love you dearly—but if you think I'll split on my twin, you don't know me.) (Oh, well. A baby is a baby is a baby. I just hope it doesn't have two heads.) (Two heads would be stretching a good thing too far. Jock, I'll settle for two balls.) (Thinking about incest, Lively Legs?) (And why shouldn't I think about it? We've tried everything else.)

(Jake, Eunice—will you two please go back to sleep? Squire Pecksniff here is searching for flyspecks on Alec's masterpiece. Trying to think up more objections—which I'll have to answer.)

"Mrs. Salomon, I find myself quite disturbed by one aspect concerning this alleged earlier child—the great likelihood that some future action may be brought challenging your disposition of your estate when this child, or some person claiming to be this child, turns up. The fifty percent of estate required—as a minimum—from any out-migrant not of a subsidized-vocation category is a source of capital to the colonies; the Commission is not willing to part with a dime of it once the Commission carries out its half of the bargain. Yet such a 'missing heir' could lay claim to all of your estate."

"Most unlikely, Mr. Barnes, but if you will look at 'Appendix G,' you will see how my lawyer handled it. A small trust to buy up any such claim, with a fifty-year conversion of any remainder to a named charity."

"Uh, let me find it. Mmm, Mrs. Salomon, do you call ten million dollars 'small'?"

"Yes."

"Mmm. Perhaps I had better look closely at the other financial provisions. Have you been advised that, even though the Commission claims only half of your fortune, the other half *cannot* be used to buy you anything on the Moon? In other words, poor or rich, on the Moon out-migrants start off equal."

"I know that, Mr. Barnes. Believe me, my attorney, Mr. Train, is most careful. He searched the law and made certain that I knew the consequences of my acts—because he did not approve of them. To put it briefly Alec Train said that anyone who goes to the Moon to *live* must be out of his head. So he tried to talk me out of what he regards as my folly. You'll find four other possible heirs in 'Appendix F'—my granddaughters. It is to their advantage to accept what is offered there . . . as they are told bluntly how much worse off they will be if they wait for me to die. A poor bet for them in any case; I am now physiologically younger than they are; I'll probably outlive all of them."

"That could be true. Especially on the Moon, one could add. I wish I could out-migrate myself. But I can't afford to pay for it the way you can and lawyers are not in demand there. Well, your Mr. Train seems to have thought of most aspects. Let's look at your balance sheet."

"One moment, sir. I have asked for one small measure of special treatment."

"Eh? All out-migrants are treated alike. Must be."

"A very small thing, Mr. Barnes. My baby will be born not long after I arrive on Luna. I've asked to have Dr. Garcia continue to attend me through that time."

"I can't promise that, Madam. Sorry. Policy."

501

She started slowly to get up. "Then I'm not going through with it."

"Uh—good God! Is this *really* your net worth?"

She shrugged. "What is the worth of one pregnant woman, sir? I suppose it depends on your values."

"I didn't mean that. This balance sheet— If it's correct, you're not just wealthy—I knew that—you're a *billionaire!*"

"Possibly. I haven't added it. That summary was prepared through Chase Manhattan with the assistance of accountancy firms listed there. I suppose it's correct . . . unless some computer got the hiccups. But give it back to me . . . since the Commission can't promise me Dr. Garcia to deliver my baby."

"Please, Madam. I have certain latitude in these matters. I simply don't exercise it—ordinarily. Policy."

"Whose policy, Mr. Barnes? The Commission's? Or yours?"

"Eh? Why, mine. I said so."

"Then quit wasting my time, you damned idiot!"

('That's telling him, Fat Lady!') (Eunice, this is one fat lady who isn't going to take any more nonsense. My back aches.)

The blast almost caused Mr. Barnes to fall out of his swivel chair. He recovered his balance, said: *"Please,* Madam Salomon!"

"Young man, let's have no more nonsense! I'm far gone in pregnancy, as you can see. You've lectured me about the dangers of childbirth—and you aren't a doctor. You've pried into personal matters with the gall of a kinsey. You've tried to tell me I can't have my own doctor when he is going in the same ship—and now it turns out that it was not a Commission regulation but merely petty tyranny on your part. Bullying. All through this nonsense—although I've appeared with a complete and carefully prepared proposal—you've kept me sitting on a hard uncomfortable chair. My back aches. On how many poor helpless applicants have you fattened your ego? But I am neither 'poor' nor 'helpless'. You spoke of a 'chill breeze.' It's an icy blast now. *I bloody well mean to have your job!"*

502

"Please, Madam! I *said* you could have your own doctor. And I *am* required to review each applicant's proposal."

"Then get your lazy arse out of that comfortable chair and *give it to me!* You come sit in this ducking stool."

"Very well, Ma'am." They exchanged chairs. Shortly he said, "I see that you are putting almost all of the other fifty percent of your fortune into starship research and development."

"It's none of your business what I do with it."

"I didn't say it was. It just struck me as . . . unusual."

"Why? My child may want to go in a starship. I want that research to *move*. Mr. Barnes, you've had time to look at that proposal; if you hadn't talked so much, you could have it memorized by now. Do whatever it is you do. Mark your X, or stamp your chop. Or hand it back and let me out of here. Now! Not five minutes from now—but *now*. My back still hurts. You're a pain in the back, Mr. Barnes, you and your petty 'policy' and your worthless talk."

He signed it. "Through that door, Madam Salomon."

"Thank you." She started toward it.

"You're barely welcome—you ancient bitch!"

Joan Eunice stopped, turned back, and smiled her best golden-sunrise smile. "Why, thank you, dear! That's the best thing you've said to me. Because it is utterly honest. Of course I'm not welcome, the way I've stormed at you—and answered your bullying with worse bullying. And I am indeed both a bitch and ancient."

"I shouldn't have said that."

"Oh, but you should have. I richly deserved it. But I would never have tried to get your job—truly, I'm not that petty. That was just backache bad temper talking. I admire your spunk in telling me off. What is your first name?"

"Uh, 'Matthew.' "

"A good name, Matthew. A strong name." Joan Eunice came back, stood close to him. "Matthew, I'm going to the Moon. I'll never be back this way again. Will you forgive this ancient bitch and let us part friends? Will you kiss me good-bye? I've no one to see me off, Matthew—will you kiss me good-bye as I leave for the Moon?"

"Uh—"

"Please, Matthew. Uh, mind the big belly; turn me a little sideways—that's better." She wet her lips, lifted her face, and closed her eyes.

Presently she sighed and nestled closer. "Matthew? Will you let me love you? Oh, I don't mean seduce you, it's too late for that, I'm about benched. Just tell me that I may think of you with love as I go to the Moon. It's a long way off and I'm a little scared—and I lived too long without love and want to love everyone who will let me . . . any who will love me back even a little. Will you, dear? Or is this bitch too ancient?"

"Uh, Madam Salomon—"

" 'Eunice,' Matthew."

"Eunice. Eunice, you're a sparky little bitch, you really are. But I kept you sitting there—even before I realized who you are—because I *like* looking at you. Hell, honey, my wife says I can love any woman I want to—ten percent of what I love her."

"Ten percent is a good return on any investment, Matthew. All right, please love me that ten percent—and I'll love you ten percent of what I loved—still love!— my darling husband. Is there enough love in that ten percent for a second kiss? It's a *long* way to the Moon—they must keep me warm all the way." She closed her eyes and waited.

(Hey, twin, lover boy is doing better this time.) (Don't bother me now, I'm busy!)

Presently Mr. Barnes murmured, "Lovely."

"All swollen and fat now, that's why I wear styles that cover them. But you should have seen Eunice—the first Eunice, my benefactrix—at her lovely best . . . in styles to show it."

"I still say they're lovely. I guess we had better stop this, I've got a roomful of people waiting out there. And you have almost four hours of processing before you go on to quarantine. If you want to go to Andes Port with your own doctor, you had better go now."

"Yes, Matthew. I love you—ten percent—and I'll still be loving you on the Moon. At compound interest. Through that door?"

504

"Through there and follow the signs. Good-bye, Eunice. Take care of yourself."

(Boss, that's either a new high or a new low. Was he kissing *us*? Or a billion dollars?) (It seemed to me—though I'm still learning compared with you two trollops—that the young man started out kissing a billion dollars . . . and wound up kissing Joan. Us. Quite well, too. Dears, I find that my animal nature has been considerably stirred—I'm looking forward to us being back in circulation again.) (Hell, yes, Jock darling, we all are. It occurs to me, Joan, that there must be lots of homesick out-migrants who will appreciate a simple country girl who learned clear back in junior high to kiss with her eyes closed and her lips open.) (Eunice, that's what I'm counting on. Seven billion people makes Earth a terribly lonely place . . . but there are only a few thousand on Luna and, if we try, we can get to know all of them and love most of them. What do you think, Jake?) (Johann, we can try. We *will*. Wups, here's our first stop. 'Physical.' Goose bumps and indignities. But what the hell?—somebody kissed us good-bye.)

29

As re-reported in the *Christian Science Monitor, Izvestia* condemned the announcement (Daily Selenite, year 35, day 69) of the Lunar Commission's call for proposal studies for terraforming Ganymede as "one more provocative example of the insatiable territorial aggressions of the mad-dog alliance of the two major imperialist, counterrevolutionary, genocidal powers, the United States of America and the so-called People's Democratic Republic of China" and demanded that the UN Security Council take action before it was too late. In Sequoia National Park three families (or possibly one extended-family) were discovered living two hundred feet up in a giant redwood. The group (seven adults, five children—two less than a year old) claimed to have been up the tree more than three years; extensive arrangements for their unique style of living lent substance to the claim. They were booked on a variety of charges but the U.S. district attorney declined to prosecute: "I ain't about to waste my time and taxpayers' money on a bunch of monkeys. Let's chase 'em back up the tree!"

The Iowa State Annual Picnic in Long Beach, California, suffered 243 cases of acute food poisoning (botulism-D), 17 muggings, 3 rapes, and was rained out. "—from the great State of New York knows that slum clearance is no answer. Must we hear the death rattle before we admit that *any* organism, be it man, or city, or civilization, in time grows old and dies?" In a letter in *Nature* (UK) it was claimed that scientists in Novosibirsk had solved both the problem of twinning replication and of extrauterine fetal development in vitro and must now be reckoned as back in the Great-Powers race with a potentially unlimited supply of workers, soldiers, and peasants. An editorial in the same issue urged the Nobel letter-writer to give up writing science-fiction or at least change his brand of hashish. Debate on proposed legislation for control of neo-psychedelics continued: "Has the gentleman on the other side of the aisle ever given thought to the potentially disastrous effect on our economy of actually *enforcing* the narcotics laws we *already* have? Or is he talking for the video audience?" Experienced observers predicted no vote this session.

In Luna City Mrs. Salomon, as with everywoman, reached the end of her nine lunar months. Her lovely navel had long since extruded, her belly was an arching dome of life pushing up the sheet. She waited in the Community Hospital eight levels down. The nurse seated near her was pregnant also but not nearly so far along.

"Winnie?"

"Yes, dear?"

"If it's a boy it must be Jacob Eunice . . . a girl must be Eunice Jacob. Promise me."

"I did promise, dear; I wrote it down as you asked me to. And I promised to take care of your baby—and that is all done, too, already recorded—I take care of yours, you take care of mine. Only we won't need to, dear; both of us are going to be all right—we'll raise them together."

"Promise me, it's important." (Johann, don't name that baby 'Jake.' Call him 'Johann—'Johann Eunice.') (Jake, I will *not* load down a boy with 'Johann'—it forced me to learn to fight too young) (Jock, don't argue with Boss. She's always right, you know that.) (Then call him 'John!') (His name is 'Jacob,' Jake—I won't have it any other way.) (Joan, you're the most stubborn old bastard in the entire Solar System—and turning you into a woman didn't change you. All *right* already!) (I love you, my husband.) (We both love you, Boss—and Jake is as proud about the names as I am.)

508

"I do promise you, Joan. Cross my heart."

"My sweet Winsome. We've come a long way together, you and I and Roberto."

"Yes, we have, dear."

"I'm ill. Am I not?"

"Joan, you're not ill. A woman never feels good just before she has a baby—I know, I've seen hundreds of them. I told you that tube was just for glucose."

"What tube? Winnie, come close and listen. This is important. My baby's name must be......"

"—rejection syndrome, Doctor. Atypical but unmistakable."

"Dr. Garcia, why do you say 'atypical'?"

"Mmm. Sometimes, when she's irrational, she speaks in three different voices and—well, two of them are *dead*. Split personality."

"So? I'm not a psychiatrist, Dr. Garcia; 'split personality' means little to me. But I don't see that it necessarily affects pregnancy. I've delivered some fine, healthy babies from women who were quite irrational."

"Nor am I a psychiatrist, sir. Let it stand that she is irrational much of the time . . . and that I see this as part of the total clinical picture, which—in my opinion—gives a prognosis of transplant rejection."

"Dr. Garcia, you know more about transplants than I do; I've never managed a transplant case in my life. But this patient seems in fair shape to me. Right here in this hospital I have seen women who appeared to be in much worse shape . . . who had their babies and were up and working in three days. With our low gravity they recover quickly. Did you think this patient was hurt on the trip up from Earth?"

"Oh, no! Those flotation acceleration cells are wonderful. Mrs. Salomon rode in one, so did my wife. I monitored them; Joan took it even better than Winnie did. I envied them, as I found the ride in a standard chair pretty rough. No, I see no connection; rejection symptoms did not show until this week." Garcia frowned. "She doesn't know that her mind isn't clear—she's lucid off and on. But motor control is decaying. That strong young body sustains her

509

metabolism—but truthfully, Doctor, I can't guess how long." He frowned again. "It could let go any moment—damn it, I wish I had proper support equipment!"

The older doctor shook his head. "This is a frontier, son. I'm not running down your specialty—but this is *not* the place for it. Here we set bones and take out appendixes and try to keep contagious diseases from racing through the colony. But when it comes time to die, we *die*—you, me, anybody—and get out of the way of the living. Now suppose we had all of Johns Hopkins here with Jefferson Medical thrown in—could you stop it? Reverse it? Possibility of spontaneous remission if you had your fancy support equipment?"

"No. The best we could do would be to extend the time."

"So the literature says, but I wanted to hear *you* say it. Well, Doctor? Your patient."

"We take the baby."

"Let's get busy."

Joan Eunice came awake as they were wheeling her down the corridor. "Roberto?"

"Right here, dear."

"Where are they taking me? Am I going in for surgery again?"

"Yes, Joan."

"Why, dear?"

"Because you haven't gone into labor when you should have. So now we do it the easy way—Caesarean section." He added, "There's nothing to worry about. It's as routine as taking out an appendix."

"Roberto, you know I never worry. You're doing it?"

"No, the chief of surgery. He's far more skilled than I am. Dr. Frankel. You met him, he examined you this morning."

"Did he? It's slipped my mind. Roberto, I must tell Winnie something very important. It's about the name of my baby."

"She knows, dear, she wrote it down. 'Jacob Eunice, o Eunice Jacob.' "

510

"Oh, good! Then everything's all right. But tell them to make it quick, Roberto; I never liked waiting around at a beachhead."

"It'll be quick, you'll never notice it. Spinal and a wagonload of barbiturate, Joan."

"That's funny, you called me 'Joan.' My name's 'Johann,' Doctor. Agnes is going to be all right—she is, isn't she?"

"Yes, Johann. Agnes—is going to be all right."

"I told her she would be all right. Doctor, I feel dreamy. If I fall asleep, will you wake me when Agnes goes in to have her baby?"

"Yes, Johann."

"Thank . . you . . Mrs . . . Wicklund. I didn't . . know . . could be so . . wonderful."

"Roberto? Where are you? I can't see you."

"Right here, dear."

"Touch me. Touch my face, I can't feel anything lower down. Roberto, what I bought was a wonderful year—and I have no regrets. Have they started?"

"Not quite. Do you want to go to sleep, dear?"

"Must I? I'd rather not. I feel sleepy—dreamy and good . . . but I'd rather not go to sleep just yet. It's on the knees of the gods now, isn't it? Time to bite the bullet and chin up and all that. But I don't need that, I'm happy. Come close, dear, I must tell you why. Closer . . can't talk . . very loud."

"Clamp! Damn it, Nurse, stay out of my way!"

"Everything always hurts, Roberto—everything. Always. But some things are worth all the hurts. 'Tie me kangeroo down, mite, tie me kangeroo down!' That . . wasn't . . what I meant to say; that's Jake, he's singing again. Always sings when he's happy. Lean very close . . so I can tell you . . before—I sleep. Thank you, Roberto, for letting me welcome you into my body. It is good to touch—to fuck—be fucked. It's—not good—to be—too much alone. You have blessed me . . with your body, dear. Now I'll sleep a while if I may . . but first I had to tell you that. Om Mani Padme Hum. Now I lay me down to sleep—"

"Surgeon, she's failing."

A baby cried, a world began.

"Heart action dropping!"

(Jake? Eunice?) (Here, Boss! Grab on! There! We've got you.) (Is it a boy or a girl?) (Who cares, Johann—it's a baby! 'One for all and all for one!')

An old world vanished and then there was none.